Praise for the novels of Gretchen Anthony

"Moving, humorous, and briskly-paced, *The Kids Are Gonna Ask* is a pure portrait of Minnesota nice, filled with empathy, wisdom, and characters you'll love to root for."

—J. Ryan Stradal, *New York Times* bestselling author of *Kitchens of the Great Midwest*

"*The Kids Are Gonna Ask* is a touching, wonderful novel about the discoveries we make when the simplest questions spark the most complicated answers."

—Abbi Waxman, bestselling author of *The Bookish Life of Nina Hill*

"*The Kids Are Gonna Ask* is a smart, engaging send-up of our modern age wrapped up in a story too delicious to put down."

—Kelly Harms, bestselling author of *The Overdue Life of Amy Byler*

"Anthony's debut successfully mixes realistic emotional responses to big life events with a sense of humor, preventing any single character from becoming a victim or a villain."

—*Library Journal*, starred review

"*Evergreen Tidings from the Baumgartners* hits all the right notes; you'll double over with laughter, but you'll also find yourself at times misty-eyed and introspective."

—Kristin Harmel, bestselling author of *The Life Intended*

Also by Gretchen Anthony

Evergreen Tidings from the Baumgartners
The Kids Are Gonna Ask

THE BOOK HATERS' BOOK CLUB

GRETCHEN ANTHONY

Recycling programs for this product may not exist in your area.

ISBN-13: 978-0-7783-3364-7

The Book Haters' Book Club

Park Row Books
22 Adelaide St. West, 41st Floor
Toronto, Ontario M5H 4E3, Canada
ParkRowBooks.com
BookClubbish.com

Printed in U.S.A.

To Bethany and Renee,
my forever book club.

Someday we shall ride camels
while sipping cosmopolitans
from our canteens.

THE BOOK HATERS' BOOK CLUB

FOREWORD

Wake up, wake up, my darling readers, because I'm about to tell you how this book ends. One of our characters will find their way home, another will discover a courage they never believed they possessed, and a third will find their heart.

Wait! you're saying. *We've heard this story before.* Ah, yes! You've spotted your first clues. Good start, darlings! But let me assure you, we've only just begun this journey of ours...because that's the power of story, isn't it? No matter what we think we remember, a good story is the source of infinite treasure, of gems yet gone unnoticed, of wisdom whispered just for us in the moments we need it most.

This story I'm about to reveal isn't Dorothy's (though she's here and practically *bursting* to pop in and say hello). It's not even Laney's, or Bree's, or Thom's, or Irma's. Oh, they do all the talking and the mucking about, but they're simply the players. This story, dear reader, belongs to you. It's yours, and your mother's, and your best friend's and your neighbor and him and her and them and all the rest. This is the story of belonging, and of the people we belong not *to*, but *with*. It's the story of dreaming your dreams, and of the loved ones who hold on to those dreams for us when they become too heavy to carry alone.

What's that? I sound as if I'm talking in riddles? Yes, yes, I know. I've always been a wee unconventional, and believe me,

I'd like to claim I only mix things up in order to make life more fun. But wait, you'll see that despite my every grand intention, I create my share of mess—and beauty!—along the way. Which is where we drop into our story.

Let me part the curtains so you can begin…

PROLOGUE

Thom Winslow swept through the glass doors of Vandaveer Investments a titan. "Good afternoon," he announced to the receptionist, his voice bold, his tenor unwavering. "I'm here for the Over the Rai-*iin*-bow—" He faltered as the word "rainbow" indiscriminately, and most unpleasantly, stuck to his throat like jelly, leaving him no choice but to clear it with a sickening "HUUCCHH!"

"I'm here for the meeting about the bookstore." This he said with the voice of a defeated man, aware that his too-narrow shoulders and pigeon neck were rapidly deflating in shame. Damn his rehearsed confidence.

The receptionist barely paid attention, his focus on the tablet attached to his hand. *(Was it glued there?)* "You're meeting in the Lake Minnetonka conference room. I'll escort you."

Irma Bedford, co-owner of the Over the Rainbow Bookshop with Thom's recently deceased partner, Elliot, was already inside, waiting. Seeing her, Thom felt a second blow, his vision for today's meeting all but stomped dead. He'd arrived early to be the first one in the room—he'd read it was a power move—and yet here she was, extending her hand.

"Thom." She stood when he entered. "They're running a few minutes behind."

She was rumpled. He hadn't expected that. Of the few things

Thom appreciated in Irma, it was her easy chic, a style that never failed to impress—well-ironed jeans, crisp white shirt, flawless foundation and knockout lips. Today they were an unfortunate shade of coral.

"Here." He plucked a tissue from a box on the side table. "Lipstick. On your tooth."

She accepted it and turned discreetly to fix herself. There was a stain on her back pocket, the flowering blue swell of ink that would never come out, and before realizing, he said, "I'll walk behind you when we leave so no one can see that spot on your slacks." It was a kindness she perhaps did not deserve, and yet he couldn't help himself.

Irma smiled, gratefully. "Before they come," she began to say but hadn't finished before James and Trevor Vandaveer, father and son, walked through the door and started the handshaking and back-patting portion of the afternoon. Trevor, the younger, pulled out chairs for Thom and Irma, as if they were elderly, joints too swollen with arthritis to do it themselves. Or in Thom's case, enfeebled by a set of useless-looking shoulders.

"Will your daughters be joining you, Irma?" Trevor asked.

"Laney's flight was delayed." She nodded toward the glass wall behind him. "But here's Bree now."

Bree Bedford exited the elevator, armpits sweating through her shirt, the voice in her head hyperventilating about what a stupid mistake she'd made by not having worn a blazer, as usual failing to avoid even one of the mini disasters that, together, comprised her average day.

"I'm sorry to keep you waiting." The clock on the wall above the crystal water pitcher that looked too fancy to touch read 2:58 p.m., two minutes early. But the energy in the room said she was embarrassingly late. She slipped silently into a chair next to her mother and pulled her planner from her purse for notes. The clasp snapped loudly, echoing against the room's hard surfaces. "Sorry. Again."

She and Trevor Vandaveer had graduated high school together, and twenty years on, he looked just as much the tailored son of privilege as he always had, wearing a suit that probably cost more than she was comfortable thinking about. His father, whose first name she kicked herself for not being able to remember, remained the only one standing. She sensed he spent too much time in the sun—though his cheeks and forehead were shiny and taut as if fresh from the dermatologist, the wrinkles on his hands betrayed his age, all but undoing the medical illusion up top.

"We waiting for more?" he barked.

"Just Laney," Irma, Bree, and Thom said in unison. Irma added, "She texted me a few minutes ago. She's on her way from the airport."

It had been upon learning that Laney was flying in from California that Bree began to feel anxious about what she might learn at this meeting. Their mother had only said, "With Elliot gone, I've enlisted an outside firm to help me make some decisions about the Rainbow." Bree was more or less the bookshop's assistant manager—it made sense for her to attend. Her sister, Laney, though, never flew in for store matters. In fact, she almost never flew in for personal matters, either. Their mom's best friend and business partner, Elliot, had died several months ago and Laney hadn't flown in for his funeral. She hadn't flown in when their mom's late-in-life boyfriend, Nestor, passed away unexpectedly last year, and she hadn't spent a Christmas or Thanksgiving in Minneapolis for as long as Bree could remember. Laney didn't come home for things, and yet she was coming home for this.

The receptionist opened the door a third time. "Laney Hartwell," he announced.

Before stepping through, Laney pulled her baseball cap low and made a wish to whatever god, genie, or fairy watching over her that Old Man Vandaveer would keep on talking. The sooner this was over, the better. She was tired. She didn't need to be here. It was too big of an ask.

"What are you doing over there?" Mr. Vandaveer saw her choose a seat in the corner and, grossly offended, slapped his notes on the table with a violent, outsize *thwak*!

She rubbed at the back of her neck, her hair at full attention. "I'm trying not to interrupt."

"Laney." Her mother tapped the chair beside Bree. "There's plenty of room right here."

"It's a big table," Old Man Vandaveer barked, a man showing off his territory—big office, big voice, big dude-jewel ring rapping on his big table's glass top. "Alright, brass tacks." He returned to his agenda. "Ms. Bedford, on behalf of Over the Rainbow Bookshop, LLC, has entered into a contract for sale of said business with Vandaveer Investments. Per her request, we've agreed to brief you all, her stakeholders, on the terms."

Trevor handed each of them a slick folder adorned with the firm's green-and-gold logo. Laney accepted hers, placed it unopened on the table, and set her brain free to wander. It was strange, flying in from her grown-up life in Oakland, only to come face-to-face with a kid she'd graduated with, now an adult with a tailored suit and a haircut too slick for his conservative, monochromatic tie.

"Let's begin with the Terms of Sale," Trevor said. The words entered the air, floated around the room. Laney didn't try to catch them.

"'...will be paid by the Seller in full upon closing in the form of certified check, agreed to by both Buyer and Seller...'"

Bounce. Bounce.

He had a tiny blue dot above his lip. She'd thought it was an ink spot, a rogue pen leaving its mark. But the more she watched, the more she became convinced. Trevor had a perfect dot of a mole above his lip.

"'—six weeks,'" the mole said.

"I'm sorry?" Bree's voice cut through Laney's foggy thoughts.

"Yes, July 1," Trevor said. "When Irma signed the Statement of Intent, we agreed to an expedited, six-week timeframe. We'll sign the final closing documents at the end of the month."

"But that's only three weeks from today." Bree double-checked the date. She was correct. "You sold the shop three weeks ago and you're just telling us now?" A panicked chill seized her; she didn't think she could lift her arms. "What about all our customers? What about the neighborhood? We're the only independent bookstore left in Lyn-Lake."

"I admit the timeframe is less than ideal." Her mother did not sound remotely apologetic. "I needed time to get Laney here."

Bree dug her fingers into the edge of the glass tabletop to keep from crying. Three weeks until her life came to a crashing halt, until the bookshop that had first been her refuge, then family, and then career, ceased to exist. "I don't understand." Tears slipped from her chin to the table. "How can you close the Rainbow?"

Irma didn't respond.

"If you'll turn to page seventy-nine," Trevor said, apparently anxious to move the meeting along, "you may understand more after hearing the details."

"Take a look at the offer price," his father said. "That oughta dry your boo-hoos."

Thom pushed the tissue box down the table toward Bree. That Irma was only now telling her daughters of the sale did not surprise him. She was a beauty with fangs, and he'd known from the very beginning it was dangerous to get too close. She and the bookshop had consumed Elliot, and just as a new chapter of their lives was to begin, just as Elliot had agreed to cut back on his work there, to consider retirement, to refocus on his life with Thom, he'd died. In a flash. Gone without warning or goodbyes.

Thom turned to the correct page and looked for the price

Irma had received for the beloved Over the Rainbow, aware that no amount of money would ever dull the resentment he'd sharpened for the woman and her bookstore over so many years. Trevor was now spewing gibberish, a tactic meant to blunt the impact of what he could see with his very own eyes: Irma had sold Elliot's life's work for practically nothing.

"Oh, Mom," Bree cried. "Is that all the Rainbow means to you?"

Laney flipped her page, assuming there had to be more on the other side. "So, is this just the first installment or what?"

Thom felt his jaw, followed by stoic resolve, go slack. "Irma," he hissed.

The woman didn't flinch. "These are the terms the Vandaveers offered, and I've accepted them," she said, her back an iron rod. "If you have questions, please direct them to our hosts."

Thom looked at the sale price again, convinced they'd misplaced a comma.

Bree shifted from being quietly tearful to a sobbing soap opera star.

Laney checked her watch.

1

45 days until closing...

Laney Hartwell wasn't sure which she wanted more: a doughnut, or a divorce. She didn't really want a divorce, obviously. It's just that this was becoming another one of those days when it would've been nice to have a husband who contributed more to the work of running their small business than simply the use of his fading celebrity. Right now, for example, she was tearing bits of rogue paper, molecule by molecule, from the jaws of their damned-to-be-jammed receipt printer while a line of customers—all anxious to be out the door and on their way—snaked deeper into the waiting area. Meanwhile, Tuck stood oblivious nearby, legs spread, knees bouncing in time to the chorus of adulation in his head, entertaining one man. "I'm telling you," he boomed, "I may as well have had fire shooting out of my ass—genuine, NASA-grade, rocket-fueled combustion!"

Laney glanced up from her gloom, fingers slathered in printer ink, just in time to see Tuck's new friend help himself to the last chocolate-glazed on the We ♥ Our Customers doughnut tray. The one she'd wanted. "Tuck?" She heard her exasperation leaking. "Could you please come help me?"

They were coming up on twenty years as "Tuck and Laney," and together, they owned Tire Stud, a tire store on Shattuck Avenue in Oakland beneath the concrete-and-asphalt canopy of CA-24. They had a crew of six mechanics (give or take, depending on who'd recently quit or been fired); 6,500 square feet of space; and as of close-of-business yesterday, 782 in-stock tires. They were nearing the five-year anniversary of its opening, and in that time, she'd had approximately 1,750 days nearly identical to the one she was having now.

As for Tuck, he was a former B-list NASCAR driver—thus, the post-racing life in tires. "Not like I was gonna retire to become a dentist," he liked to say.

"I saw you at the Stockton Invitational in 2010." The man who'd devoured the last of the doughnuts was waiting on a front-end alignment. "You blew a tire in the last lap, but up 'til that very last second, I thought you were gonna take it all."

Tuck slapped him on the back. He only had four-and-a-half remaining fingers on his left hand after a poorly chosen fight with a pneumatic wrench. "I was counting on that race to put me over the top in the standings."

"Tough break."

"Well, our treads are better here. I can promise you that."

Laney radioed the guy a telepathic message to lick the chocolate from his lips, then called, "Miss Frankie? You're all set." Frankie was one of their regulars and oddly prone to driving over a tire's worst enemies—nails, glass, and once, even her own hubcap. Her companion, Miss Pickles the Pomeranian, traveled beside her on the front seat in a custom doggy bed bedazzled with one word: *pizzazz.*

"Aren't you both looking lovely today." Frankie and Miss Pickles were in matching pink windbreakers. Laney ran her credit card, handed over the car keys, and asked if Miss Pickles was allowed a treat.

"Always!" Frankie beamed. Miss Pickles wagged.

Laney's stalled doughnut craving revved its engine.

The phone rang. The door chimed with entering customers. Laney handed a woman in a yellow rain slicker a clipboard and pen and invited her to take a seat while filling out her forms.

"Who's next?"

And that's when her mother called. Laney only picked up because she never looked at the caller ID on the store line—she couldn't tell a customer from a telemarketer, anyway—plus her mom always dialed her cell phone. Only Irma had been texting for days and Laney hadn't responded with more than Busy right now. Call u tonight, then not doing as she'd promised.

Her mother dived right in. "Isn't it you who likes to accuse me of never answering my cell?"

"Possibly." *Undeniably.* "What can I do for you, Mom?" Laney glared at the empty doughnut tray, blaming her lurching stomach on Tuck's adoring fan but knowing it wasn't hunger that had her stewing. Her sister, Bree, was supposed to handle All Things Irma because Bree was capable of sustaining a healthy, functional mother-daughter relationship. Laney lived two thousand miles away and considered the geographic distance medicinal, a necessary element for maintaining familial homeostasis—all a fancy way of saying that Laney and her mom pushed each other's buttons, and the less time they spent together, the better.

"I know you're dodging me, Laney. But I assure you, this will be painless."

Laney wanted to say that's also what they whispered to dogs about to be euthanized. She couldn't say that, however, because the woman wearing the rain slicker on a blue-sky day had returned with her completed paperwork. Laney slipped it into the pile beneath the work order for the guy putting performance-grade tires on his Honda Civic.

It had been many months since Irma's best friend and business partner, Elliot Gregory, dropped dead without warning himself or anyone else, and her daughters had been on chaos watch ever since. A recent email from Bree complained of distributor invoices going past due and online orders being delivered to the wrong customers. She wrote, "Yesterday Mom came in wearing two different shoes—one brown loafer and one blue slide."

The shoes had briefly caught Laney's attention, but then again, everyone had their days. Just recently at Tire Stud, a man in tap shoes clickety-clacked across the cement floor to drop off his keys. "Call me when she comes in wearing a stiletto-heel and bedroom-slipper combo," Laney had emailed back. "Then we can worry."

"Laney," her mom said to her now, "you know I wouldn't call you at work to chat. But since this is where I caught you, I'll just say that with Elliot gone, I've had to make a few decisions about the Rainbow. I'd like you to come home so we can review them."

Home. The word made Laney pull at her waistband, her jeans suddenly too tight. Instinctively, she scanned the room for Tuck and found him pulling up his pants leg to show off his new socks, the ones with his face and racing number on them.

"This isn't a good time for me to leave the shop, Mom. It's mayhem around here. Plus, the receptionist quit." Actually, they fired her and one of the mechanics last week for pants-down shenanigans in the restroom. "Tuck hasn't been able to find anyone new." Or hadn't put his butt in a chair long enough to decide from the very viable candidates Laney had already vetted.

"I won't keep you more than a day or so."

"Can't we just discuss this stuff over the phone? Or video conference—even criminal trials are happening over Zoom these days."

Her mother shook her head. Laney didn't know how she knew this from two thousand miles away, but she did.

"I'll pay for your ticket."

"Mom, there's just no way—" Her plea was drowned suddenly amid the noise of the customer lobby erupting in laughter. Local news was running a video of a chicken riding an elephant and Tuck had maxed out the volume on the TV in the corner.

"Two days," her mom repeated. "No more than a week."

"Those aren't the same."

"You'll fly home, we'll settle our business, and I'll get some time together with both my daughters."

The front door opened and Frankie stepped through holding Miss Pickles. "I'm not sure what I hit," she began without waiting for Laney to hang up. There was absolutely no way she could leave Tuck to handle the shop on his own for a day, let alone a week.

"Hey, Laney," Tuck called. "Check this out!" A beaming customer held up one of his early headshots. He still had a young man's hairline and he'd signed it "Tuck, yeah!!"

Her mom sensed Laney's hesitation. "I know I'm asking a lot. So before you say no again, I want you to try to recall the last time I demanded you come home."

The line went silent, and because she'd been distracted by Miss Pickles barking at a dog she saw on TV, it took Laney a second to catch on. "You mean, you want me to remember right now?"

"Yes. Tell me, when was the last time I made you do as I asked?"

There hadn't been a last time and they both knew it. Less than a week after high school graduation, Laney had ditched her college plans and her family and joined Tuck on the racing circuit. Her mother had spent the twenty years since cycling between irate, disappointed, worried, and silent. But she'd never demanded her daughter come home.

Laney evaded the question. "Are you retiring?" Their mom was sixty-seven and her business partner was gone. "Are you handing the shop over to Bree? Is that what you need to tell me?"

"Laney, I don't know how much more direct I can be. Please. Come home."

Tuck emerged from whatever he'd been doing in the office and managed to overlook the appointment card holder on the reception desk that needed refilling, the empty coffeepot, and a gooey toddler-height handprint on the front door. "Who's that?" he whispered, gesturing at the phone.

Laney pretended she didn't hear. "When do you need me, exactly?"

"As soon as possible."

She looked at Tuck, who asked her again, "Seriously. Who is that?"

"I'll call you when I get home." She was pinned. What else could she do but comply?

2

34 days before closing...

Bree Bedford held the receiver to her heart before hanging up. She'd just taken a call from a customer wanting recommendations for a book that might get her twenty-three-year-old daughter reading again.

"She's moved to Kansas City for her very first job," the mother said, "where she knows absolutely no one, and it sounds as if she spends every last waking hour at the office. I'm afraid she's using work to compensate for her lack of social life, so I thought, maybe if I could just get her reading again it would break some sort of cycle, get her thinking about something besides work, work, work. I keep suggesting she go to the library, but, well, what do mothers know? Anyway, I remembered that one of your booksellers is a whiz at recommending books to non-bookish folks. Is he working today, by chance?"

She meant Elliot.

"No." Bree sighed. She hated this part. "I'm sad to say we lost Elliot in January."

"Oh dear," the woman tsk'd. "I'm so sorry to hear that. I know it's probably poor taste to ask, but...could you tell me which bookstore he works at now?"

Ever since Elliot died, Bree felt as if they'd been swimming through a dull, gray pain at the Rainbow, a gloaming without retreat. He had been the head to Irma's heart, and no one, none of them, had prepared themselves, their customers, or the store for the cleaving.

It was coming up on six o'clock. Technically, Bree was done at five, but Irma had left hours ago for a "quick errand," and if Bree went home, she'd have to lock the bookshop behind her. Not that there were any customers to help. Even the woman on the phone had decided to call a local Kansas City store to save herself some shipping cost.

For the third time in as many weeks, she opened a file on the shop computer labeled Newsletter—Template and tried to focus. Decades ago, Elliot had set the Rainbow apart from other local bookstores by writing a newsletter targeted at people who, for one reason or another, felt turned off or excluded from the book world. He used to say, *We book people can be awful, prickish snobs. Why is a yummy romance any less worthy of a reader's love than the latest New York literary sweetheart? I say if a certain type of book isn't your preferred cocktail, darling, simply put down the glass and order something new. You don't have to act as if you've been poisoned.*

If the quip had been shorter, Bree would've had it printed on T-shirts and book bags.

Since Elliot's passing, the newsletter had become her responsibility, and she was failing. She'd completed only two editions, and neither proved her worthy of stepping up as Elliot's successor. She'd tried her best, as she was trying now, but the cursor on the blank screen was too intimidating. Not a single title came to mind, even with hundreds of them staring at her from book spines lining the floor-to-ceiling shelves.

"The Book Haters' Book Club…"

She stared at the words until the cursor, so long without moving, stopped blinking altogether. "I guess that's my cue," she said and heard the empty store swallow her voice, as well as the click of the power switch on the back of the computer that followed. It was past seven. She'd spent more than an hour not writing.

She flipped the sign in the front window. See You Tomorrow.

When she and Laney were young, Irma used to stock them up with crayons and construction paper and say, "The window needs a new rainbow, don't you think?" They devoted hours to the work because, as Bree asserted, they were decorating the street. "The people who walk by will see how happy it is here and want to come inside."

Tonight, the front display at the Over the Rainbow Bookshop featured months-old new releases. The street hadn't seen a rainbow in ages.

She leaned over to pick up a stack of discarded books that needed to be reshelved and set them on the counter to do first thing in the morning. Then she wrote Irma a note and taped it to the top of the register. "Can I help you with online orders tomorrow?"

It was late May, and summer was winning its final battle with a retreating spring, warm days overtaking the cool, damp nights. Her walk home from the Rainbow was short, just under ten minutes, and she turned the corner onto her street to find her neighbors stringing lights across porch ceilings, preparing for parties to come. Northern summers were fleeting, and winter-weary Minnesotans didn't waste them. Perhaps a change of seasons was exactly what she and Irma needed.

Irma was "temporarily frail," that's how her mom phrased it, refusing to refer to her emotional state in universally understood terms like *sad*, or *blue*, or *in mourning.* "I won't feel this way forever. I'm just not at my best for the moment." Bree recalled watching her at Elliot's memorial service, accepting the condolences of longtime customers and thanking them for coming, while wondering if this might be her mother's final blow—losing her boyfriend Nestor, the man she met too late to make a life with, followed by Elliot, the man with whom she'd been so lucky to make a living.

Regardless of what her mother called it, Irma Bedford was depressed, and therefore it followed that the Rainbow, itself, appeared the same way. The bookshop used to be antique chic. Now she just looked tired. The tartan chairs in the front window were faded and thread-worn, the glass cabinets Elliot had scavenged from an old Catholic high school needed to be restained, and the pews he'd taken from the same school's chapel were so worn their brilliant blue paint had gone gray in patches. Only the Rainbow's signature piece, the broad pink chandelier hanging from a blue ceiling filled with clouds, reflected her former glory.

Maybe this summer Bree would scrounge up the money to hire a neighborhood kid to do some repainting. School would be out soon, and someone would want the cash. She should think about finding a new part-time team member, as well. Irma didn't need to work full-time, she deserved to cut back at her age, and every business had to be smart about preparing its "next-generation staff." She'd read an article online. "Always hire for tomorrow, not just today," it said.

Elliot had done all the bookkeeping for the store, so it would probably be a good idea if Bree took some of that work off Irma's shoulders. Of course, that meant she'd need to take an accounting class or two. She'd look for one tonight after she ate dinner.

Her feet, she noticed, had picked up the pace, and she felt unexpectedly refreshed by the walk. Yes, she thought. Summer was coming, and a summer could change everything.

The Book Haters' Book Club Newsletter

Issue #1
June 1989

Hello readers,

This is Elliot Gregory, daredevil bookseller at the Over the Rainbow Bookshop, here to announce a grand new endeavor: a monthly newsletter full of book recommendations for non-bookish people.

Why? Because think of the last time you walked through our yellow door and asked our small but intrepid team—*"What would you recommend for my [son, daughter, spouse, brother, sister, niece, nephew, boss, etc. etc.]? I love books, but I don't have any idea what they enjoy."*

It's a question we get every day, and one that presents a wonderful challenge: how to turn a possibly non-bookish person into a genuine book lover.

Or, consider other variations on this book dilemma... Maybe you have a child who used to read a lot, but seems to have lost interest. Maybe your husband only reads mysteries and you're hoping to shake him up. Maybe you're on your way to your boss's birthday party and, *gasp!* you forgot your present at home.

Is there any help?

Have no fear! Whatever your situation, we here at Over the Rainbow are ready to come to the rescue.

This month I'll highlight two recommendations that I recently made for customers facing very different book dilemmas.

Our first question comes from a mother whose ten-year-old daughter reads "above her age level" and can't seem to find any books she finds enjoyable as well as challenging. If you have a young reader like this in your family, may I recommend *Tuck Everlasting* by

Natalie Babbitt. It tells the story of Winnie, a girl who discovers a freshwater spring on their family land that, if drunk, makes a person immortal. It's full of adventure, dazzling characters, and it has the added benefit of throwing in a philosophical question or two, meaning your reader won't only be enthralled, they may also find themselves pondering, "Would I really want to live forever?"

Our second recommendation is *The Cape Ann* by Faith Sullivan. I sold this wonderful novel to a customer who explained that she and her neighbor were currently arguing about how much their children really understood and observed about family life. The customer believed children observe much more than we think they do, and if our own Irma Bedford's eagle-eyed daughter is any proof, I agree! (Wee Laney will NOT allow me more than my allotted two cans of Diet Pepsi per day, even when I think I've been successfully sneaky.) The book's narrator is a six-year-old girl named Lark, who watches as her family loses its chance to buy the house they love. You, too, will fall in love with this young girl with every turn of the page. Even non-bookish neighbor ladies will say, "Yes, please!" to Faith Sullivan's story.

—Elliot

Last Hope for the Haters

Every book lover knows the novel that knocked them off their axis, as well as the one that set them right again.

3

22 days before closing...

Thom Winslow possessed an unusual genetic code. Like a fox shedding its arctic coat, he knew when the seasons were about to take their last breaths, passing one into the next. Which was why he stood now at the side of their bed, preparing winter's sweaters for their summer rest.

He arranged them left to right by weight—cashmere, wool, cotton, linen—and again by color, dark to light. Each piece was fresh from the dry cleaner's tissue wrap and ready for inspection.

The fern-colored linen pullover was unsalvageable, a pin-size hole discovered above the left cuff.

The hunter green cashmere, too, the V-neck no longer crisp.

In truth, they all needed to go. He'd grown so thin that the once-lovely pieces hung from his bones, mildewed tapestries on an aging manor wall. But, as with a gentleman to the manor born, walking away was an impossibility. These were more than yarns, they were history, the story of his life with Elliot.

Unwrap. Inspect. Fold. Box.

The repetitive sequence of tasks calmed him. June had landed. Summer was a place in which sweaters did not belong.

With the last of his pieces properly cared for, he steeled himself, then crossed to the other side of the bed. It remained empty but for the dry cleaner's bundles of Elliot's sweaters, waiting to be touched, opened, welcomed, and loved. Waiting for Elliot.

"Unwrap. Inspect. Fold. Box," Thom said to the lonely bundles. "We don't wear sweaters in the summertime. That's not the way it works."

He gently removed the first of the pile and laid it down where Elliot's chest once rose and fell. He peeled back the tissue expectantly, though his fingers already knew. The cream wool fisherman's sweater, purchased at Arnotts on Henry Street in Dublin. Just past dusk on the second Thursday in September, 2005. They'd had tea at Keoghs on Trinity Street, and Elliot was unprepared for the chill that descended on the city every afternoon. He'd left his coat at the hotel. It had been Thom's idea to buy the sweater. "A souvenir for the ages," he'd told Elliot. "You'll wear it forever."

The detail of that day was easy to recall. "For at least the first six months after losing your loved one, expect your memory to go into overdrive," his grief support group leader, Laikin, had said. "The images will come flooding—the children's birthdays and the holidays and the vacations, even quiet moments together, just the two of you.

"As a new widow or widower or surviving partner, you will have memories aplenty. Just *don't* expect to remember what your neighbor told you yesterday, or what time your doctor's appointment is, or that very important task your son or daughter asked you to write down because it's so crucial. Those things you shouldn't be expected to remember, so grant yourself lots of grace when you forget them, because right now, your heart and your brain are both saying, 'What is a doctor's appointment when I just lost my life?'"

Unwrap the paper, Thom instructed his fingers. *Lay it flat for inspection. Smooth the wrinkles. Examine it lovingly.*

The sweater looked as if it would last another hundred years.

"Bastard," he whispered. Then he folded the sleeves flat across the chest, and back against themselves in half. He brought the waist up to meet the neck and smoothed, then brought the sides together. The square was crisp, the task complete, its acid-free box awaiting its charge. Thom laid the sweater inside and closed the lid, then slid down the bed to the floor and wept for the hundredth time since dawn.

It was late when he finished his organizing. Dark, though he couldn't say for certain what time—a day's normal rhythms faltered when food lost its priority. But with the boxes now neatly at home in the guest room closet for the summer, he made his way to the kitchen. Even if he couldn't stomach anything rich, he could at least manage tea. He put the kettle on and pulled the tin of Darjeeling from the shelf. He wasn't a fan of sugar, but maybe he ought to drop in a cube. The calories would do him good. There was a roll leftover from his stop into Turtle Bread the other day. Probably hard, definitely past its prime, though he ought to at least try. Perhaps with a sliver of Havarti, if he had some. He would look. He would take a bite, even if only one.

He noticed the clock on the stove as he passed. The numbers glowed 9:05. Not as late as he thought, which he decided to take as a small victory. He had accomplished something today—the wardrobe was sorted, he was open to the idea of food, and he'd done it all before crawling into bed.

A good day.

The numbers on the clock turned to 9:06 just as his phone rang. Thom knew who it was. He'd been avoiding her calls all week. Yesterday there had been four, today there'd been six. This call made seven.

Could he answer? He knew he should, but he'd always been more skilled at avoidance than confrontation. *She's grieving, too,* Elliot would have reminded him.

Irma isn't your competition, he used to say. *I wish you wouldn't act as if she were.*

Then, why won't you retire? Thom asked. *And don't tell me that the bookstore is your life. That only makes it worse.*

If I told you otherwise, I'd be lying.

Thom picked up his phone and glanced at the screen. He'd been correct. About it all.

"Irma. What can I do for you?"

"Are you available tomorrow afternoon?"

She sounded as weary as Thom would've hoped. Their mutual despair was too heavy to carry all by himself.

"I have made some financial decisions about the store, and given that you're the beneficiary of Elliot's estate, I'd like you to hear them."

"How much did you sell it for?"

The question seemed to surprise her, and she took in a sharp breath. It shouldn't have. Of course she was selling. The Rainbow would never be the same without Elliot. The sooner they ended the misery, the better.

"It's—" She mulled her words carefully. "I intend to ensure you receive Elliot's entire share. Despite the circumstances."

He ignored the veiled "circumstances" comment and agreed to meet Irma and the brokers at three o'clock the following afternoon.

He was on-site at Vandaveer Investments by two fifteen. He found a parking space and contemplated his next move. He wondered which would make more of a statement, to enter early and make an impression on the brokers before she arrived? Or to enter late, knowing he'd forced the group to wait? Elliot would have respected the question but been offended by its target. *She's not your competition*, he'd repeat, forever looking out for that woman.

Of course, Thom knew exactly why today's meeting had him behaving like such a cad. Elliot—generous, loyal, and lovely as he was—had never finished his estate plans, despite having awoken countless Sunday mornings saying, *Remind me to call the lawyer this week and get on the schedule to finish all that.* Thom had reminded him. Many times. Minnesota did not have common-law marriage rights, so Thom had been mindful to update his estate plans. Yet, for Elliot, the simple act of making Thom the executor of his will had never been brought to paper.

The estate wasn't all a mess, thankfully. They'd bought the house together and it was paid for. Thom had his personal retirement accounts, for which he'd saved over his thirty-plus-year career as a phlebotomist ("Count von Gaycula" to friends). Elliot's commute was a five-minute walk to work, and Thom preferred to drive wherever they went, so they'd sold the second car years ago.

Only the bookshop remained unaccounted for. Perhaps he should have mentioned the hiccup left by Elliot's shortsighted estate planning to Irma before she sold. But, then again, perhaps she shouldn't have taken so much of Elliot for herself while he was alive.

He hated being angry, especially when he missed Elliot so desperately. But how could he not? Elliot's negligence left Thom feeling even more alone. Because Elliot hadn't taken the time to plan. Because he never considered what life would be like for Thom without him. Because he'd given greater care and attention to his business partner, Irma, than to Thom, his partner for life.

He was angry about having been left without a legal and financial say in Elliot's legacy.

He was angry about the small but monumentally consequential loopholes that still existed in relationships that didn't conform to 1950s ideology. That if he and Elliot had simply said "I do" in front of a judge, Thom wouldn't be in this position.

He was working himself into a stew and he hadn't even stepped out of the car.

4

21 days until closing...

Bree was in tears. Thom was muttering to himself. Laney was calculating her escape from this conference room.

Irma stood. "Thank you, gentlemen. We won't take any more of your time."

The meeting, all twenty minutes of it, had been bedlam. People talked over each other, voices raised, a circus *interruptus*. Bree's agony grew so pitched she became incomprehensible—shrill, teary, and insistent. "Why? *Why?*"

To survive, Laney distracted herself by calculating the number of hours she'd have saved by attending via video. Eleven, probably, unless you counted the sleep she'd lost trying to guess at what could possibly be so pressing it demanded her physical presence. That number was actually closer to twenty-four, a full day sacrificed for the privilege of smelling Old Man Vandaveer's circa 1992 cologne. Everything else she could have witnessed digitally, needing no more than what a series of zeros and ones dancing across the stratosphere and onto her screen could have provided. She didn't ask for this three-dimensional immersion into her mother's business decisions nor did she benefit from being close enough to touch Trevor Vandaveer's face and its infuriating lack of wrinkles.

And yet, here she was.

"There's filings and such we'll need your help with these next few weeks, Irma," Mr. Vandaveer boomed. "My secretary will be in touch."

Laney saw the receptionist open the conference room door and she raced through, out of earshot before her mother said her goodbyes. She hit the elevator button. *Down, down, down.*

"Wait!" Bree was on her heels. "Don't leave me here."

"Get a move on, then." Laney punched. *Down. Down.* She could see their mother wrapping up, handshakes all around, and didn't want to get sucked into the vortex.

"We have to wait for Mom." Bree sniffed, prowling her purse for a tissue and coming up short. "I can't believe this."

Thom came to her rescue with a crisp handkerchief, the initials *TW* stitched in navy at the corner. "It's clean. Freshly ironed this morning." Bree accepted it with teary thanks.

Irma headed for the elevators. Thom announced he preferred the stairs.

Returning to the Rainbow, Irma unlocked the yellow front door. She walked in first, followed by Bree, who made a direct line for the restroom. Laney held back, wanting a moment to herself, and when she pushed the door open, a string of small brass bells tinkled overhead.

The shop looked just as Laney remembered, and yet seeing it brought the sensation she'd felt as a young girl at her great-aunt Katherine's funeral. The person lying in the casket looked like Auntie Kate but only in theory. Likewise, this Over the Rainbow struck her as a lifeless, waxen model of its former self—the same salvaged-wood shelves, the Catholic school confessionals–turned–reading nooks, the pink chandelier beneath a ceiling full of clouds. The same, but less so.

Laney inhaled, and there it was—paper, dust, Pine-Sol, and a hint of coffee.

She walked down the center aisle, running a finger along the shelves—planks that once lined the chapel walls at Immaculate Heart of Mary School for Girls. Sometimes, when the store was empty and the lights dimmed, she'd put her ear to the wood to listen, as if the girls' whispered prayers lived on, still circling in search of answers. *Bless me, Father, for I have sinned…*

Laney had a long-held appreciation for sinners.

At the end of the aisle, she turned left and headed toward what Elliot had called "Vanity Corner." Here hung the pictures of the most-famous-of-the-famous authors who had readings there over the decades. Pat Conroy and Tom Clancy, nearly identical in white shirts and sports coats behind the same podium, years apart. Toni Morrison. Sue Grafton. Even Judy Blume—she'd been touring with her adult fiction novel, *Summer Sisters*, yet her mom got her to the Rainbow for Laney's sake. "Bring your *Superfudge* books," she'd said. "I'm certain she'll sign them for you."

Laney scanned the wall until she spotted her favorite photo: Anne Rice, 1998. She was on tour for *The Vampire Armand*, but far more important to fourteen-year-old Laney was that Anne Rice had written *Interview with the Vampire*, which became a movie with Tom Cruise and Brad Pitt and was the closest thing to sex Laney had ever seen or imagined. In the picture, Anne wore a white silk blouse with sleeves that flowed from the cuffs of her black velvet jacket, like a flower in bloom.

Finally, she looked for the article from the *Minneapolis/St. Paul Standard*, October 1, 1980. Elliot and her mom were shaking hands and grinning like goons beneath the headline, "Former Rivals Join Forces Over the Rainbow: New bookstore opens in Lyn-Lake." The photo was taken during Elliot's tight-T-shirt-and-mustache days, her mom in a white eyelet skirt and blouse. She was only twenty-six in that picture and already starting her second business.

Her first had been a bookmobile called Books 'Round Town, a smart idea for a twenty-four-year-old who couldn't afford rent or inventory, but who did have five hundred dollars and an uncle with an old delivery van. It was a great success—for one summer. Then the gas crisis hit and filling her seven-miles-to-the-gallon truck quickly ate her profits. And she had competition. Elliot had formulated his own version of the same idea, only his bookmobile was on the back of a three-wheeled bicycle. He had a lot less room for stock, but pedal-power was free.

"A Technicolor journey into the world of books" read one framed and yellowed review. "A bookshop so overflowing, it may actually have a pot of gold hidden within its stacks" said another. Laney and Bree had crawled on hands and knees into every corner and shadow of the store when they were girls. If there was treasure hidden at the Rainbow, it was theirs to find.

"He doesn't look a day younger there than when he died. Minus the mustache, of course." Her mother had sneaked up on her. "I haven't had the chance to hug you yet. May I?"

"Sure." Laney wrapped her arms around her mom's shoulders. There was less of her now, bone where there used to be muscle.

"I've shrunk, can you tell? Doctor said I've lost a full quarter inch since last year's checkup."

Laney held her at arm's length to examine the shrinking patient. "Maybe. But compared to Bree, you still look like the giant at the top of the beanstalk." Laney, whose father had been nothing more than a handsome face during a concert at the about-to-become world-famous nightclub, First Avenue, took after her mother. They were both five foot nine with child-rearing hips, a decent metabolism, and complexions that didn't cower in the sun. Bree, however, had been blessed with different genes altogether and carried a custom stepladder with her throughout the shop to reach anything higher than the middle shelf.

"Hey, Mom—" Laney lowered her voice "—Bree seems pretty devastated by your news." She scanned the store, her sister nowhere in sight. "I can't believe you didn't tell her about your plans before the meeting, or at least in private."

"I have two daughters, and I don't play favorites."

Laney bit her tongue to keep from reminding her of all the times she'd told her not to lie. "I would've been fine with a text, but Bree's made her life here. Why spring bad news on her like that? She's been locked in the bathroom crying since we got back."

"Laney, this is, and always was, a family business. Thom was Elliot's family, and you and Bree are mine. No one deserves any more or less than any other. In fact, had I told Bree first, you would have accused me of being unfair."

"Only if there was cash involved." She laughed louder than necessary, though she was only partly kidding and they both knew it.

Her mother didn't flinch before saying, "There's hardly enough cash for me," and Laney suddenly felt like the biggest heel in a two-hundred-boot parade.

"Mom, that was a joke. I'm not looking for money. Tuck and I are doing great. We're considering opening a second location." Which was true, to the extent that Tuck had been dropping hints about expanding, to which Laney typically responded with, "It's an idea."

Irma went on, "If anything, I hope that by seeing me treat you and your sister equally you'll recognize that I don't love her more because she stayed or you less because you left. I worried about you plenty, but you're okay now. And yes, Bree is going to have a tough go for a while, but you're both adults. Your lives are yours to live."

"You sound like a motivational poster." Laney glanced at her mom's shoes—a matched pair.

"Well, I'm afraid it's true. Life doesn't always give fair warning, my dear, and if anyone taught me that, it was you."

Bree was woozy with disbelief. She'd been stupid to believe there was any future for the Rainbow beyond Elliot and even dumber to think Irma would pass the legacy on to her.

"Hey, Breetle-bug." Laney eventually found her sitting in a corner of the back room and plopped down, claiming the adjacent square of concrete floor. "Mom invited us to dinner at the house tonight, but then she admitted she didn't have anything to cook and would have to go to the grocery. So, instead of waiting for that to all come together, how 'bout you and I go out?"

"Sure." Bree sniffled. "We could grab pizza at Fratini's. Or there's a new sandwich place around the corner. I'm never all that hungry after work, but I'm a mess if I don't eat something." She was babbling. Laney gave her a cockeyed stare.

"Am I making you nervous?"

"Everything makes me anxious these days. I cut my gums just brushing my teeth this morning."

Her sister gave her a sympathetic look but mercifully withheld comment. "Any restaurants around here I might miss? I was sad to see that It's Greek to Me is gone. I think food tastes better when you can hear the cooks threatening to stab each other in the kitchen."

Bree pulled a fresh tissue from her pocket. "Everything's changed. Only Fratini's is still around, and his kids changed the whole place up. More Pinterest, less Billy Joel—no curtained booths, no candles. They even painted the walls white."

Laney screwed a face. "I hate progress."

Irma offered to stay at the shop until close, which Bree thought was the least she could do, considering. She and Laney landed at Suzie Q's, a newish bistro around the corner, where they took a table by the window and stared uncomfortably at the passing traffic until one of them knew what to say.

"I know you're probably thinking I should have seen this coming." Bree decided to beat herself up before Laney got the chance to. "I thought Mom was just depressed. I didn't think she was about to pull the rug out."

Laney slowly fingered the rim of her water glass. "I've never understood her, so why would I expect you to?"

Bree said, "It took Mom an eternity to recover from losing Nestor, and they'd only been together for five years. She and Elliot were in business together for over forty. I never imagined she could be on the verge of a decision this monumental so soon after losing him."

"Again," Laney said, "don't look at me for insight."

"I'm telling you, they'd become one of those old couples you see at the grocery store, holding hands and arguing over whether to buy the superpulp or pulp-free orange juice."

"They held hands and went grocery shopping?"

"No." Bree flicked her wrist, erasing the confused metaphor. "I'm just trying to illustrate how close they were still, all the way to the end. Because in that regard, yeah, it makes sense she wouldn't want to run the bookshop without Elliot. But on the other hand, I can't believe she's just letting the Rainbow die. It was so much bigger than the two of them, you know?"

Laney, however, didn't look like she did know, and Bree needed her to understand. She felt the urgency the way you feel a pinprick, sharp and shocking. "We have customers who've been coming to the Rainbow since the day it opened. They brought their kids in when they were little, and now those kids are coming with their own kids, and even some of those kids have kids. Elliot had a woman go into labor in the gardening section, and that baby is an adult who still shops with us. Her name is Lara. She has brown hair, two of the cutest little girls you've ever seen, and she loves anything by J. Ryan Stradal."

"I've seen his stuff. Didn't they name a beer after one of his books?"

"Yeah. BLOTZ, it's a lager by Blackstack Brewing." Bree caught herself short. "Wait, how do you know that?"

"I'm a red-blooded American. I drink beer."

"I know, but—" What had she been saying before getting distracted? Her forehead was beaded with sweat. She hoped the waiter was coming soon with their water.

Laney smiled politely but turned toward the window, away from the conversation. After a time, she took a heavy breath. "I know this isn't what you want to hear, but maybe selling the Rainbow is for the best. I mean, how much longer did you think Mom would be able to work as much as she does? She's not old, but she's old*ish*, and everyone she loves is dead—besides us, of course."

Bree recoiled. "That's morbid."

"Not really. You said it yourself—from the moment Elliot died, she's had to work every day in a place that reminds her of how unhappy she is, of how much she's lost. If that were me, I'd want out, too."

Wanting out might've been easy for Laney to imagine—history had shown she had no trouble fleeing when the mood suited her—but the Rainbow was Irma's life. Since when did a woman as strong as their mother just give up on something as fundamental as that?

Laney continued speaking, apparently blind to Bree now burying her face in her napkin. "I know you love the Rainbow, but think of it this way—now you'll be free to do whatever you want. Open your own bookshop, or find an even better job. *Eat, Pray, Love* your way around the world. Get famous designing après-ski wear for dogs."

Bree sank further into her sorrow. "I don't have a dog."

She knew better than to engage with her sister's sarcasm, but every visit, it took her falling into a few traps before she remembered, and even those embarrassments weren't half as frustrating as not being able to say aloud what she really wished she could say right now. *I don't want a better job. I want the Rainbow.*

She practically ran the bookshop by herself, thanks to her mom's half-vacant state. After Irma requested three hundred copies of Stephen King's newest release instead of their usual thirty, she learned to double-check vendor orders, and she'd become an expert at performing casual walk-bys to close the cash drawer on the register or reshelve the stacks of books her mother would start to inventory but never quite finish. Bree had taken over so much of the management work, she'd convinced herself that she was almost ready to take over the Rainbow entirely and forever. Until Irma held up a shovel and announced she was digging its grave.

"I don't know what to do." Bree dropped her napkin and sank deep into the booth, deflated, humiliated, and judging from the look of relief on Laney's face, all alone.

"I get that it's different for you," Laney said. "But to me, the bookshop always seemed like an older, prettier sister—she got all the attention, while I sat in the nurse's office wearing a maxi pad the size of a pillow and waiting for Mom to drop off a clean pair of pants."

"What are you talking about?"

"The first time I got my period," Laney explained. "I was in gym playing scooter tag, and suddenly, I've got something running down my leg. It took Mom more than an hour to come to my rescue, and when she did, she made some excuse about toddler story time or a delivery delay or whatever else I couldn't care less about because I had just gotten my first period in front of my entire fifth-grade class!"

"The shop gets really busy sometimes," Bree countered, knowing better than to make excuses for Irma's poor behavior, but doing it anyway.

Laney ticked off more from her list of resentments. "Remember when she had to cancel my birthday party at the Mall of America because one of the Rainbow staff phoned in sick and Mom had to cover their shift? She kept saying, 'What choice do I have, Laney?' Meanwhile, I had to invite all my friends over to the house for cupcakes that night instead, as if chocolate frosting with sprinkles was a decent substitute for a day of shopping and gossip and flirting with boys."

Bree remembered. "Yeah, that wasn't so great."

There were the nights Irma missed school performances and softball games and forgot to pick them up from whatever event she'd promised to attend but hadn't. The dinners she didn't make. The laundry she never managed to finish. "The Rainbow took too much of her attention and nearly all of her time," Laney said. "I'm sorry this sucks for you, but I'm not going to miss it when it's gone."

I'm sorry this sucks for you, but… Bree felt the sentiment hover in the air between them, sweet like honey but also sticky and irksome. If Elliot had been there he would've looked at her and said, *Sounds as if you're on your own, sweet cheeks.*

The waiter arrived at last. Bree sat up straight and smiled politely as she ordered a glass of white wine and a full pitcher of water. When he was gone, she took a breath and assured herself that if she just kept talking, Laney would eventually hear her and understand. "I know you don't love the Rainbow, and that you're probably ready to fly home on the first plane out, but please listen to me—something isn't right. Mom would never just give up on the bookshop, or her customers, or everything she and Elliot built. Not to mention the fact she'd always implied she wanted one or both of us to take it over. This whole deal is fishy. I can feel it in my gut."

"Aren't you supposed to smell it?"

"What?"

"If something's fishy, then it stinks. You've always mixed your metaphors. It's cute."

"Laney." She dropped her face into her palm. "This isn't funny to me."

Her sister waited a beat, as if Bree were just going to snap out of her malaise. Finally, "Alright, I'm sorry. I'm wiping the smile right off my face, see?"

Bree looked up as Laney's face transitioned to sad clown.

"Thank you," she said.

The waiter returned with their wine and they both took the moment to sip and shift the energy between them.

"Does Mom have a lawyer?" Laney asked. "I assume she's had to have used someone over the years."

Bree assumed so, as well, though she couldn't remember having ever seen the name of a specific firm or attorney anywhere in the bookshop's files. "Would they even talk to us? Client confidentiality and all that."

Laney grimaced. "Probably not. What about the bank? Do you have signing privileges? Would you be able to speak with them about any financial-planning discussions she may have had?"

She didn't. "And Elliot did the accounting, so who knows how she's keeping the books now."

"Well, that's just super. We can't access any possible legal counsel she may have received, we don't know how much money the Rainbow is taking in, and the bank's not going to be able to talk to us. Hooray and huzzah!"

Bree let their frustration and limited options hang a moment, only to add, "But we have to do something, right? She's our mom. If she really is in some sort of predicament—"

Laney collapsed into herself, plucky optimism depleted. "Fine. But I promised Tuck I'd only be gone a week. I'll do my best to help you while I'm here, then I'm going home. I've got my own business to run, don't forget."

Bree felt herself release an ounce of her compounding worry. She didn't know what, if anything, they could accomplish in such a short time, but at least for the next six days, she wouldn't be left to flounder. "Thank you. I mean it."

"One week," Laney emphasized. "And you're welcome."

The waiter reappeared and Bree recognized him as the one who always wore clever T-shirts. "What's your shirt say tonight?"

He puffed his chest and moved his tray out of the way. "'Life is one long exercise in convincing ourselves we're not alone.'"

When he turned to go, Bree saw the alien head on the back of his tee, but chose to ignore that part.

5

20 days until close...

"Up and at 'em. Let's go."

Laney woke to her mother trying to drag her out of bed. "I'm not sixteen. You don't get to do this anymore."

Growing up, mornings had been the source of their most epic mother-daughter battles. Irma loved to get the early worm. Laney didn't understand how she could have possibly been born to this woman.

"Come on! You haven't worked with me since you were a teenager." Her mother pulled back the covers before Laney could get a grip on them. "Won't be many more chances. Everything green turns gold, Ponyboy."

"Mom—" Laney groaned, too fog-headed to decide whether it was worse that her mom was dragging her out of bed before daybreak or that she was quoting *The Outsiders*, as if her daughter were still twelve.

"Up! Up!" Her mother was already headed for the door. "I'll make coffee."

Laney succumbed to the inevitability of morning and eased herself up to sitting. Irma had already been asleep by the time she got home from dinner with Bree last night—it had been all of nine thirty. She'd also opened her suitcase to find she'd forgotten to pack pajamas. Her whole life, she forgot one of two things when traveling: pajamas or deodorant. You'd think she'd remember to double-check for them by the age of thirty-eight, but Tuck's extensive packing lists always took precedence over her own, and he'd grown so accustomed to her care that now he didn't even try to get himself ready when they traveled. Thus, Laney continued to forget her deodorant and pajamas, and thusser still, here she was, in her childhood bedroom, wearing a Backstreet Boys T-shirt over a pair of bedazzled Juicy sweatpants she'd found in her dresser. She rubbed her backside gingerly. Sleeping with rhinestones across your butt had its drawbacks.

Downstairs, she found her mom filling her ancient press-pot coffee maker from a steaming kettle. Unlike her friends whose parents bought gallon cans of Folgers and brewed coffee that looked like tea, their mom had always prided herself—at least when it came to beverages—on not behaving like an average Midwesterner. She made a killer martini, and her coffee poured ink black.

Laney grabbed an "Over the Rainbow Celebrates 25 Years" mug from the cupboard, cleared a stack of papers from a kitchen chair, and took a seat. If there were one word to summarize the current state of her mother's house, it would be *stacks*. Everywhere she went, stacks followed—stacks of books, stacks of bills, stacks of laundry. She even folded and stacked her grocery bags instead of stuffing them away like a normal person.

"So, tell me about how you decided to sell to the Vandaveers?" Now that she understood her mission this week, there was no reason to avoid diving in. "Did you go to them? Did they come to you?"

Her mom grabbed a carton of eggs from the fridge and began cracking them into a bowl. "Did I tell you about Nestor's sister, Helen? She has a condo in Sarasota, and her neighbor has to go to Boca Raton for a few months to help her friend recover from surgery. She wants to rent her place out while she's gone to help cover expenses, but only to someone she feels comfortable with. I'm thinking about doing it."

"Nice diversion, Mom." She meant from the topic of selling the store.

"It would be, don't you think? Summer is probably hot as Hades in Florida. But it's been such a long winter." She stopped whisking her eggs and stared at the bowl, her eyes fixed on a memory. "A terrible winter."

Laney gave her a moment. Normally, she broke through her mom's diversions by returning to the topic at hand, but this time, she sensed it was better to stay quiet. "I didn't even ask before I started scrambling these, Laney. I'm so sorry. I can get more eggs out of the fridge if you'd prefer over easy."

"Scrambled is fine. How 'bout I make us some toast to go with?"

An hour later, they walked through the yellow door of the Rainbow.

"What would you like me to do today? I'm pretty rusty, remember."

Her mother was already flipping light switches and powering up everything with a plug. "You decide. Find a quiet corner with a good book. Chat with Bree. It's just nice to have you close."

They were in the stockroom now. Her mother filled the coffeepot with water and motioned to Laney to start scooping the grounds into the basket. "Of course, I'll even be happy to pay you if you'd like to work."

Laney laughed. "Why now? You hardly paid me anything for all the hours I spent here as a kid."

Her mom crossed her arms and leaned against the counter. "I paid you plenty when you actually did something. Most of the time, you were too busy noodling around with Tuck."

Yeah, that part was probably true.

Bree startled at the sight of Irma and Laney when she opened the door. "You're here!"

Laney smirked. "I flew in yesterday, remember? How many glasses of wine did you have last night?"

"I'm just used to being the first one in these days, is all." She felt the heat rise on her face. Seeing the two of them standing there, fresh from a night together at the house where Laney and Bree had grown up, poked at her with unexpected sibling jealousy. Laney hadn't been a factor for so many years.

Irma handed her a cup of coffee. "It's no fancy latte, but it'll save you a few dollars, at least."

"Thanks." Bree couldn't help but note Irma's sudden concern for her cash flow. She caught Laney's eye and did her best to shoot her a coded message. *Is Mom ready to talk?*

Laney subtly shook her head.

Irma excused herself, explaining she didn't have time to chat, given the ten-thirty toddler story time this morning and the Murder Ladies Book Club this afternoon, for which she hadn't even begun to prepare moderator questions. Before stepping away, she said to Laney, "Why don't you join me at Toddler Time? You can read one of your favorite books as a kid."

"They have *Three's Company* in book form?"

"I didn't let you watch *Three's Company.*"

"You didn't know what I did between the hours of three p.m. and six p.m."

"Come join me, anyway," Irma said. "The kids are adorable. They'll cheer you up."

"I'm perfectly cheerful!" she called to her mother's fleeing back.

Bree waited until she was out of earshot. "What do you think? Does she seem stressed, happy, miserable, relieved, what?"

Laney scowled. "Is *Irma* an emotion? Because that's how she seems—one hundred percent Irma."

"But is she open to talking? Do you think she'll explain her decision to you?"

"She dragged me out of bed, made coffee, then got all googly-eyed about possibly going to visit Nestor's sister in Florida. But first, let's pay special attention to that first part—*she dragged me out of bed.* If she keeps that up, I'm going home early, no matter what I promised you. Tuck is the only one allowed to annoy me in the bedroom anymore."

Bree's spirits sank. She'd lain awake most of the night, despite having been buoyed by her dinner with Laney, and now even the small reserve of confidence she'd managed to salvage after yesterday's bombshell was depleted, leaving her nearly too tired to stand. "Just keep trying, alright?"

"Aye-aye, Captain." Laney's tone was a little too sharp for Bree's fledgling self-esteem, which Laney must have realized because she quickly softened, adding, "I'll look through the files for the name of Mom's attorney today. And if I don't find it here, I can dig through her office at home."

"Thank you."

"I still don't think there's anything we can do," Laney said.

"I know," Bree assured her.

"You might have to come bail me out of the county jail if Mom drags me out of bed again."

"I'll call Tuck for the cash."

"Ask for extra because I'm going to need a drink after."

Bree promised she would.

6

18 days until close...

Thom allowed himself thirty-six hours to recover from the shock of Irma's news. Then he threw himself into the task of uncovering why she was willing to sell Elliot's Rainbow for bubblegum money and what, if anything, he could do to stop it.

He went online until he exhausted his googling skills, then read the pamphlets local brokerages had mailed to Elliot over the years and that Thom had stashed away just in case. He drove to the library and stayed until the lights went out. Finally, sitting at the kitchen table with his notes and a strong pot of Darjeeling, he decided that what he'd learned was more than concerning. It was compelling. Or, at least, very informative.

This morning, he stood at the kitchen counter brewing himself a mug of elderberry tea—antioxidants being especially necessary after such a late night—while reciting an important excerpt from a well-detailed Small Business Association guide he'd found at the library... "The biggest mistake a small business owner can make when selling is failing to prepare..."

Just as Elliot had left Thom with the financial fallout of failing to plan his estate, it appeared that by being the sole handler of the bookkeeping, he had also failed Irma. Oh, how he wished he could bring himself to celebrate, but he could not. He didn't wish heartache on anyone, Irma Bedford or otherwise.

He set two legal pads side by side on the kitchen table, ready to take his twenty-four-hour business education to the next level. On the white pad, he wrote "Selling a Small Business: Best Practices" and got to work by reviewing and compiling what he now knew were the basic steps.

He flipped the page and wrote "Priorities?" Irma had obviously prioritized a fast sale. In less than three weeks, she would wipe her hands of Rainbow dust and walk away into the sunset—with about five dollars in her pocket.

He was also concerned by her choice of buyer, Vandaveer Investments. They had a long and storied history in Lyn-Lake, and he didn't think he could name a more controversial developer. A few Vandaveer projects had, indisputably, brought an economic and aesthetic face-lift to the neighborhood. For example, the grocery store, Nygaard's. It was a Lyn-Lake landmark, but it hadn't provided a pleasant shopping experience since sometime in the eighties. The carts drove every direction but forward, the linoleum floors were cracked, and the frozen foods section smelled like the ice age.

About two years ago, however, one of the Nygaard descendants finessed an infusion of investment capital from Vandaveer, and together, they remodeled the entire store. The floors were planked with salvaged wood, the once mayonnaise-filled deli selection now looked like a curated Instagram feed, and the produce section smelled like a farmer's market.

Nygaard's was a flagship Vandaveer success story.

In contrast, there was the Stone Bakery fiasco. The Stone, as locals called it, had been in the area since 1890, one of the longest-serving bakeries in Minneapolis. They baked their bread in ovens whose bricks were made of pink shale quarried from the bluffs above the Mississippi River and fired in kilns along its banks. Ruins from some of the kilns were still visible today on Harriet Island in St. Paul, making the Stone a rarely seen and vital link between history and industry.

Regrettably, the bakery fell into neglect and finally ceased operations around the turn of the millennium. The building was put on the market in hopes that a food industry investor might see it for the historical unicorn it was and bring it back to life. Sadly, none did. In 2005, Lyn-Lake residents walked past the iconic pink-brick building to find a new banner blowing in the breeze. "Future project site for Vandaveer Investments. Moving Minneapolis Forward."

Within a week, the Stone was gone. By the following spring, black-and-steel luxury condos had taken its place. Not a pink brick anywhere. Neighbors, Elliot and Thom included, had a collective stroke. Why hadn't there been public meetings? Why hadn't they been given the chance to comment? The answer was loopholes.

Always with the loopholes.

And now they had their sights set on the Rainbow.

He pushed the white legal pad aside and picked up the yellow one. Now that he'd reviewed everything about letting go of a business, it was time to develop a strategy for keeping it. He wrote "Next Steps" at the top. And then he sat, his page blank and his mind echoing, devastatingly empty.

The shop was busy for a weekday morning, and Bree was happy for the distraction. Laney had come to work with Irma again but been quick to give Bree a look that said "Sorry, no progress." Meaning, she still hadn't located the name of the shop's lawyer, hadn't discovered a trove of secret documents, hadn't succeeded in getting her mother talking. The clock was ticking while they stood still.

Irma, meanwhile, was behaving as if she'd already retired and had been on the phone in the back since she'd arrived. From what Bree could gather, she was talking to Nestor's sister, Helen, about the condo in Sarasota, and she was packing her bags.

The bell above the yellow door tinkled.

"Good morning, Mrs. Baumgartner. How can I help

you?" One of their most loyal neighborhood customers, Violet Baumgartner, diligently curated "exploratory kits" for her grandson and came in weekly, looking for books on everything from the color red to Dixieland jazz. She had exacting tastes and required a delicate hand. Elliot called her exasperating. Irma described her as a "thunderstorm—necessary, and occasionally terrifying."

"I have arranged for my grandson to spend one full day a week with me this summer," Violet began, "and I plan to use the time to immerse him in the arts. We'll spend June on the visual arts, beginning with the great painters."

"Wonderful!" Bree quickly tried to remember the grandson's age. Had he even started school yet?

Mrs. Baumgartner continued, "In my research, I found several children's books about the Impressionists, but I can't find anything on Cubism suitable for a four-year-old."

Laney suddenly peeked her smirking face from behind the door of the confessional-slash-reading cubby where she'd been hiding from her daughter-of-a-bookseller responsibilities. Bree said a silent prayer for her to keep her mouth shut. Mrs. Baumgartner, if given one's full and diligent attention, was no more volatile than baking soda, but Laney's quippish sense of humor would be all the vinegar needed to create a volcanic mess.

Violet must have sensed Bree's apprehension because she added, "Remember, my Adam is an advanced reader." Then she pulled at the hem of her sweater, straightening it with a snap. Bree recognized the tell—whenever Mrs. Baumgartner stretched her clothing, she was also stretching the truth.

"He's reading already?" she said. "What a wonder."

Violet pursed. "Well, he's not fluent *aloud* yet. But we're getting there."

They settled on a book about young Picasso; it was as close as they could find to Cubism for four-year-olds, and it could be delivered within a week. Bree completed the sale details online while trying her best to ignore the loud and ongoing phone call in the stockroom.

"Mid-June is too soon, Helen. I couldn't possibly be there before July first."

Violet departed just as a young mother with a baby cocooned against her chest approached Bree to ask, "What's the name of that book about the two women who paddled through the Boundary Waters way up to Canada? There's something about fighting off bears and losing their food… I think Kerri Miller interviewed the author on Minnesota Public Radio?"

Bree knew the book, *Hudson Bay Bound* by Natalie Warren, and led her to it. Her morning continued as such. A man needed a guide to World War II aircraft. An aunt was looking for the *Dog Man* series for her niece.

"No, I prefer to take the stairs," Irma chattered on. "It was Nestor who insisted on an elevator—"

Their mother's late-in-life boyfriend, Nestor, had been a good man, somewhat exhausting but dedicated and loyal, a retired, wisecracking curmudgeon who operated under the philosophy that if something wasn't working the way he thought it should, it must be broken—dinner didn't burn in the oven because he'd set the temperature too high, the lawn mower didn't quit because he'd run out of gas—and despite his quirks, their mother had loved him deeply. "My friends used to accuse me of putting my romantic life on hold because I was in love with Elliot," she said once. "I love Elliot dearly, but I was waiting to fall *in love* with my Nestor." They'd only gotten five years together before he died.

"Helen," she heard her say too loudly from across the shop, "I don't know why. You knew him sixty years longer than I did. You explain his button collection."

Laney would try her best to help but warned Bree she might be more dangerous than beneficial when it came to bookselling. It'd been more than half of her life ago since she'd worked in the shop, and even then, she'd have rather cleaned baby puke from the restroom walls than listen to a guy try to debate her on whether or not his favorite science fiction series could ever possibly be captured on film and remain even remotely true to its story. She didn't know, and she didn't care. And when she'd been seventeen, she would have said so to his face. But now, with their mother too busy discussing sunblock for aging skin to help her customers and Bree looking as if she'd just run a 10K, she would try.

Laney turned the corner from Health & Wellness to find a customer in a baseball hat and leggings, obviously fresh from the gym, waiting for assistance at the front counter.

"Do you have *A Man Called Ove*?" the woman asked. Her face was flushed red but glowing, the look Laney recognized as a sign of a good workout, even though it wasn't one she herself had displayed in who knew how long.

"Maybe. Do you happen to know the author?"

"Backman," the woman said. "I think?"

They found it on their first try. Fredrik Backman, right there under the *B*s. The guy had a lot of books.

"Have you read any Fredrik Backman before?" Laney asked.

"No," the woman answered. "But it's our book club pick this month." She went on to describe the member who'd chosen the book as having "a thing" for male protagonists, and Laney nodded, pretending to enthusiastically understand and agree.

"Oh, hey." The woman grabbed a copy of Backman's *Britt-Marie Was Here* from the shelf. "I've heard good things about this one."

"Great choice!" Laney beamed, having absolutely no clue what she was talking about, then sliding the store's remaining copy of *Britt-Marie* to the back of the shelf to hide it for herself. Something about the cover just looked right, the kind of novel

Elliot would have mailed to her with a note that read, "Couldn't help myself. I know how much you love a quirky character."

A few minutes later, she grabbed one of the piles of discarded books that magically mushroomed throughout the store. Whoever curated this stack had a curious mix of interests. One book about early nineteenth-century toys, the next a science fiction romance featuring an amazingly fit purple woman in a leather bikini on the cover.

"Excuse me." A man in a trench coat sidled up beside her and spoke again, low and quiet. "Are you Irma's daughter?"

"Ye-es." She eyed him in his throwback-to-noir getup. "You're not here to flash me, are you?"

He pulled something from his pocket.

Oh god, no.

"What the—" She'd expected a surprise but not the kind he shoved into her hand.

It was a note: "Thom would like to meet you. Without your mother. Please call."

"Naughty." She smirked and added, "Where?" But the stranger had disappeared. She scanned the shop only to find Bree climbing her stepladder toward the heavens in Spirituality/Religion, and her mom still in the back, now loudly discussing walking shoes.

"Did you see that guy in the trench coat?" she hissed at her sister.

Bree looked down from on high. "Where?"

"He just left." Laney walked over, handing up the note. "Before pulling his johnson out of his pocket, he slipped me this."

"He *what*?" Bree fluttered down from her perch, grabbing the note but not reading it until Laney assured her that, no, they did not have a flasher on the loose in the neighborhood.

"Who's Thom with an *H*?" Laney asked.

Bree said, "I assume it's Elliot's partner, the one from the meeting. That's how he spells his name, at least. A little snooty about it, if you ask me."

Laney thought that was rich, coming from a woman who'd spent her whole life differentiating her name from a French cheese. She let it pass. This unfolding mystery was a thousand times more interesting. "Do you have his number?"

Bree had already begun scrolling through her phone. "What do you think? Call or text?"

Practically no one called, not even their eldest Tire Stud customers, many of whom had no business even climbing behind the wheel anymore. "Try texting." Out of the corner of her eye, Laney saw her mom stand and stretch, phone still glued to her face. "It's more clandestine."

Bree knocked out a short message and pressed Send. They waited.

Several minutes later came the response: A ;;m.

"He butt-texted you."

Bree scowled. "You sure? It looks like he might have been trying to name a time—something a.m."

"No. Definitely a butt text."

It was Thom, himself, who settled the debate. He called moments later, and when she saw his number pop onto the screen, Laney grabbed Bree's hand and sprinted into the restroom, locking the door behind them. They put the call on speaker.

"My phone began scolding me when I was trying to text you," Thom explained. "It gets me all agitated when it does that."

Bree and Laney exchanged curious looks. "Your phone scolds you?" Bree said.

"It does that…oh, you know. With the words popping up all over the display."

Laney mouthed, *How old is he?*

Bree shushed her, but he'd read their minds. "I know I sound decrepit. I assure you I'm not. I just prefer a world that doesn't throw a hundred things at me at once."

Laney liked a world that threw two hundred things.

Bree clucked sympathetically, being the better all-around human being. "Listen, Thom, I have my sister here with me—"

Laney piped up with a hello.

"We got your note, obviously."

He was quiet long enough that Laney and Bree swapped glances a second time. Finally, "I thought only one of you worked at the Rainbow."

Bree explained. "We do. I mean, I do. Laney goes back to California next week. Anyway, you indicated you wanted to meet? Without Irma."

"Yes," he said.

They waited for more. "About what?" Bree finally said.

To which Thom responded by hanging up.

Bree was finally able to convince Thom that Laney could be trusted, so that night after work, they gave their mother an excuse about meeting a mutual high school friend for drinks and headed to his house. They met in his kitchen with the blinds drawn.

"You're not planning to murder us, are you, Thom?" Laney extended her hand. "'Cuz if you are, I should probably call my husband and remind him to feed the cat."

Bree shot her a look. Thom said nothing as he got to work preparing tea.

Bree placed the cake she'd brought on the counter and took a seat next to Laney at the kitchen table. Normally, she would have offered to help, but Thom seemed the sort who liked things just so. "I happened to make a lemon Bundt cake yesterday, so I thought we could all enjoy it together."

Thom acknowledged the offering by pulling dessert plates from the cupboard.

"When did you have time to make that?" Laney whispered.

"I cook when I can't sleep." Her freezer had been overflowing since Elliot died.

The tea brewed, Thom arrived with fat slices of cake on a dessert plate for each of them, along with a fourth plate of additional slices and a teapot with matching cups.

"I adore your tea set!" Bree said. It was sixties chic—baby blue bubbles on an avocado-green trim.

"Thank you. Elliot found it at a garage sale for ten dollars, if you can believe it. We... *I* have eight settings." His face flinched at his mistake.

They each took a bite of cake and sipped their tea. Bree wanted Thom to be the first to speak, given they were here at his request. Laney didn't give him the chance. "You sounded urgent on the phone. What's on your mind?"

Conversationally, Laney was often as delicate as a car wreck.

Thom examined her with his teacup in both hands, just below his chin. He returned it to the saucer and began. "I am disturbed by the price Irma agreed to for the Rainbow. Judging from your reaction in the meeting—" he looked directly at Bree "—I gathered you were upset, as well."

She nodded.

"I'm wondering," he went on. "Have you read the sales contract? The fine print, beyond the price and timeline."

Bree could see his concern manifesting in the crease at the bridge of his nose, so pinched it'd turned pink. "No, I haven't, actually." She looked to Laney to confirm she hadn't, either.

"To her credit, your mother has been very clear that she intends to award me Elliot's full share of the sale. I know that may take some finessing in probate court, but I am nevertheless grateful she doesn't seem intent on contesting my right to his proceeds."

Bree struggled to untangle the issue at the heart of his panic. "I'm pleased to hear that, but—"

He didn't let her finish. "Due to certain estate issues and much legalese I wouldn't dare bore you with right now, I don't have any standing on which to dispute the sale. That's why I reached out to you. I believe Irma is either in some sort of distress or she's being taken advantage of."

Bree dropped her fork to her plate. She'd been right. Something was most certainly fishy about this sale.

Thom went on to describe all he'd learned in the days following their meeting at Vandaveer Investments. He remained unconvinced Bree and Laney wouldn't simply run home and tattle on him to Mommy, but the pro/con list he'd created on the matter refused to budge: engaging Irma's daughters was worth the risk.

"While I will admit that I want to sell the Rainbow for every penny it's worth, I also want to be clear that this is only partly about the money for me. If the sale proceeds as planned, I won't have the comfortable retirement I'd hoped for, but I do have my own funds to rely on." He turned his face to the ceiling, fighting his tears with the help of gravity. "Without Elliot, it won't be the same regardless."

Bree touched his hand. He pulled away and stood, retrieving his papers from the bookshelf in the hallway.

"I have highlighted important sections on my copy of the purchase agreement if you'd like to see it. My greatest concerns are twofold—the speed of the sale and the conflicts of interest."

Laney said, "The buyer acting as the broker, you mean?"

He did. "Typically, at least from what I've learned in my research, the sales broker performs the valuation of the business. Normally, this would make sense—by pricing a business fairly, the broker can help ensure a timely sale at a price both buyers and sellers can agree to. But with Vandaveer serving as both broker and buyer—"

He waited to see if they came to the same conclusion he had.

"It's in their best interest," said Bree, "to value the Rainbow as low as they can."

"Exactly."

Laney began to flip pages. "Do we know for certain the Vandaveers performed the valuation?"

Thom hadn't been able to find proof of his suspicions. Laney did. "Page fourteen. 'A preliminary value for Over the Rainbow Bookshop, LLC, and its assets was compiled by Vandaveer Investments on February 27, 2022, and based upon sales of comparable…blah, blah, etcetera, etcetera, etcetera."

She looked up, her eyes widening. "They were in talks as early as February."

Thom felt his stomach twist. Elliot had been gone only a month at that point.

They sat together in a state of collective shock until Bree said, "That means she couldn't wait to sell."

"Looks that way," Laney confirmed, then after a second, added, "Though, to be fair, we get unsolicited offers on the tire shop, too. Sometimes one of the big chains wants to buy us out, other times the buyer wants our location. The Vandaveers could *coincidentally* have popped up with a deal at just the right time."

"Or not so coincidentally, knowing she was vulnerable," Bree said. "Every business owner in Lyn-Lake heard about Elliot."

"That—" Thom pointed at her, feeling his vocal pitch and blood pressure rise in pace with each other. "That's what I'm afraid of." He'd always been a boy with a thin voice and reeds for limbs. His whole life, vulnerability had hung on him like a stink.

"Alright, everybody, just calm down." Laney gestured like a rider trying to settle a horse. "Everything—besides what's in black-and-white on these papers here—is purely speculation at this point."

Thom stiffened at the recrimination but said nothing. Of the sisters, Bree was clearly the more intuitive, and this Laney, so quick with rebuff and sarcasm— Well, he didn't intend to waste his energy trying to change her mind.

"But it's not speculation." Mercifully, Bree dived in for the both of them. "Laney, you yourself just identified a clear conflict of interest, with the Vandaveers performing the valuation. How could that be anything other than self-dealing?"

"I'm not saying it's not," Laney answered.

Thom felt himself cringe at her use of a double negative.

"I'm just saying," she went on, "let's not jump to conclusions. We don't really know much of anything yet. I mean, do either of you know how much bookstores sell for these days?" She smiled, and Thom couldn't for the life of him imagine why.

Bree groaned. "I'm sure we can find one for sale on Amazon."

Laney picked up her phone and began to scroll. "Want me to buy you a new career while I'm at it?"

Bree laughed. "Yes, please."

That was too much. "Excuse me!" Thom had no tolerance for people who refused to acknowledge the seriousness of his situation. "You may not care what happens to your mother or her store or her legacy as a bookseller, but I care very much what happens to Elliot's." He could feel his heart pounding in his throat.

"Oh!" Bree reached for his hand again and he whipped it out of reach. "We're so sorry, Thom." She gave her sister a lasered look. "Aren't we, Laney?"

"We're not trying to make light of this."

"Absolutely not."

He studied them, trying to judge their sincerity.

"Gallows humor," Laney admitted. "I seem to be somewhat expert at it."

"She's quite a bad influence," added Bree.

"I don't want to be any more upset than I already am." Thom needed them to understand the murky depths he'd been trying to survive this last year. "I only want to know if you share my concerns. Because if you don't, I will endeavor to remedy the situation on my own."

COMMERCIAL BREAK

Hello again, my darling readers!

Oh yes, yes, I know, I'm crashing the party. Which means this is the point at which you throw down your book and begin to howl, "Breach of protocol! What's going to happen with Laney, Bree, and Thom?"

What's that? Can I see you? Of course I can! And I forgive you for presuming otherwise. But don't worry, you're just feeling the momentary shock of hearing from me again. You'll adjust. Trust yourself. This is nothing more than a first-person note in the middle of a third-person narrative. Go read some Ray Bradbury and come back when you're ready. Or Benjamin Percy, from our great Minnesota literary clan. He wrote a political thriller starring werewolves, so let go of your pearls and quit looking at me that way. This is a book, lovely. Anything can happen.

Now. Where was I?

Ah, yes. I'm here because Irma can't be. She is—what's the best way to put this?—not *herself* at the moment. And I'm afraid that if I don't step in with crucial context, you'll come away thinking of her as a coldhearted, cash-fisting harpy. (Bit of trivia: Did you know that a harpy is a mythological creature with a woman's face and body coupled with a bird of prey's wings and claws? They're monsters. Not surprising that they're terrifying, given how the ladies have been mythologized over the ages. *Beware! They'll make you fall in love and then eat your head.* What balderdash. (Nit to pick: Why doesn't the English language allow for a word as colorful as *balderdash* to be used in the active sense? As in, "Anyone who calls Irma a harpy is engaged in gross balderdashery.")

I've gotten myself sidetracked… Time to put down the cocktail.

Anyway. Irma. I'm afraid much of what she's going through is my fault. Poor love. She wasn't prepared. Neither was I, frankly. I cannot speak to others' experience when dying, but I certainly didn't see it coming. I had a headache. I dropped. I watched as Thom came to accept the same reality that I was already experiencing. (Experiencing? No, that's not the word, exactly, but it's the best language I have since it's impossible to describe in human terms something that cannot be known to mortals.) My point is, I had crossed over. Traversed the rainbow bridge. Joined the great disco in the sky. I was dead, dead, dead.

Now, I know what you're thinking. Poor Thom can hardly say the word, let alone accept it, so for me to state it so declaratively must sound crass. *I'm dead!* But I assure you, you're only reacting this way because you haven't yet experienced the Grand Othering. And as for Thom, we'll come back to him. I promise.

First, though, we really do need to talk about Irma…

You must trust that she isn't as cold and withholding as she seems thus far. The truth is, she's in pain, awash in a despair deep enough to toss a person upside down and inside out.

But I want you to see that our leading lady was in fact a glorious, heart-on-her-sleeve, can't-keep-from-radiating, book-loving mess from the moment I met her. *Messy*, you ask? *Laney says she has a lipstick to match every outfit.* Yes, dears, but that's because of me. And only after years of intervention. When we first crossed paths, she was wearing orange-and-yellow double knit culottes on an afternoon in July. And if you didn't immediately zero in on the words *double knit*, *culottes*, and *July*, then I have nothing more to offer you. (Although really, if those words didn't horrify you, put this book down immediately, splash your face with cold water, and scream "Wake up!" because I'm worried that something is seriously, alarmingly wrong.)

Now then… You've heard about her Books 'Round Town truck. It was a smashing idea that she did a smash-up job bringing to life. She painted the truck purple, I bet nobody told you that, with yellow stars and swirls that reminded a person of Van Gogh's *Starry Night* (if you weren't looking too hard). And believe me—no one could've anticipated that an ayatollah (*a* what *now?* said every American with a car in 1979) halfway around the world would send her bookish dreams crashing to earth.

I was lucky to avoid the gas crisis, but not because I had the benefit of foresight. I put my books on bike back because I couldn't afford anything with a motor. But, oh, that Books 'Round Town truck was a hit. She'd pull into the parking lot at Lake Harriet or Como Zoo or Minnehaha Falls, and I knew my sales were done. Kaput. Move along, little pony. I couldn't compete with that! With Books on Bikeback, I only pedaled (see what I did there?) Harlequin romances and the top-ten fiction paperbacks on the *New York Times* bestsellers list. In other words, not very much. This was 1978 and 1979, remember, so to familiarize you with my inventory, I need only say three words: *The Thorn Birds*. (Those of you unfamiliar with the phenomenon that was *The Thorn Birds* can learn yourselves via the Google machine. Or think: sheep ranch, sex, and a priest. (Ooh, naughty.))

Irma had space for ten times what I offered—nonfiction hits and picture books and not just one but multiple titles by the burgeoning superheroes of the chapter-book universe: Beverly Cleary, Roald Dahl, and Judy Blume.

So, that afternoon in July… I was having a fantastic sales day, nothing but a few scattered romances left on the bike. Minneapolis was in the heart of its annual Aquatennial Festival, and this was one of its most popular days: the Milk Carton Boat Race at Lake Calhoun. *What the what?* you ask. It was a race. For boats. Made entirely of empty milk cartons. Stop if you need a minute. Or go to YouTube and type "Lake Calhoun milk carton boat race," because there you can watch the very event where I met my leading lady, thanks to the late seventies smash-hit TV show, *Real People*. They'd come to film a segment and all of Minneapolis knew about it—the tube socks and terry cloth tank tops were out in force, the beach was mobbed, teenagers preened for the cameras. And the wax holding the milk cartons together was mmmeeeellltiiiinnngg quickly in the July heat.

(Did I mention the tube socks? Lord, how we ever survived...)

With my inventory essentially sold out and time to waste before the boats hit the water, I wandered over to my purple competitor to introduce myself, and behold, there I found the woman in the orange-and-yellow polyester culottes in all her sweaty glory. I'll admit to being instantly transfixed. I never was able to understand the attraction. It wasn't sexual. But it was fierce—the need to know her consumed me immediately.

I remember her first words: "Well, if it isn't the handsome and wise Mr. Books on Bikeback." Charm. That was Irma's superpower. "Would you like a Fla-Vor-Ice? I keep a cooler full." Now, if you've heard of Minnesota Nice but never experienced it, there you go. You're welcome. My direct competition, and she didn't even look me up and down before inviting me in and giving me treats. (Southern hospitality, my glorious ass. You're good, but you don't have the lock.)

"How many copies of *The Thorn Birds* have you sold today?" I asked.

"'Bout five."

You see what I mean?

"Michener's *Chesapeake*, too," she added. "Way more copies today than I sold last week. I suppose the Aquatennial has everyone thinking about water."

Just before the race began, she closed up shop and we climbed on top of the truck's roof for a clear view of the lake. Irma was rooting for the human hamster wheel to win. I was a sucker for the Viking ship.

"I don't think you'll have to worry about me next summer." Irma sighed, all but admitting defeat though we'd met less than an hour before. "I'm losing money. And I'm wasting hours of my life sitting in gas lines."

"I'm sorry to hear that. You have a glorious book truck. I only pedal because it keeps my legs in great shape." That last part wasn't exactly true, but I knew better than to pile on when a woman was down. "And I'll never carry the inventory you can."

Irma began to wiggle her shoulders and kick her feet in a sort of rooftop jig. "They say those who can can do the can-can, and those who can't can just watch."

"I think I want to marry you."

"No, you don't." She took my hand anyway. "But something tells me we're at the final scene in *Casablanca*. Do you feel it?"

"I do." Then I raised her knuckles to my lips and kissed them. "Hallelujah and pass the Jell-O salad!"

You see now that from its very inception, our relationship was simpatico. We required no leap of faith to join forces and open the Rainbow.

But we did have rules.

"You're the fusser. I'm the noodler," Irma said.

What she meant was, she was big picture and I was in charge of details. You may not have understood her immediately, but I did. And when you meet someone who you don't have to explain yourself to, you do everything you can to keep her in your life. Which was what I did.

"When we disagree, we rock-paper-scissors on something we can agree on," she continued.

"Example, please," I said, being the fusser.

"Well, you want to name a bookshop after a movie star. That

doesn't make any sense to me. So let's rock-paper-scissors on a compromise. I say we take an informal survey of our friends and family. If they don't like it, we find a new name."

"I can agree to that."

"But you're supposed to offer a counterproposal. If you don't counter, we don't have anything to rock-paper-scissors about."

You see, this was the noodler in Irma. So many good ideas—in theory.

"Alright," I said. "I offer this counter—if you win, we'll survey our friends because you won the game. If I win, we'll survey our friends because I did."

Irma won. As did Over the Rainbow.

As it will soon be made even clearer, Thom never understood our connection. I do love that man (you'll be pleased to know that love doesn't end when the movie is over) and I'm with him every day. (The job he did on our sweaters! And Irma thought I was the details person.) But if there was a consistent source of stress between Thom and me, it was "that woman."

Which brings us to the point in our story in which the pieces come a tumblin' down. Spoiler alert: You think they're mad now. Just wait. A train's a coming…

You go on and keep reading now. I'll be over here enjoying another vodka and grapefruit juice with Judy G. What's that? You don't believe me? Have you already forgotten that anything is possible here?

Enjoy the Jell-O salad, darlings—
Elliot

P.S. Please, dear. Tell me you already knew who this was. It's been seven pages!

7

18 days until close...

They said good-night to Thom and stepped outside into the night, Laney chattering and Bree suddenly disoriented. Darkness had swapped the day's color for shades of gray while they'd been inside, and now the cool night air bit at her bare arms, distracting as a puppy finding its teeth. She marched to the end of the block and turned left, realizing too late that if she were going home, she would have turned right.

"Your house is the other direction, Breetle-dee."

"I need to walk a bit. Clear my head."

Laney hadn't asked if she wanted company, which Bree would have accepted if only her sister were capable of going ten seconds without speaking. Bree needed a quiet moment to get her thoughts in order.

"Are you following me?" she asked.

"You said you needed to walk a bit. We're walking now."

"It was a euphemism."

"But you're actually doing it. You turned the wrong direction and said you wanted to clear your head. You can't call something a euphemism and then do it."

"For being alone. It was a euphemism for *give me some space*."

"I don't think you know what a euphemism is."

They stopped at the next corner and waited for traffic to pass. It was almost black outside, the tableau before them visible only within halos of light—a streetlamp hemming a square of baby-green grass below its footings, a car's billowing exhaust tinged red by taillights.

"And yes," Laney said as they waited. "I am following you. It's dark. Not a great time to wander the streets alone."

Bree knew she ought to thank her but instead pulled out her phone and checked her nonexistent texts, hoping her sister would take the hint.

Laney asked, "Are you going to tell Mom about our discussion with Thom? I know he hopes we won't, but why mess around with all this pseudo-espionage?" She punched the walk button a second time. Traffic refused to clear. "She's the only one who can tell us why she's selling or why she's working with the Vandaveers."

Bree didn't want to talk about this. Not here on the corner in front of Saigon Take-Out, not until she'd had a chance to think about what they'd just learned, and not with Laney, who no matter how politely or directly Bree asked, refused to shut up.

"I suppose we could try to get a neutral third party to evaluate the business for us," Laney went on, not recognizing her sister's growing frustration. "But would anyone do that without Mom's knowledge? Do you have any friends in real estate who owe you a favor?"

Bree began to hum, trying to tune out the noise. Two twenty-something guys in hoodies emerged from Saigon Take-Out and barely got to the curb before tearing into their bag of spring rolls.

Laney saw them, too. "Hmm…a ten o'clock spring-roll binge. Me thinks somebody's high. I wonder if they have any good stuff to share."

She turned as if she were about to go over and ask them, which was a step too far for Bree. "This sale may not be a big deal to you, but it's a huge deal to me."

Laney stopped, squaring her hips. "Seriously? You, too?"

"Me too, what?"

"That's the second time in less than an hour I've been accused of not caring about my mother."

"I did not—"

"Yes, you did! You and Thom seem to think that just because I'm not writhing on the floor with worry about her selling the Rainbow, I don't care about her well-being."

Bree scoffed. "You were just scheming about scoring some pot."

"*Scoring* some *pot*? Who are you? Nancy Reagan?"

"You need to focus. I just heard some very alarming details about the deal Mom made, and I need to figure out what I'm going to do about it."

"Oh, right. What *you're* going to do about it."

"What is that supposed to mean?"

"It means you practically begged me to help you, and now you're implying I can participate in this crap soufflé of a situation, but only if I agree with everything you say and do everything you ask."

"That's rich!" Her sister hadn't been an active participant in their family or the Rainbow for nearly twenty years, but *now* she felt left out.

Laney smirked. "Rich coming from me, you mean? The disloyal one?"

That was exactly what Bree meant. "You said it. Not me."

"Ah." Laney straightened and crossed her arms in front of her chest. "I get it. It's okay to make me feel bad as long as the insult comes out of my own mouth. That way, you're not being hurtful or judgmental, you're just helping me see the truth."

It was the truth. Bree did everything for their mother and for the Rainbow. All Laney had to do was send a birthday card and her mom practically farted thank-you glitter.

"You owe me an apology, Miss Holy Martyr, Mother of Cheese—"

"Quit making fun of my name."

"I will when you answer me this—what can you realistically do to change anything? You're working yourself into a state, when the truth is Mom signed a contract, and a few weeks from now she'll be laughing her way to Florida, check in hand. You and Thom can le Carré the crap out of this mystery about who double-crossed who and who put the mark on Irma as the vulnerable, mourning widow, but—"

Bree stopped her. John le Carré was one of the bestselling spy novelists of all time. "Since when do you make literary references?"

"What, the double-cross? Espionage 101. I watched *The Americans*."

That wasn't Bree's point, and she was about to say so, but Laney spoke first. "You're avoiding my question, Bree. I asked what do you realistically expect to accomplish. The deal is done. Mom sold the Rainbow. The sooner you come to terms with that reality and decide what to do with your life, the better." She stood stock-still, doing that Laney thing where she wasn't going to move or speak until you explained yourself, and if she didn't like what she heard, she was going to make you keep trying.

"I don't know what I can do." Bree heard herself teetering on the edge of hollering, a volume she never reached except in the company of her sister. "But I can't do nothing, which is why I told you I need time to think, but you keep talking, talking, blah, blah, blah!"

"Blah," said Laney.

Bree felt her jaw clamp shut but didn't let it stop her from squeezing out, "If you want me to figure this out, you need to shut. Your. Friggin'. Trap."

"But you love me," Laney mocked.

"Actually, I think you suck."

"Of course you do, but you should be glad for it, because as long as I suck, you don't have to."

"How generous."

They stood quietly for a second. Laney smiled. Bree didn't. Laney hip-checked her. Bree planted her feet, absorbing the blow. Laney slapped her bare arm. *Smack!*

"OW! What'd you do that for?"

Laney did it again.

"Stop it!"

The Saigon Take-Out twins shouted, "Catfight!"

Laney leaned in, grinning. "Slap me back."

"You're insane."

"Do it."

"No!"

Laney hollered toward the guys on the curb. "Give us some of what you're smoking and I'll get her to pull my hair."

"Pull it!" one of them shouted, the other chanting, "Catfight! Catfight!"

Laney held out her palm and flapped her fingers at them, a rebellious teenager in a woman's body, her fifty-dollar manicure visible beneath the streetlights. "Gotta pay up first, fellas."

Bree bristled, older now, and wise enough to know unexpected things happened when Laney got what she asked for. "You're going to get us arrested!"

"I live in California. It's legal there. Innocence via ignorance." Chuckling, she reached over and knocked Bree's purse off her shoulder.

"Damn it, Laney!"

Laney ignored her and wagged her open hand, calling, "Oh, boys… If you want a show, you gotta deliver."

After scanning the parking lot for cops, the guys nodded at each other in silent agreement, crossed, and slid something small into Laney's hand.

The exchange successfully complete, Bree yanked her sister's hair with such force she felt the roots barely hold on to their grasp of her scalp.

Laney screeched, "I said tug it! Not pull it out!"

"And I told you to shut up!"

The sisters quarreled.

The guys cheered.

Finally, their slurs exhausted, Laney caught Bree's eye, complimented her sparring skills, and led her away by the hand.

"You're a lunatic," Bree hissed.

Laney took no offense. "Chaos can be highly productive." They turned the corner toward Bree's house, and Laney continued, "I know you need time to think, so let me just say one last thing before I leave you alone. Which is, Mom might be getting taken advantage of."

This wasn't news. "That's what I've been telling you all along."

"Yes, and I want to make sure you know that I think you're right."

"Okay. Jeez." Bree rubbed at her arm where Laney had slapped her.

Laney stopped walking. "You're not hearing what I'm saying."

"I heard you say you were going to quit talking, but that's not happening."

"I said *you're right.*"

"Okay. Well then, thank you."

"You're a terrible listener."

"Thank you for that, too."

"You're welcome."

They walked on in silence, at last. Bree's head thrummed, an encapsulated pandemonium, the events of the past week desperately trying to settle into consonant chords. Still, no matter how she arranged them, all that came through was noise. She sensed something else, though, too, a whisper, a hint, a clue, a *something* that kept rising above the din: the Rainbow wasn't gone yet. Its loss wasn't inevitable.

"Don't say anything until I'm done talking." She stared fiercely at Laney until her sister complied, drawing a finger-zipper across her lips.

"Like I said the other night, I can't let this go until I know Mom made the best possible decision."

She waited for Laney to argue, but she only turned the lock on her lips and threw the key to the ground.

Bree said, "Mom wants to explain why she's selling, I know she does. Irma is a lot of things, but she's never been secretive."

Laney mmm-hmm'd.

"She keeps talking about how happy she is that you're here, the three of us together again. So, let's use that to our advantage—love bomb her until she's willing to talk." Bree's mind began to blink with possibility. "When we're at the store together, let's get her reminiscing about all her favorite memories, all the customers she loved, the ones who made us laugh. And I'll come over to the house for dinner every night. Or better, we can take her out, splurge on a nice place and call it a celebration. What do you think?"

Laney raised an eyebrow, waiting for permission to speak.

"Go ahead."

"See what I did there? I listened."

"What did I say, then?"

"You said we should love bomb Mom until she can't help but blurt out all her secrets, hopes, and dreams, and if it doesn't work then, hey, we still had a nice dinner."

Bree exhaled. "Exactly. So why is my stomach in knots?"

Laney laughed, reaching into her pocket. "Maybe this will help." She slipped something tiny into Bree's hand. "You need to relax, sister."

Despite her better instincts, Bree didn't argue but tucked the joint into her pocket and wondered if she would ever understand her sister's many brilliant, quixotic layers.

"I still have to fly home in a few days," Laney said. "But I'm your girl for the duration."

Bree understood, and thanked her, and kept to herself the small, crazy, entirely unrealistic suspicion that their adventure had only just begun.

8

16 days until close...

Laney and Bree let their mom choose the restaurant for her celebration dinner, then they closed the shop early and walked into Barbette, a beautiful French brasserie around the corner.

"Mom," Laney began, "besides this dinner being a chance for the three of us to celebrate your retirement, Bree and I would also like to understand the timing. Why are you throwing in the towel so soon, lady?"

Bree kicked her under the table. She'd urged Laney to go slow and let their mother be the first to mention her decision to sell, but Laney flew home in two days. Also, she didn't believe in miracles.

Predictably, Irma changed the subject. "Have either of you ordered the mussels here? I hear wonderful things."

"No," Laney answered, "given that I live in California. Which is where I was when you called me to demand I come home. You know, so that I could see Bree's face when you announced you were throwing her career into oncoming traffic."

Bree choked on her water but nevertheless managed a second, sharper blow to Laney's shin.

"Fun fact about mussels," Irma continued. "Humans have been eating them for more than twenty thousand years. They're a prehistoric food source." She began to softly hum, as if wistfully recalling her vast knowledge of the crustacean kingdom.

"Female mussels have orange parts. Males have white. It figures, doesn't it? Seems we ladies always have to put ourselves on display—no matter the species."

The waiter brought the bottle of pinot gris they'd ordered and poured three glasses. Laney took a too-long sip. Her mother's was even longer. Bree stuck to water.

"How about I start with my questions?" Laney posed the idea as a suggestion but didn't wait for permission. "I'm surprised you're selling to Vandaveer Investments. Their history is controversial, they've got a reputation for self-dealing, and I hear they've even been sued by a few of their development partners. I read your sales contract, and I don't think the Vandaveers are acting as good-faith buyers. What say you?"

Her mom hummed on and sipped her wine, dreaming of butter-and garlic-soaked hors d'oeuvres.

At long last, Bree found her voice. "Personally, Mom, I'm worried about you." She leaned close and kept a smile on her face as she spoke. "I mean, this feels awfully fast. Elliot's only been gone since January, and I've read a lot of books on grief that advise not making any important decisions for the whole first year after losing your partner. Think about how distracted you were after Nestor died—Elliot practically ran the store by himself for at least a year and just to give you the time you needed—"

Irma interrupted. "Elliot named the store, you know."

Laney rolled her eyes. Though, at least her mom was finally talking about something besides mollusks.

"It was his ode to Judy Garland. He loved that woman. Thought she was perfect in every way. I said it was ridiculous to name a bookstore after a film icon, but he insisted. Then, the more I thought about it, the more it did make sense. Books and rainbows, you know. That's where anything can happen."

Laney moved the wine bottle to the other side of the table. "That's a lovely story neither of us have heard five hundred times before."

Bree gave Laney the stink eye and turned her this-hurts-me-more-than-it-hurts-you voice on her mother. "Do you sincerely believe Elliot would have agreed to this deal?"

Their mother began to hum again, arranging and then rearranging her silverware. "He told me that if he went first, I'd be so brokenhearted I'd throw myself into the shredder." She paused, and Bree looked as if she'd stopped breathing. "But as for the sale, I think he would have said, 'Irma. I've gone to the never-ending party in the sky, and you're the last girl at the disco.'"

"Who was he, Yoda?" Laney's patience, never plentiful to begin with, was quickly evaporating. "What does that even mean?"

"You asked me what Elliot would have thought, so I'm telling you. He would've wanted me to put on my big-girl pants and make a decision."

"Yes," Bree urged. "And it's that decision that we're trying to understand."

Laney was out of subtlety. "We think you're getting screwed by the Vandaveers. Bree's too nice to say it, but I'm not."

The waiter, who'd been approaching with their platter of cheese selections, overheard and turned in retreat. Irma, however, sat forward and buckled in. "Girls, I've been trying to be polite, but that's obviously not working, so I'm only going to say this once—I am selling the store, and I'm not going to debate it with you. You have a copy of the contract, and that's everything you need to know."

Bree's mouth dropped open, clearly dumbfounded. "Don't you even care about the store, your customers, *me*? Don't you care I won't have a job when this is done? I thought you always wanted one of us to keep the Rainbow alive—you talked as if it was my destiny, my right." Her eyes began to pool.

Laney felt a rush of something powerful and wild, the anger she'd managed until now to channel as sarcasm overflowing its levies and flooding her. "Mom, I left home because of the Rainbow—you get that, right? I was barely old enough to drive, but

I followed Tuck to places I wouldn't even call towns, washed my underwear in the sink at truck stops, used my college money to buy a mousetrap of a trailer to live in. And still, all that terribleness seemed better than settling for a life I hadn't chosen. Because Bree's right—you always expected us to make the Rainbow our lives. Only, she was the good daughter. She was happy to do it, and now it's like you don't even care. I can't believe you."

Their mother remained her stony self, cold and withholding, and offering no answers. Until, at last, she found one. "Bree, I am sorry. As good as you are, you're not up to this."

Bree smashed her way through a group of would-be diners crowding the exit and fell into the fresh air just as her first tear crested its dam. She wiped it away quickly, trying to disguise the motion as if flicking away an eyelash. She didn't want Laney, who was right on her heels, to see she'd cracked.

"I'm fine." Bree held up a preemptive hand. "Really, don't make a big deal."

"She was totally out of line back there. Everyone knows that if anyone deserves the Rainbow, it's you."

Bree smiled, though her body was empty. Inside, she'd already fled for the tiny space she tucked away for moments like this. "Please don't make this bigger than it is," she pleaded as she scanned the street. "We asked for answers, and we got them."

Laney, anticipating her escape, grabbed her arm before she leapt out of reach. "Mom was a conversational volleyball game back there—*Let's talk about mussels! Let's talk about Judy Garland!* You can't take any of what she said seriously, not when she's clearly out of her head."

"Sometimes people are most honest when their guard is down." Bree could feel her sister's urgency in her grip, her earnestness in the way she refused to let go. "You said as much all along—maybe this decision is for the best. Maybe I just need to accept it and move on."

"Don't listen to me! You know I'm all hot air and BS."

"And sometimes you're right."

Laney softened, letting go of her arm, her burning expression suddenly extinguished. "Even if I am, even if she should sell the bookshop, I don't believe for one second that she didn't want you to have it. You were the one who was meant to carry on the Rainbow legacy. I mean, you literally made it your home. You followed me off the school bus and refused to go home—like, *ever.* If she hadn't adopted you she would've been arrested for kidnapping. I mean, what other proof do you need? Mom and I argued about curfew, you argued about Sylvia Plath."

Bree said nothing.

"Listen," Laney went on. "Tonight was an anomaly. The continuation of her sudden derangement syndrome. She can't have meant what it sounded like, and I still think you're right. If we keep trying, she'll eventually spill the beans about what really happened."

Bree nodded toward the street. "I need to walk. Be on my own for a bit."

Laney paused, then eventually said okay. But only after handing over another tissue. "Snot tears." She gestured at Bree's nose. "I didn't want to say anything."

The night was mild following the hot afternoon, and the sidewalks had come alive—families with strollers, girlfriends heading for cocktails, chest-puffing bachelors in formfitting tees. Their neighborhood, Lyn-Lake, was surrounded by a halo of lakes from north to south—Lake Bde Maka Ska, Lake Harriet, Lake of the Isles—and in them lay the source of Minnesotans' hang-in-there optimism.

Bree headed in the opposite direction.

She turned for the Rainbow, where she stood on the sidewalk across the street, looking at her shop. She rarely stopped to take in the store from this perspective, the way her customers saw it. Just this afternoon, she'd redesigned the front window to feature new releases by Minnesota authors: Lorna Landvik, Mindy Mejia, Boa Phi, Josh Moehling, Wendy Webb, Peter Geye, Allen Eskens, Kate DiCamillo, Kathleen West, Abby Jimenez. She'd hung a sign that even now made her smile.

"You think ten thousand lakes are impressive? Count our great Minnesota writers. (*Psst*—even more of them inside.)"

What would her life become without books? What would it become without the Rainbow?

Twenty-eight years ago, almost to the day, she and Irma had held hands in front of a judge at the Hennepin County Courthouse and made it official. Irma had adopted her and made her one of her own. Afterward, they drove back to the shop to find the front window filled with purple, pink, and white balloons and a banner that read, "Welcome to the family, Bree!" Inside there was cake, and when Elliot handed her a slice, he told her she could have as many as she liked. There was real Welch's, not generic, grape pop, and Irma let her drink a whole can.

Before the party ended, Irma took her aside. "I don't want you to ever again feel like you're a visitor here or at the house. We're family now. These places are yours."

Now Bree instinctively looked up at the Over the Rainbow Bookshop marquee. Just below the name it read, "Books and rainbows are where dreams come true." That afternoon twenty-eight years ago, drinking her pop and eating her bottomless cake while surrounded by people who seemed to genuinely love her, she had foolishly allowed herself to believe she'd found where she belonged.

Laney shot Bree a text.

Hope you had a good walk. Nygaard's at 7 tmr to chat?

Neither she nor her mother had spoken on the way home from Barbette, and they'd retreated straight to their bedrooms. She kicked off her shoes and dialed Tuck, who was at the gym when he answered. She could tell by the *ching!* of clanking barbells in the background.

"What's up, Laney-cakes? Home on Friday, right? You gonna catch the train from the airport?"

She *uh-huh*'d and, at the same moment, wondered what it would be like to have a husband who didn't simply assume she'd be happy to jump on the train after a three-hour flight. In fact, she couldn't think of a time he'd ever picked her up from the airport. She used to ask, but he always begged off saying he was "a racer, not a driver."

That adage only seemed to apply when it was Laney needing the ride, she suddenly realized. He often drove Miss Frankie and her dog, Pickles, home from the tire shop rather than make them wait out repairs in the customer lounge, and it wasn't unheard of for him to offer to pick something up at the store for a neighbor. "I'm heading out, anyway," he'd tell them. "Need anything?"

Why didn't she qualify for this same care and attention?

"Actually, Tuck, I have to delay my return ticket. There's a lot going on here, so I'm going to contact the airline in the morning." The words came out of nowhere, shocking her so she actually choked on them. She'd only called to check in, not start a second round of when-are-you-coming-home discussions.

"How's that gonna work, Laney?" A man in the background grunted, followed by a round of cheers. "It's crazy at the shop. I need you."

"There's some major stuff happening here, and I can't leave Mom and Bree to deal with it by themselves." She swallowed. Her mouth went dry whenever she tried to be evasive, and especially so when she didn't herself understand the root of her equivocation.

"How long? A few days?"

"Probably. I'm going to play it by ear. No more than another week, for sure."

"You've already been there a week."

"I'll be back as soon as I can."

"What am I supposed to do?"

"The same things you've been doing." She began to picture the shop and the state of chaos it must be in, but shut the images down before she panicked and changed her mind. "My situation is in flux, that's all. I'm sorry. But everything is going to be fine. Don't worry."

Then she said goodbye and hung up before either one of them could argue otherwise.

9

15 days until close...

The next morning, Laney met Bree at the front entrance of Nygaard's, the local grocery recently renovated, thanks to money made possible by Vandaveer Investments. Laney hated herself for liking it so much. "I can't believe I'm going to say this, given the Vandaveers' involvement, but I want to marry this new store."

"Interesting," said Bree.

"It has everything I want in a lasting relationship. It brings me coffee and pastries. I can buy pizza for breakfast, and it's not going to make me feel guilty. It's even gorgeous to look at." She ran her hand along the reclaimed wood endcaps that matched the reclaimed wooden floors. "You want to touch this. You know you do."

Bree headed for the café and ordered a large black coffee with a raspberry scone. "I didn't sleep much. You?"

Laney shook her head. "Did you know you can get a shot of espresso added to your coffee? It's called a red-eye."

"Single or double red-eye?" The barista had overheard her.

"Single, please. And a Black Forest cupcake."

Bree grimaced. "You're having a cupcake for breakfast?"

"See." Laney shook her head. "There you go, making me cross you off of my Perfect Man list."

They found a semisecluded table in the corner and fiddled with their breakfasts, not speaking. The last she'd seen Bree, she was gulping tears, and Laney had spent the night wondering how her mother could treat her favorite daughter with such cool cruelty. Unlike Laney, Bree didn't treat her relationship with her mom like a mammogram—a good thing to perform every two or three years, despite the vise-gripping pain. Bree had an actual, sincere relationship with Irma, happy when she was happy, sympathetic when she was sad.

Irma's behavior had been her trigger, Laney suddenly realized. The whole reason she'd decided to stay longer. Somebody needed to stick up for Bree, and if not her own family, then, who? Laney was the last one standing.

"I'm a little nervous to tell you what I've decided." Bree surprised her by working up the courage to speak first. "It might be asking too much." She pulled a pea-size bite of scone apart from the whole and slipped it onto her tongue, as if signaling she couldn't say more because her mouth was full.

Laney was obviously curious. "That's funny. Because I'm not sure you're going to like what I've decided, either."

"Oh, no."

"It's the only thing I can think of to do, though."

"Unless you like what I've decided better."

They both took a deep breath, their reticence stalled. Laney said, "On the count of three."

Bree did the honors. *One… Two… Three…*

"We have to fight Mom's decision."

"We have to sink this sale."

It wasn't quite clear at first. What Laney heard while she was also talking was something about stinking scales, and Bree thought she'd said something about flight precision. They backed up and got it sorted.

"I know you have to go home tomorrow," Bree pleaded, "but is there any way you can delay? Or maybe come back as soon as possible? I don't think I can manage to stop this on my own, and Thom is…" She cocked her head in the way Minnesotans do when about to declare someone *interesting*.

"He's wound tight as a tick." Laney could not have expected the amount of relief she suddenly felt. "But, actually, I'm not leaving yet. I can't leave you here by yourself to deal. I told Tuck last night, and I'll call the airline later this morning."

Bree looked more worried than relieved. "How'd he take it?" She knew how many phone calls Laney had received this week, having to talk him through everything from rebooting the credit card reader to where they kept the extra toilet paper.

"Um…" She debated how much of their circular non-conversation she wanted to reveal. "Fine?"

Mercifully, Bree left it at that. "When should we call Thom? I'm worried he'll go off the deep end without us."

Laney pointed at Bree's phone. "Early bird gets the tick."

Thom hung up with Bree and headed directly to the library, though in his haste he hadn't paid close attention to the time and had to wait in his car for thirty minutes until it opened. Once inside, however, he found his favorite reference librarian, Carol Ann, and told her he had six hours to learn everything he could about running an effective strategy meeting.

In another life, Thom would have liked to come back as a librarian. He'd been drawn to his career in phlebotomy because it gave him the opportunity to provide crucial medical care without the responsibility of having a person's life in your hands. A librarian's work was much the same. When he'd come last week in need of information on selling a business, he'd been on the verge of a panic attack. But with Carol Ann's expert direction, he completed his research with the vitality of a man half his age.

By noon, he had a legal pad full of notes and a plan for the evening. Bree and Laney were coming at six and he'd offered a light dinner. He had just enough time between now and then to buy everything he needed at the office supply store and get to Nygaard's for groceries.

"Come in! Come in!" The sisters arrived promptly. In the dining room, he'd laid a buffet of deli salads, turkey pinwheels, and a fruit salad. Plus, of course, macarons from Patisserie 46 for dessert.

"Wow!" Laney was impressed with his display, though she wasn't commenting on the food. "You sure you weren't the CEO of something before this?"

Along the wall opposite the buffet, he'd lined up three whiteboards. On the dining room table lay three copies of the sales agreement, legal pads, pens in assorted colors, as well as highlighters, dry erase markers, sticky notes, and three rolls of Wint-O-Green Life Savers. Apparently, mint was an effective tool for keeping the mind alert during long periods of concentration. "I hope I provided everything we'll need."

They ate quickly, and as soon as the work began, he walked to the center whiteboard and wrote, "GOAL: Stop this Sale."

Bree balked almost immediately. "Are we sure that's the goal? I mean, absolutely, black-and-white like that?"

Her sister balked back. "What do you mean, are we sure that's the *goal*? You said those exact words to me this morning—'We have to stop the sale.'"

"I know. It just looks so ominous up there like that."

Laney pointed her finger at her. "Don't go soft now."

Thom, eager to make as much progress this evening as possible, said, "Maybe this will help." Beneath "Stop this Sale," he wrote "to the Vandaveers."

"That works," said Laney. "Bree, you good?"

She nodded.

Frankly, Thom considered his edit slightly disingenuous but said nothing. He knew his long-term goals were at odds with Bree's, who wanted to keep the Rainbow alive ad infinitum, with herself at the helm. For him, though, if the money offered by the Vandaveers had seemed even remotely fair, he would have happily taken Elliot's share of the payout and escaped the bookshop and Irma's shadow forever. He needed the Rainbow erased, but only for a price that reflected Elliot's life's work. Bree was desperate to keep it alive and bright. (And who knew about her sister? Laney was a mystery he'd yet to crack.) In the end, only one of them could get what they wanted, but what they could—and just did—agree on was that the Vandaveer deal was no good; it could not stand. Whatever came after was for the future to reveal.

"With that settled," he said, "I'll draw your attention to your agendas. Best practices for this type of meeting would have us move from goal setting to a threats-and-opportunities assessment." This, he'd taken from a very interesting *Harvard Business Review* article. Or maybe it had been in *Fast Company*. Or the book, *An Agenda for Every Purpose*. Regardless, he had the source in his notes.

Laney asked, "Do you know how to do whatever you just said?"

"I'm pleased to admit that I do." He handed them each a marker. "Bree, your color for the evening is green. Laney, you're red, and I will use purple."

Laney accepted hers. "Will you promise to let me look at your closet before we leave? I'll bet it's exquisitely organized."

Of course it was.

The exercise took longer than expected, but within an hour, they'd highlighted some very important and potentially fertile factors. For starters, Laney recognized that for a company like Vandaveer Investments, the most efficient route to spoiling their interest in the sale was to— "Hit them in the wallet. They don't give the impression of men who have hearts, so no sense in appealing to their humanity. This is about money. As long as they stand to profit, they're going to push ahead. But threaten those prospects and you're onto something."

Thom and Bree agreed. Though, how? The board where they'd listed intervention ideas stood practically naked. Here's what they had:

Appeal to customer base
Protest Vandaveer involvement
Seek help from neighboring businesses

"That's all squishy stuff," Laney said. "It may be helpful in theory, but we need to translate it into concrete actions."

Thom referred again to the myriad highlighted selections in the sales contract. "The agreement is nonbinding all the way up to closing. Whoever backs out may be subject to financial consequences, but from what I can tell, they're nominal, at most."

He'd bought and sold two houses in his lifetime. This appeared comparable. "You don't think there's any chance Irma can be persuaded to back out?"

The sisters exchanged glances. "Are you a betting man?" Laney asked.

He was not.

Thom took out the notes from his morning at the library, recalling that he'd recorded several tactics for reinvigorating a lagging brainstorm. "I have an idea." He directed them to set everything aside except the sales contract. "For the next ten minutes, let's each reread the agreement with fresh eyes. Review it as if for the first time. At the end of ten minutes, we'll compare our findings." He turned the knob on his kitchen timer and smiled to himself. He was proving very effective at this sort of thing.

It was Bree who found it, and Laney who identified the potential. The clause read as follows:

Notwithstanding anything to the contrary contained in Section 3.04, neither Buyer nor Seller shall take any action, or appear to commit to take any action, that would result in, or would reasonably be expected to result in (1) a material adverse effect on Over the Rainbow Bookshop, LLC, or (2) a material adverse effect on Vandaveer Investments, LLC.

Thom asked one of them to please explain why they found this so intriguing.

Laney responded by reciting the clause again. "'…neither Buyer nor Seller shall take any action, or *appear to* commit to take any action…' It's right there in black-and-white. We don't have to prove the Vandaveers took advantage of a vulnerable woman mourning the loss of her business partner. It just needs to *appear* that they did."

"Public perception is a powerful thing," Bree added.

It took a moment to process, but Thom finally connected the dots. "You mean the appearance of self-dealing?" He'd caught on now. "You're saying we don't have to prove the Vandaveers purposefully undervalued the Rainbow knowing Irma's emotional state, we just need to generate enough public suspicion about it to put the deal in jeopardy."

"Bingo," answered Laney.

Bree grinned at him from across the table. "People don't like to see little old ladies get beat up by bullies."

It seemed like just the loophole they'd been hoping for. And yet, "I'm not comfortable in gray areas, legally or otherwise," Thom said.

Laney beamed. "Then, you're in luck because gray areas are where I happen to thrive."

He ignored her. "What I am comfortable doing," he went on, "is tapping into Elliot's and my large community of friends for action and support. We're seasoned activists." They'd had to be for too many reasons. "We can organize a crowd in virtually no time."

"Perfect!" Laney stood and wrote, "Thom: Activists" on the board. "Meanwhile, I'll muck about in the dark recesses of the

Lyn-Lake gossip party on a potential whisper campaign. And while I'm at it, I'll take point on Mom. Keep her distracted while you all do your thing."

"Are you sure you can handle that much time with her?" Bree asked. "Maybe you ought to let me take Irma."

Laney didn't budge. "She's been mad at me for years, so what's another week? Plus, if you really do want to take over the Rainbow someday, it'd be good to have the support of other local business owners."

Thom agreed. "They might also know a thing or two about the Vandaveers that we don't."

Bree looked a bit ill. "Can't I just keep selling them books? They seem to like me fine when I'm doing that."

"Sorry, Breetle," Laney answered. "If you want to reach the rainbow, you gotta survive the storm." Then she slapped Thom's table and laughed. "Who sounds like a motivational poster now?"

10

14 days until close...

The next morning, Laney got dressed, took a long pull on her coffee, and did her best to buck up before arriving at the Rainbow. Her tasks weren't impossible, she told herself—all she had to do was keep her mom distracted while Bree and Thom got to work, and maybe tiptoe into the gray with a whisper campaign. When Tuck was racing, she'd gotten one of his main rivals pulled from a crucial race by just happening to mention to one of the other racing girlfriends she'd heard that a particular driver was using illegal additives in his gas, and she just happened to mention this while in the concession line in front of an assistant to a very important member of the compliance committee.

Tuck won that race, by the way.

Her mother had been up early this morning and Laney arrived at the bookshop to find her at the customer desk humming "Surrey with a Fringe on Top" while reloading register tape.

"Morning," Laney said.

"And a beautiful one, at that," Irma answered, chirpy like a jay.

Laney slipped into the back room as the bells over the yellow door tinkled. A moment later she heard a woman say, "I asked the girl to recommend something interesting enough that my grandson would see there's a whole world outside of his computer screen."

Laney recognized herself as that girl in question and peeked around the stockroom door to see their unhappy customer holding the same copy of Matt Ruff's *Lovecraft Country* she'd sold her yesterday. Elliot had first mailed her the novel, along with a note that read, "A mind bender, where I found myself wondering which was more terrifying…the imagined monsters or the real ones. Best read with a drink in hand." Now hearing the distressed woman return, she wished she'd ducked into the back room yesterday, too.

The customer said, "Did you know they play video games together from their own homes? Complete strangers, miles apart."

"Your grandson plays with the girl?" Her mom looked confused.

"Oh, I'm sure he does."

"Our girl?"

"Which girl?"

"The girl you said sold you this book."

"Are you even listening? I said I asked for a book appropriate for a fifteen-year-old and she sold me one in which creatures descend from out of nowhere to eat people."

"Sorry, not sorry," Laney whispered, and then crept back into the shadows.

As soon as she heard the register beep, clatter, and shut, she rejoined her mom on the floor. "Bet you're not gonna miss that anymore, huh? All the grumpy customers?"

"Oh, she wasn't so bad. Just an old woman like me, frustrated by a world she no longer understands or seems to belong in."

Laney hoped she was lucky enough to have an accidental howdy-do with a speeding truck before old age ever happened to her. This moment was about Irma, though. "You're not out of touch, Mom. You're too curious. You'll always keep up-to-date with the interesting stuff." Flatter. Praise. Cross fingers.

"Oh, you say that now, but you'd be surprised how quickly

life slips away." She patted Laney on the cheek and retreated into the stacks.

"Won't you be bored when you don't have the store keeping you busy anymore? I mean, think about it. You'll have to start paying for books!" Laney was on her heels, determined not to let this opportunity for real talk slip by.

"That's what libraries are for, my dear." She grabbed a book cart and began to empty its paperbacks onto the end of the *N-Q* shelf. "Anyway, I suspect my well-connected friends will slip me a few copies here and there. They won't forget this old bookseller too soon."

That was the second time in as many minutes her mom had referred to herself as old. Calling Irma *old* was fine when she and Bree were having a laugh, but not when it came out of her own mouth. Because she wasn't. She'd just had a rotten couple of years. "I'm sorry I didn't come home for Elliot's service." It was a non sequitur, but Laney needed to say it. "Or Nestor's. I should've been here for you."

"You're here now, aren't you?"

"Yeah, but it's different. During the funeral I would have fawned on you and been your Sweet Laney. This trip, I'm disappointing your customers and yelling at you for putting Bree out of a job."

Uh-oh. She'd flown too close to the sun with that last comment. Cue the mollusk trivia.

Her mother placed the last of the paperbacks on the shelf and looked at her. "I told you, Laney. I'm not going to discuss the sale."

"But Bree—"

"Drop it. Whatever you don't know you don't need to know."

The yellow door jingled, and just like that, their moment was spent.

Bree didn't have any idea how to perform her assigned job. As far as she understood, she needed to approach the small-business owners in the neighborhood and get them all riled up about Vandaveer Investments buying the Rainbow, while at the same time not being too obvious about doing so. Selling books was so much easier.

Alstrop's Ace Hardware next door was her first stop. The hardware store and the Rainbow were the only two buildings on their block and shared a small customer parking lot in the back. The parking alone probably doubled the value of their location.

"Mornin', Al." Al Alstrop Jr. had inherited the family business from his father, Al Alstrop Sr., and every time Bree saw him, she felt as if she'd walked through a wrinkle in time. Father and son looked identical, all the way down to the tape measure clipped to the waists of their jeans.

"Mornin', Bree. How's things at the Rainbow? Clear and sunny?" Father and son also shared a love for a good weather joke.

"Oh, you know. Always trying to outwit the Empire."

"I hear ya. Had a kid in here the other day with a ratchet set he bought online. Tryin' to use it to assemble a bike he'd also bought online and couldn't for the life of him understand why it wasn't tightening the bolts." He waited to see if she'd be able to solve the mystery.

"Hadn't flipped the direction switch on the ratchet, huh?"

Al beamed. "You're a woman who knows her tools."

She had to. Her barely-more-than-living-wage income never afforded the luxury of hiring out the repair and maintenance owning a house required, so she'd taught herself—with plenty of help from YouTube and Al, himself—to fix leaks and clear gutters, install faucets and light fixtures, even retile a bathroom last decorated around the time of the moon landing by a person enchanted by the color teal.

Suddenly, the realization she could lose her house in this mess hit like a rock between the eyes, and she pinched the crook of her nose in response to the pain.

"What brings you in?" Al reached into his pocket and offered her a Werther's butterscotch. His father had always kept a pocketful of Chiclets gum.

"Browsing, really. I have the morning off, so..." Why hadn't she planned this more carefully?

She plucked a doodad from the spinner beside the register. It looked like a miniature version of a pirate's hook, if the pirate wore it on their finger and the hook part were covered with a rubber tip.

"Nah." Al scowled. "That's cheap made-in-China stuff. You don't want to waste your money."

Good. She didn't know what it was for anyway. "Say, Al." She took a breath and dived in. "You heard anything about Vandaveer trying to scoop up more of the buildings in the neighborhood? I thought I heard something, so I guess I'm just, like, curious." Too subtle? Laney was so much better at this sort of thing.

He paused before answering, appearing to measure his words. "Yeah, they're in here about every six months offering me some sort of deal on this place. Never very serious offers, though. Laughably low. I tell 'em I'm not in the market to sell, but they keep coming back anyway."

Laughably low. Their instincts about Irma's contract had been right.

"Now, that thing you were looking at..." Al changed the subject. "Lemme show you a different option." He motioned for her to follow and led her down an aisle crowded with everything from Windex to kitchen timers and pulled a slightly larger, obviously more substantial version of Captain Hook's finger puppet from the shelf. "Here's the one you want. Pricier, but it's not gonna bend in your pocket."

The smile on his face was so earnest, Bree couldn't muster the nerve to turn him down. She took it.

"Anything else you need?"

"Uh, no. Just this, I think. Thanks."

They returned to the register. "You know, about the Vandaveers," he said finally, "it's hard to know whether to trust 'em. Sure, the work with Nygaard's grocery turned out nice enough, but that Stone Bakery fiasco..." He whistled through his teeth. The register clicked and bleated while he slid Bree's new whatchamacallit into a brown paper sack the size of a postcard. "That comes to $14.37. You wanna do cash or credit card?"

Nearly fifteen dollars and she didn't even know its name.

Uptown Vintage wasn't open yet when she passed by—their customers weren't shopping for midcentury prom dresses or go-go boots at ten thirty in the morning. And Judith at Scout & Morgan Real Estate had an officeful when Bree got there. They waved at each other through the window instead.

Up next: Lady of the Lake Distillery, a lucky coincidence given that she was thirsty and tired and hadn't worn the right shoes for a day of hitting the pavement. The distillery had gone in kitty-corner from the bookshop just over a year ago. Daisy and Lou, the owners, were nice enough, but their entry into the neighborhood had also spelled the end of the Rainbow's beer and wine business. Customers who once met at the bookshop for a drink and a browse now went across the street.

"Dibble-dibble doo, dibble-dibble dee, it's Bree!" Daisy had seen her coming up the sidewalk and opened the door to usher her in. "How's it hangin', princess?" She didn't know Bree well enough to have given her a nickname, but Daisy also didn't seem the sort of woman who cared about formalities.

"Oh, you know." Bree disentangled herself from her purse and followed the owner toward her bar.

"You come sit with me, Double Cream. We'll have a drink and a good ol' bitchfest. Catch up on what's been happening across the street." Daisy pulled out a stool next to where she'd presumably been sitting, judging from the stack of papers awaiting her return. "What's your pleasure?"

Bree looked at her watch. Eleven fifteen. "If I have alcohol this early, I'll be a waste for the rest of the day."

"Which is why most people come here—to *not* drink." Daisy poked her playfully with an elbow and rounded her way behind the bar. "How's about a Rhuby Gin?"

Bree sat up to protest. Daisy grinned. "It's ginger ale with a shot of our house-made rhubarb syrup. You'll love it." Moments later she placed a tall glass of ice and pink fizz in front of Bree. "Now, what has you wandering the block instead of selling books this morning?"

"I'm not wandering. I just have the morning off, is all."

"Uh-huh." Daisy nudged the Rhuby Gin toward Bree and waited for her to take a sip.

"Wow, that's good."

"That's more like it! Alright, let's roll back the tape a bit. Starting with, who's the new gal over there these days?"

Bree swallowed more, then explained. "That's Laney. Irma's daughter. She's visiting from California."

"I thought you were Irma's daughter."

"I am."

"So, Laney's your sister."

"Yes, but—" Bree rolled her shoulders back and tried to stretch out the knots in her neck. It'd been nearly thirty years and she still clammed up trying to explain her family. "Irma adopted me when I was ten. Up 'til then, I'd just been Laney's friend who followed her to the bookshop every day after school. My home situation was pretty bad."

Understatement.

"Adopted or not, still sisters, though." She raised a single eyebrow.

"Right. I just. You know. Some days my relationship with

our mom feels more complicated than others." She bobbed her head the way people do when pretending there isn't much more to say. Daisy bobbed back, meaning she either believed her or was fluent in the nonverbal code of uncomfortable conversations. Bree didn't care which.

The chat was interrupted anyway by the appearance of a live-action version of Paul Bunyan, if Paul were in his forties with graying auburn hair.

"You met Witt?" Daisy hooked a thumb toward the man. "C'mere and say hi, Wittaker. This is Bree. She's the whirlwind from the bookshop across the street."

Bree accepted his outstretched hand, noticing how soft it was, despite it being the size of a small bear paw.

"Witt Blake," he said. "Welcome to Lady of the Lake."

"Witt's our distillery genius. Among other things, he's the mastermind behind that rhubarb syrup in your Rhuby Gin, there."

Bree took a perfunctory sip. "Tastes kinda like a SweeTART." *Ope.* Was that an insult? "I mean, in a good way."

"Enjoy." He winked. Bree choked, coughing at the shock of it.

"Whoa, slice!" Daisy laughed and slapped her back. "He's not gonna bite."

"I know!" If there were a fork nearby, Bree could stab it into her thigh and look less ridiculous than she did right now. She allowed herself to meet his gaze, just briefly enough to see that the blue in his eyes was flecked with tiny white crystals the color of ice.

This was a disaster.

"Well," he said, "I need to grab a case of bourbon. See you soon?" This he directed at Bree.

"Sure. Of course. Probably. Yeah."

Daisy leaned in close enough to growl in her ear, "Flirting's good for the blood pressure, hon." She began to shuffle her papers into a neat pile, readying to clear the bar for the noon crowd. "You need anything else? Don't worry about your Rhuby Gin—that one's on me."

Bree shook her head, uncertain whether she felt mortified or flattered. "Thanks."

Daisy was nearly gone when Bree remembered. "Oh, hey. Just wondering. You heard anything about Vandaveer Investments? I caught whiff of some rumors and thought I'd ask around."

"Those two." She *hoowee*'d and shook her head. "They handed us an offer on this place not even a month after we opened. Lou kicked 'em to the curb with the pointy end of her boot. Whatcha heard?"

"Oh, just—" She reminded herself she wasn't lying if what she was saying could possibly be true. And something about Daisy made her feel safe inching just a little further out onto her limb. "They plan to knock down the Rainbow and replace it with condos."

Thom blocked his afternoon to work on the tasks assigned to him. This morning, however, he had a meeting to attend.

"Who have you lost?" Laikin, the support group moderator asked. "I don't mean the loved ones whose death you're grieving. I mean, who have you lost that once played an important role in your life? Maybe for some of you it's a former neighbor. Or a friend. Or family. Even a lover."

Thom saw a few people nod. One or two jotted names in their notes.

"The loss may be circumstantial—a neighbor who moved away for a new job. More likely though, if they're at the top of your list, the split may have been deeply worrisome or even hurtful. A loved one you had a falling-out with. A friend who quit returning your calls with no explanation. A generalized friction you were never able to fix with someone in your life.

"The point of this week's discussion is to ask ourselves, 'Who have I lost?' Because whether we're aware of it or not, there's often guilt leftover from those lost relationships, and guilt is what?"

Thom joined his fellow group members in answering. "Stressful."

"Right," said Laikin. "And what's one of the struggling spirit's main enemies?"

"Stress," came the group's reply.

Afterward, Laikin approached Thom as the other members of the group made for the exit. "Terrific to see you again, Thom. Big plans coming up? Are you going to try to get out and engage?"

Laikin loved for everyone in his group to try to "get out and engage" as often as possible. What he didn't know, and which Thom had no intention of telling him, was that he was about to head home and begin making some potentially pivotal phone calls, starting with his closest friends, Brian and Michael.

Every year, Brian and Michael hosted a birthday dinner in Elliot's honor. Michael made boeuf bourguignon and homemade spaetzle. Brian mixed the cocktails and the playlist. Their friend Timothy brought cake from the Buttercream Bakery. Elliot played piano after dinner while the lot of them clustered around love-worn sheet music, belting drunken Broadway tunes.

This year, they couldn't pretend everything hadn't changed. He'd spent Elliot's birthday in a dark house with the blinds drawn.

Now, he was about to emerge.

"I have a few things coming up soon," he answered.

Laikin studied him with piercing eyes and a generous smile—a disconcerting mix of friendship and alarm. "Your attendance here has been outstanding, but I haven't ever seen you bring a friend or partner or family member." He held out a fist for Thom to meet with his own, the moderator's preferred form of physical connection with group members. Thom complied, and Laikin held them there, knuckle to knuckle.

"Loss is cruel enough as it is. I don't want you to go through it alone."

Thom promised to consider his advice.

COMMERCIAL BREAK

Hello, book darlings,

I promised I'd be back, and here I am! In fact, you may be thrilled to know Judy just reminded me that every great artist benefits from a timely reappearance. It took her four years to land after MGM fired her from the set of *Royal Wedding* and the contract she'd been under since 1935. But when she came back, she did it in style with an Academy Award nomination for a little 1954 film called *A Star is Born*. And even with all that glorious acclaim, she didn't land her next role until 1961. For those of you at home, that's four years for Judy's first comeback, and seven years until her second. A real star always returns when the time is right!

She says "thank you" and sends her love.

Anyhoo...you've been worried about Thom. I hear you. I know. You just want to wrap him in a bear hug and tell him everything will be okay, and that yes, I was awful to overlook him in my estate the way I did. Oh, friends, how I wish I could tell you you're right. But you know, I can't do that. For one, you're not as right as you think you are. And two, telling you all the juicy details now would ruin the story. Don't get off the bus in Omaha and declare it Disney World—you're not there yet, people. Patience.

I will give you a few nuggets to keep you reading, however.

Irma. Did I love her? Yes! I don't know what I need to say to prove that already. But listen, we get hung up on the idea of romantic love between men and women, and that's just cheating ourselves. Our spirits have the capacity to love in infinite ways, and if you don't personally know that to be true, go make yourself a cup of tea and sit down because you have a lot to learn.

As for me, I lived to make people happy. It was lemonade on a hot day, chocolate chip cookies dipped in milk. But I knew I was feeling the presence of real love when I wanted nothing more than to make the object of my affection smile. And Irma was my number-one gal. After all, I was a gay man born into 1950s America, remember. It was my God-given, Wonder Bread, and Whirlpool manifest destiny to meet a pretty, young thing with an hourglass figure and head on down to the chapel with her on my arm. I was to drive an American car with chrome fins and earn a degree in any profession with initials: Elliot Gregory, MD, JD, CPA, PhD.

But I was taught to believe myself a miscreant. A pervert. A Uranian. (That last reference is today's history lesson. Enjoy.) I was not born of I Like Ike DNA, and therefore no more pro forma *Americanus* than the *Hyla cinerea* ("Ribbit," he said).

I could, and did, however, love Irma. How do I know? Because when I was with her, I felt "right." I craved her laugh, her ideas, her way of being in the world. I could be vulnerable without fear of rebuke. I could be Elliot and do so without hating every part of myself, because she loved me so much. Yes, she was my foil. Your word choice is linguistically correct, but don't attempt to squeeze everything we were to each other into a term from your Introduction to Literature class. When I stood with Irma, she threw light onto all the parts I had for so long tried to keep in the dark. The more sunlight she threw, the more I craved and needed her.

Because, you must understand that when I was alone, my spirit went black. And there, one cannot live.

"Do you believe in magic?" she asked me one day.

"No," I answered. How could a child who'd spent every night praying and wishing upon stars that he'd awake in the morning somehow "cured" believe in magic? "I do, however, believe in skilled trickery."

"Hmm." She studied me in that cocked-head, golden-retriever-with-the-gorgeous-amber-eyes way she had. "Too bad. Because you have a skill for reading a person. I would call it 'looking into their soul,' but that's a little—you know." She flitted her fingers in the air, mimicking the flight of one's reason.

We were at the Rainbow for this conversation, likely sometime in the mid-to-late eighties because I had just finished running around the store in my puffy Reebok high-tops for a grandmother distraught by her inability to choose a high school graduation gift for her granddaughter. "She's leaving for college, and I don't think she's even read Chaucer."

"Where is your granddaughter going to school?" I'd asked.

"The University of Washington. Though from what I can see, she's spent more time planning the decorations for her dorm room than she has studying the course catalog."

I'll admit. If the girl's mother was as judgmental as her grandmother, I couldn't blame the child for fleeing to Seattle. I may have chosen the University of Hawaii, myself. But her grandmother's fretting did give me an idea. "We have a beautiful set of leather-bound classics. Brontë. Austen. Woolf. Morrison. I promise your granddaughter will love them."

"No Sylvia Plath," she'd admonished.

"I wouldn't dare."

One hundred dollars later, old Grandma Chaucer walked out the door with thirty pounds of fiction.

"You know her granddaughter won't read those books, right?" Irma smiled, and I drank her sunlight, like a flower.

"Of course not. But they'll make her look good, sitting on her shelf, gilded and IQ heightening. She will love that."

And that's when Irma asked me if I believed in magic. I didn't then. I do now.

The problem with basking in the sun, however, is that with time, we all get burned. It's the reason I could never eat cupcakes—the first bite always tasted so good. But the second sent me soaring to sugary heights, then crashing to a sour, sluggish mire just as quickly. Irma was my sugar high. I loved her. She fed me. But her nutrition was not sustainable, because it did not feed all of me. Let's not be prudish about it, I'm talking about sex. Sex matters. And good sex matters a hell of a lot more.

Enter: Thom. No! He wasn't just sex to me. He was my partner. My love. My caretaker. The day he walked into the Rainbow was the only other moment in my life in which I felt that certain something I'd felt when I met Irma. Except, with Thom, it was a certain something-plus. Need I remind you, the reason I wanted to tear off Irma's clothes was because she was wearing orange polyester. Thom was sexy. I fell into him, and when I did, I released a breath I didn't know I'd been holding. It wasn't the sex—I'd had plenty. Our connection was all-encompassing. Physical + Intellectual + Spiritual + Emotional + Vulnerable + + +. He was my other, and I, his.

Oh, I know I'm beginning to sound like a greeting card, but as I've made perfectly clear, words cannot capture spirit. My point is, we fit. I didn't ask Thom to move in. He came to my apartment one night and never left. The next thing either of us knew, we were signing mortgage papers, an act that proved no more dramatic or anxiety provoking than brushing one's teeth before bed. If we wanted to live, we needed to be together.

And then I died. We had nearly twenty years, but my death was a betrayal. I wish I could have made him happy by living forever (though I don't wish that for myself—trust me when I say that what lies beyond is—*beyond*. (And enough with the fountain of youth fixations, darlings. Just live, already!)).

Now, here's the second nugget I'll pass along: Thom has more living to do, and his next chapter is better without me. Yes, it does sound maudlin. But it's true. I had quit loving him the way he deserved to be loved. I don't know when it began; these things sneak up on us. But Thom loved me so fully, it sparked the embers of self-hatred I thought I'd finally extinguished. I don't have the words, obviously, but let's do this—picture a moment in your life when you felt fabulous from head to toe. Your hair was perfect, your makeup brought out your best features, your dress was unlike anything anyone had seen you in before. Every piece of you sparkled.

Now go find a picture of yourself in that moment. Maybe it was a wedding, or a trip to Paris, or the first long weekend away with the one you love. For me, I think of the day we opened the Rainbow. The *Minneapolis/St. Paul Standard* sent a photographer, and I made sure to wear my 1980 best—tight jeans, tight tee, tight trim on the mustache. The article still hangs on the bookshop wall in Vanity Corner. I tried to hide it many times and Irma always scolded me for my pride, but I hated that picture because all I saw when I looked at it was my ridiculous clothes and how much pain that all-too-human jackass was bound to cause in the years to come.

The Elliot I thought I was wasn't fabulous at all.

That's what happened with Thom. His love became a poison. As true as it was in the moment, its cumulative effect was to remind me that I didn't deserve love. The better our nights together, the bigger the pervert in the mirror the next morning. The gentler he handled my vulnerabilities, the deeper I had to wound myself to keep them fresh. I hadn't been born into love. I was born to a mother so cold she wore a cashmere coat in Miami Beach. (I know that sounds like a line from a bad lounge act, but it's true; the coat was the color of warm caramel and as soft as my shell.) With a woman like that as my maternal foundation, to have a love as complex, and vibrant, and simple as I felt with Thom could not be anything but wrong.

Oh, bother. Sometimes I don't like remembering.

Judy has just offered to mix me a second grapefruit juice and vodka. She also suggests I take a break. Or as she says it, "You're sinking, darling." And she is correct, as ever.

I will be back, though. You can bet your bottom dollar on it.

11

13 days until close...

Thom had never been much of a joiner, but that didn't mean he wasn't aware of exactly which local gay men's groups to target with his unfolding mission.

Brian agreed. "If I had to rank Minneapolis in order of most likely to take on a cause, the Gay Men's Kickball League tops the list. Michael couldn't even make it a whole season, he was so exhausted from their activist extra-extracurriculars."

Thom wrote "Kickball" on a yellow sticky note and hung it in the "Tier One" column on his whiteboard.

"After that," Brian continued, "and I know it sounds counterintuitive, but I'd have to say the chess club."

Thom asked which, the Gay Men's Chess Club of the Twin Cities, or the Gay Men's Chess League of Greater Minneapolis.

"The League. The Twin Cities club is really just an excuse for people to escape the suburbs for an afternoon. They're too concerned with kids and school boards to care about anything else."

Thom made a second sticky note.

"What is this for, by the way?"

"Vandaveer Investments is attempting to force Elliot's store to sell so they can put up condos there instead."

"NO!"

Forcing them to sell? Perhaps that was a stretch.

Brian said, "I have running club tonight. You okay if I spread the word?"

Thom smiled, proud of his immediate success. "The faster we organize, the better."

Brian could not agree more.

"Oh," Thom said. "Could I bother you for another favor? I have a need for a deliveryman again."

"You really need to adapt to the times—this is becoming absurd."

They hung up. Thom pulled out his planner and found the number for their friend, Timothy. He wasn't on the kickball league, but he played trivia on Tuesdays with people who were—two groups with one call.

"Drip. Drip. Drip," he said as he dialed.

Laney was at the shop, trying to help a young woman choose a belated birthday gift for her mother.

"I'm not really sure what she likes to read, but she is kind of into murder." Moments ago, they'd been in the gardening section until she realized she didn't know if her mom kept a garden anymore.

"I know." The woman snapped her fingers. "Do you carry other books like *50 Shades of Grey*?"

"Right over here, my dear." Laney hadn't expected it, but lots of daughters seemed to buy their mothers sexed-and-saucy romances. She and Bree, on the other hand, usually gave their mom geraniums.

It had been like this most of the day, but whenever traffic lulled, Laney did her best to take advantage.

"MOM?" she hollered, knowing how crazy it drove her mother. "YOO-HOO! IRMA!"

Irma appeared at the stockroom door, wearing a neon-pink Rainbow tee that, judging from its equally neon-green appliqué, had to be a relic of the Madonna Ascendancy. "May I help you, daughter?"

Laney's eyes popped in her skull. She pointed at the shirt. "Where? What?"

"I'm clearing out boxes. I always liked this design. The eighties are back, you know."

"Not that part." She squinted, trying to see if there was any angle at which she could tolerate her mom's fashion homage to Wham! "Anyway, quick question."

"Yes?"

"Does Al next door know you're betraying Bree and selling the store for five dollars and a bucket of peel-and-eat shrimp?"

"I don't eat shrimp. It makes me burp."

With her mother returned to the bowels of the stockroom, Laney wandered over to the front window and looked onto the street. There was plenty of life out there to keep a bookshop like the Rainbow alive. For example, there was a couple on the corner arguing about directions, each of them holding phones, one of them pointing left while the other pointed right. If she wanted, she could walk out right now and offer them any number of books they might find useful, from communication strategies to relationship counseling to geocaching. Instead, she hollered, "MOM? YOU HUNGRY?"

Twenty minutes later she returned from Saigon Take-Out with a bag of spring rolls (no, she wasn't stoned, they were just really good) and planted herself at the table in the back room, facing her mother.

"I'm going to sit here until you talk to me."

"Wonderful. I couldn't think of a greater blessing than to spend time with my wayward daughter."

"I'm hardly wayward. You have my address."

She hmm'd. Then dropped an entire folder of yellowed somethings—old invoices or bills or correspondence—into the recycling bin.

"I know you wish I'd stayed home to work at the store like Bree did."

"That's not true."

"Yes, it is. You've always hated that I ran off with Tuck. I know you don't like him. I know that's why you don't come out to visit very often."

Her mom placed a fist on her hip and turned. "You seem to know an awful lot all of a sudden."

"Or maybe I've known it for a long time and I'm finally saying it out loud." She took a bite of her spring roll and got an unexpected mouthful of cilantro. The taste of Irish Spring. Either the Saigon Take-Out cooks were the ones smoking pot today, or someone new and in training had been set loose in the kitchen before they were ready. She spit it into her napkin, but the scent of freshness in a bottle was overwhelming, fouling both her appetite and her mood. "The irony is you're cutting and running on Bree the same way I did to you. Who's the kettle and who's the pot now?"

That did it.

"I'm insulted that you think so little of me." Her mom slapped another yellowed and overstuffed folder onto the desk. "I'm hardly cutting and running. We make our own choices in life, Laney. And we live with the consequences, come what may."

"You don't think I know that?"

Her mom went silent for a moment and sat down. "I think you know it all too well, actually."

Laney ran her fingers across her napkin, though the grease from her cooling lunch had been long wiped away.

"I miss you, Laney. Yes, I wish you wouldn't have run off the way you did. Yes, I wish you wouldn't have lived so far away for the past twenty years. But I've only ever wanted you to be happy. To pursue the life you want. That wasn't the bookstore for you, and you wanna know a secret? I'm glad it wasn't. Now more than ever."

"What is that supposed to mean, now more than ever?"

She just shook her head. "Doesn't matter."

Later that afternoon, Bree blew through the bookshop door like a child running for the bathroom.

"ANYTHING NEW?" Laney was shouting because she'd put Neil Diamond on the sound system and dialed the volume up to *Crackle*.

"WHY IS IT SO LOUD IN HERE?"

"I'M TRYING TO FLUSH MOM OUT. SHE'S GIVING ME THE SILENT TREATMENT."

Twenty or so minutes ago she'd started playing "Sweet Caroline" on an endless loop. The tactic had been inspired by a bit she'd heard from the comedian John Mulaney, who, when he was a teenager, went into a diner and played "What's New Pussycat?" twenty-one times on the jukebox. The people in the restaurant went nutters.

"TURN IT OFF!" Bree hollered, then didn't wait for Laney and did it herself. "You are insane."

Laney wagged a finger. "Uh-uh. I am an agent of chaos. It's very different."

Bree ignored her and ducked into the stockroom only to emerge a few seconds later, grinning. "She's not in there, you know."

"Yes, she is. I've attached myself to her, as directed."

"She sneaked out the receiving door."

"Dang it! So obvious."

The bell above the yellow door tinkled and the man in the flasher's trench coat walked through.

"Oh! Hello again," Laney said. "Are you actually going to do it this time, or are you just a tease?"

The look on his face made it clear he didn't know what she was talking about. Then he handed her a note. "I'm supposed to stay until you write down your answer."

Bree took the folded slip of paper and read it.

Meanwhile, Laney said, "By the way, I'm very impressed you wear a Burberry trench when you do this. Classy touch. Not many flashers have a good sense of style."

Bree asked Laney to join her at the counter. She read the note aloud. "Given our ticking clock, I would like to meet as soon as possible for a progress check. Please consult with each other and indicate your preference."

Their choices were:

☐ 6 pm
☐ 7 pm

"Is he serious?" Bree asked.

Trench Coat said, "Just tick off the time slot you prefer."

"If we're going to have secret meetings," Laney said, "we ought to have a code name, don't you think?"

Bree grinned. "Most definitely."

"Like Operation Barbecue Fest?"

"Or Operation Doggy Rescue."

"The Tea and Biscuit Society."

"The Agatha Christie Book Club."

"The Book Lovers' Book Club."

"The Book Haters' Book Club."

They locked eyes. "That one!"

Bree wrote the name on the slip of paper, along with the 7:00 p.m. slot and a suggested meeting place: Lady of the Lake Distillery. "Thom shouldn't have to host us every time."

Trench Coat took the note and slipped away into the afternoon.

"Why is he wearing that when it's seventy-something degrees outside?" Laney asked.

"Better question," Bree replied. "When is Thom gonna learn how to text?"

***

Lady of the Lake gave Bree the sensation of stepping into the life she never lived. She'd always preferred the sorts of environments in which expectations of her were uniform and clear—at school, she took careful notes and spoke when called upon; at the bookshop, she answered customers' questions; at home, she put her clothes away and washed her dishes. Here, a young woman in black leather leggings sipped a highball flocked by three men who mysteriously laughed only when she laughed and drank only when she drank. Over by the window, a couple nuzzled awkwardly across a broad-plank table, while a second couple nearby repelled each other physically, magnets of the same pole. And behind the bar, Witt, brawnier than ever and looking directly at her.

Bree heard herself forget how to breathe.

Laney nodded sympathetically. "I know. I forgot how the Minnesota humidity fills your lungs like soup."

"No, I think I'm having an anxiety attack."

"Either that or you picked up one of those parasites that cripples you without warning." Laney tracked her line of sight toward the bar. "Oh, I see now. Little Miss Breester has a case of the crushing crushies."

"You're the worst."

"But I'm right, aren't I? Which one—the Brawny Paper Towel Man?"

"The Paul Bunyan look-alike."

"He's cute. Go tell him you need a cleanup on aisle nine."

Bree turned, more dumbfounded than disgusted. "You never grew out of that, did you?"

"*That* being…?"

"I don't know." She circled her palm in front of Laney's face. "Your overall Laney-ism. Quick with the comeback. Vaguely offensive."

Laney gave her a pitying look. "You've always been a little

bit country. I've always been a little bit rock and roll. Those are the cards we were dealt." She gave Bree a shove. "Now, go chat with your lumberjack before Thom gets here."

She complied, helped along by Laney's fist in her back, and Witt nodded as she approached. "Hey, Bree, welcome back." He extended a hand to Laney. "I'm Witt."

"I'm Laney. Bree's mom."

He believed her, if only for a millisecond. "You nearly had me. Who are you, really? Friend? Coworker? Cousin?"

"Sister," they said in unison, as if Laney were Marcia Brady and Bree were the less fortunate Jan.

"Whatcha recommend tonight, Witt?" Laney asked.

"You like bourbon?"

"As long as it doesn't burn a hole through my nasal passages."

He got to work and moments later produced a highball with a single ice cube swimming in an amber-pink pool. "I call it a Barbed Bourbon. Basically, a bourbon sour with rhubarb instead of simple syrup."

Laney sipped, grinned, and passed it to Bree, who wasn't a bourbon gal, but always the Jan when her sister was around, stepped up as wannabe good sport.

"Holy cow." She brought a hand to her lips. "Oh my god, that's delicious." It was.

"Glad you like it."

"I'll have one of these, too, please." Bree's first sip was already sliding into her toes, inviting them to dance, and she realized she needed to take it slow because if she wasn't careful, she might start telling Witt secrets she didn't know she had.

Witt mixed, and Laney craned her neck to scan the crowd. "Any sign of Thom?"

The distillery was busier than expected. And louder. Bree wondered if they'd be able to hear each other or if they'd even find a table.

"I'm going to step outside to give Tuck a quick call." Laney leaned in, not quite yelling but too loud for such close proximity to Bree's ear. "We've been playing phone tag all day."

"Everything alright?"

Laney didn't respond but suddenly pointed across the room. "There's Thom. He's got a table."

"I was beginning to think you weren't coming." Thom wasn't fond of his alarmist tendencies, but he disliked being kept waiting.

Bree said, "We were sitting at the bar. Laney just stepped outside to call her husband."

He examined her cocktail. It looked fresh. "Good?"

She said it was.

Laney appeared. "More phone tag," she told Bree. "Lovely to see you, Thom."

He acknowledged her arrival by getting right to it. "Jumping into the business at hand, I accept your code name suggestion, the Book Haters' Book Club. It's a fitting nod to Elliot and his legacy." He made a tick by the first item on his notepad and wished he had a gavel. Naming their mission felt propitious. He lifted his water glass an inch from the table. "All in favor?"

Aye.

The knock of glass on wood made it official. Project Book Haters' Book Club.

"Before we move on—" Laney interrupted before he had the chance to introduce the next item on his agenda, "Sharing Recent Successes." "Sweet list you have there, by the way. Thanks for coming prepared. But first, how are you?"

"I was just about to suggest we share our progress. Would you like me to go first?"

"In a second." Now she was smiling at him as if expecting he could read her mind. "That's business. I want to know how you are doing. Let's chat before jumping under the sheets."

Bree chided her sister by way of apologizing. "Ignore her.

She's been away from Minnesota too long and forgets her manners."

"No, I suppose Laney's right." Thom heard his group leader Laikin's voice in his head—*try to engage every day.* "I am feeling energized, thank you for asking. It's been nice to have a project. Something to work toward."

Laney leaned closer, face propped on her hand. "How long were you and Elliot together?"

The question made him blink. He couldn't remember the last time anyone had asked. "It would have been twenty years in April." April 11. He'd kept the lights off all day and tried to force down a handful of saltine crackers. "That's one of the reasons we went to Machu Picchu in January. An early anniversary trip."

Adding that last bit may have been a mistake. Whenever he told a relative stranger about their last dream trip together, they cooed at the romance of it and said "at least you have the memories."

He would have rather died himself if it meant not having them. They were still too painful to touch.

Laney, mercifully, skipped the trite condolences. "Elliot taught me how to ride a bike. Did you know that? In the MTC bus corral near the shop. I thought I took to the challenge like a champ, but I also remember asking him what those stains were under his armpits on the walk back to the store."

Thom suppressed a smile. Elliot's biggest muscle by any measure had been his heart. "I like that story. Thank you for sharing it."

Bree looked at her watch, feeling the urge to get a move on. "Thom, you went to the effort of putting together our agenda, so why don't you go first?" Maybe if she had another drink, she might loosen up a little. Was Witt watching her?

Thom removed a slip of notepaper from his materials. "It seems my attempts to organize against—" he paused, glancing at the nearby tables "—against our friends, the *Varsity Interlopers*, has proven remarkably fruitful."

"Gotta love a good whisper network," said Laney.

"Recently," he continued, "I *may* or *may not* have been privy to the speculation that our Varsity friends aren't just, in fact, planning condos, but very expensive units, at that. I received a call this afternoon from the husband of a friend whose college roommate plays in the Gay Men's Soccer League, and he just happens to work in city development and therefore has access to the information to prove definitively that, yes, the Varsity Interlopers have indeed filed the necessary building permits."

"Which one is 'he,'" Laney asked. "The husband, the friend, or the soccer player?"

Bree's head felt ready to pop. "He just confirmed they plan to demolish the Rainbow, and you want clarity on who's married to whom?"

Laney, thankfully, took her point and buried her face in her drink.

Thom smiled. "The point is that's excellent information with which to shake the neighborhood hive."

"Cheers to that!" Laney and Thom celebrated while Bree clocked Daisy from across the room. They spotted each other, and Daisy pivoted in their direction.

"Well, if it isn't Breetle-dee and her circle of rum-tum-tums!" Daisy peered over Laney's shoulder to inspect her drink. "Almost dry. You need another?"

"Depends. Do you have a rule against sudden and possibly tone-deaf a cappella ABBA medleys?"

Daisy's guffaw came out like an unequivocal approval, and she punched Laney on the shoulder. "I like this gal." She turned to Bree. "How 'bout you, dancing queen?"

Bree decided another drink would land her facedown on the bathroom tile. "I'll just stick with this one, thanks."

She moved to Thom's side of the table and extended her hand. "I'm Daisy."

"Thom Winslow." He accepted her handshake like a schoolboy accepting the stern congratulations of his headmaster. "Very pleased to meet you."

"And you, Mr. Thom Winslow. Now, tell me this—how do you feel about the prospect of a little cask-aged whiskey?"

Laney answered for him. "He's never been so excited."

As soon as Daisy left, Laney decided it was her turn to share. "Alright, my turn," she said. "I got nothin' from Mom. She shuts me down as quickly as I can formulate my questions and her only consistent answer is 'You know everything you need to know.'"

"Is she willing to get a second opinion about the offering price?" Thom asked.

Laney had tried that approach. "All she'll say is that she made an informed decision."

"But with whose help? Did she rely solely on the Vandaveers' information? Did she engage outside counsel?" She could see Thom begin to twitch, he was getting himself so worked up.

Bree sighed. "The way she's acting, she may as well have consulted with the magical leprechaun who visits at night."

She meant the magical Over the Rainbow leprechaun. Laney had forgotten all about him. Or her. Or them. Did leprechauns need a gender?

She and Bree were little when the mystery began. She remembered sitting at the small table in Children's Corner eating peanut butter sandwiches and studying the small golden nugget that had mysteriously appeared on the table overnight.

"It has to be gold," Bree said. She jumped from her chair and returned with a copy of *The Miners '49er*, a picture book about the California gold rush, and one of her recent favorites. She opened to a page showing a single shiny nugget in a miner's pan. "See?"

Laney put their nugget into her mouth and bit down.

"What are you doing?" Bree grabbed her by the arm, trying to shake it free.

She didn't need to. It was too bitter to stand for more than a few seconds. "We're supposed to bite it. That's how to tell if it's real or not."

"Well?"

"It sort of tastes like when you suck on a penny."

Bree flipped the pages of the book, looking for answers.

"Hi, gals." Her mom happened to wander by at just that moment. In hindsight, it was obvious she'd left the fool's gold out for them to find. She probably saw Bree's budding interest in *The Miners '49er* and decided to bring a bit of history to life. In the eyes of two six-year-olds, it was nothing less than magic. "Looks like the store leprechaun dropped a bit of his gold last night. Must've been in a hurry."

"We do not have a leprechaun!" Laney knew because she would have found it by now. She'd explored every inch of the store.

Her mother didn't budge. "Well, I've never seen the leprechaun, but every once in a while, Elliot and I find little nuggets like this one just lying around." She picked it up and twirled it slowly between her fingers. "You're lucky. This is a biggie. Last one we found was on the floor behind the front counter, but that was barely the size of a piece of sand."

"You can't see something as small as a piece of sand, Mom!" Laney was not going to be fooled.

"Can so." Again, Bree flipped to the relevant page in her book. Sure enough, there was another miner with a pan full of dirt and one brilliant speck of gold shining through. "That's why they had to sift so carefully. Because most of what they could find was small like that."

"Just goes to show," her mom said. "I guess you don't necessarily have to see something to believe in it."

Adult Laney snapped free of her thoughts. "I wish the leprechaun would drop some gold again soon. Then we could sell it and buy the store with cash."

"I don't follow," said Thom.

Laney laughed. "I'll catch you up later." Which reminded her of something she didn't understand. "By the way, who is Trench Coat and why does he keep delivering notes for you?"

Thom looked momentarily confused. "Oh. That's my friend. Brian."

Bree said, "Why do you send him instead of just calling?"

"Because I never know whether Irma is nearby. The first time I needed to reach you, I didn't have your cell phone number and I certainly couldn't risk calling or stopping by the store. And the second time, I wanted to ensure you didn't answer by saying 'Hello, Thom.'"

Laney laughed. Bree dropped her face into her palm. "I am capable of answering my phone with discretion."

"Well, I know that now."

Daisy reappeared with their fresh drinks. "Been thinking about your dilemma—" She placed a cocktail in front of Laney, so strong her brain began to buzz from the smell of it. "You need Lou and I to stand up on your behalf with the neighborhood development board? We could dispute the sale at the public hearing."

"Maybe," said Bree. "I hadn't thought about that."

"Well, let us know." She passed the table a round of three small glasses with a half inch of clear liquid in each. "In other news, I brought you a taster of our new aquavit. Compliments of Witt."

Bree's head immediately snapped. "Witt sent these over?"

"Sure." Daisy winked for Laney's benefit, who thought she'd just made a new best friend.

Laney brought the glass to her nose. "Dill?"

"Lil' bit," Daisy confirmed. "Now, if any of you are driving home, let me know right now so I can get you a ride."

They were all walking.

"No offense," Laney warned the group when Daisy was gone, "but I've suddenly become more interested in drinking than scheming."

Thom frowned. Then drank. "I can choose to be satisfied with this evening's progress."

"Me, too," said Bree, scanning the room.

Laney elbowed her. "You get less subtle the more you drink, you know. You may as well be wearing a sandwich board that says I Heart Witt."

Bree slid down in her seat until her head was no longer visible above the crowd. "I think I'm having a nervous breakdown. Or a midlife crisis. Can you have one of those before you turn forty?"

Thom said maybe. "I'm not sure mine ever ended."

Laney's phone buzzed in her pocket. Tuck. *Ignore.*

Bree pushed the rest of her aquavit away. "I should get home."

Laney's phone buzzed again. This time Tuck tried texting.

Why aren't you answering?

Because, she didn't reply, *this is easier.*

The Book Haters' Book Club Newsletter

Issue #381
February 2021

Ah, February. A month for lovers…

Oh, *phbphbphbt*! If you want to express your devotion to those you love, *please* don't wait for the one day a year the greeting-card-and-chocolate-industrial complex would like you to do so. Love is everywhere, and when we're lucky enough to experience it, we ought to celebrate that blessing with our every thought.

This issue, I'm choosing to celebrate friendship, and in particular, a dear friend of the bookshop, Nestor Nivens. He passed away recently after an admirable fight against cancer. The illness eventually took his body but can never steal our memories of his kinship and kindness.

Nestor was not the sort of friend I would have made on my own—we were the unlikeliest of alliances. He wore a belt with a special pouch for his utility knife; I wear a belt to keep my belly from pouching. He kept his eyes on the sky, while mine were in the pages of a book. Nestor was my Rainbow co-owner Irma Bedford's friend first. I never would have met him if it weren't for her. But once you meet a man like Nestor, he's hard to let go. I don't think I ever saw him frown—his two expressions were smiling and grinning. "Good day today, no?" he'd say. Or, "Hard to complain about a day like this, I tell ya." And all while fixing a leaky pipe or a running toilet. One day, when replacing a bowing floorboard he spotted long before I would have, he accidentally hammered his thumb and hollered, "Well, Mary, *that's* gonna make me late for supper!"

Which brings us to this month's recommendations…

The Friend by Sigrid Nunez is the story of a woman who, upon losing her dearest friend, feels compelled to adopt his grieving Great Dane. She is not a dog person, and, being in such deep pain herself, the care this creature requires nearly causes her to lose her sanity. A National Book Award winner, the novel demonstrates a human truth: the love we need often comes from unexpected sources.

I should add, too, that I once recommended *The Friend* to a woman who told me "I prefer dogs to books." She returned to the shop later to tell me specifically how much she enjoyed "the Great Dane character."

Coming February 9 is *Crossing the Line* by Kareem Rosser. Talk about unlikely alliances. This is a memoir, the story of young brothers growing up in crime-and poverty-stricken West Philadelphia who go on to become polo champions. Yes, you read that right: *polo*, the sport of rich white men and royals. These young brothers take an interest in a barn full of horses in nearby Fairmount Park, and Lezlie Hiner, founder of the Work to Ride stables, trades the brothers' labor in exchange for free riding lessons. It's a galloping tale of determination, hard work, and loyalty, and, don't fret, we'll have a stable full of copies ready for you.

Hug the ones you love today, readers. Better yet, come in and let us help you pick out the perfect book to place in their hands.

—Elliot

Last Hope for the Haters

Words alone cannot express how it feels to love and be loved. And yet, to write, to speak, to search for and piece together just the right words—those acts themselves, are love.

12

12 days until close...

Laney could have woken up with a headache, but she'd sprung out of the sheets, thrown on a vintage "The Spice Girls are trying to kill you" tee from her dresser, and hustled to the bookstore. Maybe sabotage was the new antihangover cure.

Bree was in a good mood, too. Though for her, it was probably on account of having spent the previous evening in the gaze of her urban lumberjack. Moments ago, she'd been in the stacks with the barcode scanner, beeping and singing. "I do my hair down—"

"'Toss,'" corrected Laney. It was a well-established fact that anyone who misquoted Lizzo was going straight to hell, and so it was only right she do what she could to save her sister from such a terrible fate.

"Paint my nails—"

"'Check'! She *checks* her nails. Do you even listen to the lyrics?"

"Don't step on my gown, hater!" Bree chirped.

OMG, now she was mangling Taylor Swift.

Laney needed to find something to keep her hands busy and her mood up. Traffic at the shop was proving about as reliable as a clown car parade, and they'd only had one paying customer all morning—a man in cargo shorts who'd been dispatched to pick up a fresh copy of Kelly Barnhill's *The Girl Who Drank the Moon* after their puppy ate his daughter's beloved copy.

Tire Stud was never this slow, and on the rare occasions their customers trickled to a stop, Laney had a bottomless list of tasks to keep her occupied. At the Rainbow, though, her main job was to act as the devil on her mother's shoulder, and she'd already popped up this morning, only to be quickly flicked away.

Over coffee: "Still in the mood to sell, Mom?"

"I'm not discussing this, Laney."

Making breakfast: "You know who loves books more than eggs? Bree does."

"You know who loves talking more than listening? You do."

Now she popped into the back room. "Mom? You need anything? Maybe some help calling the Vandaveers?"

Her mother had her head buried in a decaying cardboard box labeled Misc. Tees. "Triple-XS? Who on earth did Elliot think would buy these?"

"What's that you say? You've decided to pass the store on to Bree? That's great news. I'll tell her right now!"

"Polyester blend? No thank you."

Having nothing better to do, Laney began to shuffle the display where they kept the month's picks from the big-name book clubs—Oprah, Emma, Jenna, Reese.

Bree put the scanner down on the sales counter and wandered over. "Does it look like we're selling through those?"

"Actually, I thought I'd just spruce the piles up. See if a little rearranging would help."

At first, Bree didn't spot it. Laney had been deceptively careful with her camouflage. Until, "Oprah's Book Club is not reading *Mourning Your Guinea Pig*."

"No! But can you believe that cover? The pink-orange sunset is almost identical to the real pick."

"Oh, come on. *Potty Training the Reluctant Child*?"

"Hey, can we help it that rogue packs of mischievous teenagers roam bookstores during summer vacation and have a penchant for disrupting book displays? If you want to know what I think, children should be forced to go to school 365 days a year. Boredom is the number one cause of all merchandise-related chicanery. Look it up."

Bree went back to barcode scanning. "You're going to make our customers think we're losing our minds."

"That's an excellent point. You should probably send me home for insubordination."

"Can't. Daisy just texted and wants me to come over. Says she has an update."

"What sort of an update?"

"Do I look like I know yet?" Bree grabbed her bag and was out the door, leaving Laney to watch at the window like a pup waiting for her person. *How long until she's back?*

"Girls?" Her mom walked out of the back room unrolling a poster. "Do you remember this?"

"No girls, Mom. Just me."

She stopped short, surprised to find a bookshop without her bookseller daughter in it. "Where'd Bree go?"

"Job hunting." Sure, it was twisting the knife, but it may as well have been true. "Rumor has it she'll be unemployed soon."

Her mother held out a warning finger. "Don't start." Then as if they'd been discussing nothing more controversial than pineapple on pizza, she stepped to the front counter and unfurled her find. "It's a poster from one of our annual summer tent sales. This one's dated 1990. We always held it during the Aquatennial to take advantage of the crowds—" She didn't finish the thought. "Those were the days, weren't they?"

Laney scowled. "No, crazy lady. You hated the tent sale." Because she remembered clearly. For her mother, the tent sale always turned into a stress-ridden, irritable-bowel-producing nightmare.

"About a week before the event, you flipped out about how

much work had to be done, a mini roller coaster of a tirade that went on for several days until Elliot cried uncle and produced an army of friends to erect the gigantic white tent you rented every year from AAA Rentals—which, if you'll recall, never went up the way it was supposed to, and always ended with someone on the way to the ER for stitches. Meanwhile, the remaining lot of suffering souls set up every long table available for rent in the metro area."

"It wasn't that bad."

"I'm not done yet. Because even when the setup was under control, you still had to stew about the weather forecast, despite the fact that July only ever brings one of two possibilities in Minnesota—you either get thunderstorms or the kind of heat and humidity where your underwear sticks to your butt."

Her mom was unmoved. "We made a profit every year. It was an extremely popular event."

Laney laughed. "How could it not be with a gazillion random people crowding in to hold up books and holler 'Have you read this one?' at each other?"

"Even so." Her mom carefully rerolled the poster. "Wouldn't it be fun to hold one last sale? I wonder if the tent company has any last-minute deals."

Laney looked at her fingers and debated which one she was willing to sacrifice to the AAA Rental gods.

"I'm not serious, of course. It would've been the perfect send-off, is all."

"To what, your sanity?"

Her mother gave her a stern look. "It's important to say a proper goodbye, Laney. You should try to remember that."

"Ooh, nice dig." Her mom was, of course, reminding Laney of how she'd abruptly left town and leashed her future to Tuck's. "*Insult Enthusiast* rated you as 'subtle, yet biting.'"

"I wouldn't call it subtle."

"What do you want me to say? You wouldn't have changed

my mind then, so what's the point of rehashing it all these years later?"

Her mom's face burned red. "Because I'm your mother. I thought you were in trouble and it's my job to protect and care for you. I was desperate with worry."

There were nights Laney had lain awake, wishing she had left differently. So many of those nights that it frightened her, sometimes to the point she had to get out of bed and pace, put her head between her knees, tell herself everything was going to work out. That living in a mouse-infested trailer without plumbing or running water wasn't permanent. Tuck was going to make it. And she was going to help. And as soon as that happened, the trailer and the panic and the memories of the desperation in her mom's voice when she called from somewhere on the road in Arkansas or Alabama or Kansas would melt away like the fog only to reveal the happy, safe, lush life she was bound for.

The life she suddenly wondered if she'd ever found.

It was also why she knew her mother would never treat Bree this way, vulnerable and scared and soon-to-be unemployed, if there wasn't something larger at play. Like Irma said, it's a mother's job to protect and care for her children. Laney may not be a mother, herself, but she had instincts enough to know that something was hurting their family.

Thom was walking so fast he had to keep stopping to pull up his pants. Even his belts were too big with all the weight he'd lost. But he had to hurry. He'd stopped at Nygaard's for a cup of coffee on his way home from his grief support group and spotted Irma buying a salad cone from the deli (just what in the world a salad cone was would have to wait for another day). If he hustled, he could catch Laney and Bree at the shop before their mother returned.

"Try pushing it to the left, maybe?" He heard Laney's voice

before he saw her or the oversize orange couch lodged in the Rainbow's front door.

"I swear I didn't know, fellas." She groaned, though she smiled as he approached. "Mom decided to start liquidating the furniture before measuring any of it. Who knows how they got this monster into the shop to begin with."

The young man holding the street-side end of the couch—presumably a college student currently questioning his choice of summer job—slowly lowered his load to the cement. "I don't think it's going to fit, ma'am."

Laney tented her fingers beneath her chin. "Maybe if you took the feet off?"

A young mother pushing a double stroller headed down the sidewalk, paused, and turned around.

"You just lost yourself a customer," Thom said.

Laney looked in the woman's direction. "Actually, we just got lucky. Bree says her little boy likes to rip the covers off the picture books and we lose money every time they come in."

And to think that was the sort of petty mayhem Elliot had been dealing with for forty years. Which reminded him.

"You're going to love what we've got people handing out in front of Nygaard's." He pulled a postcard from his back pocket and handed it to Laney. "You can keep it. I grabbed extras."

She scanned the card with one eye, keeping the other on the doorjamb. "'Knix the Knickerbocker Condos?'"

"The Knickerbocker, can you believe it? That's what the Vandaveers have decided to name the development. I can't even begin to list the reasons why the name's a travesty. Except, yes I can, and number one, it's desperately striving. The Knickerbocker Club in New York is the most prestigious private club in the country. The Vandaveer's Knickerbocker won't even be the most prestigious on its street." He hoped he was making sense. He was spinning with adrenaline.

Laney continued reading. "'Call Vandaveer Investments and

tell them Lyn-Lake wants to keep its only bookshop. Make your money matter. Support these and other local businesses targeted by developers.'"

Thom flipped the card over for her. "On the back is a list of every neighborhood business the Vandaveers have tried to buy out recently—and these are just the ones we know about." The Quickie Oil Change. Spin Vinyl. And Fringe, a high-end vintage clothing boutique that turned young women into chic, modern renditions of his own Eisenhower-era mother.

"This is exciting," Laney said. She gave Thom a quick squeeze. "Something's happening! I'll stop by Nygaard's as soon as I can to do a little speculating with your friends about a poor, vulnerable bookshop owner being taken advantage of."

It was all just thrilling. "Word is getting out." He paused as another idea shot the circumference of his brain. "Come to think of it, I should ask Bree if she's seeing any discussion about this on the neighborhood business association Facebook page."

"Ma'am!"

Laney excused herself and returned her attention to the evolving couch fiasco. Thom needed to keep making phone calls anyway. He grinned as he walked down Lake Street toward home. "Can't expect this pot to stir itself now, can we?"

Laney was lying on the orange couch jammed in the entrance when her mother returned. "I hope you stopped at Vandaveer Investments on your way home to cancel the sale because you can't move out. The couch is too big for the doorway. You're stuck here. Sorry."

Her mother scowled. "I told you the movers had to take it out through the receiving door in the back. Were you ignoring me or just not listening?"

She yawned. "Little of both, probably." She'd forgotten how comfortable this couch was. Maybe she could lie here in protest until her mother changed her mind.

No such luck. Irma pulled out her phone and called the movers, insisting she didn't care if they were on their way to another job, they'd left a couch jammed in the front door of her store. "Would you prefer I call the police and have the truck pulled over?"

That must've done the trick. "They'll be back in twenty minutes."

"Perfect." Laney stretched. "I love a good power nap."

"Funny girl." Her mother stepped onto the cushion beside Laney's head and crawled into the store.

Not long after, the yellow door, having been freed of its orange interloper, burst open with a gust akin to a tornado. "It's a travesty! And we're not going to let it happen!"

Laney had been weeding out mis-shelved books and startled so at the disruption that she dropped a hardcover edition of *The Lord of the Rings* trilogy on her foot. "Mrs. Baumgartner!"

Violet must have been on grandmother duty because she patted the back of her grandson and said, "Adam, run along and see if you can count the number of books whose titles begin with the letter G."

He did as he was told.

"Is it true?"

Laney pulled a smile across her face. "You've heard about the sale, I take it."

"Public notice was posted on the internet this morning." Violet shook her head hard enough that her product-controlled hairdo shimmied. "It's a travesty! And selling to condominium developers, no less! What is Irma thinking?"

Laney licked her lips and tasted opportunity. "Oh, Mother, dear! You have a visitor." Then she excused herself to the stockroom. "Mom? You back here?"

"Sssshh!"

There was either a snake in the corner or her mother was hiding.

"Mrs. Baumgartner has a matter of some urgency to discuss with you." She found Irma behind the last row of metal shelving, lodged between a broken chair and a pile of moving blankets.

"Everything with Violet is urgent. I'm not going out there."

"She knows you're here."

Her mother gestured at her hiding spot. "Do I look like I care? Tell her I left. I had to run to the bank."

"Do you have to run to the bank?"

"Of course not."

"Then, I'm not telling her that."

"You can tell her I had to run to the potty, for all I care. I'm not going to speak to her."

Laney crossed her arms and grinned. Just when the day looked too boring to endure. "Can I tell her you have Ebola?"

"If you wish. You'll sound ridiculous."

"Uncontrollable diarrhea, then. I can tell her you look like Melissa McCarthy crawling onto the restroom sink in *Bridesmaids*."

"Be my guest."

Laney didn't think she'd ever seen this side of her mother. "Are you actually afraid of little ol' Mrs. B?"

Her mom let her head fall back against the wall. "I wasn't ready to announce our closure to customers yet. It's too emotional."

A familiar flame shot up Laney's spine, hot and quick, angry and hungry. "There are so many things wrong with that statement, I don't even know where to begin."

Mercifully, she didn't have to. Violet knocked on the stockroom door. "Yoo-hoo, Irma?"

It gave Laney the escape she needed.

"I guess Mom ran out for a moment," she lied, leading her back into the heart of the store, out of earshot. Laney knew a coconspirator when she met one, and Violet Baumgartner was practically begging for the job.

"I've known Irma Bedford for more than forty years," Violet said, "and I know that she would never willingly let go of this store. She is clearly not acting of her own accord." She moved farther into Laney's personal space and lowered her voice. "My husband maintains a number of important judicial and legal connections. If your mother is being manipulated in some way, you just say the word."

WORD! Laney wanted to scream.

But Violet wasn't finished. "I am also a member and founding president of the Lyn-Lake Historical Preservation Committee. Razing this building—which you must know was first built in 1926 and is nearing its centennial—is exactly the sort of tragedy we work to prevent."

Whichever god or fairy was looking down on Laney today must have been in a generous mood, and she wished she knew what she'd done to please them so she could make a regular habit of it. "Between you and me, Violet, the timing seems awfully suspicious. A couple of rich developers swooping in with an offer mere weeks after Elliot died?"

"How many weeks?"

"About a month, from what I've heard."

"No one is capable of major financial decisions at that stage of their grief. I have gone through extensive training in lay ministry. I know this for a fact!"

Laney mmm-hmm'd and tsk'd accordingly. "Sadly, what can be done?"

She was about to plant a seed about the Vandaveers acting as both broker and buyer when Adam returned and reported to his grandmother, "I can't see past here." He stretched his little-boy arm above his head. "I don't know if any books taller than me start with G."

Violet gushed with the effusiveness acceptable only for grandmothers and promised to help him count the rest. Before departing for their task, she added one last thought. "We are not finished with this discussion. A neighborhood without a bookstore is as dull as a life without books."

Laney was shocked to find that she could not have said it better herself.

Bree was unaware there had been a couch strike, because she was at the distillery following Daisy's text. They retreated to Lou's office and closed the door as soon as she arrived.

"What's up?" Her palms sweating, she felt like she'd been called to the principal's office.

Daisy and Lou exchanged glances. Daisy nodded, agreeing to something unspoken between them. "We've got news, Double Cream," she said. "And you may not like it."

Maybe it was on account of her surroundings, but Bree's thoughts immediately leapt to Witt. He was married. He'd quit. He was getting investigated for embezzlement.

In fact, she couldn't have been more astonished when Daisy said, "Did you know your mom talked Al at the hardware store into also signing an agreement with the Vandaveers?"

That was impossible, and she said so.

Lou shook her head. "We chatted with him this morning. Got it straight from the hardware man's mouth."

"I needed parts to fix the dripping sink in the women's restroom," Daisy said. "You know Al. He's a genuine guy and we got to talking. He mentioned he'd be calling it quits soon, so of course we asked why. He hemmed and hawed for a minute, but eventually, he said your mom had been working on him to sell for months. She knew they'd both gotten offers from the Vandaveers and she was full speed ahead on getting out."

This didn't make any sense. "Alstrop's Hardware has been there since the 1950s. It's so iconic-looking it's been in three movies. His grandfather started it." Even as Bree spoke, she knew nothing she said contradicted what Daisy and Lou were trying to tell her. It wasn't that Al was selling out; it was that her mother had somehow pressured him into it. "Tell me exactly what he said."

Lou did. "I told him I was surprised by the news because it's always looked like they do a pretty good business. He said the same thing every other small-business owner says—that online retailers have left a deep gash in their profits, that the real estate is worth more than the business. Said he'd considered a number of offers over the years. But Irma was the one to ultimately change his mind."

Interesting. Irma could change other people's minds, just not her own.

Daisy gave her a gentle punch on the leg. "Given what you told me about you and your sister being so upset about the sale, we thought you'd want to know."

"I was just in there the other day, and Al didn't say a word." Bree's head felt so light suddenly, she dropped to her knees for fear of keeling over. "What do I do now?" The words rose muffled from between the folds of her pants. Daisy and Lou were probably exchanging "uh-oh" glances and she was relieved not to be able to see them.

After a pause, Daisy said, "My father was a Navy man, so I tend to follow his advice at times like this."

"Which was?"

"Maintain course and speed until instructed otherwise."

Bree sat up. "That would be great if the person leading this mission weren't heading directly for an iceberg."

Lou interjected. "Actually, I think it would be useful for you to speak to Al yourself. He might be willing to go into more specifics with you."

It was tempting. She had hundreds of questions. "Did he seem open to that? I don't want to show up and put him on the spot. It's a little awkward, Irma being my mother and all."

Lou offered to ask him for her. Daisy added, "We need to go back anyway. I bought the wrong size washers for that sink."

13

11 days until close...

Thom was positively burning up the phone lines. Brian had learned from Michael who'd learned from a friend that Vandaveer Investments had taken notice of their flyers.

"Of course we didn't put our names on the materials!" Brian said. "We want to honor Elliot, not get sued."

"But how did we gain this much support so quickly?" Thom knew average chatter speed, and this was much, much faster. "I only just learned of the sale last week."

"Because of the Treehouse," Brian said.

The Treehouse Nightclub. Thom had forgotten. Or rather, he hadn't at the time possessed the capacity for outrage. Knowing that the most iconic gay bar in Minneapolis was forced to close after more than fifty years in business was sad, but having to constantly relive the memory of watching your partner die on a patch of dirty airport carpet was devastating. His grief center had been fully occupied since January.

He asked Brian to remind him of the details.

"Long and short of it, the Vandaveers took advantage of a vulnerable buyer and earned a whole lot of enemies in the process. The original Treehouse owner, Gary Bushnell, retired and sold the bar to a couple of guys somewhere around the early 2000s. One of them had a smack habit, though, and they had to get the other guy's brother to come in as a third investor to keep from losing the whole thing. Then, once things got back on track, he decided he was done with the bar business and sold his share to the Vandaveers, who must have performed some sort of voodoo ceremony, because by the time we all heard that the Treehouse was in serious trouble, there was nothing anyone could do to help."

He let out a long, defeated sigh.

"Have you seen the design for the condos they're planning there? Walking past the hole in the ground feels like a lobotomy—all that history ground to dust. And the designs. No style. Their architect stacked milk crates on top of each other and called them *condos*. A one-bedroom starts at just under a million."

Thom's entire body deflated. A single condo worth more than double what they'd offered Irma for the Rainbow. How was any of this fair?

"I'm glad you called, though," Brian said. "Because I just heard there's a rally at Alstrop's Hardware to protest the destruction of another neighborhood icon. Michael and I are heading over around five. Can we pick you up on the way?"

"Alstrop's is selling, too?" He instinctively glanced at the ceiling to make sure it wasn't about to fall in on him. "I'll see you there."

That afternoon, Thom was ready to rally, handmade sign and all. "If you love your neighborhood, fight for it!"

It wasn't the pithiest poster he'd ever created. Elliot was the wordsmith. But these Vandaveers acted as if Lyn-Lake was theirs for the taking, and they needed to be stopped. He had a voice. It was time he used it.

Before he left, he walked into the bedroom and laid a fingertip kiss on Elliot's pillow. "Here's to not giving up the fight."

Brian and Michael were late. Michael accused Brian of being a perfectionist with his sign, and Brian claimed Michael spent an hour putting on sunblock. Regardless, the rally had already begun by the time they arrived. A dozen or so people had formed a marching circle in the parking lot kitty-corner from the hardware store. Sadly, neither the rally-goers nor their signs stood out as particularly noteworthy.

Vandaveers, stay out of our businesses

Keep Lyn-Lake the Lyn-Lake we love

You can't order a friendly smile on Amazon

"No *bueno,*" said Michael. He swung left into the lot and parked at the far end. "This needs a lot less *Norma Rae* and a lot more fantastic."

"Did anyone think to call the TV stations?" Brian pulled his phone from his pocket and swept it open, ready to dial.

"Don't!" Michael stopped him. "Not until we rid ourselves of the sad sacks." They watched in silence as the circle marched with barely a peep.

In a sudden spark of inspiration, Thom snapped his fingers. "Is Tim's nephew still a referee for the kickball league? Call him and tell him we need everyone we can get. Tell them to come wearing their uniforms and bring every whistle, every noisemaker, and every loudmouth they can rustle up. We don't need signs. We need energy!"

By seven, the lot had transformed from an empty square of potholed pavement into a hooting, tooting street party. A sign strung across the fence read Knixo Disco, bookended by gigantic, thumping speakers and a DJ spinning the retro seventies and eighties sounds that happened to be having a cultural moment thanks to Gen Z having "discovered" the likes of Earth, Wind & Fire, Lou Rawls, and The O'Jays. Hair was natural, the mustaches bushy, and the dancing couples were of every combination. Parents swung toddlers by the arms. Twentysomethings celebrated until the sweat ran. Even Thom, Michael, Brian, Tim, and all their friends reverted to their younger selves, as if the years between had never happened, the losses had never come, and the wrinkles had never appeared.

"I can't believe this," Thom hollered. "It's magnificent."

His friends bobbed heads while keeping on dancing.

"I just worry most of these people don't know what this is about." Thom didn't want the night to end, though neither did he wish for the event to have been just an excuse for a party. "Shouldn't we make some announcements or something?"

Brian grabbed his hand and spun him until his vertigo acted up.

Bree stood next to Laney at the shop window watching the protest shindig.

"I want to go out and join them," Laney said. "I'm a sucker for a street party."

Because that's what the rally had become—a full-blown see-and-be-seen social coup. The few people who'd originally brought signs dropped them when the dancing started, which was probably good since nobody wanted the headline in tomorrow's *Minneapolis/St. Paul Standard* to read "Man concussed while doing the Hustle at neighborhood protest."

Worries aside, it did look like a lot of fun. She pictured heading across the street to the distillery and grabbing Witt by the hand, dragging him out the door and down the street to dance until they could hardly stand. She could never do that, though. She wasn't confident like Laney. He was probably working, anyhow.

Laney's face began to glow red, green, and yellow as a dance strobe lit up and began to spin. "Elliot would've loved this, don't you think?"

Bree's eyes glazed with unexpected tears. "Absolutely."

"I can only imagine how much you miss him. I miss him and I've been the family flunky for twenty years."

"You're not a flunky, you're a subversive." Bree winked, causing the first tear to drop. "And I do miss Elliot. So much."

For not being her father, he'd nevertheless crept into the corners in her life the way a glass of cold milk fills the nooks and crannies of a cookie. He never announced "You need a male figure in your life, so I'm volunteering." He just listened when she needed an ear, joked when she needed a laugh, offered a hand when she needed a boost.

"He helped me navigate the whole messy process of getting a mortgage. Did I ever tell you that?"

Laney shook her head.

"He even offered to loan me money for the down payment, but I wouldn't let him. I'd been saving, so I had what I needed." She'd wanted to feel the accomplishment of doing it on her own. Sometimes money was a lot more than money.

"Do you know why I didn't come home for his funeral?" Laney took a long breath and blew it out slowly, the echo of tamped emotion. "I was afraid I wouldn't be able to handle seeing Mom so upset. It was a total cop-out, I know." She shrugged. "But hey, I seem to excel at those."

In many ways, Laney and Irma were too much of a good thing, too interconnected as mother and daughter, in that they saw the other's vulnerabilities so clearly that when they hurt each other, they did so with clean and swift precision.

"You need an Elliot," Bree said. She'd thought about that sometimes, listening to him and Irma carry on in their private world built for two, a place without fear of betrayal or rejection. What would her own life be like with an Elliot? People attribute that kind of intimacy to a marriage or romantic partnership, but over the years, Bree had heard them say things to each other she was certain would have ended other relationships. Marriages could head for divorce. Partnerships could be dissolved. The friendship between Elliot and Irma looked as if it could never be killed. "Who's your best friend?"

Laney looked flummoxed by the question. "What do you mean, who's my best friend? You are, dummy."

"Yes, but family comes with baggage. I mean, who else do you turn to?"

"I guess I'm just one of those losers whose best friend is her sister. Because, let's be honest, you're the only one who can't leave me." She heard it as soon as she said it. "Bad logic. Sorry."

Bree shook her head. "I think everyone deserves an Elliot. He never let me down. Not once. And I'm afraid I'll never find my own."

"I thought that's what Tuck and I had. But I've started to think maybe not."

Bree waited, hoping she'd say more. It didn't come. Maybe a best friend ought to push, but she didn't dare. Instead, she said, "Irma and Elliot might be unicorns. What they had together probably isn't even possible for normal people."

"Well, I make a point of not being normal. And you mangle Taylor Swift, which normal people don't do."

"I mangle Lizzo."

"You mangle both. You're a broad-spectrum mangler."

The song, "Dancing Queen," began to fill the night air and Bree laughed, hearing it. "Elliot despised this song. He much preferred 'Waterloo' when it came to ABBA."

"'Ooh-Ooh, Waterloo,'" Laney sang. "Knowing his fate was to be with Irma."

"'Waterloo,'" Bree sang back. "Couldn't have changed if he wanted to."

They threw their hands in the air and sang the chorus again, laughing because they knew they looked ridiculous, and also because they didn't care.

The Book Haters' Book Club Newsletter

Issue #368
January 2020

We dedicate this month's newsletter to all those Haters who claim a book has never made them laugh…

Perhaps it's the dreary weather, but we've been seeing a lot of dour faces walk through our yellow door recently. One woman told me, "I just need to laugh!" Her husband said, "Give her something, please. We've been stuck inside so long she's even bored with me." I sent both husband and wife home with enough humor therapy to fend off even the gravest threat of weather-related divorce.

For her: Mrs. Reader was a smart, go-getter of a gal who told me she doesn't read because she can hardly bear to sit down, so I chose *The Garden of Small Beginnings* by Abbi Waxman. Why? Because gallows humor is just what this weather calls for! In the novel, a recently widowed mother with fleeting suicidal thoughts begins to get a handle on her life with the help of a quirky group of gardeners. Also, Waxman writes with such quick wit, the pages turn themselves (even for a reader who refuses to sit).

For him: I wrapped Mr. Reader's fingers around a copy of *Hollow Kingdom* by Kira Jane Buxton. He warned me he was a man who appreciated a kooky turn of events, and what's more kooky than the end of the human race, a talking crow who loves Cheetos, and an opening scene in which a fellow's eyeball falls out of his face? It's *Zombieland*, book-style. Only this time, the hero is a lowly crow.

Don't worry, dear readers. The sun will shine soon enough! In the meantime, come in and let us help you find a few laughs.

—Elliot

Last Hope for the Haters

Every one of us holds the entire universe inside ourselves. Books are the means through which we can explore it.

14

10 days until close...

Judging by the number of calls Thom was receiving, the rally-turned-disco had attracted better-than-expected attention. He'd heard reports of hardware store employees delivering bottled water to the crowd and of the appearance of at least one, if not both, Vandaveers at the scene. And there was a hashtag, #KnixoDisco, which Thom didn't understand but he'd been told by several people was very good and in widespread use.

The question remained: How could they make their momentum matter?

He dialed Laney and found her in the bookshop with Irma, who, she assured him, was too busy on the phone saying farewell to other booksellers to either eavesdrop or care. Now that the hardware store closing was getting press, Irma was also having to answer questions about her own decision to sell.

"My concern is that we can keep rallying but to what end?" Thom began. "Our energies are only well spent if your mother takes notice of them."

"She called the rally 'ridiculous,' if that helps," said Laney, who sounded as if she enjoyed her own flippant attitude a mite too much.

"It does not."

"Look." She rightfully adjusted her tone. "Unless we discover some sort of smoking gun that forces her to reconsider the sale, this is a game of increasing pressure. You're working on building public momentum. Bree's working on getting assistance from neighboring businesses. I'm working on Irma. Nothing's changed. We just have to keep at it until we either succeed or the clock runs out."

Patience had never been one of Thom's greatest skills. Lists were made to be completed, not studied. Problems were better solved than stewed upon.

Not that his preference for a tidy life had made any difference with Elliot. Thom retired four years ago. He'd been planning it for twenty-five. Elliot only promised to consider retiring after Thom threatened to leave him. That's how the trip to Machu Picchu came about. Elliot promised to cut back on his hours at the shop, and when he predictably did not, Thom purchased two insultingly expensive tickets on a luxury, two-week tour of Peru. He packed Elliot's bags and set them by the front door.

"You can either come with me or clear out while I'm gone," he announced that night over dinner-gone-cold. "I'm tired of waiting for you to choose me."

"I choose you every day. You are the only one I want to come home to. You are my solace." Elliot tried to grab his hand.

Thom stood and walked out of reach. "What a lovely thing for you to say, repeatedly, as if by rote. It's a wonder you've not yet remembered to behave as if it's true."

It was their preferred argument. Thom accusing Elliot of treating him like a housekeeper and cook. Elliot professing he couldn't survive even a day if it weren't for the love Thom showed him. Demands for change. Promises that "after" the current concern of the day was over, things would improve.

Not this time. "You have ten days," Thom told him. "Clear your calendar and inform Irma of your vacation. But know that I'll be on that plane with or without you." He would have gone, too. The tickets were too expensive to waste, which was why he'd purchased a first-class trip. Elliot had proven himself willing to ignore his partner, but he never threw money at the wind.

The bitter irony of it.

He was washing his lunch dishes when the idea came to him. Again, Thom picked up the phone and within minutes was connected through a friend of a friend of a friend to the owner of the vacant lot where they'd held the rally.

"An outdoor disco?" Maxwell Klingerhorn spoke with the clenched-jaw tenor of a man who slept with a cigar between his teeth. He was also a man with a good eye for opportunity. "How long do you want the lot?"

"Nightly until July first, though hopefully less," Thom answered.

"But you don't have money to rent it?"

"Are you currently making use of it?" The answer was obviously no. The space contained the remnants of a drive-through bank without the bank.

Their tit for tat went a few more rounds until Max said, "Tell you what. I've been trying to get the attention of those Vandaveers for a couple of years now. You don't want their condos going up, but I do, and I want 'em in my lot. If you can figure out a way to get your crowd to promote the idea of moving the development across the street, you can use my land for your kicks-o disco."

"Knixo Disco," Thom corrected.

"If there's any trouble, you and I never spoke. Got it?"

"I excel at forgetting names when necessary."

Bree was anxious, which made her overeager and early for the meeting with Al, Daisy, and Lou. Witt was behind an empty bar when she arrived at the distillery, which may also have been what she was secretly hoping she'd find.

"Hey," he said as she pulled herself onto a stool. "Rhuby Gin or something stronger?"

She said she'd better keep it nonalcoholic. "I have an important conversation in a little bit. Gotta keep a clear head."

He nodded and began to mix. "Sorry to hear about you losing the store to condos. Always had a hunch those Vandaveers were no good."

"Yeah?"

He shrugged. "Got a good nose for bullshit."

Daisy appeared and slapped the bar by way of hello. "Well, if it ain't my favorite troublemaker. You hanging in there, el Bree-ablo?"

"Been better," she admitted. "I'm a little worried about what I'll hear from Al today."

"May be rough, may be nothing." Daisy raised her coffee mug in honor of the sentiment. "Either way, you'll figure your way through."

This sounded like a very Daisy philosophy. Bree appreciated the optimism she and Lou always extended, but she'd begun to wonder if she'd rather not have known about Irma's involvement in Al's decision. What difference could it make now, besides sharpening her already sour feelings?

Witt placed a cold, fizzing glass on a napkin in front of her. "Somebody want to fill me in?"

Daisy turned her eyes on Bree. "Up to you."

She didn't know if she wanted to explain. It felt disloyal to expose Irma's possibly underhanded influence. What she knew at this point was no better than gossip, and if she told Witt, she'd be responsible for helping spread it.

"Like I said—" Witt tapped his finger to his nose "—got a pretty reliable BS meter."

Daisy turned with a wry look that suddenly relieved Bree of the feeling she was going to have to answer Witt's request. "How 'bout you two revisit the topic after we know more?"

She then redirected Bree's glance to the front entrance where Al stood, scanning the room. "Here's the guest of honor now."

They met in Lou's office. It was tight, but Bree thought she'd have a better conversation with Daisy and Lou asking follow-up questions, and if they all trekked over to the hardware store together, it might catch Irma's attention—rational intentions that now, in execution, made the meeting feel unnatural, a secret back channel between warring families. She could feel her heartbeat in her throat.

"Thanks for meeting me here," she began finally.

Al had eyes that darkened and lightened with his mood, and right now he looked at her as if he'd accidentally run over her cat. "I wasn't entirely forthcoming when you asked me about the Vandaveers. It's true they made me a lot of lowball offers, but I'm sorry I didn't tell you about finally deciding to take them up on one."

It hadn't crossed her mind until just now that her mother hadn't been the only one lying to her. "Why didn't you?"

"Oh—" Al shuffled his loafers across the floor "—just a hunch, I guess. You were in the hardware store asking about possible sales when your mom and I had already signed agreements, so I thought maybe you didn't know, and if that was the case, I sure as heck didn't want to be the one to tell you."

"When did you sign your contract?" Daisy asked.

"Shortly after Irma. Although I've got more time to close my store than she does. I'm not going anywhere until Labor Day."

Bree, Daisy, and Lou exchanged glances.

Bree said, "I'm hoping you can shed some light on your decision to sell. I've only known about the Rainbow closing for about a week, when Mom called us all together over at the Vandaveer offices to deliver the news—me, Elliot's partner, Thom. Even Laney flew in from California. The big mystery is why? Why is she selling? And why so fast? She'd made this big thing about keeping the shop in the family, and now it's like she doesn't care she just stabbed me in the stomach."

None of this appeared to make Al feel any more comfortable. "Well, I don't know if it's my place to say—it must be difficult for her to carry on after losing Elliot."

"It's been tough, yes. Which is the main source of my concern—that she's making a rash decision. That she's being taken advantage of. This isn't like her. Not at all."

Al said, "When we lost my dad, my sister and I felt like the world crash-landed on our shoulders, and there was too much to be done to make time for feeling sad. She was trying to help my mom sort through everything at home, and I was trying to take over at the store. I'd worked there my whole life, but still, it's different when you're on your own and in charge. You don't have anyone to ask for advice or even where the extra paper towels went."

Bree thought of Tuck calling Laney eight times a day with the same sorts of questions. Yesterday, he'd called to complain that the new receptionist Laney had hired from two thousand miles away, Sylvia, made him mop the restroom after a customer got sick in it. Apparently, Tuck wasn't used to cleaning up other people's messes.

"Daisy and Lou told me about the conversation you had," she said, "that Irma put a lot of pressure on you to sell to the Vandaveers."

"I don't know if I'd call it pressure, but she was a woman on a mission, sure enough. At first it was just a few questions. Had I received an offer? Was I considering it? As the weeks went on, she stopped in more often until it was a couple of times a week. *I intend to sell, Al, but they want the whole block*, she'd say. Or, *We're better off if we negotiate together. If they want all our land, we've got leverage.*"

Bree told herself that if Al had already been planning to sell, she'd quit with the questions. It would mean he and Irma were both ready to move on and there was probably nothing she and Laney and Thom could do to alter the course of things. "And were you considering it?"

"Nope," he said. "I mean, it'd crossed my mind. It's a tough time to be a small business when everything you've got on your shelves can be shipped free overnight. But I hadn't planned for my next move yet. My kids don't want to take over the store and my sister's kids haven't shown any interest. If I didn't leave it to one of them, would anyone want to keep it going?"

His answer didn't do much to quell her concerns. "Doesn't it bother you that the Vandaveers are going to knock Alstrop's down for condos? The store has been in your family for three generations."

"It bothers me, sure. But I have to say, it bothered me a whole lot less when the Vandaveers sweetened their offer the way they did. I can retire now and pay out my sister for her share. I didn't realize how much stress I was holding about being able to do that until I saw that I could."

The Alstrops had a tradition of making people happy. When Bree and Laney were kids, they loved to take the dollar bills they earned for dusting shelves to buy treats next door. Al's dad had a sweet tooth and kept one whole end of the front counter stacked with Jolly Ranchers and bubble gum, gourmet caramels, and every color of saltwater taffy. He let them buy five taffies for a quarter, which should have equaled twenty for a dollar, though when they opened their paper sacks, there were always at least two dozen.

Hearing Al's relief at being able to treat his sister with the same generosity made Bree sit back in her chair. Of course he'd made the decision that he did.

"Thank you," she said, taking a breath. "I guess we were just concerned that Irma had roped you into a bad deal."

Al went quiet.

Lou heard it, too. "Something else on your mind?"

"Well," he said after a pause. "Again, it's not my place to tell a dead man's tales, so I'm not going to get into specifics, but let's just say that Elliot—may God rest his soul and I hope you know how much I liked and respected him, because gosh, I sure did—he came to me a few times for money. Once, he said it was a personal loan to fix his car, another time something unexpected like that. One time, I remember he said it was for your mom, that she was having a hard time covering her boyfriend's medical bills during the cancer. Nothing he didn't pay back, and I was always happy to loan him what I could, but it was odd."

Bree hadn't recovered from the shock of Elliot borrowing money to help Irma pay for Nestor's cancer treatments when Lou asked, "You thought it was odd how?"

Al chewed on his answer for a moment. "I'd just never thought of us as the loaning-money sort of friends."

15

6 days until close...

Thom was at the Knixo for the third night in a row.

"We've come to disco en plein air," said Brian, arriving with Michael and Tim and a carful of others in tow. He dropped a fistful of bills into the Cross the Street Project donation jar and wrapped Thom in a hug. "Good crowd. Better than yesterday, even."

It was Super Funk Night, and right now, Chaka Khan wanted someone to tell her something good and tell her that they liked it.

"Jar's filling up, too," Brian added. "What are you going to do with the money?"

Thom had agreed to Maxwell Klingerhorn's request and commissioned two large vinyl banners to hang on the lot's fences that read, "Cross the Street, Vandaveer Investments!" and "We're going to disco until you knixo the Knickerbocker!" It wasn't until after he'd had them hung that he realized the mixed messages; did they want the Knickerbocker canceled or simply moved? He supposed he didn't care.

"If tonight's donations are good," he told Brian and crew, "we might have enough money to start running some decent digital ads." Listen to him, speaking like a millennial. He nodded in the direction of one of the dancers. "That one over there in the purple roller skates works in an ad agency and offered to handle it pro bono."

Brian turned toward where he was pointing and wiggled a suggestive eyebrow.

"Don't be crude." Thom would be sixty-nine next year, but he was still easily embarrassed. "My point is, they said they could design the ads in a way that is sure to catch the Vandaveers' attention."

Knixo Disco was a hit. Perhaps it was just a temporary fascination, but the lot had been crowded every one of the five nights since it began. The seventies were all the rage among the soon-to-be and recently graduated, a crowd with plenty of energy but less cash, who threw their loyalties behind any venue with a zero dollar cover charge. Daisy and Lou had pitched in, too, sending over packets of ten-dollar Lady of the Lake drink tickets, five dollars of which went to the Cross the Street Project fund.

And the magic didn't stop there. The duo who brought and ran the sound system for the first rally agreed to return for the duration, in exchange for free fence advertising and the ability to promote their DJ services. "We already have gigs this weekend," the taller of the two had said, "but we'll try to help you find someone to cover for us." Typically, Thom would have found such a noncommittal commitment stress inducing, but he'd become Knixo Disco Thom. He rolled with uncertainty and trusted the fates. He made to-do lists during work hours and left them behind as soon as the music started.

Kool & the Gang began to "Get Down On It," and Thom let his hips sway, ignoring the dull pain on his left side, which no longer liked to move that way. He closed his eyes and imagined Elliot when they'd first met, both already in their forties and battle scarred, but desperate to leave the heartbreak of years past behind.

Elliot, for all his charms, wasn't a dancer. He said he wouldn't dare insult the memory of Judy Garland or the living legacy

Elaine Stritch with his "discoordinations," and Thom had to admit that if he were to describe Elliot's style, he'd have called it "adolescent gorilla." Even so, his was a hand to hold, even as other couples swirled around them, and he let his mind fall into the memory of how their fingers fit together, puzzle pieces that had finally found their mates.

"Thom?"

He heard Elliot's morning voice, the one that hadn't been awake long enough to work out its rasp. He saw the stubble on his chin. The puffed pockets beneath his eyes.

"Thom?"

He was a beautiful thing in ways distinctly his own. There never was a face like Elliot's, and there never would be again.

"Hey! You have company."

He opened his eyes to find Brian pointing across the lot toward the fence line. On the other side stood Trevor Vandaveer talking to Hardware Al.

"Oh my goodness. Is this a good sign or a bad sign?"

Brian hmm'd. "I'll put five dollars on good."

"Out of how much?"

"Fifty."

Oh dear.

They stood and watched as the men talked for several minutes. Every once in a while, one would gesture to the crowd, but mainly they faced each other, engaged in lively discussion.

"Do you think he saw the opinion piece in today's paper?" Brian asked. The *Minneapolis/St. Paul Standard* had published a letter to the editor written by a woman named Violet Baumgartner in which she blamed the explosion of condo development on new retirees trading their suburban family homes for what she called "egg carton condominiums" in the city. "They may be available by the dozen," she wrote, "but you wouldn't like them splattered across your lovely neighborhood any more than you enjoyed cleaning them off the side of your house each November 1."

Her letter rang with imperiousness, though she didn't provide any data to prove that retirees were, in fact, at fault for the spike in development. Nor did she give any indication as to why her house appeared to be an annual target for rogue trick-or-treaters.

"I doubt anyone would connect the author of that letter to the Knixo Disco," he said. "And I believe I've seen Trevor here on previous nights. Though I've never seen him with Al."

Al was shaking his head now, fists shoved deep into the pockets of his Carhartts.

"Trouble in paradise," Brian whispered. "Maybe you ought to turn up the music."

Laney stood at the shop window again, always the watcher, never the dancer. Tonight, she was with her mother, whose scowl had grown so deep it threatened to turn her face inside out.

"Ridiculous," Irma said.

"That kind of attitude will get you dragged outside by the scruff of your neck, young lady. You could benefit from some time on the dance floor."

"That's not a dance floor, it's an empty lot—a lot we use for overflow parking."

"The disco is hardly causing parking issues."

Her mother gave her don't-argue-with-me eyes. "I know it's Thom who's behind all this, and you can tell him I know. While you're at it, tell him it's not going to make a lick of difference. The sale closes in six days."

Laney was well aware; she was plenty good at counting. Also, Bree reminded her of the time remaining every 7.38 minutes.

"You ought to go out there, Mom. At least say thank-you to all the people who came out to support the store."

"They're not out there for the store. They're out there for the free party."

"That's a pretty crass attitude from someone who's made her living thanks to the goodness of strangers."

Her mother turned, hands on hips. "I didn't realize I'd been running a charity for forty years. Funny, it hasn't felt like that."

Laney knew better. Tire Stud wasn't a charity, either. She retreated. "Fine. But you have to admit all this attention has been good for your sales. We've gone through a ton of stock."

News crews had begun to come out every night to capture the discoing crowd, and to the last, each person interviewed favored the idea of moving the condos in order to save Alstrop's Hardware and the Rainbow. Also thanks to the news coverage, store traffic had increased. People who'd never heard of Over the Rainbow came to see what all the fuss was about, and past customers arrived with their credit cards and cash, ready to express their outrage and support.

Laney examined her hands. "I think I got carpal tunnel today from standing at the register so long." She plopped down on the window ledge, drained. Increasingly, she'd lost track of what she was fighting for. Bree was fighting for the Rainbow; Thom was fighting for Elliot's money. But her? She'd spent most of her days acting out some kind of delayed adolescence, answering a deeply coded reflex that demanded she argue with her mother because she was a daughter and that's how their DNA had designed their relationship. She'd told herself she was in Minneapolis out of loyalty to her sister, but not for the first time in her life, she was also beginning to recognize the ocean of gray between loyalty and its lesser cousin, stubbornness. Laney had gone swimming and lost track of the shore.

"Is there anything that would convince you to change your mind, Mom? At least tell me that much."

"We all have the right to certain privacies, Laney."

"I know I lost the privilege of family confidences twenty years ago, but Bree devoted her life to this place. At least talk to her about why you're selling. She wants to carry on your legacy and your work. You're her idol. Her savior. And Elliot was the closest thing to a real father she ever had."

Then, like a flash, Laney's brain lit up. As if whatever she'd just said had been a match, a flame dropped to a dead and dry forest floor. *You're fighting for family.*

Laney sank from the window ledge to the floor, splaying her arms and legs wide in surrender. "Well, crap."

Her mother scowled at her dramatic daughter, then softened just as quickly. "You've gone white. Is your stomach acting up again? Do you need water?"

"No, it's not that." Back in high school, Laney had been diagnosed with IBS, an acronym she refused to explain because it included the word *bowel* and, as Tuck would put it, required her to talk about "butt stuff." Stress was her main IBS trigger, and given the growing family tension of the past week, she'd begun running to the restroom on the regular, calling, "Land shark!" the family code word for *bathroom emergency.*

"But you're right. I don't feel good. I've got my life flashing before my eyes and a hangover from feeling so pissed about how you're treating Bree. And that's not even the worst part, because the worst part is that I miss you. I miss my family. I miss Elliot. I miss my sister. But most of all, I miss you. And it sucks. I want to throw up it feels so bad."

Her mother was quiet for a beat before sinking to the floor beside her. Only, Irma wasn't angry, and she didn't reach out with a consoling hug. To the contrary, she began to laugh, filling the shop with great hoots and snorts.

"What are you— Oh my god! It's not funny, Mom!"

"Oh, Laney, face it. You just threatened to throw up because you miss us. Everything's funny with the right perspective."

"Not this! I'm pouring my heart out and you're acting like a Frenchman at a Jerry Lewis movie."

Irma took a steadying breath, forcibly stuffing her guffaws back down her throat. "Well, if I'm the pot, then you're the kettle, my dear. Just the other day, I told you I was too emotional to talk to Violet Baumgartner and you threatened to tell her I had Ebola."

"I'm being vulnerable here. Trying to have a moment with you."

"Of course. I apologize."

"Plus, if everything's funny from the right perspective, how come you're in such a sour mood about all those people out there trying to show their support?"

As usual, her mother didn't have an answer, except to mutter, "I laughed at several of the outfits." She did, however, reach over and take Laney's hand in her own. They sat without speaking until at last Irma said, "I've missed you, too, you know, every day since you left. Losing you wasn't the same as losing Nestor or Elliot, but it was its own devastating loss. I was so sure I'd failed you, and there didn't seem to be anything I could do to fix it."

"You didn't fail me, Mom." Which for the first time, Laney actually believed. "I left because I didn't want to stay here. And I stayed gone because I didn't know how to come back."

They'd fought like wildcats that spring. Laney wanted to spend her last summer before college on the racing circuit with Tuck, but Irma told her she needed to stay home and work, that there wasn't nearly enough money saved to let her flit it away roaming the backwaters of the nation, one minor racetrack to the next, eating into the money meant for college and her future.

Now her mom said, "I should have let you go, at least for part of the summer. I shouldn't have belittled Tuck's racing ambitions the way I did."

Irma had called him a "greaser," which made Laney holler, "Well then, I guess that makes me Sandra Dee!" As if her eighteen-year-old self even knew who that was, her cultural understanding of her mom's generation no deeper than what she'd learned from the movie *Grease*.

Laney groaned. "Being home has been frustrating, obviously,

but maybe it's good, too. I always told myself this big story about how I'd been brave enough to leave, that I took a chance on Tuck, and that we were on a great adventure together. But I think the truth is that I didn't know what I wanted, and Tuck gave me an escape."

She felt her mom melt further into the floor. "No mother raises a child hoping that someday they'll want to escape her."

Laney could've kicked herself. She didn't have kids, though she'd wanted them, tried and failed to conceive. But even with zero parental experience, she could sense how completely she'd just confirmed her mother's worst fears about failing her daughter.

"Whether you believe me or not, Mom, this really isn't about you. It's about me realizing that if you keep yourself busy enough worrying about someone else's needs, you don't have to think about your own."

16

4 days until close...

Bree was at the front desk when the mail carrier arrived.

"Sure are gonna miss you all," Gerry said. She'd stopped into the Rainbow nearly every day for the last decade, just one of the myriad faces on Bree's growing list of losses. "Your news seemed to come out of nowhere."

"You're not kidding." Bree was done being diplomatic about the store closing. It was killing her, and she wanted people to know. "I didn't have a say in the matter."

"No, I 'spose not." Gerry shifted uncomfortably, then remembered, with visible relief, that she had a job to do and dropped a pile of mail on the counter. "Anything to pick up?"

Bree shook her head.

"Alrighty, then. You have yourself a good day. Get out into the sunshine for a bit. It's hard to be in a bad mood when it's beautiful. Did you see Belinda Jensen's forecast on Channel 11? Low eighties all week. That'll keep your spirits up, sure enough."

Bree swept the stack of mail off the counter. "Did you know Belinda's an author? Children's books. In case you have any parents on your route with budding meteorologists." The recommendation was pure instinct, a bookseller's predisposition to put the right books into the hands of readers, even when she wouldn't have those books to offer in less than a week.

"I will keep that in mind." Gerry headed for the door. She never stayed long. Neither rain nor sleet and all that.

When she was gone, Bree flipped through the mail, and among the bills, she found more than a dozen postcards from concerned members of the Lyn-Lake Heritage Committee. They'd been arriving all week, and no one—not Bree nor Irma nor Daisy—had ever heard of such a group. But they had a logo. And they had the know-how to design, print, assemble, and mail postcards in bulk.

Please reconsider selling to developers
who are willing to sacrifice Lyn-Lake
history and heritage for their own profit.

Each card was hand-signed, though most senders made themselves unidentifiable by giving only their first name.

"Nineteen more postcards today, Irma," she called. It wouldn't make a difference, but it felt wrong not to highlight their arrival. She carried them into the back room and dropped them onto the desk where her mom sat emptying more files.

"Tell Thom to quit wasting his friends' money on stamps," she said, barely looking up.

"I don't think this is Thom's doing." Thom had no reason to withhold his machinations from her, given their extracurriculars, and he had denied having any part. "Maybe there really is a Lyn-Lake Heritage Committee."

"Not that I've ever heard of." Irma dumped the remainder of a fat folder into the recycling bin and grabbed the next one on the pile.

"So, I know you sign the papers on Friday, but when do we actually have to be cleared out by?" As far as Bree knew, Irma hadn't hired movers or a cleaning crew or any of the other resources necessary for dispatching 4,500 square feet of items like floor-to-ceiling wooden bookshelves and the ancient confessionals Elliot transformed into reading nooks.

"The Vandaveers take possession on Monday morning."

Bree flinched. That gave them only forty-eight hours to move out. They wouldn't sleep until it was finished. She did her best to calm the panic in her voice. "Want me to call around to some movers?"

Her mother flicked the offer away. "Liquidators come Saturday morning. They'll take care of everything that's left."

"Ah." She pasted a smile onto her face just long enough to add, "Good to know." Three words, and they took everything she had.

She fled and shut herself into the farthest confessional, pulling the door tight behind her. Liquidators. The thought hadn't even crossed her mind, but of course. Irma didn't need six chipped chapel pews in her living room. No one had the space for even a single confessional, let alone eight. And these antiques were probably worth some money. How much, she didn't know, but something, at least.

She ran a hand down the wall and felt the knotty oak grain beneath her fingers, the varnish nearly gone, worn away by decades of readers, and before them, generations of confessing teenage girls.

"Forgive me, whoever's out there," she whispered. "But I have had disrespectful thoughts about my mother. I don't think she's in her right mind. And to be honest, I kind of wish I'd never fallen in love with this family or this store, because if I'd known how much this would hurt—" She stopped. She was being too polite. "Okay, let's just be honest for once. I hate this. I hate that I'm supposed to just stand around and smile while my life goes down the toilet. I hate that Irma doesn't think I'm smart enough or deserving enough to know the truth. And you know what? I think I even hate the Rainbow. This stupid, everybody-be-happy-'cuz-books-are-miracles fantasy that, most days, is nothing but long, crappy hours trying to get people to take a chance on a book they're just going to drag home and drop on a TBR pile. Nobody reads even half the crap they buy. But what do I care? I'm just a lowly shopgirl working the register. I don't have a big enough brain for opinions!"

There was a knock on the confessional's door. "Bree?" It was Laney. She was whispering. "You need to come out here."

"Not yet." Bree didn't see the point in keeping her voice down—Irma didn't even listen to her when they were face-to-face.

"Seriously. Al's here and he's pretty worked up."

Hearing this, she pushed the door open without warning Laney, who took a knob to the hip.

"Ow."

"Sorry."

Laney cradled her side. "That really hurt," she whispered, then urged Bree silently toward the stockroom. They crept, *Mystery Incorporated*–style, until they reached a spot near the door, out of sight but within eavesdropping range.

"This is awful, Irma." Al was back there, alright. "If I'd known there'd be such a strong reaction, I never would have signed the deal."

Bree and Laney exchanged wide-eyed glances. From the sounds of it, he was second-guessing his contract.

"Al, I close on Friday."

"I'm aware, believe me. Nevertheless, my agreement has an exit clause, and I may have to consider it. I'm sorry."

Irma sputtered more of the same—that he couldn't, they had a deal, timing was imminent. But Al didn't budge, and before Bree and Laney were ready for it, he walked out of the stockroom and straight into their path.

"Girls." He nodded.

"Al." They nodded back.

Then he was gone. Out the yellow door and down the sidewalk toward his own store.

Laney turned to Bree. *What just happened?* she mouthed.

I have no idea.

"I know you're standing there listening!" Irma hollered. "You may as well come in here and get it over with."

They did as they were told and turned the corner.

Bree said, "I'm sorry. We couldn't help but overhear."

Laney said, "Who was that and what did he say?"

Irma looked at Laney but responded to Bree. "You may think this is good news, but believe me, if Al backs out, then what's coming will be infinitely worse." She shook her head and slumped into her chair. The desk was strewn with papers, the floor covered with recycling that'd missed the bin. And Irma's face was clouded with something Bree hadn't seen in a long time—fear.

Her mom closed her eyes and brought two fingers to the bridge of her nose. "Al's sister is having second thoughts about selling her share of the store. She'd never cared before, but apparently, the news coverage and the dozens of postcards she's received in the mail has her second-guessing the decision."

"Al didn't think of that before signing a contract?" Laney asked.

Without thinking, Bree blurted, "He was going to buy her out. He said the Vandaveers offered him enough money that he could retire and make sure his sister got a decent sum, too."

"How do you know that?" Bree's little disclosure suddenly had Irma wide-awake and paying attention. "Did you go running to Al?"

"No!" she said. Except, yes, she had. "At least, not the way you make it sound."

"How would you make it sound, then?"

Bree looked to Laney for help, but she only shrugged. Because, of course, Laney didn't know any more than Irma did;

Bree hadn't disclosed her behind-the-scenes discussions to either of them. "More like—" Her brain was panic spinning when it hit her. "Daisy and Lou came to me. Because Al told them you'd pressured him into selling." She flinched, remembering that he'd specifically said she hadn't pressured him. "Or that you were a 'woman on a mission' is what he said. And he thinks you were acting as a go-between to the Vandaveers, because as soon as he gave you a number he would consider selling for, the Vandaveers came back with an offer that matched. He hadn't been planning to retire, but he decided he had to because the money was so good."

Laney's eyes looked as if she were caught in a tractor beam.

"Sorry," Bree said. "I didn't get around to telling you any of that."

"Uh—yeah."

Irma, however, had questions. "Daisy and Lou came to you? Why is this any of their business?"

"Because they're trying to help!" Bree threw her arms in the air and realized too late that she was hollering. "Because they knew I was upset and because they try to be a good neighbor and because AL ACTUALLY ANSWERED THEIR QUESTIONS!"

"Whoa, there, Bree-sta." Laney put a hand on her arm, attempting to quell the storm. "Maybe take it down a notch."

"WHY?" She stomped onto the sales floor and hollered, "HEY, RAINBOW CUSTOMERS! YOU BETTER GET WHAT YOU WANT NOW, BECAUSE IRMA WOULD RATHER CLOSE THE STORE THAN LET HER OWN DAUGHTER STEP UP AND HELP!"

She'd thought the shop was empty. Instead, a mom with a baby who likely had been sleeping in its stroller mere seconds before, walked quickly toward the front door.

"Sorry!" Ugh. That would be on Google Reviews tomorrow. Good thing nothing mattered anymore.

Irma stood so abruptly she knocked her entire stack of file folders to the floor. "I can't take this another second." She grabbed her purse from beside the desk and hustled toward the door. "Close up whenever you want. I won't be back today."

"Mom!" Laney called. "Where are you going?"

She didn't answer. Which was exactly why Bree hadn't even wasted her breath to try to stop her.

17

3 days until close...

Laney stared at her phone. She needed to call Tuck to update him on her return plans, having lied yesterday about the airline's website being down, preventing her from rebooking.

"What's going on?" he'd asked her. To which she'd replied, "Terrible thunderstorm here," knowing that wasn't even remotely close to what he'd wanted to know.

This morning, she got a text:

I checked the website. Working fine.

It was now past 7:00 p.m. and she still hadn't been able to force herself to respond.

"Hey." He answered on the first ring.

"Hi."

Fat silence filled the line. They both knew a storm really was coming—a metaphorical one. They saw the clouds on the horizon and felt the dew point dropping. It was potent.

"What's so terrible about our life together that you'd rather lie about being stuck there? You used to hate going home. Now you won't leave?"

No one, especially Laney, would ever describe Tuck as particularly *astute.* He was not deep, his interest in the voices outside his own head about as thick as an orange peel, and yet he was right about this. Laney didn't want to go home, and not him, or their marriage, or their life together was proving enough to draw her back.

She tried to explain. "It's not so much about what's there, as what's not. My family's going through a tough time. I'd feel irresponsible if I left before everything gets sorted out."

Tuck asked what that meant, what it would take to sort it all, and how long. She didn't know. Not because she couldn't make a decent attempt to guess, but because *everything* was a big word, and because it felt powerful, and good and right to resist defining its boundaries.

Tuck hissed, "You're a mess." He meant it as an insult, to hurt her because he was hurting. Laney had always been the barrier between him and life's messes, the one who prevented them when possible and cleaned them up when they happened. She wasn't supposed to cause them.

"Actually." She straightened and felt the infusion of whatever physiological strength came with it. "I don't think I am. We're a mess. Our relationship is a mess. But I'm not." She looked out the window at the party across the street. "In fact, I might even go dancing tonight."

Tuck understandably mistook this to be an admission of her staying in Minneapolis to continue with some illicit love affair, which he'd already begun to suspect her of having, and only quit accusing her of when Laney threatened to put her mom on the phone as a character witness. "I'm running to the bathroom every ten minutes, and I go to bed every night at nine o'clock. What sort of wild sex do you think I'm having?"

"Whatever," he said finally. "Just come home, Laney."

Thom's back and hips hurt, and the Knixo Disco was having its first slow night. It was Tuesday. The lot had a crowd, though smaller than Friday and Saturday, when they'd had to turn people away. Still, he could really use a chair.

Maybe he'd convince someone to run across to Al's and buy him one of those canvas jobbers that folds up small enough to slip into a bag. He felt for cash in his pockets. Six dollars. Could he justify taking a few bucks from the donations? Getting caught with his hand in the cookie jar wasn't a good look. He'd have to suffer through.

Have to, or want to? Those were very different considerations, which his back spasms were swift to remind him. One *had to* wait their turn in the emergency room. Had to stand in line at the grocery store checkout. One did not *have to* insist his sixty-eight-year-old body endure another night standing upright without reprieve. Just a few years ago, he spent entire shifts on his feet. Somewhere since, he'd gone soft. Gotten old.

His body and his brain told him he didn't have to do this at all. He was choosing to sacrifice his temporary comfort for Elliot's sake. In his honor. And who was he kidding—he was standing up for the money. Even if the cash was mired in probate purgatory until Thom joined Elliot in the skies above, the money meant something. It meant Elliot was worth more than what Irma had assessed him for, that his life had meant something, that his value on earth had been considerable.

He looked at the scene he'd created in his partner's honor—dancers on a mission to convince a set of slick developers to renege on a too-good-to-be-true deal. Folly. He'd known it all along. Their chance of success was laughable, and yet he'd tried. There was pride in the having done something, or as his father would have said, in not being a "fence-sitter."

Thom's father would not live to see the day his son felt comfortable enough to tell him he was gay, nor would he have liked hearing it. But on this, on the issue of legacy, he would have liked knowing his son was taking a stand. He looked to the fence where the "Cross the Street, Vandaveer Investments!" and "We're going to disco until you knix the Knickerbocker!" banners still hung. When it came to defending Elliot, Thom was a fence-hanger, not a fence-sitter.

But, lordy, he really did need to sit down soon. He looked at his ankles. They were the size of mangoes.

"Howdy-do, Thomas."

The name made him flinch. No one had called him Thomas since his mother passed away in 1984, because no one had been allowed to. He was Thom. And yet, Daisy, who'd said it, was Daisy, and she didn't seem to hold much to convention.

He did his best to straighten and smile. "Good evening."

"Still going strong, I see. Just stopping by to see if you might need adult refreshment." She winked. "My treat."

He cocked his head, studying her. Such a mix of contradictions, this one. Brash and bullheaded and yet driven by heart. "What I really need is a chair, actually. But I don't expect you to drag one of those out here for me."

Daisy shook her head. "No, can't do that. But I can offer any one of the wooden crates we have out back. Suppliers think it makes 'em look fancy to ship that way. Really, they're just a pain in my ass."

Thom accepted her offer with pitiful-sounding relief.

Tonight felt like an afterthought, a habit. Brian and Michael had bowed out for a few days, pledging their devotion while crying uncle. The DJ was a substitute, and his playlist felt perfunctory and discombobulated. The Bay City Rollers followed Judas Priest who'd followed John Denver. In what universe did "Grandma's Feather Bed" qualify as dance music?

Mercifully, Daisy returned after only a few minutes. "Plop your keister on this, mister." She placed a wooden crate etched with faux French passport stamps at his feet. "Just be careful of getting a splinter where it don't belong."

Thom laughed. Snort-laughed, surprisingly, his mood lifting immediately as he sank to his seat beneath a chorus of seraphim and cherubim giving praise to the heavens above. "Thank you, Daisy. You don't have any idea what an otherworldly relief this is."

"And you're sure you don't need a drink—pop, even?" she confirmed.

"I'll stick to my water bottle." He'd thought to bring that, at least.

Daisy gave her best wishes and farewells as the DJ took to the microphone. "Alright, Knixonians," he announced. "Thanks for coming out to support the Cross the Street Project tonight. Just say no to bulldozing our businesses. And on that note, get out your cowbells, 'cuz here comes Blue Öyster Cult hoping you '(Don't Fear) The Reaper.'"

Knock. Knock. Knock. Knock. Knock. Thom found himself striking his own imaginary cowbell in the air high above his head. His attitude really was improving, and who could resist a little more cowbell anyway?

"Thom?"

"Al!" Embarrassed, he shoved his pretend percussion into his back pocket and stood, grimacing and wondering about his sanity. "Hope we're not disturbing your customers. Do you need us to turn down the volume?"

Al shook his head. "In fact, I was hoping I might be able to say a few words to the crowd? Whenever you think it might be a good time. Don't want to stop the fun."

"Of course!" This was curious. Al had been plenty generous with the bottled water on past nights, but he'd never asked for time on the mic. "Wanna give me a sneak peek of what you plan to say?"

"Well." Al considered the offer. "Actually, I think I'd better just go right ahead and say it. Don't want to lose my nerve."

"Certainly." Thom felt the rock return to his stomach. And just as his night had begun to look up. "Let's head over to the DJ right now."

Moments later, Al began, "Friends, first let me say what an

amazing few days this has been. I don't think Alstrop's Hardware has ever been in the newspaper so much—and we've been paying for ads in it for nearly fifty years!"

The crowd whistled and clapped appreciatively. Al had a certain old-timey Minnesota charm, appropriate for a hardware man—he pulled hard on his *O*s when he spoke and looked most comfortable with his hands shoved in his pockets. Thom imagined that the highest compliment he gave was to say, "Well, now, ain't that something."

Someone in the crowd hollered, "Show us your moves, Al!"

He laughed. "No. I think I'll spare you that. But I do want to say thank you for the support you've come out to show. My family and I genuinely appreciate it."

More whistles and clapping.

"And that's why I'm making sure to tell you first that Alstrop's isn't closing after all. My sister's daughter, my niece Kaarin, has stepped up to continue the family business. She's an artist and real good with a blowtorch. I guess I just never realized she had an interest in the business, too."

By now, the crowd was cheering so loud they didn't even hear the part about Kaarin having her own welding videos on YouTube. The DJ answered their excitement by starting a low, thumping beat that got them jumping up and down as if on pogo sticks.

"Yeah! Yeah! Yeah!" they chanted.

Al was trying to explain how much Alstrop's was going to need their business going forward, but Thom could see they were too far gone to care. "I think you gave them what they wanted to hear," he said, gently taking the mic from Al's hand. It was sweaty; he'd obviously been anxious. Thom shook it anyway. "That's some amazing news, Al. Congratulations. And thank you. For hearing us out and responding the way you did." His heart was thumping, threatening to leap from his chest. And it wasn't because of the oversize speaker blasting beside him.

"Well, we'll have to see how it goes," Al said. "It's still gonna be tough for Kaarin to make it."

"I promise to remain a loyal Alstrop's customer." Thom felt his smile stretch wide enough he knew he must look like a goof. "Tell Kaarin I'll buy everything there. Toilet paper. Dish soap. Even tools I don't need!"

Al began to argue that wouldn't be necessary, but people had started pulling at him to extend their congratulations. Thom gave the DJ the signal to continue. He needed a minute to digest what he'd just heard. Of all the nights for his friends to stay home (probably with heating pads and Tiger Balm, the lucky fools). And Laney. And Bree. Where were they for this wonderful moment?

Bree had one too many bourbon thingies. Her tongue felt too thick to talk.

"Hey, Witt." She tried anyway. "Since I'm going to be out of a job on Friday, can I come work here as one of your bartenders?"

He smiled—more like, laughed—at her, but either way, she liked his face, and his hips, especially the one leaning against the bar.

"Do you know the difference between whiskey and vodka?" he asked.

"Yes! One is white and one is brown."

"White? Like milk?"

"No—" She wiggled her fingers, erasing her answer from the air. "Clear-ish. You can see through it." Now her hands were in front of her eyes, and she peeked at him through finger blinds. "I see you."

"I think that's your last drink." Witt withdrew her glass, though it was only half empty. "But, yes, you are correct. Vodka is clear and whiskey is brown."

"Can I have a job, then?"

"I suspect you have greater things awaiting you. Let's shoot for those."

A sigh escaped before she knew it was coming. "What, though? I've never done anything except read books and then get other people to read them. It's not like selling cars. I'm not pushy enough to do that."

Witt hmm'd. He looked like he was enjoying this. Maybe she ought to ask.

"Are you in happy with this?" *Try again.* "With me, that is?"

Now he was full-on laughing. "Definitely. Yes, I'm *in happy* with you."

"I'm making a fool of myself, aren't I?"

"Nah. We bartenders see lots of stuff."

That didn't sound reassuring at all. Now she wanted to crawl under the bar and hide. "Don't look at me. I think I'm drunk."

"I think you're right." He took a moment to pour her a glass of ice water. "But I don't think you have a future in selling cars, either. You love selling books, right?"

She nodded.

"There are other bookstores in town."

"Bookstores are just bookstores. The Rainbow has a leprechaun." Because what did she know—maybe they really did.

"Why doesn't your magical leprechaun step in and save the store?"

Bree dropped her face to the bar. "Because he's a dick."

Witt left her to sulk while he served a couple down at the other end of the bar. She really didn't like being drunk. It made her feel out of control. Messy. Problem was, her non-drunk life was out of control and messy now, too. She couldn't win.

She felt a gentle slap on her back.

"Has our friend here had a bit too much?"

"Hi, Daisy." She didn't lift her head. She preferred disappearing.

Daisy sat down next to her. "I was just out at the lot. Your friend Thom looks like he could use some company."

Bree brought her face to her palm. "I'm hiding."

"From little ol' Thom?"

"From everything. The Rainbow. Irma. My desperate, unemployed future."

Daisy frowned. "Nope. Not gonna do that." She pointed at Bree's face. "No feeling sorry for yourself at Lady of the Lake. C'mon." She stood and pulled Bree up with her. "Hey, Witt, she's gonna take a mosey for a bit. Set her tab aside. She can pay it later."

A protest began to rise in her throat, though Bree didn't know what for—that Daisy was being supportive and trusting? That Witt hadn't tossed her out for pouting and complaining?

"Where are we going?" she asked.

"You're going to get some fresh air and keep your compatriot company while you're at it." Daisy opened the front door and gave her a gentle push. "He's over there behind the stage. Can't miss him." Then she left Bree standing alone on the other side of the entrance, nowhere to go but forward.

"Fine," she muttered to no one. "Quit your pushing."

The music was loud tonight. Or maybe it was always this loud. She'd been trying to keep her distance so it didn't look to Irma like she and Laney had joined the revolutionaries, even though they had. As she walked, her pace began to match the beat… *Knock. Knock. Knock. Knock. Knock.* This song. What was it? Her brain answered with an image of Will Ferrell in a curly wig and too-tight sweater on *Saturday Night Live.*

"We need more cowbell!" she hollered. "I got a fever!" Suddenly, she had her own imaginary cowbell in the air, and she was all twisting hips and throttling percussion. *Knock. Knock. Knock. Knock. Knock.* "Don't fear the what-what," she sang.

A car honked. She startled. The driver didn't like that she was cowbell-ing in the middle of 28th Street. "You don't have to use your special finger, dumbass! It's the cowbell song. Have some respect."

The music quieted and she was close enough to the lot to see someone take the stage, though not close enough to see who it was. Her gut told her to run. She heard, "…for nearly fifty years!" Then the crowd responded, apparently happy to hear whatever this guy was saying. Then a person yelled, "Show us your moves, Al!" and everyone laughed and clapped too hard for her to hear his answer. But it was Al, she recognized him now. Her stomach threatened to turn itself upside down onto the street, but she kept up the pace. There was something happening.

"My family and I genuinely appreciate it. And that's why I'm making sure to tell you first that Alstrop's isn't closing after all. My sister's daughter, my niece Kaarin, has stepped up—"

Bree made it to the fence, and she hung there, fingers and face to the steel mesh. She couldn't see Al from this vantage point, but she knew what she'd just heard. The Alstrops had gone and backed out of their contract.

"They backed out!" She was jumping up and down and hollering. "They backed out!"

As if seeing her excitement, the DJ turned up the bass with a thump, thump, thump to which she and a hundred or so of her fellow Knixonians began to bounce in unison. "Yeah! Yeah! Yeah! Yeah!"

Where was Laney? She had to go get her. No. She and Irma were together at the shop tonight. Bree couldn't go screaming across the street with glee. She'd call. Or text. Where was Thom's friend in the trench coat when you needed him?

"Laney!" she shouted into her phone. "Did you hear what Al just said?" Laney answered, but Bree couldn't make sense of it with all the mayhem. "What? I can't hear you. But you need to go outside. You need to see what's happening!"

Laney kept talking. Bree hung up.

Then she leaned over and threw up all over the grass.

Way, way too many bourbon thingies.

Laney put her phone down and looked at her mom. "I suspect you know what Al just announced out there."

"That he prefers red wine with lamb?"

"Funny girl. Wonder where I get it." She walked behind the counter and found her mother's keys. "C'mon. We're going outside. I'll lock the door behind us."

"I'm not going anywhere." Arms folded across her chest, Irma looked like Nellie Oleson throwing a Walnut Grove tantrum.

Laney tsk'd. "Silly lady. Don't you know I can drag you out by the hair if I need to? I'm younger and stronger."

"I'll sue you for elder abuse."

"And I'll sue you right back."

Her mom raised a for-what? eyebrow.

"Kidnapping. No, body snatching. Alien abduction. Whatever you are—" she swirled an open palm in the space between them "—it's you who've stolen my once-sane mother."

Laney grabbed her mom's hand and pulled her toward the door. Her resistance wasn't as dramatic as their repartee, and soon, she and her mother were standing on the curb outside the store. She wanted to hustle across the street but knew that would all but stop their progress. One step at a time. Let Irma adjust to the world outside her window for a moment.

"So, let me guess, Al announced he's not going to sell after all." Irma harrumphed.

"Which is what he was trying to tell you yesterday, isn't it?"

"You were listening at the door. You heard what he said."

Laney shook her head and smiled as the thump, thump, thump of the bass tried to crack the neighborhood's windows. She would never understand how Thom had gotten away with such a loud stunt. Or how a trio of nincompoops like themselves had potentially crippled the Vandaveers' plans.

★★★

Thom didn't see Bree at the fence nor did he see Irma and Laney on the sidewalk across the street. All he saw was stars in his eyes—mostly from his excitement over Al's news, but also because he'd just sat down too hard on his wine crate and felt a *snap!* zing its way up his spine and out to his extremities. He'd probably just paralyzed himself. How nifty.

The microphone squealed, and again, the DJ brought the music to a stop. Thom was too busy trying to keep from splaying out on the asphalt to notice that another person had taken the mic.

"Hey, all you Lyn-Lake rockers!"

Thom cringed. Whose voice was that? And why did he fancy himself Wolfman Jack?

His back seized. He grabbed for it and winced.

"If I can have your attention, please." Little Wolfman was starting to sound pitiful. "As you just heard from Al, we've been busy these last few days with our plans for the Knickerbocker. A little bird tells us you haven't been too pleased about the location we picked."

Thom perked. *Our* plans for the Knickerbocker? This had to be Trevor Vandaveer. He strained to look, but his muscles told him he wasn't going anywhere until they were good and ready.

When the crowd jeered at the "little bird" comment, he knew he was right. It was Trevor. Who continued, "Didn't like that last part, huh? Well, maybe you'll like this better."

He paused like a good showman should, then directed their attention to the fence along the west side of the lot. "Maestro?" he said. There was quiet, then a roar that outshone Al's announcement a hundredfold.

What had happened?

"That's right," Trevor said. "We heard you. And we listened."

The DJ began his thumping bass routine again—this guy was a real one-trick pony—and whatever comments Trevor added were quickly drowned out. Thom couldn't sit on his little stool like a child, he had to see what had just driven the crowd mad. He stood, easy-easy, pushing his thumb deep into the muscle that complained the loudest, trying to massage it into submission. He was halfway up. A forty-five degree angle. Now fifteen. Just a little more, that's all he needed. But the crowd was pogo-sticking again, a hundred heads bobbing to block his view.

"Damn it," he said to his protesting bones. "Just do me a favor. For once!"

He eased one foot on top of the crate. *Okay.* He took a breath. Blew it out. Now for the hard work. He threw everything he could into straightening his leg, just enough to guide his other foot up onto the wood. Almost there. His thigh shook. His back screamed. Almost…and, there! He did it! He was up. The crowd was still bobbing, but he'd gained sixteen inches. He scanned the fence—his signs were still hanging. But where—?

Why did Vandaveer Investments cross the road?

He saw it, a giant white banner with the Vandaveers' green logo at its heart.

To show everyone the future home of the Knickerbocker
Lyn-Lake's finest in condominium living
Arriving Soon

Arriving soon? Across the road? They'd done it! Oh my god, they'd really—

CRACK! CRASH! THUD.

INTERMISSION

Mr. and Mrs. Elliot Gregory Sr.
of Miami Beach, Florida,
announce the marriage of their son
Elliot Martindale Gregory Jr.
to
Irma Juliette Bedford
Officiated on Friday, the 30th day of November,
in the year 1979

The couple will reside in Minneapolis, Minnesota

Oh yes we did!

I know, I know. It's confusing. Judy's urging me to explain, too.

First, let me set the scene.

It was the last day of November and Minneapolis was seeing the season's first snow. Irma was all smiles, as was I, though I also took very seriously my responsibility to keep my new bride safe on the icy courthouse steps.

"Easy does it," I said, having never navigated such weather in open-toed heels.

My parents were inside glad-handing the former colleague who'd performed the ceremony. Before retiring, Elliot Sr. had been a district judge in the same courthouse as our officiant, a man with an "infallible" reputation. It's an irony at which you may now chuckle, given that moments before, he stood by with pride as his gay son married his platonic best friend as a means of getting at his parents' money.

"What's next?" Irma asked me.

"Martinis and steaks at Charlie's on 7th, then off to the airport. Mumsie and Dadums are on the six o'clock plane back to Miami."

"Won't they want pictures?"

"Not with this mustache."

Irma looked lovely in white chiffon ruffles and a rabbit-fur wrap or, as Mumsie put it, "perfectly appropriate." My suit was crisp, freshly acquired from the Dayton's men's department. Even it, however, couldn't outshine my parents' distaste for the "growth" on my face. Dadums called me a hippie, even though hippies hadn't been en vogue for nearly a decade.

Irma said, "We can go right back inside and have the marriage annulled if you're having second thoughts." The offer was so typical of her, as she was always willing to fly wherever my whims took us, but not too proud to admit when we'd made a mistake.

This marriage, however, was no mistake. I said, "Do you still want to open our bookshop?"

"Of course. Very much."

"And do we need fistfuls of cash to do so?"

That remained true, as well.

"Then, to the Bank of Gregory, we go."

On that auspicious day in November 1979, Irma and I were both twenty-five years old. In my parents' eyes—they having been born before the roaring twenties and in their sexual prime when Emperor Hirohito surrendered to the Allies—it was about time we got down to the business of marriage and family. I ought to be well finished sowing my wild oats, and Irma was practically shriveled.

"Do the poor woman a favor and marry her quickly," said Mumsie.

"You'll get more of my money when there's children," said Dadums.

It's obvious now, right? We did it for the money. You see, I was deemed unworthy of any portion of the Gregory wealth until I could show proof of my red-blooded American male credentials. And though I'd tried to get a loan before dragging Irma to that altar, we had no real income, no credit to leverage. The banks laughed us right out the door.

Judy says she's not surprised to hear this at all.

So, there! Now you have the inside scoop on our bookshop's origins, and the answer to the question you've been asking ever more loudly with every page. We got the money for Over the Rainbow because my parents insisted I marry and because Irma had no hang-ups about social constraints.

The next day, as we signed our new, fat check over to the bank, Irma turned to me and asked, "Our children don't need to look like you, do they?"

Heavens, no.

18

3 hours after stopping the sale...

It looked like a dinner party migrated into a hospital room. Thom lay in the bed, moaning, his back bent and his ankle twisted. Irma sat rigid in the corner, her chair as far away from the room's other inhabitants as possible. Bree sat with her knees tucked into her chest, still drunk, stinking of sick.

And Laney? Well, she was just trying to keep it all together. Keep the herd of cats in the room, the seams from bursting, the match away from the gasoline.

"You." She pointed at Bree, then pulled the garbage can from beneath the sink and placed it beside her. "If you're going to glarf again, do it in this." Bree had been sick in the car on the way to the hospital, which of course she had, because that's just what their night needed—more bedlam.

"And you." Laney pointed at her mother. "You're not going anywhere until you spill the beans about what's really going on. I know you're feeling defeated, but you'll see that stopping the Vandaveer sale is the best thing that could have happened to the Rainbow. I mean it. Start talking, or I'll make a doctor give you a shot of truth serum, if that's what it takes." She knew that wasn't a thing. She also knew her mother hated needles.

"And as for you." She moved to Thom's bedside and adjusted the pillow under his ankle. After the Vandaveers' announcement, she'd run to the Knixo to celebrate but, instead, found him lying on the asphalt, his back locked at ninety degrees and a wine crate wrapped around his foot. He said he'd stepped on it, fallen through, and landed wrong. Laney wanted to ask if there was a correct way to land when falling through a crate but stopped herself when she saw what looked like a watermelon at the end of his leg. His ankle was so red it was almost green and visibly throbbing.

Now every one of them was on their worst behavior, stuffed into an exam room at Swedish Memorial Hospital.

"Thom Winslow?" Their second visitor of the evening arrived. A few minutes ago, a young man with a laptop strapped to his chest like a robot in a low-budget sci-fi movie had been the first to visit, there to take Thom's medical history and reconfirm his medical insurance.

Their second visitor wore pink scrubs and a watch pinned to her shirt. "So I hear you're having some pain tonight?"

Thom moaned, tried to point at his ankle, and gasped when the movement made his back seize.

"Hmm," said Pink. "Looks uncomfortable."

Laney's inner cynic wanted to scream, *He's in labor, can't you see?* Only, she couldn't because Bree had pulled the garbage bin to her face and began to make sounds more sea mammal than human.

"She alright?" Pink asked.

"Sure. She just hates Tuesdays," she said, and her inner cynic smiled with relief.

Then Thom screeched as Pink touched a fingertip to his ankle.

Bree covered her ears with her palms, still doubled over the trash.

"I'm going for a walk." Irma stood and made for the door.

Thom was now making a terrible, syncopated hissing noise—maybe he really was in labor—and Laney couldn't blame anyone for wanting to escape. But her mother required a short leash.

"Oh no you don't." She was closer and quicker and able to block Irma's path. "We're in this together. Which means none of us are walking out until we're all walking out."

Hearing this, the nurse was swift to object. "I don't think Mr. Winslow will be walking out tonight."

"Thom's dying?" Bree pulled her head out of the bin. Just in time for Nurse Pink to lift his ankle for inspection.

"AAAAAAAAAAAAAIIIIIIIIIIIEEEEEEEEEE!"

Somewhere in the midst of the mayhem, Laney turned her back long enough for Irma to slip out of the room. Maybe it happened when the doctor arrived to make Thom scream again or perhaps when the nursing assistant arrived with the prescribed muscle relaxant and ended up with a face full of water. Turns out, it's difficult to swallow properly when your body looks like a bedsheet at the end of a tumble dry, twisted and knotted and a little inside out.

"Sorry," Thom dribbled. "I think I got the pill down, though."

"S'alright, man. Been sprayed with worse."

And now there were two, Laney and Bree. An orderly had wheeled Thom off for X-rays, and for all the sisters knew, their mother had hitchhiked home.

Bree stood, wobbled, and made her way to the bed.

"What are you doing?"

"I need to lie down."

She pulled the blanket across her legs. Laney watched the clock tick off a full ninety seconds. The room became too quiet.

"Where do you think Mom went?"

Bree groaned. "Talking makes the room spin."

"Fine."

Two minutes. Three minutes. Four.

"If she's not back in ten minutes, I'm going looking."

"Why?" Bree hiccuped. "Don't answer. Rhetorical question."

Laney thought about the answer anyway. Why should she go looking? Did she have a self-punishment streak she'd never been aware of?

She thought of that day in the tire shop, the one that started this snowball rolling. There hadn't been anything different about it—the customers were as quirky as ever, the doughnut tray in need of refilling, the lobby television was set to max-volume-plus. And yet, she'd agreed to fly home.

And here they were.

"Bree," she whispered, "do you ever wonder what life would be like if I hadn't stayed with Tuck?"

She groaned, but found words enough to say, "Sorry to disappoint, but I don't spend a whole lot of time thinking about my sister's husband."

"No, not for him. For me. For us. Would you and I have stayed close, or would we have gone our separate ways? Would we be one of those families with unbreakable bonds you see in Hallmark movies?"

Bree eased herself up onto her elbow and squinted across the room. "That's like asking 'What if I'd been born as a man in China?' It's impossible to know, so what's the point?"

Laney scraped the toe of her shoe across the linoleum. She didn't know why she'd brought this up now, with their current circumstances being hardly ideal and nerves already raw. But she had, and that meant something whether she understood it yet or not. "I was planning to break up with Tuck that summer. I was going to stay with him on the circuit until August, then leave for good. I never set out to ditch my college plans for a life on the road. And, to be honest, I was getting tired of all his brawny bullshit."

"His brawny what?" Bree squeezed one eye shut, trying to decipher.

"You know—his *real man* attitude and everything that comes with it. The ego. The constant talk about 'making it big.' And god, those freaking protein shakes. Always with the damn shakes. I never want to hear another blender my whole life."

Bree lay down again and opened her eyes to the ceiling. She laughed. "I remember those. Mom asked me once if I thought he was 'juicing.' I assumed she was talking about Jamba Juice until she mentioned an article about 'roid rage."

Laney chuckled. "He didn't need steroids. He hated bulking up, said he couldn't move in a tight car unless he was lean and strong. It made me feel disgusting every time I wanted a burger."

Again, Bree was up on her elbow. "What are you trying to tell me? Spit it out." She was glaring, which could legitimately have either been because she was angry or because bright lights were a drunk's Nosferatu.

Laney took a breath. "I'm saying I'm worried I don't actually want to be married to Tuck anymore. I don't know if I ever did." She closed her eyes, avoiding the glare of the Big Truth that now floated in the space between them. The Truth was ugly. It frightened her. It grabbed her guts by the fist and twisted.

But the Truth didn't shake Bree at all. "I know," she said. "You'd be trying harder to get home to your life in California if you wanted to be there."

"That's not fair. You need me here."

"Yes, and you need you here. You promised you'd stay one week, then two. It's been nearly three weeks since you arrived, and I don't hear you making flight reservations. I think there's a reason." She eased herself further upright and dropped her feet off the side of the bed. "Home is where you're supposed to go when life gets too confusing to deal with alone. It's an instinct."

"But in my case, home *is* my confusion. It has been for twenty years."

"I'm talking about your people. Your loved ones. We have a homing device, and when we're hurting, we turn toward love. Sometimes we turn before we even know we're in pain."

Laney smiled. *We turn toward love.* Maybe she'd print that on a T-shirt.

The door opened with the click-hiss of hydraulics and the orderly rolled Thom through. "He did great. Just waiting on results now."

"Any idea how long?" Laney was drained. She wished the room had bunk beds.

The orderly frowned. "It's busy for a weeknight. Sorry."

Thom waved a gentle hand. "No worries, young man."

"Those relaxers kicking in, huh?" The "young man" took him by the elbow and eased him out of the chair into bed. "I call 'em Dreamy Jeannie's, myself."

"Magnificent," answered Thom.

Laney raised her hand. "Can I have one?"

They resettled. Thom in bed, Bree in a chair with her head in Laney's lap. Laney threaded chocolate strands of Bree's hair between her fingers and ran her hand down the length of her sister's neck, loosening the snarls of a tumultuous night.

"That feels good," Bree whispered, while Laney closed her eyes and fell into the spell of its repetitiveness—soothing, soft, and silent.

Thom, feeling pharmaceutically enhanced, began to quietly sing.

In the Blue Ridge Mountains of Virginny,
Stood a cow on a railroad track.
She was a good old cow, with eyes so kind,
But who'd expect a cow to read a railroad sign?
So she stood, cha-cha-cha, in the middle of the track,
And the train, cha-cha-cha, hit her whacky on the back.
Oh, in the Blue Ridge Mountains of Virginny,
There's no tail on a lonesome spine.
Onnn a looone-sommmme spi-i-iiine. Cha-cha-cha.

Bree clapped. Laney asked him to sing it again. Thom obliged.

They were alone that way for some time and, had the circumstances been any different—had they not been exhausted or confused or numb or even remotely aware that life was about to change—they would have taken advantage of the privacy to celebrate and plan their next move. Instead, they settled into the quiet, a trio of unlikely friends at a fork in the road, watching the dust for clues about where the wind was likely to blow them next.

"Well, Mr. Winslow." The door swept open, and the doctor began speaking before it even closed behind him. "Looks like you're going to be off your ankle for a good six-plus weeks. X-rays showed a Grade II sprain—in other words, you've messed it up good, but it doesn't look like you'll need surgery. Just the RICE routine—Rest, Ice, Compression, and Elevate. We'll wrap it before you leave. Do you have crutches?"

Thom was still singsongy. "I have a lovely cane we bought in the Andes before he died."

The doctor, confused, looked to Laney for clarification.

"His partner died earlier this year. But I can get him crutches if you tell me where to go."

"Can I choose the color and pattern?" Thom asked.

The doctor chuckled and, again, deferred to Laney. "I'll leave that up to your fearless leader, here." He winked. He was very handsome. And the ring on his left hand said he was very married. Of course he was.

Doc started to explain Thom's treatment directions. How much ibuprofen he could take and when. How to properly elevate. How often he needed to ice his ankle. Thom had just asked how to shower when the door burst open again, and Irma barged through.

She didn't wait for it to close, either, before blurting, "You wanted the truth, so here it is."

The doc looked at his watch and began to object, but Irma

steamed ahead. "Elliot left the store deep in debt. He maxed out our credit cards. There's at least forty-five thousand on our accounts. The sale to the Vandaveers was our last chance to get out with any money in our pocket."

Laney heard herself moan and her sister gasp. Thom, still muted, said, "Ghosts don't pay bills."

Laney, Bree, and their mother instantly began to argue. How could this have happened? Why hadn't she said anything? How were they going to pay it all off? What was going to happen if they couldn't?

"Hate to interrupt," said the doc, who sounded as if he didn't hate it at all. "Busy night around here. Any final questions before I send the nurse in to discharge you?"

Thom was humming his cow song again, peaceful despite Irma's bombshell. He stopped. "One question, actually. Have you ever been to the Blue Ridge Mountains?"

The Book Haters' Book Club Newsletter

Issue #177
February 2004

I'd like to kick off this issue by reminding all you haters why we humans can't survive without stories: they show us we're not alone. Everyone experiences tragedy, and laughter, and mystery, and delight. It's other people's stories that teach us how to deal with our own.

So, in this issue I'm racing to the rescue of any book hater who's even the slightest bit intrigued by history, architecture, medical quackery, our Big Sister City of Chicago, or even murder. Have I hooked you yet?

The book is *Devil in the White City: Murder, Magic, and Madness at the Fair That Changed America* by Erik Larson. And, wowza, it will make you wonder why history class had to be so boring, when you could have been reading it the way this author writes it.

Unless you are a history buff, you may not have known that during the Chicago Columbian Expedition (World's Fair) of 1893, there was a serial killer on the loose who lured his victims by using the once-in-a-decade event as bait. Dr. Henry H. Holmes, our killer, is dark and devilish, and it's easy to see why his murderous charms give the book its title.

At the same time, however, Larson somehow manages to bring to life the masterful politicking, money, and architectural wizardry that, over the course of eighteen months, reshapes Chicago into the international destination it remains today.

The book is a ticking clock, and while none of us need any more stress in our lives, every so often, it's good to recognize that you're not the only one facing what feels like an impossible task. You're not the only one to be shocked to discover the people you trust can betray you. Or to be reminded that the hero you need may arise from the unlikeliest of places.

We've got copies aplenty. Come nab yours.

—Elliot

Last Hope for the Haters

Humans don't need stories the same way whales don't need oceans.

19

18 hours after stopping the sale...

Bree needed another tissue—tears had soaked the one in her hand to the point of disintegration. Her head ached, and the last place she wanted to be was in the back room of the Rainbow, staring at financial documents she didn't understand.

"This was supposed to be a day of celebration." She sniffled before a line of snot dropped on the page in front of her, which she may as well have been reading upside down for all the sense it made. "I never thought things would look worse than before. I was going to buy balloons."

Laney had been shuttling back and forth between the shop and the back room all morning, helping visitors and Bree in equal measure. She was too calm, and when Bree told her so, she defended herself by saying that someone had to be.

"I'll have my breakdown later. How's that?"

"Very un-Laney-like."

"Well, don't say I never gave you anything."

Right now, Laney sat cross-legged on the cement floor with a three-hole punch, trying to organize the potpourri of bank, credit card, and loan statements they thought might, possibly, could be important. "If you want to buy balloons, buy balloons," she said. "Just don't expect the store to pay for them."

Bree picked up a supplier invoice stamped as late. "This was past due two years ago. How am I supposed to know if it ever got paid?"

"Toss it down. I'll start a binder for invoices."

Bree felt a tear drop off her chin. Then another. She realized she'd recycled a cluster of other invoices, and the thought of digging through the bin to find them was more than her emotional dam could hold.

"I need a minute." She grabbed a fresh tissue and laid her head on her knees. In the span of eighteen hours, she'd taken every single ride at the mental health amusement park she once named Six Flags Over Your Feelings. The Reality-Tilt-A-Whirl. The Courageous Carousel. The Long Log Ride of the Persecuted and Bitter. She snapped to her feet. "Why are we even here? It's hopeless. We should just close the doors and cut our losses."

Laney looked at her with a told-you-so smile. "Okay, Irma." She returned to binder assembly. "Here's what I'm trying to figure out—Mom spent days emptying out these filing cabinets, and yet she saved the stuff we're looking at now. Why?"

"She needed it to pay Elliot's debts! These are all bills. She's trying to keep herself from getting sued or going to debtors' prison."

Laney looked up. "A—not a thing. And B—what if there's more to it? Nothing about this screwball comedy has turned out to be what it seemed."

"Maybe she's in, what do you call that—" Bree snapped her fingers "—where you believe two contrasting things at once even though they can't both be true?"

"Psychotic delusion."

Bree scowled. "Cognitive dissonance." It was the only concept she remembered from her college psychology course. "She wants the sale to go through but also hopes it doesn't."

Laney shuffled a stack of papers into a messy pile and snapped them against the floor until straight. "No way of knowing."

"I think I need some fresh air." Bree scanned the desk for her wallet. "Can you manage the store on your own for an hour?" Her eye caught on a draft of the Book Haters' newsletter she'd been trying—and failing—to write for weeks.

"I'll text if I need you."

She got outside into the sunshine. Vitamin D was good for something, she couldn't remember what, but right now she'd take a good something over the whole lot of bad nothing at the shop.

The next few weeks were going to be humiliating. They'd have to close the store, and this time, it was going to be obvious that it wasn't because of the Vandaveers or rampant development or even the rogue suburban retirees Violet Baumgartner had blamed in her op-ed. They were going to be exposed; the curtain pulled to reveal the ugly truth that the Over the Rainbow Bookshop was in deep debt and beyond saving.

"Are you sure?"

The voice stopped her. So abruptly, in fact, that the woman behind her on the sidewalk smacked into her, broadside.

"Ope!" they said in unison—because Minnesotans have a strange habit of apologizing for things that aren't necessarily their fault, and they do so with a single syllable that no one can really explain but everyone understands. The woman moved on. Bree stood still, listening for more. That had been Elliot's voice she'd heard. And if there was one thing she absolutely did not need on her list of catastrophes-in-the-making, it was hearing dead people.

So, of course, she answered him. Though not out loud. She didn't need to look crazy on top of feeling it. *If that's you, Elliot, please know I love you. But if you want to help, start dropping money from the sky. Otherwise, keep your mouth shut.*

She waited for him to answer, right there on the Midtown Greenway, eyes to the heavens. When nothing came—because of course nothing did—she raised both arms and used her special fingers to give him a double-barrel salute. *Just messing with me, huh? Because it's fun? Is that it?* She gave her salute an extra one-two punch and walked on.

That voice hadn't been Elliot. She was being crazy. She was exhausted. Her brain was too full to function. The only thing she needed was to keep walking until she either collapsed or got hit by a bus and had to spend a month in the hospital.

Her feet hit the pavement—*crunch-slap, crunch-slap.*

Bicycles cruised by and whipped her hair.

The sun kissed her shoulders.

The voice echoed in her head. *Are you sure?*

Are you sure?

Are you sure?

"Knock it off!" she screamed, this time out loud. This time at herself. Because now her own brain was giving life to the crazy seed Elliot had planted. Was she sure the store was past saving? No. Irma said it was, but did that make it true?

"No!" she yelled.

A woman on a fat-tired beach cruiser passed just in time to pretend she hadn't heard a thing from the woman fighting with herself on the Greenway.

"Don't worry about me!" Bree hollered at her. "I'm just losing my mind over here, but I'm harmless!"

The woman looked back. Mortified, Bree turned and ran the opposite direction.

Minutes later, she threw open the distillery door and marched straight at Witt, who was unlucky enough to be sitting nearby with a glass of iced tea and a stack of reports.

"Tell me I'm nutters, and I will walk out this door right now."

"Well, you do look a little—" He made wild fingers around his head. "Did you go running in jeans?"

"I'm upset." She pulled out a chair and sat down.

"Sure. Have a seat." He pushed his iced tea toward her, smirking, enjoying himself a wee too much. "Are you here to tell me you built a time machine out of a DeLorean?"

"What?"

"You know. *Back to the Future.* You remind me of Doc Brown right now with the—" He made the crazy fingers again.

"I'm UPSET!" It came out louder than she'd intended, but it got the point across because Witt immediately changed his tune.

"Alright. Sorry. No more jokes." He pushed the iced tea an inch closer.

This time, she took a sip. "I'm just..." How does one phrase the complete crap-out of her life, sanity, and family? "Let me put it this way—Irma dropped a bomb on us last night, and I don't know how to tell if she's telling the truth or not. Except I have to find out somehow because if I don't, we're gonna lose the store. Which is IRONIC—" she threw her hands in the air "—because I thought we'd saved it last night!"

"Wait. I heard the Vandaveers are moving the development—just like you wanted."

Ha. *Like they wanted.* Funny how much could change overnight. "They are. The sale is dead. If the Vandaveers can't get the whole block—bookshop and hardware store—they don't want it at all. Which is why upon learning this, Irma finally decided to tell us that the store is dead, too. We're broke. No, worse. We're not just broke, we're buried in debt." Then she laughed a hysterical laugh like the madwoman she'd become. "Up to our eyeballs. Dead. Dead. Ding-dong dead."

"Yikes."

"I know. Although I do feel slightly less guilty about throwing up in her car last night."

"Double yikes."

"I don't like bourbon anymore."

Witt picked up his pencil. "I'll make a note of it."

Bree dropped her head to the table. There had been way too much head-dropping in her life lately. She picked it up again. "I don't know what to do. I don't even know what I'm doing here, except that I know if I walk back into the Rainbow, I'm going to lose it."

He sat silent for a moment. "What is it that you're trying to figure out?"

What kind of a question was that? "Where all our money went? How much do we owe and how are we going to pay it off?"

"Are you a shareholder?"

Bree looked at him with an expression she very much hoped said, "Do you speak English or is your hovercraft full of eels?" Also, the fact that ancient Monty Python skits were now taking up space in her brain was of absolutely no help to her sanity, especially since 'roid rage Tuck was the one who'd put them there twenty years ago.

Witt clarified. "Is the business in your name? Do you own part of it?"

"No." That, at least, she knew.

"Do you have access to its financial statements?"

"Well, I spent the morning swimming in credit card statements, if that's what you mean."

He frowned. "Not exactly. But you can probably get the information you need from your accountant. Have you contacted them?"

Funny you should ask! she wanted to say. *I was just talking to him on my way over.* "Elliot did the books."

"Okaaay." He began to drum his fingers on the table.

"How do you know so much about this stuff?"

"Financials?"

"Yeah, if that's what you call it."

"It is. And I know because I'm a CPA. Or, was. I quit renewing my certification when I became distillery master here."

"You're a CPA."

He nodded. "Surprised I'm not wearing my pocket protector?"

"A numbers guy."

"I like them all, yes."

"Who makes booze."

"We call them craft spirits, but that's the gist of it."

"How." She didn't phrase it as a question because she didn't need to. He was going to explain himself.

First, he laughed. "I know. We accountants aren't known for our beards." He ran a hand down his cheek and what looked like a few days' worth of stubble. "What do you think, by the way? I thought I'd try something new."

She studied him. "I prefer to see your face." Oh lord, please tell her she hadn't just said that. "Because, I mean, it's a nice face. And you asked, is all I'm saying. Is the AC on in here?"

He grinned too handsomely for comfort.

"Anyway." She tried to get back on topic while also trying not to panic at the realization she'd worn her lazy bra this morning—the one with 0.0 percent padding—which meant her nipples were right this second *yoo-hoo!*ing at him through her T-shirt. *Hi, Witt! Hey, there!*

"Um, accounting." Stop it. Stop it! "You understand this stuff?"

"General Mills thought I did," he said, his eyes noticeably glued to her face.

"You were an accountant at General Mills?"

"For eighteen years."

"Did they find out you were a moonshiner?"

"Well, I didn't exactly do it on company time."

"What, then?" Was it possible to air out her armpits without him seeing?

He shook his head. "It's a long story, and someday, I'll tell you. For now, though, how much time do you have before you're out of operating capital?"

"If I knew where our capital was, I would move to it." She

flapped her shirt against her chest, creating a breeze and throwing the girls into hiding.

He began to explain that *capital* wasn't a place but—then he spotted the glint in her eye. "Funny. I see what you did there."

"I've already lost my mind, so I figure, why hold back?"

"I like a go-get-em attitude." He winked. "But seriously, do you want help looking at your financials? I'm off the next few days. I don't know how much I'll be able to figure out, but I'm happy to give it a go."

Bree shook her head quickly. "Too mortifying."

"But it's not your fault. You weren't the accountant."

For a brief second, she thought she might leap across the table and lick his face, changing the subject via shock and awe. Then again, gross. What was happening to her?

"Still. No, thanks." She wanted to say yes. Why couldn't she say yes?

"Well, if you change your mind—"

"Yeah, yeah, of course." She began nodding so hard her forehead began to throb. "I probably should get back to the shop. Thanks for the tea."

COMMERCIAL BREAK

Of course it was me, darlings!

Here in the Ethereal Embrace, miracles are like vacation days—use 'em or lose 'em—and our young Bree needed a swift kick in the intervention, if you know what I mean. Our book lover was losing her rose-colored optimism, so I spoke to her.

Fine, yes, I scared her. But look where she ended up. Even if she's a bit rattled, she won't stay that way (especially not with the Brawny Paper Towel Man's arms available to keep her steady, am I right? (Time-out: Judy insists I clarify that, no, we cannot see the future. But I say, really, do you need more Bree + Witt clues?))

Back to the subject at hand: the Bree Miracle. You heard what she said last night—that those who are hurting turn toward love. She knows of which she speaks. Give her story time to unfold.

Now, on to the money and the debt. It's awful. You're right. In fact, I believe I died of shame. Doctors can give it whatever fancy name they like, but I call my fatal blow, "devastated beyond repair."

However, let me be clear: I'm not ready to discuss it yet for reasons I shall not enumerate. You will understand when you need to understand. Again, I remind you to give it time.

For now, I need to lie down. Miracles are handy but they take everything you've got.

Mwah! Mwah! Mwah!

20

20 hours after stopping the sale...

Laney wasn't calm, she only looked that way for her sister's sake. In fact, she'd managed to transform her body into a metabolic pinball machine, packing all her anxieties into a tiny steel ball slamming around her insides. *Ping! Ping! Tilt!*

She'd had to unbutton her pants, she was so stress-bloated.

So, no, she wasn't feeling as coolheaded as she'd let Bree believe. Yet, of the two of them, her sister deserved the wider freak-out zone. If the shop closed, Laney could fly away, but Bree was stuck in the jobless, directionless mess she'd tried so earnestly to avoid.

Tuck had called again last night, too, and it was getting harder to justify her absence with vague declarations, like "I can't leave yet" or "I still need to be here." He wanted real answers.

"Why, Laney? Your mom's already sold the store. Hire some movers and get out of there. It's not rocket science."

"Golly, thanks, Einstein." She didn't actually say that. No, she being her wilting-in-Tuck's-presence self, attempted more superficial weaseling. "I can't explain, it's just important I stay."

"I want a date. When are you coming home?"

"Are you planning to leave for vacation or something?"

"I mean it, Laney. Do you hear me laughing?"

This was Tuck-speak for "I'm not joking." But in that moment, it hit her that he never did joke or laugh. She couldn't remember the last time they laughed together. The man who made a point of signaling seriousness by highlighting his sudden lack of bonhomie was neither breezy nor light. And if you never laugh anyway, how was saying "Do you hear me laughing?" a monumental announcement? The arrogance made her want to tear her hair out.

She was exhausted, and so unable to focus, she thought her eyeballs might have actually exchanged sockets. Regardless, she ignored every last ounce of better judgment and said, "Actually, Tuck, I'm not sure I've ever heard you laugh."

"What?" he hollered. "I'm a frickin' barrel of laughs."

That second part she knew he'd said with a straight face—she didn't need to see his flaccid expression to recognize it. "Okay, one—being the source of laughter is not the same thing as actual, physical laughter. And, two—you're wrong."

"Oh, is that so, smarty-pants?"

"You say 'That's funny.' You say 'Nice one.' I heard one of the mechanics tell you a joke—that one about the broken pencils—and you said, quote, 'Ha.'"

"Duh. That's laughing."

"Uh-uh. Those are statements. Laughter is an exclamation. In fact, grammatically speaking, what you do doesn't even require an exclamation point."

"Ooh, I'm being schooled by the grammar police. So sue me."

Laney wanted so badly to clarify that police don't file lawsuits, nor do they teach third-grade English. Instead, she closed her mouth and went silent.

"Laney?" he said.

"Yeah?"

"I feel like you're quitting me."

As if receiving a text directly to the logic center of her brain, Laney heard her mind go, *Ping!* When had her nonlaughing, thickheaded husband become so astute? Because once again, he was right. She was quitting—not just Tire Stud, or California, or even their marriage—she was quitting Tuck. Quitting everything she had thought she got from him, from escape to purpose to ambition.

This whole three-week exercise had been her brain finally forcing her to stop. And look.

What she saw was this: Tuck no longer provided liberation; their life together was a sentence she continued to place on herself. His dreams weren't also hers; she'd merely borrowed them for lack of her own. He didn't owe her more; she was in debt to herself. And though he was far from a perfect man or a perfect husband, he at least deserved her honesty.

Relationships don't survive without truth.

She closed her eyes and told herself to act like a grown-up. "Just give me a little more time to figure things out. I'm sure everything will be fine."

Later, she stood in the shop, grieving her cowardice. She was weak and pitiful and a liar.

Then again, was she? Maybe things really could be fine. Maybe, when this hoopla with the bookstore was all over, she'd fly to Oakland and tell Tuck she was unhappy and they'd refocus on their relationship, fix it, get happy again.

"But you never liked it. Don't give me that crap."

Laney looked up to find a young mother with a phone on her cheek and a preschooler on her heels. "You say that now, but last night when I asked you what you thought, you said, 'It's fine.'"

She put the phone to her chest and asked Laney, "Do you gift wrap?" then didn't wait for a response before returning to her call with, "No, *fine* does not mean *it's fine*, it means you hate it. It was the same with the house in Vail, and it was the same when my colorist changed my undertones from cinnamon to bronze, and it's the same with this couch."

Phone to chest: "We need a birthday gift for a four-year-old."

Phone to cheek: "I already returned it."

Phone to chest: "Anything you think is great. Just make it around a hundred dollars."

Phone to cheek: "I can call them back, but don't say you like it if you don't."

Phone to chest: "Yes? Is there something else you need?"

Laney: "Girl, boy, or gender neutral?"

Phone indeterminate: "I said do whatever you want."

Laney mumbled under her breath on her way to the children's section. "That clears things up immensely. I can't believe your husband doesn't understand you."

Sometime later, Bree returned looking more discombobulated than when she'd left.

"What's with the—" Laney waved her fingers around her head. "You get into a scrap with a badger or something?"

"Why does everyone keep asking me that?" She stormed off toward the restroom with Laney close behind. This story sounded too good to miss.

"So, were you in the lake when it happened, or did it jump at you from the bushes?"

"What are you talking about?"

"The badger. Water attack or land assault?"

"God, Laney, I'm just stressed. Because, gee, it's not as if anything's happening around here these days."

Laney reached for a clump of Bree's snarls. "No, this is definitely an attack of some sort. How much blood have you lost? Any loud ringing in your ears?"

"Badgers aren't water animals, you know." She reached for the restroom door and opened. "Oh my god! What died in here?"

"My colon." Laney blushed. She should have hung a warning flag on the handle. "You're not the only one under stress, you know. I'm—" There were only so many bathroom euphemisms a person could come up with. "Let's just say it's Groundhog Day, but Punxsutawney Phil refuses to budge."

"And you accuse me of having animal problems." Bree opened

the door wide enough to examine her shock-evoking appearance from afar. She tried to smooth her hair, wiped the makeup streaks from beneath her eyes. "I'm a mess."

When she turned, Laney saw fat tears about to drop from both eyes. "Hey, there! No! No more tears today. We've used up our daily allotment. We can cry again tomorrow." She ushered her to the nearest bench and sat them both down. "We have to pace ourselves or we'll burn out."

"Oh heavens!" Bree's laugh cut with scorn. "We can't let that happen. How will we file for bankruptcy if we're too burned out to pick up the phone?"

A phone call probably wasn't the proper way to file for bankruptcy, but that wasn't a point Laney needed to make right now. "I'm saying we have to keep going until we understand the situation and our options. And to do that, we need to stay strong."

Bree sniffled and wiped her nose on the hem of her T-shirt. "I just made a moron of myself in front of Witt."

"You were drinking at—" she checked her watch "—eleven o'clock?"

"Of course not! I couldn't keep walking anymore and I was too upset to come here, so I ended up at the Lady. Then Witt might have gotten a little bit flirty but, really, what do I know, because I can't tell when a man is flirting any better than I can see the color of a person's underwear through their pants. I got all embarrassed and weird, and I think I may have given him a nipple parade."

"Macy's Thanksgiving Day or small-town Fourth of July?"

"I didn't look. But my best guess is 'Seventy-Six Trombones'-style."

"Wowza."

"No kidding. It was a dumpster fire."

"What did Witt say to get you so riled up?"

Bree took a steadying breath. "That he's a CPA."

"He's a what?" Laney recoiled just far enough to give her sister the are-you-for-real? special. "An accountant! Did he offer any advice? Can he help us?"

"In what universe would I ask him to do that? It's mortifying enough that we're going to have to put Going Out of Business signs in the window, let alone admit to the cute guy across the street that our bookshop sank forty-five thousand dollars into the hole without any of us noticing!" She crossed her arms, defiant, but not before Laney noticed the display of lights across her sister's chest.

"I have just two things to say to you, so listen up. One, if you let your vanity get in the way of accepting help when it's needed, you're making a gigantic mistake." She meant it. She could feel her heartbeat in her ears, she meant it so completely. If only she could follow her own advice.

"And?"

"And, nothing. Haven't you learned by now that a job like this requires several doses of humiliation a day? At Tire Stud, I put doughnuts on a tray like Betty Draper and pretend that I like it."

"I thought you said two things? Laney, I'm so sad."

"I know. Me, too." Laney reached for her sister's hand and squeezed. "But how's this for a deal? You didn't let up on me until I did the right thing and promised to get the truth out of Mom, so now I promise not to let up on you until we know what we're up against and try everything we can think of to save the store. You stepped up first, and now it's my turn."

Bree laid her head on Laney's shoulder. "Okay. Deal. But I can't promise I'll be easy."

Laney chuckled. Instead of answering, she knocked her knuckles gently on top of Bree's head, a sister's promise, noogie-style.

They sat in the silence for a moment until Bree said, "What's number two?"

"What's what now?"

"You said you had two things to tell me. So what's the second?"

"Oh." Laney smirked. She remembered. "The second thing

is you really need to wear a different bra under that T-shirt. You're like a walking marquee. A billboard over Times Square."

"Stop it!" Bree slugged her.

"An alert from the Emergency Broadcast System. The Rockettes' Christmas Spectacular."

"I will punch you in the boob if you don't shut up."

"Breaker, breaker, one-nine, we've got a caravan of high beams on the move. Take cover."

21

Thom didn't see any reason to get out of bed. Not when everything hurt, and nothing—not medication, nor food, nor person—could rescue him from his depths. Ibuprofen eased the throbbing in his ankle, but without the distraction of physical pain, his mind was left free to steal its way into forbidden emotional territory—where the confidence he'd fed himself during the battle for Elliot's legacy was but a paper tiger, and where, even in death, the man he'd loved without fail continued to break his heart.

There was no money. There hadn't been an estate. Irma, the source of all the tension in his twenty years with Elliot, hadn't carelessly thrown the Rainbow to the first bidder. She'd released it to the only bidder. More, despite Elliot having left her mired in debt, she intended to split her piddling proceeds with Thom.

He rolled toward the wall, unable to face a reality in which Irma was a good witch, and Elliot lay dead beneath the spinning house.

These past few weeks, he'd frequently awoken in the dark to an unfamiliar sensation. The type of occurrence that daytime allows no space for, with its busyness and hunger and worry, but which capitalizes on midnight's silence to make itself known. As he lay in its haze, he sometimes named the sensation "purpose," attributing its appearance to his fight for Elliot's legacy.

On more exhausting occasions, he called it "grit." Once, he even flew close to the sun and dared to name it "happy."

Now he called it delusion.

What he felt wasn't the presence of something new, but the absence of the familiar. He missed his rage, his anger, his despair, and that was what he now called on, as he sank into the terrible, awful memory he so desperately needed.

The fall. The screams.

Speakers blaring. *Medical emergency, Gate F17.*

A pair of white sneakers against gray carpet.

The hot, electrical smell of the defibrillator.

Elliot's glassy, dead eyes.

He died on the floor of Miami International Airport. They'd just stepped off the plane after two luxury weeks in Peru, the trip Thom presented as his final ultimatum: join me or lose me.

In Lima, they'd held their breath and made a wish on the Bridge of Sighs, kissed beneath the trees at the Parque del Amor, indulged themselves with ceviche and *picarones* and *anticuchos* on the narrow streets of Barranco until their buttons popped.

They hiked a postage stamp of Amazon land. Visited the Nazca Lines. Cusco. The Inca Trail. Machu Picchu. Lake Titicaca.

All the while, Elliot's blood cells began an aggressive round of bumper cars deep within his veins, a silent game with deadly consequences.

Elliot was tired on the flight out of Lima. "I can't keep my eyes open. The travel yesterday took it out of me."

"You slept nearly the whole trip down the mountain." They'd ended their tour at Lake Titicaca, the world's highest, bluest lake, in a room on a rocky hillside where sky met water. It was every bit as lovely as he'd imagined it would be, but all things come to an end, and on their last day they descended to the town of Juliaca in a tourist transport van, where they boarded a small plane bound for Lima. It was a full-day trip, followed by an eight-hour wait at the terminal before at last boarding their international flight to Miami.

"Have you been drinking enough water?" Thom instinctively signaled the flight attendant.

Elliot shooed her away. "I don't want to have to get up for the restroom."

Later, a doctor would explain that two sedentary days combined with the extreme change in elevation most likely led to Deep Vein Thrombosis, DVT, a blood clot left behind by the bumper cars. "When he stood to walk off the plane," the doctor said, "he gave the clot the clear path it needed to shoot straight to his heart."

They weren't even out of the gate area when he collapsed.

Thom told their friends, "I thought he was having a heart attack. He was gray almost immediately. I slapped him, trying to bring him to, as if he'd fainted."

"Did anyone help?" they asked. "Don't they have those defibrillator things in airports?"

They'd tried to defibrillate him. The voltage did nothing but leave the sick, sweet smell of ozone arcing through the air.

When he pictured the scene now, he focused on a white pair of sneakers against the gray carpet. They belonged to a nurse on her way to her flight, who immediately began CPR. What they didn't know, of course, was that the clot had already killed him.

What was her name? Thom spent entire days trying to remember. He had so many regrets with which to torment himself, yet this one stood out. The nurse had told him. It was a lovely name, and he'd let it slip away. All that remained were her white shoes. This was more than Elliot left. In his wake, he'd left a hole, a negative, a vacuum. The nurse's shoes were at least something, a tangible, functional sign of life, but Elliot left debt, which Thom soon learned was not so much a financial statement as an emotional one. Debt was deceit—lies upon lies of things purchased but not owned.

It was enough to make him sit up and grab for his crutches. He hobbled to the guest room and stood at the closet where he'd so tenderly packed away Elliot's sweaters. He could touch them, smell them, pull them over his head and feel them on his skin, but that didn't make them real. Not if they were purchased on borrowed money that grew into debt that became a secret that became a lie that could never be untold.

He began pulling them from the shelf, boxes crashing to the wooden floors, lids flying, wool and cotton strewn across the room.

When there were no more boxes to throw, he returned to their bedroom, where Elliot's shoes lay tucked in protective sleeves and slotted into tiny shoe condominiums. He ripped them from their hidey-holes and threw them, one by one, some hitting the bedroom wall, some scuttling down the hallway out of sight. Pieces of a deceitful partner Thom never wanted to see again.

The bedrooms undone, he navigated his way through the mess toward Elliot's desk in the corner of the living room. The computer certainly wasn't paid for, but he'd wait until he was walking again to enjoy smashing it to bits on the sidewalk. There were notepads and pens and doodads, none of it consequential enough to bother eliminating. He opened the top drawer, the middle, the bottom. The bottom drawer was where he'd been throwing Elliot's mail—the credit card statements and bank notices of a dead man. A stack fatter than a handful. Now he wanted to see every last charge, every last lie. He emptied the drawer onto the floor with a satisfying *splat.*

It was an action, he would soon come to learn, with life-altering consequences.

22

4 days after stopping the sale...

Why was it so mortifying to ask Witt for help? Bree was still at the shop, shuffling papers, though they'd closed hours ago, and she'd gotten nowhere. Basic money-management skills weren't her problem; she kept herself on a budget, got her bills paid on time, had bought a house. But the puzzle in front of her was so much more complex—cash in versus cash out plus all that stuff that happened in the middle. What the hell was an offset?

She sat in the back room beneath a flickering lamp, trying to solve what was beyond her—because she'd rather wither away at this very desk than expose how little she actually understood about the bookstore where she'd worked her whole life. It felt as hypocritical as voting for a candidate based entirely on looks, then complaining about their policies. Or like the woman she and Laney met in Oakland who swore California was the absolute best place in the whole world, then had to admit she'd only left the state when skiing over the border into Nevada in Lake Tahoe.

"Why would I go anywhere else?" she'd said. "We have everything here."

"Except for everything you don't know you don't have," Laney had answered.

Bree hadn't known anything close to what she needed to know about the Rainbow to try to save it. And now the one person capable of helping her unravel the mess was also the last person to whom she wanted to look ignorant.

"Oh, sure," she said into the darkness. "I can run the store. I mean, who needs to understand accounting—the numbers just work themselves out, right?" Irma had been smart not to leave the Rainbow in Bree's incompetent hands.

Operating capital. Net sales. Capitalized depreciation. Fish waltz. Brambleberry stew. They all made as much sense as the last.

Laney said she was letting her vanity get in the way. Laney was right, but if anyone knew the allure of not wanting to answer for one's stupidities, it was her sister.

She looked down at the copy of *Small Business Accounting First Aid* she'd pulled from the shelves. It read: "This chapter will provide you an overview of quarterly accounting tasks, including tax estimates, quarterly payments, and preparing a revised annual P&L estimate."

Did they keep a hammer in the bookshop? She may as well knock herself in the head.

"I'm glad you called." The next morning, Witt arrived at the shop with two mugs of fresh coffee and a calculator capable of launching the space shuttle.

Bree accepted his generosity with a meek smile. "I don't know why it took me so long to accept your help." The coffee was rich, like a Colombian mountainside tumbled through Witt's press pot into her cup. "Except that I don't like looking like an idiot."

"Are you a CPA, too?" He smiled at her from behind his mug. "Because we really, really hate making mistakes. It's sort of a no-no in our profession… Accidentally reverse a few digits and send the company into Chapter 11."

"No wonder you changed careers." Bree's brain, ever the miscreant, pictured her sipping this same cup of coffee between Witt's bedsheets. *Stop it.*

Eventually, he asked her to show him everything they'd uncovered, which so far consisted of scattered piles on the floor and Laney's half-constructed binder.

"But you haven't come up with any financial statements? P&L reports, or balance sheets—even tax returns would be helpful."

She shook her head. "Sorry. I would've assumed Elliot kept that on the store computer, but there's nothing."

"Any chance he kept them on his home computer?"

She promised to get a hold of Thom to find out.

Without any of the historical documents, Witt explained that they were going to have to try to re-create them. "It's not ideal. There's always a chance we'll miss something. But it's better than what you have now, and at least, you'll gain insight into whether Irma is right about the debt or not."

"We've been asking her for information and she refuses to cough it up. She must have Elliot's documents, though. She wouldn't know the store was in so much trouble without them." Bree and Laney were in a near panic, trying to rescue their mother from a burning building, and she refused to move, waiting for the walls to fall in. "I don't know why we keep trying, but we do."

Witt looked up from his calculating. "You're family. Families are a sticky mess."

They still had a couple of hours until the store opened, so she agreed to run over to Irma's for additional documents while Witt stayed put to review what they'd found so far.

"I'll tell my mom to be nice to you since you're being so nice to us."

"I'm a fan of her daughters."

Had he meant *daughters* or *daughter's*? It was impossible to answer, but regardless, two full blocks, she fixated on a single apostrophe, her entire future dangling at the edge of a financial cliff while she drew mental bubble hearts around the cute distillery guy who may or may not have just complimented her. She was starting to sound like a Jane Austen character. Not one of the redeemable ones like Elizabeth or Jane but a tiresome, ridiculous one like their mother. If she started fretting about her "poor nerves," someone was going to have to do something drastic.

She opened her mom's front door without knocking and found Laney in the kitchen, who said, "Lady Irma won't get out of bed, so I'm cleaning out the fridge to keep from strangling her with a pillow."

Bree looked at the empty trash bin beside her in front of the open refrigerator door. "You haven't thrown anything away."

"Third time I've done it this week." She pulled out a carton of yogurt. "Can this stuff really expire? I mean, isn't it technically expired to begin with?"

Bree wrangled her sister's full attention and closed the fridge. "Mom obviously has Elliot's bookkeeping files stashed away somewhere, and if they're not at the shop..."

They turned in unison and hollered, "Mom!"

Bree opened the bedroom door. Laney pulled back the sheets. "Up and at 'em, young lady. Let's go. Early bird gets the bookworm."

Irma grabbed for her pillow. "I am not a child and this is my house. I will stay in bed as long as I want to."

Laney looked at Bree. "You get her shoulders. I'll get her feet."

"Who's gonna turn on the shower?"

"Whoever has a free hand when we get there."

They pulled. Irma struggled. "Leave me alone. I'm grieving."

"Oxygen is good medicine," said Laney, which made Bree giggle, having heard Irma say the same to Laney on approximately three thousand school mornings.

Bree added, "You can't really know how you feel until you're on your feet, Mom."

This made Laney snort, and now they were both laughing, except for Irma, who kicked and grabbed for an anchor.

"An active body is the best way to fight a low spirit."

"Better to get lost between the pages than between the sheets."

"Even bad books make for good toilet paper."

Bree looked at Laney. "Gross. That's not a saying."

"It is now."

"No, it's not."

"Enough!" Irma pounded her fists on the mattress. "You've caused enough trouble, the both of you. Please, finally, just leave me alone." Her anger sucked every last wisp of merriment from the room. Bree collapsed onto the side of the bed, Laney on the other.

"You keep fighting for something that's not going to happen." Irma sat up against the headboard, rumpled and red-faced. "Even if we could wipe out every cent of Elliot's debt, the bookshop isn't salvageable. It's become too expensive."

This part Bree refused to believe. "If it's too expensive, how do the other local independents survive? Magers & Quinn. Moon Palace Books. They're both within a few miles of us and they've managed."

"That's them," Irma sighed. "Not us."

"Prove it." Laney didn't appear angry but neither did she sound as if she were going to let her mom refuse their demands. "Show us the numbers. You must have them or you couldn't have sold the shop."

"The Vandaveers were buying the location, not the business."

"Even so." Laney stood and began to straighten the room, channeling her frustration, folding discarded clothing and pairing strewn shoes. "You had to get the forty-five-thousand-in-debt number from somewhere. Where are the financial statements? We've torn the filing cabinets apart at the shop, so we know they're not there."

"What does it matter? Elliot's dead. The Rainbow is going to close. The creditors will get whatever they can."

Bree shot to her feet. "It matters because you might be wrong.

Have you ever thought of that?" She grabbed a corner of the bedspread and pulled it straight with the force of a tractor. "I've got a friend who's a CPA and he's willing to look everything over for us. But he can't do that if he doesn't have all the information he needs."

Irma became angrier than before. "You plan to give a complete stranger access to my private financial information? Without my permission?"

Laney dropped a stack of folded clothing on the dresser and left the room.

Bree didn't flinch, having mired herself too deeply in Irma's plight to escape now. "He's not a stranger. He's a friend. A friend who's a CPA."

Irma, having no cover under which to hide, got to her feet, pulling items from the stack of clothes Laney had just straightened. "You don't have any right." She pulled on a pair of jeans beneath her nightgown.

Laney appeared in the doorway waving a fistful of papers. "Got 'em! Let's go."

Bree wasn't sure what Laney got, but she knew enough to hustle. Irma grabbed for her shirt as she passed, but she swerved just in time.

"That is my private property!" Their mom followed them out of the bedroom, trying to tuck her shin-length nightie into her waistband before recognizing the futility of the task. "I do not grant my permission to show anyone that information!"

Laney was already opening the front door. "You can try to stop us, but you're gonna have to put on your clothes first!"

Bree slammed the door closed and they ran like children down the street. "Are you sure you found what we need?"

"Nope, but I've got a pretty good hunch. These papers were in a folder titled 'This Is the Way the World Ends.'"

The Book Haters' Book Club Newsletter

Issue #253

June 2010

This month: Books for Haters who need a shot of paperback courage.

My Over the Rainbow cofounder, Irma, and I have a long-standing argument about which of us is the braver human being. Irma says I am, but anyone who's met us knows she's wrong. Irma Bedford is brave; I'm just fabulous. And because this is my newsletter, I get the last word.

Since we're approaching the Fourth of July, the day our forefathers chose to tell King George "Enough!" I'm recommending two very different books about courage.

The first is a book we've kept in stock since it was published in 1994, titled *Healing After Loss*, by Martha W. Hickman. I'm a brick wall of a man who doesn't like to admit to things like feelings, so when we sold our first copy to a woman grieving the death of her husband, I'm sure I handed over her purchase and said something easy like "I'm sorry for your loss." Then we sold more copies, and more, and I still didn't think about that little book until one of our customers returned to tell us just how helpful it had been. "You need to recommend this to everyone who comes in looking for a book about grief," they said.

Haters, I just looked at the numbers, and we've sold at least one copy per week since the day we got it in stock. Maybe you'd expect that for a runaway bestseller, but I bet you've never even heard about this book until now. I bet you didn't know it's small enough to fit in the palm of your hand. I bet you didn't know a woman going through a divorce told me, "It gave me the courage to feel sad."

The courage to feel sad? Remember, I am just a dummy with sponge cake for a brain, so until she said that I didn't even know that being sad could be an act of courage. But take it from the Rainbow customers who keep returning to tell us how much this book means to them: we may not get to choose what happens in our lives, but we can choose not to act like fools in the face of our hardships. (The author puts it better.)

In a completely different interpretation of bravery, last week, a young woman bought a copy of *Piano for Dummies* so she could play "Happy Birthday" at her grandmother's 80th birthday celebration. She said she'd never touched the black & whites in her life, but she loved her grandma and her grandma loved the piano. We wish her luck, and we applaud her courage for taking on something new!

What subjects are you brave enough to learn? How about making yourself a new bookshelf with *Woodworking for Dummies*? Expand your horizons with a travel guide to any country on the continent of your choice. Personally, my eye was recently drawn to a copy of the *Lonely Planet Peru* with its beautiful picture of Machu Picchu on the cover.

Have you thought about learning French?

Need to brush up on your personal budgeting?

How about finally organizing all of your photos with a how-to guide on scrapbooking?

Go for it. Be brave. We're here to help.

—Elliot

Last Hope for the Haters

Books are like people. The ones who stay on the shelf look like beautiful porcelain dolls, but it's the page-worn ones that have the best stories.

23

"The state of my house is a reflection of my mood, so consider yourself warned." Thom moved aside from the door and swept an arm across the disaster that was his foyer/living room. Having a small house had always served his need to keep a tidy home. "We don't have space for mess," he loved to say, picking up Elliot's strewn books and magazines as he bustled. Now the space reflected the chaos he'd been trying to stifle for years.

The look on Bree's face said she wasn't sure the mess suited Thom. "I—" She entered carefully, as if she might step in something. "Well, I guess I'm here to check on you." Her eyes roamed the blast zone, eager to judge the extent of his disaster. She wanted to ask what the hell happened but didn't know how—he could see it in the way she held her purse close to her hip, her smile too broad, her gestures too calculated.

"Come in," he instructed. "My condition isn't contagious."

His crutches made navigating the paper-strewn floor tricky, difficult for the rubber nubs to find purchase, and he'd already slipped once this morning, landing hard on his injured ankle. The pain reconfirmed his emotional state, searing and red and in want of retribution.

He sat in the leather craftsman, raising the footrest to elevate his injury. Bree squatted and began to straighten.

"Stop!" Thom didn't mean to bark, but he no longer had patience for subtlety. "I find the agony of living in disarray therapeutic."

"Alright. Thom—" She perched on the couch across from him, full of concern and clutching her purse ever closer. "Are you sure you're okay?"

"Of course not. I never claimed to be. I am in physical and emotional agony and no matter what treatments I take, the ache only worsens." He pulled a lap blanket across his legs. Outside, the summer heat was fat with humidity, but inside, the air-conditioning left an invalid chilled. "Enough about me, though. How are you?"

"I'm fine, I suppose. Are you sure you don't want me to pick up some of the paper on the floor?"

"Why would I want you to do that?"

"Isn't it dangerous? You being on crutches and all?"

"Very. I've fallen once already today."

"Thom!"

"Bree." This was becoming increasingly unpleasant. "I am aware of the state my house is in. I did warn you from the beginning, did I not?"

"Yes." She lowered her head, shamed by her own compassion.

He knew she wanted to ask, "Why?" Why were there torn papers and files thrown about his living room like leaves to the wind? Why was he adamant she leave it alone? Those were not questions he wished to answer. "What can I do for you?"

She took one last glance at the surroundings. "If you're sure you don't need anything, then I guess I just wanted to tell you we have a CPA looking at the shop's finances. To confirm whether Irma's right about the amount of debt or not, and to learn about our options. Supposing we have any."

"Kudos. Good for you for not sitting back while everything falls to pieces."

"Thank you." It came out more as a question than a statement, for which he couldn't blame her. He sounded at least patronizing, if not sarcastic and even accusatory.

"I should tell you, however," he said, "she's correct to worry about the debt. It will likely crush her and the Rainbow."

Bree's eyes widened in accordance with her surprise.

"I found Elliot's files. It seems he had been working down the bookshop's debt for a while. At one point, it was close to a hundred thousand. Impressive, no?"

She closed her eyes and tried to shake the confusion from her face. "If you have new information, we'd be really grateful if you let us take a look. Irma has the shop's financial statements. Laney and I found them in her home office." At this, Bree let out a quiet laugh, a memory she didn't plan to share. "Anyway, she brought several years' worth of files to the bookshop for the accountant. She claims it's everything she has. But if you have more..."

It shouldn't have felt so satisfying to be in possession of something Irma knew nothing about. But it was, and he took a moment to enjoy it. "He was actually using his personal inheritance to pay the bookshop's debt." That was among the treasures he'd found in Elliot's desk drawer—a spreadsheet compiling every asset in his name, along with its estimated value and date of sale. To his credit, Elliot had been careful not to touch or borrow against anything he owned with Thom. He hadn't mortgaged the house, hadn't suggested Thom sell his Mercedes for something less expensive. He had, however, slowly and effectively eaten away at tens of thousands of dollars in assets he'd kept secret from the beginning.

His father's rare coin collection fetched nearly eleven thousand dollars. His mother's mink coat brought a thousand, and her ermine stole three hundred. He'd sold rare books. Hermès scarves. His comic books and baseball cards. A Pairpoint lamp. The jewelry that once graced his mother's neck, ears, and wrists—a Mikimoto pearl choker, two-carat diamond studs, a gold-and-ruby tennis bracelet—were listed at several thousand each.

It made Thom's stomach lurch again. He'd known Elliot's inheritance was sizable. When they decided to buy their house together, he'd claimed to have used much of it to pay off Thom's existing mortgage so they could move into their new home debt-free. "For us," he'd said. "For our future."

Elliot hadn't written a will or made arrangements for his estate, but one single act of generosity guaranteed Thom a house and home for as long as he wanted. It was a benevolent cruelty he didn't know if he'd ever be able to forgive.

"I don't understand," Bree said. "He was using your money to pay down the Rainbow's debt?"

"Aha!" Thom thrust a finger in the air, a distinctly Sherlock Holmesian gesture he would never have made if he'd felt master of his own sanity or affairs. "But that's the quandary, no? Is it *our* money if Elliot never blessed it as such? Legally speaking, we were not married, and as Minnesota does not recognize domestic partnerships, I hold no indisputable claim over his estate. I may have considered my possessions shared property, but in the eyes of the law, what was his is his, and only those items in both our names—the house, the car, the season tickets to the Guthrie Theater—are mine."

"But didn't you know about everything he was selling? I mean, his mother's mink coat—you would have noticed that hanging in your closet."

He wondered if he could use the word *alas* here without sounding like an erudite ass. "I'm afraid there are many things I never knew about Elliot."

Bree sank onto the couch, deflated and once more disappointed by the man she'd loved so dearly. It hurt to see Thom echo her feelings about Elliot.

"It should've been your money," she said finally. "I don't care about legality. It was his, so now it should be yours."

A quiet fell while they each muddled in their thoughts. Thom didn't know what his role here was supposed to be—was he to play the victim of a deceptive partner? Or was he expected to act as a resolute optimist, determined to overcome the adversity of life? Maybe she needed him to comfort her, to reassure her of Elliot's love and good intentions?

Grief was too messy to be anything but exhausting.

"I'm absolving you of paying off any more of what we owe," Bree said. "I know I don't have the right to do that, so this may be a symbolic gesture at best, but I want you to know. It's the bookshop's debt. Not yours." She puffed briefly, happy to be capable of such generosity. "Although," she deflated anew, "I don't suppose that helps any when it comes to Elliot's estate."

Thom poked at a Mastercard past-due notice with his crutch, leaving a satisfying smudge on the paper. He was embarrassed to admit he hadn't yet informed creditors of Elliot's death, meaning the bills kept coming and the interest growing. He'd simply been too angry to deal. "I presume the creditors will come for his share of whatever's left after Irma closes the shop."

"If she closes it," Bree corrected.

"Of course." He could allow her this one dream, unlikely though it may be.

"I know it sounds silly for me to hold on to hope, but I can't help it." She paused for a breath. "I'm not sure what Elliot told you. My dad was in and out of jail for beating my mom. And my mom was in and out of rehab. So, without the Rainbow, I don't know who I am. The school bus dropped Laney off in front of the store, and one day, I followed her because I knew wherever she was going had to be better than everything waiting for me at home."

Thom had heard portions of Bree's story, though mainly its scaffolding. That Bree had practically adopted Laney and Irma and Elliot as her own by the time the state formally stripped her parents of their rights. That her father was doing a life sentence for armed robbery gone tragically wrong. That her mother left her alone one too many nights for authorities to ignore—especially given that Irma had taken to calling them almost daily to report the neglect. He'd respected Irma for that. The list of her good qualities was longer than perhaps he'd allowed himself to see.

"It's like, I am the Rainbow and it is me." She took in a heavy breath that turned without warning into heaving tears. "Oh my god." She rocked, cradling her head on hands and knees. "I can't handle this."

His crutches made for an awkward hustle, but he managed to cross the debris on his floor and land at her side. He rubbed her back quietly, aware there were no words.

"Everything is upside down. We thought we were doing a good thing, cratering the Vandaveer deal. I mean, we did, right?"

Yes, yes, their intentions had been good.

"But we ruined Irma's chance at getting out of there with any money at all. I've probably damaged my relationship with her forever, but she was selling the one thing—the *one place*—that saved my life. Just selling it! No explanation. No warning. Of course I had to do something."

Of course. Of course.

Thom's back was cramping, not fully recovered from his fall through the wine crate onto the pavement. "I'm sorry, hon, but I need to lie back for a minute. Keep talking." He stretched out against the stack of throw pillows, which, he was finally willing to admit after a years-long battle with Elliot, was too many for a couch this size. He pulled out the most unwieldy pillow of the pile and threw it to the floor.

Bree went on, "The saddest thing of all is that, even if we are able to keep the bookshop going, Irma's never going to feel the same about it. It hasn't been the same for her since Elliot died. I tried to make it a happy place after losing him, but the two of them were just so—you know. Just so—"

"Just so Irmiot," Thom said. Elliot had hated that name. Accused him of using it as a passive-aggressive way of calling Irma an idiot. Which Thom wasn't. He'd been calling them both idiots. He regretted it now.

"Irmiot." Bree snorted through her sobs. "That's fantastic."

"Isn't it, though? During my darker moods, I sometimes pictured them picking nits off each other like apes at the zoo. No matter how close the rest of us got to them, they still only trusted each other with their most intimate moments."

Bree reeled. "You're not about to make some big revelation about catching them in bed together, are you? Please tell me you're the only one he was sleeping with."

Thom would have reeled at her the way she had at him—if his back weren't spasming itself into a steel rod. "Good lord, girl, I said 'intimate,' not sexual. No. They were not sleeping together. They never even consummated the marriage, as far as I know."

"Their what?" Bree jumped to her feet, bouncing the couch with such force Thom squealed in pain.

"Aaaaaeeee!"

"Oh god, I'm so sorry!" She tried to help him sit up but that only made it worse, and he squealed again. "I thought you were serious about them being married. Don't joke like that!"

She began throwing pillows willy-nilly behind his neck, under his knees.

"I wasn't joking. I found their marriage certificate in Elliot's files. They've been married since 1979. Which means I finally have an answer—"

She tried to put a pillow beneath his feet but grabbed his ankle, sending his pain receptors into full tilt.

"WHY ELLIOT WOULD NEVER AGREE TO GET MARRIED GODDAMN IT ALL TO HELL QUIT TOUCHING ME YOU MONSTER!"

Bree drew her hands to her mouth, shocked, frightened, and again bursting with tears.

"I'M SORRY!" Thom couldn't not scream. "PLEASE DON'T CRY!"

It was too late. She'd sunk to the floor, sobbing, devastated and confused, and Thom was too far away and too physically twisted to offer comfort.

"Bree," he pleaded, doing his very best to stifle the anguish in his throat, "give me a minute to recover. You can get my muscle relaxants. That will help. Then we can talk to your mom or the CPA or whoever we need to call to get to the bottom of this whole, bloody mess."

How he wished the list of sold jewelry was the only secret he'd found in those files.

24

Tanking the Vandaveer deal may have crushed Irma's hopes of retirement, but it'd done just the opposite to the Rainbow's customer traffic. By six o'clock, Laney's feet throbbed and she had a headache running up her spine and over the crest of her skull. She'd run the shop end to end a hundred times, juggled phone calls between ringing up purchases, and told the same story to every customer who asked: No, they weren't selling out to the condos. Yes, they did hope to stay open.

The last time she said it, she felt her voice change, stronger and with no shift in pitch, which could only mean one thing: she meant it. She didn't want the Rainbow to close.

Right this minute, however, she needed a break. Irma had joined Witt in the back room to crunch numbers, and Bree had vowed to return from Thom's house over an hour ago, so she flipped the sign in the doorway to See You Tomorrow and walked out. Disappointed customers could come back later. She was going to head to the park and watch some baseball.

She'd seen a kid in the store wearing a Nilssen Mortuary jersey, and when she told him she'd played on the same team back in the day, his mother suggested she come watch their game against Johnson's DIY Dog & Car Wash over at the Cedar Playfields.

It sounded like the perfect escape.

She walked the six blocks from bookshop to field and ignored two of Tuck's phone calls. He'd all but given up texting her—too easy to dismiss. A ringing phone demanded a response—hang up or pick up, but make your choice.

Ignore. She pressed it for the third time in as many minutes, each time cursing herself for doing so. The veil she'd hung between Oakland and Minneapolis was beginning to tear, and Tuck, needy and impatient by nature, was becoming angry and desperate. She had to get her head on straight.

At the field, the scoreboard read Home: 2 Away: 0. Miniature black-shirted bodies speckled the bases and the outfield while a bench full of blue shirts cheered for their own: a player at home plate holding a bat the size of their torso. Were ten-year-olds really this small? At that age, Laney recalled taking on a certain swagger, a soon-to-be fifth-grader, oldest in the school, master of the playground. Fifth grade was the year kids received "the talk," were taught about periods and erections and their *changing bodies.* Surely these little creatures spotted across the dirt weren't ready for all that. Were they?

She plopped down on a bench by the sidewalk, avoiding the bleachers so as not to interrupt the proud parents and grandparents with an actual child in the game. The grass smelled greener here than in California, and the scent brought her back to lazy summer nights, riding her bike to the playfields whether she had a game or not, giggling with friends, a pocketful of change ready to spend on snow cones and Big League Chew Bubble Gum at the concession stand.

Kid summers were the best.

It wasn't until Laney was in her thirties that she realized Tuck was never going to want children. When they first left home, they both knew they were too young; they'd never met anyone who became a teenage parent by choice. Pregnancy was nothing but a "stupid mistake," and Tuck became so militant about birth control—condoms plus whatever else she could attain on the road without a prescription—that sex lost its appeal. Bad enough that her mother spent years stashing condoms in Laney's sock drawer; now it was her boyfriend.

As they rolled into their twenties, parenthood became an age-appropriate decision, and still, Tuck remained vigilant. Every month it was "Did you get it?" meaning her period, and every month he looked ready to cry with relief when she said yes. "I can't stall out on my career with a baby right now," he'd say. "I gotta keep focused." Of course he did. She understood. There was plenty of time.

He retired from racing when he was thirty-two. A year later, they opened Tire Stud. A year after that, on her thirty-fourth birthday, Laney stood in the bathroom hoping for a blue line to appear on a white stick. She was weeks late, which never happened. She was also on the pill, but had recently changed prescriptions after the last one left her pocked with adult acne. So maybe? Could it be?

It wasn't. Her period came the next day and when she told the story to her doctor, he laughed with an almost cruel flippancy. "If I had a dollar for every woman who thinks she's pregnant because she's a few days late."

At home, Tuck said, "But you got it, right?" Then sighed with relief and added, "It's just, you know—us being so busy with the new store and all."

Of course. She understood. They were never going to have children.

"Play's at first, everyone!" The sound of an eager Little League coach brought her back to the field. The pitcher, all of four feet tall and ready for his next batter, brought his mitt to his waist, focused his aim, and delivered the ball straight down the middle to home plate.

"Ball!" the ump called.

"What?" Laney yelled. "That was a strike!" A few of the parents in the bleachers looked her way with curious stares. Who was this invested stranger? She didn't see the mother who'd invited her to come.

"Play's at home!" Coach hollered. "Get ready! Play's at home."

And at that, Laney started to cry. She wanted to go home. Not to Oakland. Not to Tuck. Not even to her mother's house. Just home. To know what home was, what it felt like to *be* someplace, not itching for the next thing, not leaving her clothes in her suitcase because what was the use in unpacking. She wanted to sit down in the middle of the room and not have to get up. Because it was hers, and she belonged there, and her people knew where to find her.

The tears were streaking her cheeks now as she used the hem of her shirt to wipe them away. Fatigue had worn her mascara away hours ago. She was losing weight, thanks to her stress and her old friend IBS, and if she stayed in Minneapolis much longer, she was going to have to buy new clothes, a pair of yoga pants, at least, something that wouldn't fall down when she walked.

Her stomach lurched and she doubled over to throw up into the grass.

"Where have you been?!" Bree didn't like to yell, but everything was topsy-turvy. "I've been calling and texting you for an hour! I thought you'd been hit by a car."

"I was over at Cedar Park."

"What were you doing at the Little League fields?" Bree did not have time for diversions.

"I don't know," Laney stammered, which upset Bree even more; Laney never stammered, ever. "I needed a break. It was something to do."

"To watch other people's kids play baseball?"

"I got to thinking. Maybe if I'd stayed, I'd have gotten married and had a kid in a game tonight."

"What are you on about, all these questions about what-ifs?"

Bree felt her insides snap, threatening to break. "Here's one for ya—what if Mom's married to Elliot?"

Laney squinted, confused. "What's that, now?"

A voice, lulled but loud, ascended from the chapel pew where Thom lay in the Rainbow, immobilized since arriving. "Your mother and Elliot are husband and wife. I found the marriage certificate locked away in the vault."

Laney looked as if her brain didn't know which word to stick on. *Marriage* or *vault*?

"He means Elliot's desk at home," Bree explained. "He found a marriage certificate inside, from 1979. They got married. Did you know this?"

As Laney was shaking her head, Thom piped up again with, "And an annulment form."

"They annulled it?" Bree screeched. "You could've mentioned that!"

"Blank," he bellowed back. "A blank annulment form."

Then, as so often happens in books and movies, the bells above the yellow door tinkled, and who should walk through but Witt and Irma, arm in arm and laughing as if they didn't have a care in the world.

"Oh goody!" Bree threw her hands in the air and giggled with a tinge of hysteria. "My mother, who's secretly married to that man's husband—" her fingers were spinning and pointing at the accused parties like a dial on a broken scale "—is now hitting on my boyfriend!"

Witt dropped Irma's arm. "Your boyfriend?"

Bree felt every eye in the room. "Friend!" she corrected. "I meant friend." She couldn't muster the energy to act embarrassed. It was a truly awful day when a Freudian slip as big as the one she'd just committed barely registered on your list of concerns.

Witt smirked. "I usually get to kiss a woman before she calls me her boyfriend."

"And I get my hair done before someone declares me his bride." Irma clutched a fat manila folder to her chest, but dropped it onto the front desk, freeing her hands for the gesticulation to come. "But, yes. Elliot and I got married because it was the only way to get the money we needed to open the Rainbow. However, if you're imagining we found ourselves wrapped in some great, secret love affair for the ages, I'm sorry to disappoint. The marriage was annulled decades ago." She opened a drawer and began to rustle through the random detritus of time, pens and clips and notepads and magnets and, unexpectedly, one thin gold band. She slipped it on her left hand and held it up for all to see.

"Why do you keep your wedding band in the junk drawer?" Laney asked—a question that wasn't even close to winning the battle for center stage among the misadventures littering Bree's head.

"It's actually an earring." Irma took it off, held it to her face to demonstrate. "Elliot gave me a family diamond during the ceremony, but we stashed it away in case we ever needed the cash. This pair was a gift from my grandmother when I graduated college. I lost the other earring at some point, but one afternoon, I needed a ring for a last-minute trip to the bank." She slipped it back onto her finger. "It worked like a charm. So I kept it here. In case of matrimonial emergency."

"Brilliant," Laney said.

Irma batted her eyelashes and curtsied.

Bree squeaked, "Can we please get back to the part where you *got married*?"

The voice from the benches bellowed, "May I present, Mr. and Mrs. Elliot Gregory."

"Rubbish," said Irma. "We went for martinis at old Charlie's on 7th after filing annulment papers at the courthouse. It's where his parents took us after the wedding, so it's where we went after the *Great Dissolution*." She emphasized the words, giving the impression this wasn't a title she'd just created.

"Irma—" Witt stepped to the front desk and opened the folder. "You being married to Elliot likely changes everything about the financial strategy we discussed."

"But we weren't married anymore!" She slapped the desk playfully for emphasis, a behavior that the Irma of just a few hours ago would have been incapable of performing.

"You're cheerful!" Bree pointed at her accusatorily. "What is going on?"

"Maybe we ought to sit down," Witt suggested.

Laney began to pull chairs toward the seating area beneath the front window.

Irma continued defending her status as a single woman.

Thom bayed from his bench, "I need help!"

When they settled, the four of them in chairs and Thom on his relocated pew, Irma began.

"First of all, I owe you my thanks." She looked pointedly at Laney, Thom, and Bree, in turn. "Your brilliant friend Witt just spent the afternoon showing me what a disaster the Vandaveer deal would have been."

Witt elaborated. "The contract included the purchase of the Over the Rainbow name and all related intellectual property, but the money they were offering only accounted for the real estate. In other words, they were buying the whole business while only compensating Irma for part of it."

No one looked surprised by the revelation, though Bree wasn't sure she understood completely. "What does that mean, only compensating her for part of it?"

"Even before Elliot died, I knew our building was worth more than the bookshop," said Irma. "It cost us sixty thousand dollars in 1979, but last year the dry cleaners on the corner sold for nearly a million. Can you imagine? We never made that sort of profit selling books, and so, when I discovered the massive debt we'd accumulated, I panicked. There was no way a small store like ours could overcome a gap like that—not in today's environment, especially."

Laney, apparently stuck on the same point as Bree, said, "So, what part weren't they paying you for?"

"Our name." Irma puffed, straightening in her chair. "The sale would have prevented me—*us*—" she looked directly at Bree "—from ever using it again."

"But you were planning to close anyway," she answered, stung by the fact they were having this discussion now instead of months ago.

"May I?" Witt asked Irma, who nodded. "Legally, a business's name is considered its intellectual property, and the name's value increases the more widely recognized it becomes. It's basically the reason you can't open a store and name it the Gap. But the opposite is also true. A business that makes, say, highly specialized widgets, can sell everything—its manufacturing facility, customer contracts, patents—but keep its name."

"It's as if the Vandaveers were saying," Irma continued, "'You can't have the Over the Rainbow brand anymore, and we're not going to pay you for it, either.'"

"So, you couldn't have rented a place down the street and moved the shop there," said Laney.

"Exactly." Witt nodded.

"But you didn't want to!" Was Bree the only person who hadn't forgotten this fact? "You spent a full week on the phone with Helen, planning your escape to Florida. You told me I *wasn't capable* of running the Rainbow."

"I meant because of the money." Irma fiddled quietly with her hands in her lap. "Admittedly, I could have handled this whole situation better. But think about it from my perspective. When I lost Elliot, I was in shock, and then, to discover all that debt and to realize that it began when I suggested we add the café..." She placed a hand, heavy with shame, on her heart. "I knew we'd taken a loan to cover its construction, but I didn't know we had to begin paying our bills with credit cards because all our cash was going to the bank. And all because I'd said, 'Let's sell wine and coffee, too.' Then Nestor got sick, and I all but disappeared—"

Bree exchanged a tentative glance with Laney, trying to judge how well Irma's pitiable tone was landing on her side of the circle. Either Laney was as unmoved as Bree, or she had a better poker face.

"Secrets, secrets, everywhere." Thom's voice arose from his bench, breaking the quiet. "May I remind you, Mrs. Gregory, that you married the man who claimed to love me only and always? The man who declared, 'If equal affection cannot be'—" his voice rose, a mix of mimicry and sarcasm "—'let the more loving one be me.'"

"Auden," said Irma, always the bookseller.

"Elliot never understood me, never recognized that his choices weighed much more heavily on our relationship than his words."

Irma bristled, and Bree realized it was the first time she'd seen her mirror Thom's territorial behavior. His cold war stance toward the Rainbow and everything associated with it—namely and especially Elliot—was a poorly held secret, and on the rare occasions he came to the shop, Bree and her mom busied themselves scarce, granting the men their privacy. Never, however, had she seen her mother show any ill feelings of her own toward Thom.

Irma's eyes narrowed on him, prone and immobile on Elliot's bench, as she calculated her response. "Yes, we were married. For the money. It was over as soon as it began. I don't know why it upsets you so much, but I recommend you get over it quick because you're really going to hate what comes next."

Bree and Laney exchanged dubious glances. Thom bellowed, "Oh, marvelous. More secrets! I suppose you're about to tell me Laney is Elliot's daughter. But please, just save your breath."

Laney, understandably shocked, yelled, "I'm WHAT?"

Bree turned to Witt with an expression she hoped he understood as "Did you know about this?" But he only dropped his face in his palm and groaned.

Irma was now out of her chair, towering over Thom. "For once in your life, quit trying to stir up trouble. I mean it. The hours upon hours I listened to Elliot on the phone, coddling you, having to defend himself against everything from missing dinner to having an affair. I want those hours back! I want them back! I swear, if I have to listen to your whimpering, sniveling voice for one more second, I'm going to lose my mind!"

Thom, powerless except for his baritone, bellowed, "WOMAN!"

"Yes, sir?" Irma let loose, collegiality and pretense dissipated. "May I help you? May I share any more of my life or my business or *my money*? You may wish to remember that I was about to give you half of what I would have gotten from selling the bookshop. A half that I was in NO WAY legally bound to give up!"

"AND YET YOU WOULD NEVER GIVE ME ELLIOT!"

Irma let out a roar, so frustrated, so abounding, Bree thought she heard the chandelier rattle. Laney jumped between the feuding duo, ensuring neither punched the other, shrieking for SOMEONE to explain why they never told her Elliot was her real father.

Witt mouthed, *What is happening?*

"HELLO!" Bree clapped her hands once, twice, stomping her feet. The crowd tittered itself into a reluctant silence. "We are better than this!"

Irma tried to interrupt, but Bree shot a finger in her face so quickly she swallowed the words.

"Now," Bree continued, "we're going to speak one person at a time. Pleasantly and calmly. Understood?"

The room murmured its reluctant agreement.

She looked directly at Irma. "I'm sure Laney would like to know if Elliot is really her father. Is it true?"

"Of course not!" Irma could have taken this moment to reassure her confused daughter. Instead, she pointed at Thom and sniped, "He's either delusional or a liar."

"I didn't say Elliot *was* her father—" Thom started, though Bree was quick to silence him.

"One person at a time." She returned her attention to Irma. "So, there's nothing Laney needs to know right now? No bombshell paternity secret in the wings?"

Irma shook her head, then finally remembered that it was her daughter she ought to be reassuring. "No, Laney. All this Elliot mess has nothing to do with you. Everything I've ever told you about how you came into this world was the truth." She grabbed her hand and squeezed.

"Good. Because I like telling people I was conceived during a surprise Prince concert at First Avenue. It's very rock and roll."

"And you may keep doing so."

"Alright," Bree sighed. "That's one crisis averted." She took a deep breath. This was exhausting. "Now, can you please explain to Thom what you meant when you said he was 'really going to hate what comes next'?" She couldn't believe that in the midst of all this mayhem, she was actually doing a pretty good job of keeping track of the bombshells.

Irma exchanged glances with Witt, then sighed. "I'm sorry to have to tell you this, Thom, but it appears only a portion of the remaining debt belongs to the shop. Most of it is on credit cards taken out in Elliot's personal name."

Thom, who'd been refusing to look at the group for several minutes, turned his head and gave one slow blink. "And?"

"And," Witt stepped in, "depending on how Elliot's will was written, the credit card companies can seek repayment from his estate. Meaning, if he left you any money or property, they could claim it as settlement."

He rolled his eyes. "Irma's his wife. They'll have to collect their money from her."

"Jiminy Cricket!" Irma threw her hands in the air, exasperated.

Witt, however, put the matter to rest. "No, Thom. Not if they weren't married at the time of his death, and it sounds like the annulment was granted long ago. If you still harbor doubts about Elliot's marital status, I can help you find the relevant documents online. It would take about five minutes."

Thom harrumphed, too stubborn to acknowledge defeat. "I suppose it doesn't matter anyway. He didn't leave a will, and there was no estate. The only things I got were already jointly held—the house and the car." In a sudden moment of realization, his eyes shot wide and he tried to sit up. "Oooh!" He grabbed for his back. Witt hustled to help. Thom flicked him away. "They can't take my house, can they? Am I about to be homeless?"

Witt shook his head. "I'd have to see the title to say for certain, but generally speaking, claimants can't come after your primary residence."

"They'll have to come after Elliot's garage full of yard tools, then." Thom's voice remained bitter, but his expression looked distinctly relieved. "He loved to buy them but never had time to use them."

"Is that really all he left?" Witt asked.

"That and a lovely collection of Italian leather shoes." He sighed. "The man had wonderful taste."

Bree chuckled. It was true. Elliot called his style "sunshine on a rainy day."

"Hold on a second." Laney lifted her head. "Mom, you said most of the remaining debt is on his personal credit cards. So what does that mean for the Rainbow? Good news, right?"

Irma nodded toward Witt, allowing him to explain.

"It's good news in that we thought the store owed close to fifty thousand, but it's actually closer to nineteen."

"Dollars?" Bree squeaked.

"Thousand," he answered. "Many businesses would be able to absorb a debt of that size. The trouble here, though, is that the

Rainbow is also running a loss—it hasn't been profitable for a while. I'm sorry I can't give you specifics yet. I will with time."

Bree looked at Irma, confused by her placid expression. If she'd understood Witt correctly, they were broke. Less broke than they thought, but still floundering, a rainbow-striped sunfish flopping on the beach at Lake Harriet. It didn't matter how far up on the sand they were—two inches or twelve—unless there was water soon, they were going to die.

"Should we have taken the Vandaveers' money after all?" Laney asked.

Witt said absolutely not. "It was a terrible deal."

"But we're twenty thousand in the hole and losing more every month."

"Nineteen," he corrected. "And, yes, you're probably looking at some major changes sooner than later, but I haven't had enough time to identify your full range of options. If you do have to sell, I can at least help you get a fair price."

Sell. Maybe it was just Bree, but the word seemed to hang in the air, the fading peal of a bell. She'd heard it a thousand times this past month, said it a thousand more. This time was different. It sounded rounder, fully dimensional, mournful. Real.

"What now?" Thom's voice had lost its edge. He turned his head to them, his expression finally more considered than angry.

"Now," Witt said, "I'll dive more deeply into the numbers. It's going to take a few weeks. But until your options become clear, I say maintain course and speed."

Bree perked. "That's what Daisy says."

Was he blushing? She matched his smile with her own.

It had been a terrible day with a terrible conclusion, yet despite it all—the fighting and screaming and lying—she'd kept her cool. She was calm, confident they'd passed the peak of their crisis. "Maintain course and speed," she repeated.

"Until instructed otherwise," he added. "That's the last part."

"Until instructed otherwise." She held up a finger. "No. Until *advised* otherwise. I like that better."

Witt lifted a finger to his nose and tapped.

Irma interrupted their private reverie. "We have a bookstore to run in the morning, debt or no." She glanced at Bree and locked eyes on Laney. "Out of bed early, a good breakfast, and at the shop by eight thirty. Yes?"

Yes, they answered.

Thom moaned, a pitiful child forgotten on his bench. "I hope someone is planning to drive me home before then."

25

Witt promised a free drink at the Lady, and Laney intended to take him up on it. Lord knows she needed one after what had just gone down. The past few hours had left her drained, as if Pandora hadn't just opened her box, but jumped out naked and high, hallucinating and screaming "RUN FOR YOUR LIVES!"

Or, maybe today was just another day at the Rainbow.

Before heading to the distillery, however, Thom needed a ride home. He wasn't in any shape for a night of carousing. She helped him into her mom's car and threw his crutches into the back seat.

"So, tell me," she began. "If your mind were a Volkswagen right now, how many clowns would be trying to climb in?"

He lifted his chin to consider. "Four. At capacity, but *finally* not overflowing." He said that last bit with a sigh so breathy it fogged a small circle onto his window. "I am sorry for that bit about Elliot being your father. It was flippant and cruel."

The idea of having known her dad shot a zing through her belly. She would've loved Elliot as a father. Sometimes he'd even acted as if he were, with their talks about boys and grades and first heartbreak—all the childhood disappointments that look minor only in the rearview mirror of adulthood.

"If he had been my father," she said, "my one regret would be not knowing until after he was gone."

"And I would have had yet another reason to act the jealous fool." His voice sounded so pitiful her instincts flashed instantly, urging her to reassure him he wasn't any such thing. She slapped them back. He had acted like a fool. He had been a little cruel.

Instead, she said, "What next, then?"

"It's a long list, too mortifying to enumerate. But one of the first items is to revisit my grief support group. I thought I was doing so well, with the disco and the fight to save the bookshop. Now I see that without those distractions, my grief has nowhere to hide."

She kept her eyes on the road, not wanting to interrupt until she knew he was finished. "Can I ask you something personal?" The word *personal* rankled as she said it—as if her paternity and his grief were as impersonal as a grocery list.

He graciously nodded without pointing out the obvious.

She said, "Were you always unhappy with Elliot, or do you think it would have subsided? Like, do you think your unhappiness could've been a phase?" It was a big question for such a short drive. They were already pulling into his driveway.

"Why would you think we were unhappy?" He recoiled as he spoke, wincing as his muscles were forced to shift without warning.

"Because, you know." She put the car in Park but left the motor running. She hadn't expected to have to defend the observation. "What Irma said about the phone calls. And it just seems like you're mad at him, or at least, it sounds that way when you talk about your life together..." She didn't finish the thought. Thom looked horrified. She'd obviously leapt to some very wrong conclusions.

"I threatened to leave him."

It came out so quietly, Laney had to rewind in her head to convince herself she'd heard correctly.

"I booked our dream trip to Peru and told him he had to choose—he could come along or he could get out."

"But you went together, right? He went with you." This much she knew, and the words flew from her lips with relief.

Thom nodded, though without the enthusiasm she craved. His skin was already pale, he was in pain, but now his mouth hung open and his eyes were teary. "I know everything looks rosier on vacation, but that trip. Those two weeks together. To laugh, and talk, and remember. We fell in love again."

She reached for his hand, alarmed to find herself frightened. The moment was too raw to experience without connection, and she was too afraid to let either of them travel memory lane alone.

"I was so lonely, and he was so gone. Before, I mean. The last five years. Maybe more. All that time, I knew I was being lied to, and still, he'd come home and tell me I was acting crazy. And now I know I wasn't wrong—he was lying to me, just not about what I thought. It was that inescapable cycle— the more I tried to talk about it, the further he slipped away. We began living in different realities. I didn't wake up angry one day. It was years and years of loss, of missing him, even when we were face-to-face."

"But the trip was a turning point?"

He squeezed her hand and smiled. Like a grandfather about to bless her with his most sacred advice, like the older, wiser friend who tells you that life is better when you're finally able to quit fighting and just accept whatever comes.

Instead, he said, "That trip was a giant *F. U.* from the universe."

Now it was her turn to recoil. "A what, now?"

He laughed a little. "My friends urge me to think of it as one last glorious chance to remember what we'd been, how well we'd loved each other. But I can't. No matter what I try, I'm convinced it was Fate handing me an ice cream cone on a hot summer day, allowing me one delicious, delirious taste, and then snatching it away." He snapped his fingers, startling her, making her blink.

"Uh-uh," was all she could muster. "That can't be right."

"How else do you explain it?"

Her first instinct was the same as his friends' had been, that the trip had provided a chance for closure, for happy memories that would soon help to dull the pain of loss. Except, that really was a load of crap. She understood suddenly, with a clarity just as black as the night outside their windows. A loss was a loss was a loss.

And just as unexpectedly, she was in a phone booth again in a nameless town, telling her mother she wasn't coming home. That the college money was gone. She'd cashed it in for the trailer they were living in (rust-eaten and mouse-infested), and Irma was just going to have to accept her decision. The decision Tuck had made, and that she now saw she hadn't mustered the strength to overrule.

"You know what I think it was?" She emerged from her thoughts and looked at Thom. "I think the trip was the universe offering you a chance to prove something. I mean, consider what it required of you. Instead of allowing yourself to be lied to anymore, you drew a line in the sand. But it wasn't just an ultimatum. You said, 'We can try to find *us* again, or we can give up.' That's different than saying 'Straighten up or get out.' You turned toward love." She felt her skin tingle at the chance to repeat her sister's wisdom. "You bet on your love for each other, and you were right."

He let out a quiet harrumph as if her insight surprised him. "Well, look at me. Smarter than I thought I was."

"Braver," she corrected. "What you did took bravery. It's hard enough to end a marriage—and I don't care what the state of Minnesota says, let's face it, you were married. But it's a lot more difficult to work to save a relationship, to create the conditions in which something good can grow from poisoned soil."

"You're mixing your metaphors." He smiled. "But I understand what you're trying to say."

She snickered. "You see? Sometimes it's good to act like a hard-ass."

"A hard-ass? These days, I'd settle for an ass that didn't wobble while I walk."

"Hobble," she corrected. "You're more hobbling than walking in your current state."

He groaned. "Wonderful. So now I wobble while I hobble."

"But you're brave enough to do it, my friend. And that's the point." They hadn't let go of each other's hands, and she brought their laced fingers to her cheek. "I didn't realize I would miss Elliot this much. But I'm so grateful that losing him gave us you." They were words she hadn't planned, didn't even know they were waiting to be spoken, but they emerged full and true and ripe with blessing.

"You are a dear," he whispered. "A lovely gift."

They sat, listening to the purr of the engine, lulled by its pulse.

Finally, Thom freed his hand and readied his exit. As if an afterthought, he stopped to look her in the eye and said, "Leaving is also brave."

To anyone but Laney, it would have sounded like a quip, a throwaway line from a man with a broken body struggling to make his way to his front door. Instead, it was as if he'd stepped inside her head, picked up her most vulnerable and frightened thought, and cradled it gently in his hands. "Believe," he whispered. "It's your specialty."

"What sort of odds would you give us?" Bree slumped across the bar, face on her fist, watching Witt mix and promising herself that from now on, she would always order a cocktail that required shaking. This one, a chilled Rhuby Gin (no bourbon for her tonight), was stirred, and she missed watching his muscles flex beneath his T-shirt.

He placed her drink on the bar and cocked his head, considering her question. "What sort of odds would I give us, huh?"

Slowly, teasingly, he inched forward until he was just a breath away from her face. She could smell the mint he'd popped into his mouth and his shampoo from his morning shower, something woody, like pine.

"You're mocking me." She huffed, pushing him back, because even if he was flirting, this was their game, forward and then retreat.

He grinned. "You mean, I'm not your boyfriend anymore?"

That was gonna stick. In the past twelve hours, he'd peered into the depths of the Rainbow's fiscal distress, served as financial therapist to her mother, and witnessed the David Sedaris–level absurdity that was her family. And yet, his takeaway was that she'd called him her boyfriend.

"I meant, us—the bookshop." The glint in his eyes told her the odds of the other "us" didn't look good, either, that teasing her held more appeal than the idea of kissing her. "What are the odds the shop will survive?"

He shook his head and straightened. "I can't tell yet. Too many unknowns. But I will say it's too soon to lose hope." Then with a smirk added, "I haven't lost hope yet."

"You're mean."

"Or am I delightful?"

"You're embarrassing me, so you're definitely mean." She suddenly pictured diving across the bar to kiss him, the woman in the romantic comedy who overcomes her awkward inhibitions to win love, even though Bree also knew such a bold move was an impossibility for her, given the fundamental disconnect between her imagination and her personal reality. She told her brain to behave itself.

He changed the subject anyway. "I'm going to make you another drink. Just a small taste, but I came up with this one the other day with you in mind."

"More rhubarb?" She waited until he passed her a mini cocktail. She sipped. She was wrong. The first thing to hit her tongue was peach, ripe and fresh, followed by a flash of tart. As she swallowed, the lazy flow of whiskey washed across her tongue. "Wow."

"Like it?" He beamed, surprised or happy or both. "I'm calling it Peach on Rye, though I'm open to suggestions."

"The peach is delicious." She took another sip. "Is it a syrup, like the rhubarb?"

He shook his head. "Peach nectar. I get it directly from a distributor in Colorado. Everyone talks about Georgia peaches, which are great, but that flavor is rounder. Palisade peaches from Colorado are brighter. They pop on the tongue."

She found herself smiling as he talked. He knew something about everything. It made her chuckle as she sipped.

"Now you're mocking me," he said.

"I didn't say a word."

He scowled. "You're smiling like I'm some sort of fruit pervert."

"No!" Her laugh shot across the room. "Actually, I had been hoping you'd teach me everything I need to know about doing the accounting for the Rainbow, but now I realize that listening to you talk about cocktails is much more interesting than numbers."

"Oh." He lowered his voice to mock-purr levels. "Just wait. We haven't even touched on General Accounting Principles yet. They call it… GAP." His lips popped on the *P* so hard he couldn't help but laugh. She repeated it back, popping even harder, and now they were both laughing, lost in a shared, ridiculous moment. She let herself close her eyes and enjoy it. When she opened them, Witt wasn't laughing. He was looking at her, watching her, and liking what he saw.

So she did it. She hurled herself across the bar, grabbing for his shoulders, aiming for his lips, consumed by the thought of what it would feel like to kiss him.

"Ow!" Unfortunately, she'd misjudged, crashing her forehead straight into his nose.

"Oh my god, I'm so sorry!" Was he bleeding? She tried to lift his face to see, but she was mid–belly flop, her upper half straddling the bar, her bottom half tangled in the rungs of her toppled stool, all of her floundering about helplessly. Finally, gravity pitched her to the floor and she hit bottom, literally, where she lay, basking in her humiliation.

"You okay down there?" Witt peeked at her from above.

"I think I'll just stay here until I die, if that's alright."

"Whatcha do to her this time?" A pair of boots appeared next to Bree's head. "I'm going to have to start charging you rent if you lay there much longer."

Daisy extended a hand and pulled Bree back onto her feet.

"It was my fault," Bree said.

Witt agreed. "All her," he said, but holding a towel to his nose, the words came out, "Uller."

Daisy walked away, hands in the air. "What am I going to do with the two of you? It's like an insurance claim just waiting to happen."

Witt pulled the towel from his face. His nose was cherry red, but it wasn't bleeding or pointing in a new direction. "Don't worry. I think only half of the room saw your acrobatics."

Bree resettled on her stool, her face on her fist where it began. "I'm invisible. Sorry. Can't hear you."

Mercifully, she didn't have to wait long before Laney showed up.

"What can I get you?" Witt asked. "Remember, first one's on me."

Laney thanked him. "Do you have plain ginger ale? I'm still a little unsettled."

He obliged, and Bree stood. "Let's get a table."

"I dropped Thom off," Laney said, following her. "I thought he was going to be an emotional salmagundi, but he was strangely calm. He told me the story of their trip to Peru." Until tonight, every time she heard the word, Laney thought of Paddington Bear having come from "darkest Peru." Now she would think of Thom and Elliot, falling in love and heading for tragedy.

"I always thought it was weird how that happened." Bree stuffed herself into the very corner of their corner booth as if expecting a surprise attack. "Elliot didn't mention the trip at all until a few days before. Then suddenly, *bam!* He's going to be gone for two weeks. If we'd known two weeks would become forever..."

Laney stopped her. "He went on the trip because Thom gave him an ultimatum. Basically, it was either 'Come with me and let's try to save us' or 'Stay, but don't be here by the time I get back.'"

Bree rolled her eyes. "I always wondered what that relationship was really like. Mom stayed out of it, but we heard the phone calls."

"Thom was lonely," Laney said. "And he didn't realize it until he'd felt that way for years."

Bree scrunched a face, the way she always did when she was willing to accept whatever you said, but also wanting to know, "So?"

Laney answered. "That's my marriage. I've been lonely for a long time. Only, that's hard to see when you're so busy you have to steal toilet paper from work because you ran out at home and don't have time for errands. I think that's how we've survived, Tuck and me. When he was racing, it was all about stats and sponsors and which city we had to be in next. I did our laundry in the sink, and sold cheap leather bracelets in the parking lot before races for grocery money, all of which I had to squeeze in when Tuck didn't need me glued to his side like an emotional-support animal."

"When did he become so needy?" Bree sounded as sapped as she looked.

"Apparently the day we met." She took a sip of her drink, mainly because her mouth was dry. She was glad she'd asked Witt for ginger ale sans whiskey. If her head were a Volkswagen, she had a dozen clowns clamoring inside, and they'd begun to shake the car so much her stomach was now begging them to get out. Her body was too confused to handle alcohol.

"Anyway," she went on, "I think I've finally admitted to myself that, on top of everything going on here, I also need to make a decision about my marriage."

"As in?" Sometimes, one of the best things about Bree being less confrontational than Laney was that she tended to ask open-ended questions, forcing her to think before answering.

"As in, do I want to fight for it?" The question had evolved since her conversation with Thom. Before, it was did she want to stay? But she'd already answered that. Every day she remained in Minneapolis was a day further away from her marriage. The question she really needed to resolve was one of intention, not geography. "I keep thinking, running toward something is so different from just running."

"You won't really be anywhere until you know where you want to be," Bree said.

"Thank you, Instagram." She patted Bree's hand. "I know what you're saying, though. I used to think I wanted to be wherever Tuck went. I'd see other racing girlfriends or fans paying him just a little bit too much attention and I'd get up in their faces like, 'Back up, coochie coo, he's mine.' Now sometimes I wonder if I'd be willing to pay someone to take him off my hands." She held out her palms as if waiting for confirmation to fall from the sky. "That's a sign of an unfulfilling relationship, am I right?"

"You're asking me?" Bree's voice rose three octaves and hit the ceiling. "I'm thirty-eight and I spend all day with my mother." Then she leaned in and whispered, "I tried to kiss Witt tonight, but instead I nearly broke his nose and ended ass-up on the floor."

Laney felt her eyes pop. "You what?"

Bree scanned the room conspiratorially. "He was flirting. Or at least I thought he was, so I figured, 'Go for it, Bree! Just do something for once!' Only, I kind of slipped when I was trying to lean over the bar, and I smashed his nose in with my forehead."

Laney lost it now. There was no holding back the image of her sister in a rom-com disaster.

"It's not funny!" Bree was pleading. "I have to meet him again in the morning to go over more of the accounting and it's going to be humiliating. How am I supposed to look him in the eye if all I see is the nose I tried to break?"

"You could always stare at his boobs. That's how men seem to handle it." She was definitely feeling less nauseous. Laughter as Alka-Seltzer.

A waitress appeared with two glasses of water. "From Witt," she explained. "He says he's looking forward to examining your bottom line tomorrow."

Laney howled so loud, she didn't know if she'd be able to breathe ever again.

By the time they opened the door to leave, both women were so tired their feet dragged. Even so, Laney suggested they take the long way home. "I could use the fresh air."

Her sister followed.

"If I leave California, I'll lose parts of my life I actually like."

"Name them," Bree said. "Make a list."

"Oakland," she began. She liked the weather. The grand, magical mix-up of people and personalities and food and culture and madness.

She sort of enjoyed managing Tire Stud. Working in an office held no appeal, and although being a small-business owner was often as serene as the opening scene of *Jaws*, she'd just as soon stay in the ocean than a cubical. She liked dealing with their customers. She liked her independence.

"You know what you didn't say, though, right?" Bree asked when she'd finished.

She did. "I didn't include Tuck."

They turned onto Bryant Avenue, away from the Greenway and into the front-porch parade that was residential southwest Minneapolis. Nearly every house had one. Many were enclosed, screened over to keep the mosquitoes at bay, and on nights like this, residents made full use of their open-air charm. Every third or fourth house, Laney found herself waving to people she would likely never meet, but who, at least for tonight, performed as her costars in a living tableau.

"I love Lyn-Lake almost as much as Oakland," she said.

Bree mistook a discarded sock for something dead and gave it wide berth. "Isn't that sort of like comparing the United States to Delaware? The size difference is apples to basketballs."

"Yeah, but what I'm saying is, if I leave Oakland, it's nice to know I'd be happy here."

"Did Laney Bedford Hartwell just admit to liking Minneapolis?" Bree giggled. "I *knew* you'd come around eventually." She plunged her thumb into her chest in celebration of such majestic wisdom, though misjudged her own force and hit too hard. "Ow. I just bruised my breastases."

"Your breastases bone," Laney corrected, neither confirming nor denying her sister's claims. "You hit the spot between your breastases."

Bree whispered, "Do you know Elliot was the first to tell me I needed a bra? He said, 'Girl, go ask Irma to take you to JCPenney today. If she doesn't know what for, tell her to come see me.' I came home with a size triple-A."

"Jeezers creezers. Was that weird for you?"

She stopped walking so she could think. "No. I wasn't embarrassed at all. I guess I just felt bad for giving Irma more to do."

"Why? That's a mom's job. Plus, I would've been happy to take you instead. Wouldn't the salesladies have loved that—two preteen girls digging through the Maidenforms."

Unexpectedly, Laney felt Bree slip a hand into hers. "You always did so much for me. I still feel guilty about it. And don't you dare tell Mom this, but I couldn't blame you for leaving. Not really. I missed you like crazy, but you needed your own life, to go do your own thing without having to always take care of me."

"I didn't take care of you. You're exaggerating."

"No? Well, how come you always brought me along when you went out with friends? How come we kept sharing a room even after Irma said one of us could have the basement?"

"You didn't move out, either."

"You rewrote all my papers," Bree said. "You didn't have to do that."

"Yeah, but you read all my books for me."

"I was reading them for my own classes anyway."

"Liar." Laney teased her rib with an elbow. "Bree, seriously. I liked being with you. We were friends and sisters. I don't get why you feel guilty about any of it. We had a mutually beneficial relationship."

"Like the bee and the flower?"

Laney smiled. "Shark and remora."

"Fly and cow pie."

"Gross. I don't want to be either of those." Laney kicked a broken piece of asphalt down the street. "Although it's a fitting description of Tuck and me."

Bree laughed, clearly assuming she was being sarcastic. "Don't refer to your husband as bovine dung," she teased. "It's unladylike."

"Heaven forbid." Laney played along, though the words didn't come out as lightly as she would have liked. "Except, that is the state of things right now between him and me. It's not a pretty companionship."

"Has he always been so helpless?" Bree was referring to the never-ending questions Laney received about things a typical small-business owner ought to know about their own shop. This morning, it had been a text about whether to pay a vendor invoice by credit card or check, though, now that she thought about it, at least he was paying them.

Laney opened her mouth to admit, yes, Tuck had always required a babysitter, but stopped herself. "I think maybe some of that is my fault." He needed her, obviously, but early in their relationship she'd needed him, too. "I remember going to bed at night with my feet aching because I'd run around all day in these crappy two-dollar sneakers—making food for Tuck and the crew, doing laundry, sprinting all over whatever town we were in, playing errand girl. And the whole time I'm telling myself, 'Pull your weight, Laney. Don't be a slacker. You're no groupie.'"

"What was that supposed to mean? Of course you weren't a groupie. You were his girlfriend."

It had taken decades, but Laney finally understood her compulsion to belong. "It was my twisted way of believing that if I kept him needing me, I could stay. He wouldn't dump me for someone else, and I could go on justifying my choice to be there."

"Good grief, Laney." Bree sounded judgmental, but Laney knew she was just acting sisterly.

"Yep. Totally gross."

"Did he cheat on you?"

She'd wondered the same a thousand times. "I don't think so, but I don't know for sure. Those guys are pretty good at covering for each other."

"Are you okay not knowing? I can't imagine wondering about something that huge."

"It bothers me a lot less than knowing I probably would've put up with it if he had."

Bree responded by not saying a word.

"I can't believe it, either, but I think it's true," Laney admitted. "I've got this thing about always wanting something to fight—I fought Mom's expectations for me, I fought the Rainbow, and once I was gone, I had it in my head that everyone here expected us to fail, so I spent the next however many years fighting that, too."

"Are you saying that's why you stayed here—to fight for the Rainbow?"

Laney wished so badly that she were. "That was part of it. But if I'm being totally honest, I've been fighting against Tuck. I created this marriage where our roles are clear—he's the big, bright light and I'm the socket. I do all the work so he can shine. But what happens now that I've realized I'm sick of it?"

"I don't know," Bree whispered, as if afraid to show how impossible that question was to answer.

"Tuck can be a total idiot, but he's not an asshole. He was never abusive—physically, emotionally, or otherwise—and he didn't use manipulation to get his way. He's a jackass, and a baby, and he's got an ego that's almost too heavy to lift, but I saw a lot on the circuit—the horrible, awful things men do to their partners. But Tuck? Never. He never pulled that crap."

"Still, do you want to be with him now?" This time, Bree's voice came out loud and firm.

And this time, it was Laney who whispered. "I don't think I do."

They stopped walking, saying nothing, staring at the ground.

Then suddenly, Bree was like a winner on *The Price is Right*, jumping and clapping, punching the air, kickboxing with ghosts. "I'm Laney and I'm done with you."

"What are you doing?" Her sister had lost her mind.

Bree kicked. "They say words are power, so I'm helping you use yours. Say it! Do you want to stay in your marriage?"

"No," Laney answered.

"Say *what*?" Bree hollered.

"I'm done with you, Tuck."

"Like you mean it, now!"

Laney paused, checked the street for witnesses, and filled her lungs. "I'M DONE WITH YOU, TUCK!"

"SAY IT AGAIN, SISTER!"

"I'M DONE WITH YOU, MOTHER TUCKER!"

"KNOCK IT OFF OUT THERE!"

"Oops! Sorry, sir!"

Bree was slightly mortified at having just been yelled at by a grumpy old man on his front porch, but she also really, really had to pee. All the ginger ale and water she'd drunk at the distillery. "Think I can squat over the rain gutter?" she whispered. "I have to go so bad."

"Sure." Laney pulled her in the opposite direction by the elbow. "I'll pick you up at the police station later."

Squirming, crossing her legs, then squirming some more, Bree scanned the street for a plan B. "Where, then? I'm desperate."

"We're right by Thom's."

"No! The poor guy's like seventy. Let him sleep."

Laney was already sprinting toward his house.

"Wait! I can't run with my knees locked together!"

It was less than two blocks to his front door. They rang the doorbell, which brought no response, so they knocked on the back door, and when that didn't work, put their faces to the kitchen window.

"Oooh, Thom," Laney sang. "Where are yoooou?"

"I'm sure he's asleep." Mentally, Bree gave him two minutes before she watered one of his bushes.

Laney crept around the corner in the dark. "Which is his bedroom window, do you think? *Oh, Thom, I know you're in therrre.*"

"You're gonna see him naked!"

"Make up your mind! Is he sleeping or is he naked?"

"Both!" They were shout-whispering, trying not to rouse the neighbors, and her throat had started to burn. "I feel like I swallowed a comb."

When Laney didn't respond, Bree swept the dark blindly with her arms, trying to find her. "Where'd you go?"

"Over here!"

"Where?" She tried to move toward the voice, but her foot caught on a tree root and she went down, boobs first in the dirt. "Holy Dave Grohl, I just popped the girls!" She rolled up to her butt, groaning, then remembered the neighbors and dropped to her elbows, army crawling toward the house. "We're going to end up in jail."

"Shit! Roses! They've got me!" Laney was close.

Bree found her a moment later, half-swallowed by the rose garden. "How am I supposed to get you out of there without getting stuck myself?"

"Pull!" Laney reached out a hand, though she could barely get the words out, she was laughing so hard. "Save me, Rhett!"

Bree saw the branch whose thorns refused to let go and gave it a tug. *Rrrriiiiiiip.* "Oops!" She snort-laughed so hard she had to crouch down cross-legged to keep from wetting herself. "I just ripped your pants off."

Laney inspected the damage, twisting her leg side to side. "Holy crow, I'm bleeding. My jeans look like I got my period from my knee."

"Stop!" She was really gonna do it. She was gonna pee her pants in Thom's backyard.

"Give me your purse."

"Why?"

"I need a tampon!"

"Stop!" Bree panicked, she was at the point of no return, where no leg crossing, crouching, or Kegels could hold back the dam. "Stop!" she squealed again, barely catching her breath.

Suddenly, the floodlight on the neighbor's porch went on and a man hollered, "Who's there?"

Laney grabbed Bree by the hand. "RUN!"

"I can't!" She half crouched, half trotted as Laney dragged her across the yard. "I'm not going to make it!" She had a drizzle going in her pants that hadn't yet turned into a full-blown storm, but Laney kept pulling, and she had no choice but to yank herself free and do the Quasimodo two-step toward the neighbor's pine tree.

Laney gasped. "At least do it in Thom's yard."

"Too late!" She felt a trickle start down her thigh. "No." Waddle. "No." Waddle. "No." The trickle became a small stream and with one *jerk*, she ripped down her pants as she ran; the stream became a river mere seconds before reaching the tree.

The relief was sweeter than chocolate ice cream with caramel syrup and a cherry on top.

Laney pulled her phone from her back pocket, blinding her with the flash from her camera. Bree couldn't have cared less. "Ha. Funny. Sell it on eBay."

Laney snapped another. Then—sirens.

"Shit!"

Bree struggled to pull her pants over her butt while Laney zigzagged toward Thom's backyard, trying to tuck behind one bush, then another. "I'm not going back into those rosebushes," she hissed.

"Here!" Bree grabbed her hand and pulled her toward the dark shadows behind the garage.

The sirens were close. They turned onto Thom's street.

"Do you have an attorney?" Laney asked.

Blue, red, and white lights broke through the black, turning the night into a carnival, colors flashing on the houses, on the grass, and in the next moment, on Thom's driveway.

"It's an ambulance." Laney's tone went from panic to dread as she stood to get a closer look, running toward the house.

"Come back here!" Maybe it wasn't the cops, but Bree still wasn't eager to explain why she'd been prowling through neighborhood backyards, even to a team of medics.

She heard Laney stumble. Then, loudly, "This is our friend's house? Can I help you?"

Someone was already knocking on the door, announcing themselves. They asked Laney if she knew the location of a spare key. Then pounding. "SIR?" the medics called.

Finally, somehow, the medics opened the door, and Bree saw light flood the kitchen. She quit thinking and ran to find paramedics pushing their way through the door with what looked like tackle boxes, two of them lifting a stretcher off its wheels and into the house.

She found Laney and took her hand.

"It's Thom. I can't believe it."

"Call Mom."

The Book Haters' Book Club LIVE

Thursday, March 15, 2018
Beware the Ides of March…

Calling all Friends of Book Haters!

We had such a great turnout for last summer's BHBC LIVE that we're doing it again. Here's a refresher:

☐ Bring a nonreading friend with you to the store on March 15th. While you're here, you can show them a few books you think they might love and introduce them to our Over the Rainbow family. At checkout, mention BHBC LIVE and you'll get 10% off your entire book purchase.

☐ Even better! Call ahead to register for a 10-minute personal shopping session with me, your favorite book whisperer, and you'll both receive 20% off. You can't do that online!

In anticipation, here are a few books for you to start thinking about. The upcoming BHBC LIVE falls on the ever-auspicious Ides of March (remember *Julius Caesar* from high school English, anyone?), so I'm recommending a few of my favorite just-when-you-thought-it-couldn't-get-worse titles. *Et tu, Brute?*

Station Eleven by Emily St. John Mandel is the sort of dark, twisty book I love to recommend when people say "I want something that reads like a movie." After a flu pandemic wipes out civilization, survivors flock together in camps. And, you guessed it, a few of them are nothing but trouble. Just when you thought it couldn't get worse…enter the cult leader and his merry band of enforcers. This one's been out for a few years, but we'll have plenty of copies for you *and* a friend. Believe me, this novel will leave you with plenty to think and talk about.

While we're talking civilization meltdown, the wildly talented Minnesota writer Kaethe Schwehn is out with her first novel, *The*

Rending and the Nest, and the plot couldn't be more upside down and inside out. In a bonus for us Twin Cities natives, the trouble all starts for protagonist, Mira, at our very own Mall of America, where she experiences a rending of the universe and 95% of the world's population disappears in a flash. Like *Station Eleven*, camps form and survivors try to make their way in a world that no longer makes sense. And just when you thought things couldn't get worse…women start giving birth to things that were never alive to begin with. This book is a brain twister I'll be recommending to readers who say "Give me something set in Minnesota that's *not* Lake Wobegon." Fair warning: after reading this one, you'll never see the Minnesota Zoo the same way again.

It's authors like Mandel and Schwehn who remind us that the people we love most dearly can hurt us most deeply, but they can also be the source of our greatest surprises. Tell that to your book-hater friends!

—Elliot

Last Hope for the Haters

The more picturesque the cover, the messier the story inside.

26

Laney and Bree were at the front desk of the emergency room when their mother arrived. "At the risk of sounding crass," she said, "it seems like we were just here."

Bree gave her a kiss on the cheek. Laney kept her distance. "My stomach's upset." She probably ought to ask for a bucket. They got lucky and found three seats together in the waiting room.

"Full house tonight," Irma said.

"They can't tell us anything since we're not family." Bree was clenching her hands together so tightly her knuckles were purple. "What if the worst happens and Elliot is still listed as his next of kin?"

Irma placed a gentle hand on hers. "We don't know enough to worry yet. Let's save our energy for when we need it."

Laney was only partly listening because there was an alien invasion underway in her gut. Her top half roiled, threatening to toss up the nothing she'd had for dinner, while her bottom half was constipated to the point of bloating. She straightened and unbuckled her pants.

"What are you doing?" Her mother scowled as if she'd pulled them all the way off and was now dancing in her underwear.

"I'm bloated. All this stress is like candy to my IBS." She doubled over, fighting the sudden urge to barf all over the carpet.

Bree wasn't paying attention. "Do we know if he has a heart condition? At his age, a heart attack is the most likely culprit, right? Or he could've fallen. Oh my gosh, maybe we ought to tell them about his injuries at the disco."

"They'll have his records from a few days ago," Irma said, speaking to Bree but turning toward Laney, rubbing her back. "Did you overdo it at the distillery?" she whispered. "Is that what's bringing this on?"

Laney shook her head, compounding the dizzy. "I had ginger ale. Bree's the drunk one."

"I am not!" This, she heard.

Laney inhaled a swift, sharp breath. Could she lie down on the floor? All she wanted to do was curl up in a ball.

"I'm getting you looked at." Her mother stood and made for the front desk. Laney lifted her head to argue, but the movement was too quick and she urped in her mouth, not enough to spew it all over her feet, but bitter and vile. Her stomach whipped in protest as she swallowed it back.

"Miss?"

She opened her eyes onto a pair of blue scrubs and bright pink clogs in front of her.

"Your mom tells me you're not feeling so good." The voice crouched down revealing a concerned face and an ID that read Talia (they/them). They took her wrist gently between two fingers and took a quick pulse. "Your heart's racing. Are you light-headed?"

Laney nodded, stupidly forgetting that movement of any kind woke her alien invaders. "Yeah." She gulped. "And I think there's a spaceship blocking my colon."

Talia must have looked to her mother for interpretation, because Irma said, "She speaks Hyperbole. I think she means she's constipated. She's had IBS since she was a teenager."

And so it was decided that Laney was getting her own trip to the emergency room. Talia left and returned with a wheelchair. Irma said, "Give me your purse. I'll find your insurance card and get you registered."

Moments later, Laney gasped with relief as she crawled onto the exam bed. Finally, she had a clean, white place on which to curl up and die.

Talia took her vitals and launched into the standard Laney Hartwell 101, health-history questions. Did she have underlying conditions besides IBS? When was she diagnosed? What medications did she take?

"Any chance you could be pregnant?" they asked.

Laney laughed. "No more than the Virgin Mary."

"So you're not sexually active? Your mother indicated you're married, and your husband is in California."

"He is. We're just—" Well, golly. How to explain the current quagmire that was her marriage. "We're just not *that* active, if you know what I mean."

Talia clicked away on their keyboard. "When was the last time you had sex? An estimated date is fine."

She was tempted to say, "When Elle Woods was still a Gemini vegetarian." But Talia was too nice and too busy to have to decipher her wandering mind. Instead, she made her best guess. "Maybe around Valentine's Day?" That sounded about right. She'd been in Minneapolis since early June, and she'd brushed Tuck off before leaving, claiming she wasn't in the mood given everything going on at home. Before that, he'd had his typical spring allergies and before…*oh*. "Make that early May. Or maybe the end of April." They'd gone out of town for a mini spring break, and Tuck had a thing about sex in hotels. "It's better in a strange place," he liked to claim. "More mystery."

Talia did some quick calculating on their fingers. "So, around eleven or twelve weeks, then?"

She nodded slowly. "But I don't think that's it. We're crazy careful. I've had false alarms in the past and it's always just the result of my body acting temporarily lazy. You know, unpredictable like my intestines. Lazy ovaries, lazy colon."

"We'll have you take a pregnancy test, anyway, just in case. But with you being constipated and with your history, it's likely IBS related. The nausea could be a result of the bloat, or you could have something more serious going on like an infection. The doctor will examine you. It's good you came in."

My mother made me, she wanted to say. But again, Talia didn't deserve her sass. Plus, she was suddenly feeling very, very curious.

After they rolled Laney away, Bree curled up across their two seats and laid her head in her mother's lap; Irma didn't hesitate to stroke her hair as she'd done countless times.

"Thank you for coming tonight," Bree said. "I know you're mad at Thom, and we didn't even think before calling you. It was instinct."

Irma took a deep breath, raising and lowering Bree's head gently as she sighed. "I was simply trying to protect him—or maybe I was trying to protect Elliot. I don't know. Regardless, I hid the debt because I knew how much it hurt me, and I didn't see any reason to inflict that on Thom. Or you. Or Laney."

She paused to smile at an elderly man who, with the help of his daughter or aide or another Good Samaritan, carefully navigated his walker through the crowded waiting room.

"The debt was as much my fault as Elliot's anyway. It began with improvements I suggested, and the Rainbow was our store, a shared responsibility. If I'd been paying closer attention, we never would have gotten ourselves into this situation."

That wasn't fair. "You were busy caring for Nestor and mourning his death. No one expected you to pay attention to anything beyond that. Plus, don't forget I saw Elliot every day, too. He acted like he had everything under control."

Irma's fingers continued their slow, soothing journey down

Bree's scalp. "Still. I regret leaving him the way I did—emotionally, at least. I don't think I've been thinking clearly for years, frankly. Now with Elliot gone, maybe I never will again. He was so much of me."

Bree smiled, knowing that to be true.

Her mother went on. "He used to call our relationship 'a love story for the ages, without the sex.' Then he'd laugh and say, 'Harlequin would never buy it.' One time I was up on the stepladder, and I caught my blouse on one of the shelves, ripping it. He ran for his camera and said, 'Quick! It's our book cover!'"

Bree remembered that day. She'd believed him, thought they really were writing a book together, even though she never saw the two of them work on it and couldn't imagine how such an enormous project would ever get finished. It wasn't until hours later when Elliot crawled on top of the front counter to pose for a customer who wanted a picture of "that gorgeous pink chandelier and the man who designed it" that she realized the book project wasn't real; it was simply a manifestation of Elliot's spectacular creativity and imagination, his way of stating, "Obviously we're worthy of a book. We just don't need to write one."

She looked up, into her mother's eyes. "Promise me that if you do sell the Rainbow, you'll at least keep the chandelier. It's iconic. And it's so Elliot."

"Where in my tiny house am I going to hang a six-foot chandelier?"

"The master bath." Bree grinned, picturing it. "You'll have to knock out a wall, but it'll be fabulous."

"Sounds perfectly practical." After a moment's pause, she tapped Bree's head lightly. "What would you take from the Rainbow?"

Bree had always loved the confessionals but doubted she could ever find the right place to put one. "I'd take the chapel pews. I'd line them up in my living room small-town-meeting style like they do at Miss Patty's on *Gilmore Girls*. I'd also put one on my front porch for people watching."

"Why am I picturing rows of red handmaidens with white wings about their heads, filling your house?"

"Because you always said Gilead was your idea of hell, but Margaret Atwood just happened to put it on paper."

Irma hmm'd. "Little did I know the hell of losing so much wouldn't require a costume change."

Bree found her mom's hand and squeezed it. "I've been thinking about a few options for what we might be able to do with the shop. Tonight's not the time to discuss them, but I do think one or two of them might have some promise."

Irma thanked her by squeezing back.

The automatic doors to the exam rooms opened and they both turned, looking for Laney. A mother and a young boy with his arm in a sling walked through.

"I wonder what's taking so long," her mom said. "I'd like to go see for myself, but Laney told me to stay put."

Bree brought her phone to her face to look for texts. Maybe Laney had an update. Maybe Thom knew they were there, waiting for news.

Nothing.

At five minutes after midnight, Laney hit the wall button and watched the emergency room doors swing wide with their telltale hydraulic hiss. She'd had an enema, taken a stool softener and an uber-antacid, and farted almost nonstop for the past twenty minutes. She couldn't remember a time she'd felt more relieved.

Bree, who'd been half asleep on their mom's lap, sat up with a startle. "Well?"

"What did they say?" asked Irma.

Laney shook her booty. "I was right. My chute was as backed up as the Suez Canal after that cargo ship blocked the entrance.

The doctor recommended I get an appointment with a gastroenterologist to keep it from happening again."

Her sister squinched her eyes shut, clearly trying to wipe the image of Laney's GI track from her brain. "Glad you feel better."

"Do you have any follow-up care?" her mom asked. "Do we need to stop by the pharmacy to pick up any prescriptions?" She began to ready her purse, as if leaving immediately.

"No, I'm fine." Laney held out a hand, gesturing for her to sit back and relax. "The only other thing she said was… I'm pregnant."

And, just like it happens in the movies, Laney's feet left the ground and she began to float—arms wide to the sky, her face to the sun, her spirit as light as the wind.

(At least, that's what it felt like.)

27

Thom stirred to the sound of snoring. Elliot must have eaten spicy food for dinner; peppers always swelled his sinuses. He reached over to nudge him awake and found a cold steel rod in his place.

Of course, Thom reminded himself. *Elliot is gone. And I am here.* Though—where, exactly? He opened his eyes onto a hospital room, the gray light of dawn seeping through the blinds, sketching the outlines of his bed and the thin white blanket covering him. He wiggled his toes and saw them dance, even with the immobility boot on his left ankle. A good sign.

He was wearing a hospital gown, could feel the ties digging into his back, and a long tube snaked up from deep under the covers. What did that connect to? He tugged it and felt—oh. *Oh!*

"Thom?" A figure he hadn't yet noticed stirred in the corner. "Are you awake?" It was Bree's voice. Suddenly, she was beside him, her face expectant even in shadow.

"What happened this time?" he asked.

"We were hoping you could tell us. An ambulance was called to your house last night and they brought you here. Privacy rules prevent the doctors from saying much more than that." She glanced back into the dark side of the room where faces he couldn't make out waited for him. "At least they let us stay with you once they moved you out of the ER."

She wanted him to explain an incident requiring an ambulance. The memories were faint, but his mind stirred with images of blue light, a room crowded with strangers. "I thought they were astronauts," he said, finding more detail as he spoke. "They all wore the same uniform and carried the same kits. I told them they were going to be late for launch."

Bree snickered. "Did you get high last night?"

"No." He tried to sit up straight, but he was so tired. He felt the tiny IV needle in the crook of his arm. "I haven't smoked pot since the seventies."

His eyes wanted to close again, and he let them. He felt Bree's hand on his. The air was a cotton-candy cloud into which he fell. Happy and light.

The next time he opened them, Bree was there with her sister, Laney. "Hi, again," she chirped. The room was no longer gray, but peachy.

Laney squeezed his forearm. "Just so you know, we're not astronauts, and we're not going to be late for anything." Her eyes smiled as she continued, "Mom just left to open the Rainbow."

Irma had been here? "Tell me again what happened," he said. Bree got to the part about the ambulance when the doctor walked in. She looked as tall as the ceiling, and as much as Thom believed in looking a person in the eye when they spoke, he had to close his eyes to the strain of such an angle.

In the end, Dr. Boerger explained he'd had an adverse reaction to pain medication. Paramedics found a bottle of Vicodin on the kitchen table. She asked Laney and Bree to step out of the room.

"The Vicodin was prescribed to Elliot Gregory. Do you know this person?"

"He was my partner of twenty years. He died in January."

She expressed her condolences but didn't soften her stern tone. "Vicodin is a controlled substance. It's never safe to take a medication not prescribed to you, but it's especially dangerous with a Schedule II drug like the one you took. You were hallucinating when paramedics arrived. You weren't able to tell us how much you'd taken, so we had to intervene to prevent overdose."

That explained the astronauts. "I don't abuse pills. In fact, I've never taken any of Elliot's medications before. I only took the Vicodin as a last resort. I fell recently, spraining my ankle and throwing my back out, and I'd run out of muscle relaxants." He thought about last night's decision. The stress had left him wrung out, and he was so tired. "I just wanted a good night's sleep."

Dr. Boerger nodded slowly, doing her best to judge his sincerity. "The prescription was written for seven pills. There were four left in the bottle when paramedics found it. Did you take three?"

No, no he was certain. "One. They were left over from surgery Elliot had to correct a broken wrist that hadn't healed correctly. He fell on the ice. He hated going to the doctor, even though I told him how important it was to treat his body with respect." Why was he telling her this? He let go of a long-held breath. "Anyway. I suppose last night shows I need to learn my own lesson."

The doctor nodded, then patted his arm gently. "You had a rough night. We're going to keep you a few more hours for observation and we'll take another look at your back. See if we can't do something more for your muscle spasms." She made a note in his chart, then smiled at something she saw. "Any memory of the moth invasion?"

He groaned. He remembered. In his hallucinated state, moths had descended on Elliot's sweaters, the ones Thom had ripped out of their boxes in his rage. "How many sweaters was I wearing when they found me?"

Dr. Boerger chuckled. "About half a dozen. A few on top and at least one on your legs."

He didn't mention he'd also tied one sweater to a broom handle as his battle flag.

★★★

When he was cleared for discharge, Laney and Bree drove Thom home. "Are you sure you don't want us to come in and help you get settled?" Bree asked. Her poor face was white with worry and exhaustion.

The last thing he wanted right now, however, was company. He planned to crawl into bed and sleep as long as his body needed. Only after that would he make a list of what to do next.

"Don't panic if you don't hear from me tonight," he said. "When I'm rested, I promise to call."

Laney said okay. Bree made him pinky swear.

They guided him up the porch stairs, but he entered the house alone. The kitchen looked like it really had seen battle—discarded wrappers and tubing and miscellaneous detritus left by the paramedics, a heap of sweaters, broken dishes, a tipped-over planter, its dirt spilling onto the windowsill. He maneuvered his crutches carefully over it all, not looking back until he reached the bedroom. The covers were still neat, and he pulled back the corner on his side of the bed. He slipped his shoes off and nestled deep. Then he reached over, letting his arm span the width of where Elliot lay. "Sleep tight, sweetheart," he whispered. "Don't worry about me. I'm going to be fine."

He knew it to be true because the piece of last night's puzzle he hadn't shared with anyone—not the doctor or nurses or even Laney and Bree—assured him of it. It had been a voice that saved him, a voice that cut through his growing terror and provided just enough space between the imagined and the real for his fingers to dial 911. "Oh, Thom," the voice had called. "I know you're in there..."

COMMERCIAL BREAK

No, darlings, it wasn't me! This time it was our lovely Laney, knocking on Thom's bedroom window and calling his name. Remember now? (Slight sidebar: Judy is worried for my rosebushes, but let me assure everyone they'll be just fine. Roses are practically weeds in Minnesota, they grow so well in our rich, black soil.)

But back to the point of my having popped in again…

I think this little misunderstanding between Thom and me is a wonderful turn of events. The perfect collision of belief and circumstance. Thom thinks he heard me, and that's just fine, because I am the connection he yearns for. Oh, I realize it seems I'm encouraging a fallacy, but the heart believes what it wants, and he wants to have heard me, just as I want him to want to believe that.

Anyway, you know I would've stepped in had Laney not been there, alive and in person. I could never have let him lie on the floor, alone and suffering. At the very least, I would have hollered at him to "Get up! It's not your time yet, you brokenhearted fool!"

(Judy agrees. "Of course you would. You adore that man." (Notice her use of the present tense?))

I'm not here merely to defend myself, however. I'm here because I need you to know that Thom and Laney and Bree and even our gal Irma aren't done with their pain, yet. They have more to do, more stretching and growing and reaching for their goals.

Getting to the rainbow isn't easy. It's not supposed to be. If it were, anyone could do it—and that wouldn't leave much gold in the pot, would it?

28

Violet Baumgartner was at the Rainbow when Bree and Laney arrived from having dropped Thom at home, though Bree was the first one through the yellow door and the one to hear her exclaim, "Irritable Bowel Syndrome!"

Her mother shot them a look across the room, pleading for help. Bree thought Mrs. Baumgartner was the sort of woman who never left the house without her hair and face done, but she was apparently also the sort who held no compunction against howling the word *bowel* for all to hear.

"My husband, Edward Baumgartner, spent his career as one of the world's most respected IBS researchers. He's since retired, but his reputation remains, and he travels all over the world consulting with other researchers on their work."

Laney stopped briefly to take in the scene, then shook her head and mumbled, "Nope. Can't." She made straight for the stockroom, leaving Bree with no choice but to step up and help their increasingly red-faced mom.

"Hello, Mrs. Baumgartner," Bree said. "No Adam this afternoon?"

"He's attending Theatrical Movement Camp this week. Are you the one with the blockage?"

Bree quickly shielded a grin with her hand. "No. That's my sister. She's resting." *About ten feet away*, she added silently.

"It seems that Violet," said Irma, changing the subject, "came to congratulate us on not selling to Vandaveer Investments."

The woman straightened, puffing with pride. "I give credit to the *Minneapolis/St. Paul Standard*. They published a very strongly worded opinion piece I wrote about retirees flocking to buy new condos and ruining our historic neighborhoods in the process. I'm very lucky to have several connections at the newspaper."

"And we appreciate it," said Irma. "Don't we?" She raised an eyebrow, and Bree got the message.

"Very much," she said. "What would we do without customers like you, Mrs. Baumgartner?"

The bells over the yellow door tinkled all afternoon, leaving Bree's feet to feel as if they were weighted with bricks after a night of no sleep, though she powered on, refusing to slow. At seven, just as she was flipping the sign in the window and turning the lock, she saw Witt jog across the street. She gasped and threw open the door. "I can't believe I forgot you this morning!" She'd promised to meet him at 8:00 a.m. "Thom ended up in the emergency room and so did Laney and I should have texted you—"

He held up a hand. "You did text me. Middle of the night. You don't remember?"

That's right. She had. "The last twenty-four hours are such a blur."

"Listen, I know you're probably exhausted, but I have a little more information now. Think you'll be up for coffee in the morning? I work tomorrow, but I can at least run you through the highlights."

She nodded, eager to hear the latest. "Coffee's on me this time," she said.

"Deal." He was grinning. Did that mean he had good news?

"Hey, before you go," Bree said. "I've been tossing around a few ideas. We don't have to go into detail now, but do you know anything about pop-up kiosks?"

He cocked his head. "Like, in the mall?"

"Yeah." Or, not exactly. "Sort of. But not really. I'll explain tomorrow."

It wasn't until they'd said goodbye and she watched him go that she remembered: she'd tried to kiss him last night.

"I'm going to be a grandma!" Laney, Bree, and their mom sat in her living room waiting for pizza delivery. They were each desperately tired, but also at the point beyond exhaustion where the body goes on autopilot and the brain cuts back its processing to handle one need, one decision at a time. It's slow, and a little foggy, but with no energy to handle stress or emotion, it's also enticingly blissful.

Laney lay back against the couch cushions and stretched her belly. Apparently, pregnant women were prone to constipation—especially women with divas for digestive tracks, like hers.

"I don't think I want to be called Grandma, though. What's a younger-sounding name? Mimi? Meemaw?"

"How 'bout Granny Gray Hairs?" Laney teased. "I hear that's all the rage these days."

Her mom flicked the comment away. "Funny girl."

Bree sat with her eyes closed, present but too tired to listen, speak, and look all at the same time. "When are you going to tell Tuck?"

Ah, her sister. Always the buzzkill. "Soon. I just don't know if I should wait to tell him in person?"

"That depends on how long you're planning to stay here," said her mom. "I hate to pile on, but you have a lot more decisions to make than you had yesterday."

Had Laney told her mother her marriage was in trouble? It was possible that Bree could have mentioned it, but as sisters, they didn't tend to triangulate their relationships with their mom. Regardless, Irma sensed something. "I take it you've figured out that Tuck and I aren't exactly Cinderella and Prince Charming right now."

Her mom gave her a sympathetic smile. "You've been in Minneapolis for nearly a month, you have a business and a husband in California, and more often than not, you press Ignore when he calls. I had a hunch, yes."

Of course she had.

"Yesterday I'd almost made up my mind to leave him. I'm not happy in our marriage, and I didn't even want to try anymore. I think if you asked Tuck, he'd say the only problem we have is that I'm not there to run the shop."

"I suspect he knows more than that," her mom said.

Bree nodded, her eyes still closed but her brain still on. "Have you asked him what he wants?"

Irma said, "A smart woman never assumes, Laney. Ask the questions you need answers to."

Bree mmm-hmm'd behind closed lids.

"I know he has the right to play a role in this baby's life," she said, "and our child deserves a loving, responsible father. But I don't know that I can be the mother I want to be if I'm with him."

Her mom leaned forward, her elbows on her knees and her eyes dark with determination. "Go home, Laney. If you learned anything from your time here, let it be from my mistakes. You can't make any decisions until you ask the questions you need answers to."

29

Seven o'clock fell like an anvil to the skull, but Bree made it to the bookshop, coffees in hand, to find Witt waiting outside. He grinned, an easy smile meant just for her, the kind worthy of bragging rights. *See that, ladies? Back yourselves up 'cuz he's all mine.*

"Hiya." Her voice cracked when she spoke; she was not a morning person even in the best of circumstances.

Witt took the coffees, freeing her hands to unlock the door. "The neighbors must really love the Rainbow, because in the three minutes I stood here waiting, I got the once-over from two different people. As if I was trying to break in."

The lock clicked and Bree pushed her way through. "Hang on—" She motioned for him to stay there. "Gotta turn off the alarm. Neighbors are great, but security systems are good, too."

She punched the code on a keypad hidden behind the coatrack.

"In my neighborhood," Witt called, "the neighbors yell at you to stay off their part of the sidewalk."

"Alarm… Off," said Electric Keypad Lady.

Bree reached for her coffee. Witt handed it over, then refused to release his grip on the mug. "Just to be clear—I'll happily be your number jockey this morning, but I draw the line on kissing." His smile was half-imp, half-propriety cop.

"Yes, sir."

"I know I'm sexy as a bull, but I'm a human being, not a piece of meat."

"I promise to keep my hands to myself. But I'll warn you, your analogy has me craving breakfast, and I may just hold you responsible." Holy cats, she was actually flirting without risking her safety or her dignity.

No matter how deliciously their morning had started, though, numbers weren't sexy in the least nor were Witt's soliloquies on taxes owed, quarterly projections, annual projections, quarterly adjustments, just-in-time inventory, the small-business benefits included in the latest tax bill, and on and on… What she did enjoy, however, was discovering she understood far more than she'd expected.

"So, the business is salvageable," she confirmed, "but we have too many assets and not enough income?" She pictured their building tilting steeply to one side, a vessel in the midst of capsizing.

Witt nodded. "It's a good problem to have. You started this process believing you were debt heavy, and if given the choice, I'd almost always choose to be asset heavy. But, a problem is still a problem."

Irma should have been here for this meeting, but Bree, wanting time alone with Witt, had selfishly *forgotten* to mention it, and now there were decisions to be made. She pinched her thigh under the table. "You said there were a few options for moving forward. Let's run through those."

He scratched at the not-quite-beard stubble on his chin. "In order to make the best decision about next steps, you need to be clear about your priorities. Is your family determined to save the business, or does Irma still want to sell and retire? Are you open to considering a change in location? And if you do save the Rainbow, what's the transition plan after Irma's gone?" He paused. "Where is your mom this morning, by the way?"

"I let her sleep. She's understandably exhausted." None of that was a lie.

Witt dived into his folder and pulled out a thin packet. "Are you familiar enough with what we discussed to explain it to Irma? These may help." He slid the stack of brightly colored graphs across the table. "You could have your discussion over at the distillery, that way if either of you have questions, I'm around. I've got a full day, but I'll carve out as much time as I can."

Bree thanked him and flipped through the pile. "I'll take a shot at it. The sooner we know which direction we're headed, the better." She came to a sheet with two columns, one with Vandaveer numbers, the other, Witt's numbers that he'd labeled Current Market Estimate.

"They really were going to hose us, weren't they?" she said, scanning.

They were, he agreed. "You're a quick study, Ms. Bedford. A pretty, good student."

"Well, I hate to correct your grammar, sir, but it sounds as if you've got your comma in the wrong place."

"No. I placed it exactly where I want it."

"*Pretty, good*, huh?" Bree leaned in and tapped a finger to her chin, studying him. "I always strive for 'excellent.'" She lowered her face to his. "May I, Professor?"

He answered by kissing her.

30

Thom spent the next several days practicing self-care. That's how he'd chosen to refer to it. "I'm doing home care," he'd told Brian when he called, leaving his friend with the impression that a medical assistant was stopping by regularly to check on him. But Thom was nursing himself, finally willing to admit that he deserved the R & R. Not because he was injured and forced to slow down. Not because he was depressed and unable to get out of bed. He was caring for himself because he ought to.

The hospital had sent him home with a new set of prescriptions that helped his back immensely without placing waking nightmares into his brain. The doctor also recommended he rent a sort of scooter for around the house. "It works two ways," Dr. Boerger said. "You can rest your injured leg on the seat and push yourself around with the other—the wheels aren't as cumbersome as a walker. But it's also wide enough to sit on, meaning you've got a seat with you anytime you need one."

He stood in the hallway now, holding the handles and pushing himself off toward the kitchen. It glided effortlessly, proving once again that he'd been right to insist they never carpet over the house's hardwood floors.

The kitchen was clean, as well. That had taken the better part of a day, given the extent of his Thom-made disaster and his commitment to rest. He'd sat on the seat of his scooter and pulled a broom alongside as he slid across the floor. When that was finished, he placed the garbage can on the seat just below the counters, sweeping them free of debris with his arm and aiming the pile straight for the trash.

He was growing quite fond of his small but mighty assistant-on-wheels.

At the stove, he set the kettle to boil and selected a bag of Irish breakfast tea. He was even going to put sugar in it without a hint of guilt for what he may be doing to his teeth. He'd been malnourished for months, he recognized that now, and though he was no dentist, he knew that a cube of sugar held far less potential for damage than starving his body of calories and necessary nutrients.

Finally ready, he sat down at the kitchen table and pulled a fresh yellow legal pad in front of him. He had a new assignment. Though he'd stayed home the past few days intentionally, he did make one trip out, to his grief support group, just as he'd told Laney he would.

This week, the subject was "the back-and-forth of grief," the reality that it doesn't just subside one day and disappear.

"I choose to think of grief as a season," Laikin had said. "We've experienced enough springs in our life to know that most of the time, the temperature is cool but not cold. The grass is greening but mostly brown. There are going to be sunny days but also a lot of rain. And yet, we also expect that every spring is going to vary from the last. Some years, March is nothing but rising temperatures and melting snow, but other years, we'll get a blizzard with a foot of snow or more."

Thom remembered one such spring. He'd begged Elliot to take time off so they could escape the endless winter, even if only for a few days. He found deals on trips to Florida, to Mexico, to New Orleans. Elliot rebuffed every one of them. Now he understood why—his partner had been consumed with panic and regret over the debt he'd compiled, and he was probably loath to spend any extra money but couldn't explain why.

Knowing that, however, didn't magically resolve the hurt. Thom could look back on those days and say, "Ah, I see." But that didn't keep him from wanting to scream and cry and slash a deep gouge into their beautiful kitchen table with his pen.

"The fewer expectations we have for our grief," Laikin had said, "the less it can disappoint us. We all have those moments—we're going along, happy or, at least for once, not thinking about being sad, and *boom!* That contentment vanishes in a flash and you remember, *Oh yeah, this is awful.*"

Thom had lost himself in the work to save the Rainbow. He'd danced and laughed with friends and drowned himself in so much sensation he didn't have any space for despair. He'd told Laney it'd been nothing but a place to hide from his grief. Maybe, instead, he had stumbled upon joy?

"Some people talk about the grieving process as two steps forward, one step back. But to me, that's a negative concept—the idea of *losing* ground. I want to encourage you to reshape your concept of what it looks like to live in the season of grief. Whether today brings sun or the third blizzard in a row, those things are gonna happen whether we like it or not. We need both sunscreen and a good snowblower."

Thom looked at the blank pad before him. He didn't know where Elliot was now, didn't have an ever-comforting image of what "beyond" held for us. He did know he'd been lonely for a long time, and that he was still here, and that in living, he would have new stories to tell the man he loved.

Dear Elliot, he wrote.

Maybe you're looking down as I write this, saying, "I see you! I already know all this!" But I've taken too much for granted for too long, and the thought of living my life without you is unbearable. I may not be able to hear you anymore, singing as you shower, but

I need to believe that you are here, that you and I continue on together. You may be laughing at me this very moment. But please, indulge me. There is so much I want you to know.

First up, we thought we saved the Rainbow, only to find out we hadn't, only to find out later that maybe, in fact, we had. There's a disco in this story, you're going to love it, so hang on. I need to explain a few things first…

"I don't feel like it's real." Laney was on her way to the airport, the trip she'd spent the last month unconsciously dreading. Her mom insisted on driving her, wouldn't even hear of her daughter and grandbaby-to-be crawling into the back seat of "some stranger's claptrap car." Now here they all sat, stuck in construction traffic on I-35W. There had been construction traffic on I-35W since the day Laney was born.

"I know there's a baby inside me—" she'd seen the grainy flutter of Baby's heartbeat on the hospital's ultrasound "—but it's as if I don't know how it got there. Or why."

Her mom gave her the side-eye from behind the wheel. "I presume you know *how* it got there."

"Mechanically, yes. But now? After years of hoping?" The part she really wanted to say but didn't was that, if it weren't for this baby, leaving Tuck would have been so much easier. But saying that part, even allowing her brain to acknowledge it, lay the blame at Baby's microscopic feet, and even the barely awake mother in Laney knew that was unfair.

"Sweetheart," her mom said, "motherhood is a lifelong lesson in learning to let go. Even if you had planned this child, gotten pregnant when all the pieces of your life seemed just exactly right, hand selected your doctor and hospital, and gone to the classes and read the books and done all that good stuff, the kid would still manage to surprise you. Because you're creating a life other than your own. A child that, from its very conception, is its own being with its own biology and personality and path. All a mother can really do is try to ensure safe passage along the way."

"But what if I don't know how to do that?"

"You don't." Her mom turned and gave her an apologetic smile. "Nobody does. But you'll do your best to figure it out, because every day will be a new challenge, and just when you think you know what you're doing, kids have a way of pulling a trick from their sleeve. You certainly did." It struck her so funny, she guffawed and hooted. "Oh lord, if this child is anything like you, we all better buckle up!"

Laney threw her head back against the seat, preemptively exhausted. "And it's got Tuck for a dad. The poor kid is doomed!"

"Nooo." Her mom pulled at the long Minnesota *O* like taffy. "This child will be full of adventure and heart." She reached over and patted her knee. Laney, though, was still unpeeling the realization that this baby, her child, would someday be capable of doing all the things she'd done and be responsible for all the consequences that followed.

"I know I've said it a thousand times, Mom, but I'm so sorry I disappeared on you all those years ago. Then, once I'd chosen Tuck, I had to prove I'd been right to go. I look back now and see so many moments that could have been turning points, when I could have called it quits. I could have picked up the phone and said, 'I want to come home,' and you would have gotten me on the next plane. But I never did."

Her mom nodded. "Loyalty is tricky like that. It's a priceless gift and so easy to give to the wrong people."

There was no ride waiting for Laney and Baby on the other side, only five midflight texts from Tuck about ordering more disposable cups, and calling the plumber, and had she paid the Amex bill? Her first instinct was to be annoyed. Her better instinct told her to have some compassion; he knew things had changed. They were both struggling to make sense of it.

She'd also spent the flight debating with herself. She could go straight to Tire Stud and close the office door and tell him she was pregnant. She could also go home, make a nice dinner, and tell him over dessert. Maybe she'd go home, then call him to get a read on his mood and decide after that.

The Lyft driver pulled up in front of her requested address. "Ma'am?" he said, questioning if she'd really intended to be dropped off at an empty lot.

"Oh," she said. Tire Stud was down the block and she'd gambled, thinking that as soon as she saw the shop, she'd know whether to go in or go home. "If you wouldn't mind, my real destination is three doors farther. Could you let me out there?"

Tuck's manic calls and texts recently had her expecting Gomorrah inside, but she opened the door onto a lobby as clean and organized as she'd ever seen it. The smell of fresh coffee was so strong, it almost overtook the rubber scent emanating from hundreds of tires. The customers looked no more or less agitated than an average day, and, was that music she heard on the sound system?

A square-shouldered woman with neatly trimmed hair stood behind the front desk. "Welcome to Tire Stud," she said, not realizing this stranger was her boss.

"Hi, I'm Laney." She extended a hand.

"Laney!" Recognition came as soon as they heard each other's voices, having spoken on the phone. She cupped Laney's hand in her palms, giving her a lovely squeeze. "I'm—"

"Sylvia!" Tuck came around the corner, stopping in his tracks at the sight of Laney. "Hey, everybody, look who's back!" Tuck put his arm around Laney's shoulder and squeezed exactly one ounce too tightly. "You been gone too long."

She'd spent hours imagining her return, rehearsing what she might say, anticipating what he might say back, preparing her replies. The one thing she promised herself was that she wouldn't pick a fight. And yet, the touch of his arm across her back, once a sense of protection, now felt unfamiliar, as if he were a stranger who hadn't asked permission. She nudged him off. "Well, I'm back now."

She told herself it had been right to come to the store, but she was suddenly exhausted, drained of the adrenaline that had gotten her here. "Think I can steal you away for a little bit? Or could you maybe even drive me home? I'm more tired than I thought."

The muscles holding Tuck's grin taut fell ever so slightly, and he inhaled a quick breath as if to decline her request. Then just as quickly, as if realizing they were merely dancing, trying to hold the impending argument at bay until alone in private, he righted himself. "Why don't you go on home? I'll be there soon."

Had he even heard her? She wanted a ride, not his permission. She owned this place, owned the car in the parking space out back, made sure the loan payments got to the bank on time and that the credit cards stayed under limit and employee payroll went smoothly and that an upset customer didn't try to tank their business with a scathing online review. All of it stuff he either was or would need to learn to be capable of doing.

"You know, Tuck." She was smack in the middle of the customer lounge, chin up and chest out. "The least you could do is drive your pregnant wife home from the airport."

He waved her off. "I'm not a taxi. You've known that since the very beginning."

The room was quiet with only the sound of distant hydraulic drills and darting customer eyeballs.

He turned, anticipating a response but hearing none. "What? No quippy comeback, Laney?"

She caught Sylvia's gaze and they locked eyes, conversing in the intimate and silent language women speak only with each other.

Are you really?

I am.

Are you happy?

Very. She smiled and shrugged and waited for Tuck to catch up.

"Why are you just standing there?" The man who'd recently made so many astute observations looked genuinely confused.

Sylvia silently asked for Laney's permission, then turned slightly and said, "Did you hear *every* part of what she just said?"

He threw his hands in the air, losing patience with this game.

"Laney said she's pregnant," Sylvia whispered, though loud enough for the room to hear. "Your wife is expecting."

"No, she's not." Even as he said the words, his face betrayed the growing realization that she might actually be. "When?"

"That long weekend when we had our mini spring break," she answered.

He nodded slowly. Didn't smile. Didn't frown. Just checked his memory for confirmation and did the math. "Alright. Let me grab my keys."

The discussion that followed reminded Laney of the night Tuck finally surrendered to the fact it was time to retire. That night, there were three of them—Laney and Tuck and his coach. Then, as now, Tuck did most of the talking. He knew the facts but needed to process them aloud.

"I don't understand how this happened. You're sure you remembered—" He made a vague gesture toward Laney's bottom half, as if birth control were a pair of magical panties the woman puts on before sex.

"Yes, I'm sure. And I don't know, either. I haven't seen an OB yet, but the doctor at the hospital said it could have something to do with my age. Thirty-eight doesn't seem old to me, but apparently to my hormones, I'm on my way to ancient."

"And you're sure you're, I mean, the test couldn't have been a false positive or anything?"

She shook her head. The ultrasound pictures were in her

purse. She would show him, but not yet. "I heard the heartbeat. It was pretty amazing."

He said "Uh-huh" the way their tax accountant took in their yearly information, punching numbers into his program, tabulating as he went. He asked how she found out, how long she'd known, if there were risks because of her age. She answered as best she could with the information she had, trying to keep from coloring his world in her own rosy palette.

She was due in February, just before Valentine's Day. "I've been told winter newborns are great. By the time I feel rested and the baby is on a schedule, the weather will be nice enough to start getting out." This last part she said to save them both the agony of having to answer what he really wanted to know—was she planning to keep it? *Ask the questions you need answers to*, she heard her mother say, and she suddenly recognized how hard she was working for Tuck's benefit, preemptively offering details he hadn't yet requested, taking care of his feelings before he had time to feel them. *Ask the question*, she said to herself. *You know what it is*.

"Tuck." She pulled his hand into hers and looked him in the eye. "I know this wasn't in your plans. It wasn't in mine, either. Frankly, though, I'd be lying if I told you I never wanted to be a mother. I always have, and I think you've always known that. So I don't want to make any secret of how much I want this baby. Of how much I already love this child."

She leaned in and squeezed. Took a breath. Waited for the moment.

"But I know being a father was never something you wanted. And so, I guess I'm just trying to ask, do you want me to release you from your responsibilities to this child?" She laughed and squinched her face. "That sounded so cheesy. I'm sorry."

"Glad I didn't have to say it." He smiled back.

She brought his hand to her cheek. "You know we're done, right? Regardless of whether you choose to be a part of this baby's life or not, we're not going to be Tuck and Laney anymore. We've hit the end of the road."

Yeah, he knew. He'd figured it out, just like she had. He curled his fingers and knocked his wedding ring on the kitchen table. "Do you want me to move out for now? I can get an apartment closer to the shop."

She said no. That wasn't necessary. "There's one more thing I need to tell you. I'm going home."

31

Bree knew how they would save the Rainbow. With Witt's help, she'd drawn up a rough business plan for what she was loosely calling OTR 2024, which she planned to present to Irma this evening.

Problem was, the shop was busy these days, and with Laney back in California, it was just Bree and Irma all the time. Their bodies and minds were beginning to read like bands of sedimentary rock, one period of fatigue layered atop another. Still, she flipped the sign and turned the lock at closing time, determined to carry through as planned.

Her mom took one of the tattered wing chairs and ushered Bree to the other. "I'm all ears," she said.

"As I've told you, I've always loved my work selling books, and I can't imagine another place I would rather be. This was where I first felt safe, where I learned what it meant to belong, and, not only that, but to be loved." She pushed down the emotion creeping into her throat, determined to get through everything she needed to say without tears.

"It's like, I didn't just get adopted into a family that ran a bookstore, but that the bookstore was a family—you and Elliot and Laney and the books themselves. I got to learn for myself how it feels to hand a copy of *Anne of Green Gables* to a young reader and imagine what it would be like to read it again for the very first time, to know the joy waiting for them. The Rainbow was this magical, secret club and I got to join."

Irma leaned in. "Don't underestimate the role you played in coming to us. You were the little girl brave enough to get off the bus and follow Laney here. And you did it day after day, until seeing you was as natural as anything. You chose us, Bree. That's the truth of it."

"Maybe." She could feel her face flushing. "But I wouldn't have kept coming if you didn't welcome me. Did I ever tell you that every night, when I had to go home, I would get to the door of my apartment and tap the doorknob like this—" She closed her eyes and extended her right index finger, tapping the flimsy faux-brass handle in her memory. *One, two, three.* "I never went inside without first saying to myself, 'This place isn't real. This lady isn't your mom. These people are trying to hide you away from your family. But if you keep really, really quiet, they'll forget you're here, and then you can escape, and your real parents will find you, and they'll be so happy they'll throw a party for the whole town, and you'll never have to be with the bad people again.'"

Irma's eyes pooled as she spoke, knowing as well as Bree that her story had unfolded almost exactly that way. A fantasy become reality. Bree could easily have given way to tears, but she steeled herself, determined to finish. "Given all that, I'm sure you think I'm going to try to convince you to stay here and try to keep the Rainbow alive. But I'm not."

Her mother was quiet, shocked into speechlessness. "Really?"

Really, and she wasn't sure she believed it herself, yet. "As much as it's going to break my heart, I know you've lost your passion for this place, and I know you want to retire from full-time bookselling. Plus, given what we've learned from Witt's accounting, the money you need to do that is wrapped up in the value of this building."

Her mother sighed, a pitiful, reluctant acceptance of the truth.

"It's hard to justify staying when, some months, our entire revenue goes to paying the property taxes."

This was the central dilemma, what Witt had been referring to when he said the business had too many assets and not enough income—a bookshop and its building at the point of irreconcilable differences.

Bree said, "I don't see a way to stay in this location and help you retire. Selling books is just never going to turn the sort of profit we'd need to have it make sense."

"It barely did in our heyday," Irma acknowledged. "Though Elliot and I had a fabulous time trying."

"I remember."

"Oh, honey. You don't even know the half of it."

Bree was tempted to ask, but now wasn't the time. "Are you ready to see what I am proposing?" She flipped the cover page on the presentation she'd prepared. "I'm calling the idea OTR 2024. We sell the building and allocate a proportion of the funds to your retirement package." She pointed her pencil to a pie chart in which the largest segment was labeled Mom.

"We'll also need to set aside a significant portion of the sale to pay the various taxes you'll incur, as well as the remaining debt on the store credit cards and loans." This piece of the pie was smaller, though not small enough for comfort. She pointed to the last segment, the slimmest by far, labeled OTR Future.

"If we're able to sell the building for what we think is current market value, we *should*," she emphasized that last part, as their projections came with no guarantees, "have a small bit of seed money to begin transforming the Rainbow." This was more fun than she'd expected while rehearsing last night, alone in her bedroom. "The seed money won't be enough to fund all of this. I will need to obtain my own loans and funding. But, here's the plan…"

By the end, Irma was speechless. "You came up with all that?

Not that I doubt your ability or your smarts, it's just so...inventive."

Bree thought so, too, and the ideas had come to her in such a piecemeal fashion, it took a long time to recognize them as part of a larger solution, not simply Elmer's glue on a broken chair. "I had a lot of help. Witt, obviously. Daisy and Lou at the distillery have taken me under their wing. And—" Time for the final reveal. "Laney is coming home to help me do it."

Laney and Tuck were over. She hadn't made him move out of the house, but he had been in the guest room since the night they decided to cash in their chips. They'd hired attorneys, pledged to keep the settlement negotiations as civil as possible, and managed to only break that promise a few times. It was good that she was leaving for Minneapolis tomorrow. Baby had been reason enough to keep them on their best behavior for the past several weeks, but even its power was waning. Divorce hurt, they were both angry and sad, and they needed space to act that way.

Right now, she was on the phone with the movers, revising her earlier estimate about how much stuff she'd be taking to Minnesota. "I won't be moving any living room or bedroom furniture." Red leather didn't suit her, and Bree had invited Laney to move in with her until Baby came, or until the Rainbow stabilized, or until they were just plain sick of each other, whatever came first. "I only need the crew to load my boxes and drive them to Minneapolis."

Laney, herself, would fly, taking one suitcase and the only carry-on she needed, tucked safely inside her belly and just beneath her heart.

32

Thom parked and pulled his scooter from the back seat of his car. His ankle and his back were vastly less angry these days, and he didn't need his go-anywhere contraption nearly as much. But this visit would be difficult. He may need a place to sit down. He may need a safe place to cry.

He smiled at the woman behind the desk and pulled a key from his pocket. He'd found it in Elliot's files the day he discovered his partner's attempts to sell his way out of debt, as well as the marriage certificate that had started it all. "My partner, Elliot Gregory, recently died and I found this key in his belongings. It's stamped with your name and location, so I presume it's for a safe-deposit box here."

The woman accepted the key and examined it. "I'm sorry for your loss. Do you know if you're designated as a spouse or co-renter on the box?"

He was neither, of course. But he'd done his research and had come prepared. "I have a copy of his death certificate with me, as well as the deed to the house we owned together on which I'm listed as his beneficiary." He dropped them to the desk. "I also have documentation demonstrating that items belonging to Mr. Gregory's estate may be inside." This was the list of valuables he'd sold from his inheritance.

The teller, however, pushed them all aside. "That won't be

necessary. It looks like Mr. Gregory listed you as a co-renter on the box. I just need your driver's license."

He couldn't believe it. Nothing about Elliot's death had been easy. He may not have even found this key if not for losing his temper. It was taped to the inside of a file labeled Just in Case, along with a cryptic note that read only… "Thom, my love—I did try. I'm sorry."

Together, he and the teller entered the vault where she located the correct box number, and they inserted their matching keys. When it was out of its cubby and safely on the table at the center of the room, she said, "I'll close the door for your privacy."

Last night, Thom had lain awake trying to picture what he would find here. With any luck, it would be remnants of Elliot's inheritance—stocks or bonds that weren't valuable enough for him to have already sold but that may help chip away at his remaining debt. He'd finally notified creditors of Elliot's death and tried to convey to them the fact that there was no estate to plunder for payment. And yet they continued to call, as if one day, Elliot would answer, miraculously alive and flush with cash.

"What surprises have you left for me here, my love?" He pulled open the top, and as he did so, he felt a warmth rush the length of his spine. It wasn't a reaction to what he saw inside—the box was less than half full and nothing but tattered envelopes. He felt Elliot, the presence of him, fleeting and thin, yet beside him nonetheless.

The envelopes contained little treasure. Elliot's birth certificate, a copy of the deed to their house, business registration filings for Over the Rainbow Bookshop, LLC, and the deed to the building in which it stood. He found birth and death certificates for both of Elliot's parents, social security cards for all three of them, and a black-and-white photo of a young man, handsome in his morning suit, standing beside a stern-looking woman in a white silk veil and pearls. There were no names or dates written on the back, but this had to be Elliot's parents on their wedding day. He'd had the man's eyes and, when he slept, the stern, set face of the woman. "What a miracle you were, coming from all that," Thom whispered. Elliot, he knew, laughed and agreed.

He'd brought a tote along with him, unsure of what he would need to remove from the box, and he transferred the papers into his bag. Thom had his own safe-deposit box, and he would store these items there. No reason to pay two rental fees when he was the only one left.

The box was nearly empty but for one last packet, a manila envelope just bigger than his palm and lumpy enough to indicate it held more than paper. He undid the clasp and slid the contents into his hand. It was a stunner, a diamond brooch in a laurel-wreath design, at least three inches in diameter. He wanted to count the gems but refrained. It felt uncouth, like a grave robber rubbing his grimy hands.

This was the same brooch Elliot's mother wore in the only picture displayed of his parents. It was taken on their fortieth wedding anniversary. They'd thrown a party for themselves, and Elliot said he'd attended, with Irma as his date. He and Thom hadn't even met yet, but the idea of Irma traveling to Florida on Elliot's arm always steamed him, that he'd had to hide his real self from his parents in the arms of a woman and that Irma had been the one willing to shelter him.

Now, of course, he knew why.

The brooch was pinned to a piece of jeweler's stationary, which he unfolded to discover was a notarized certificate of authentication, the weight and clarity of each diamond listed, along with the weight of the gold in which the gems sat. Beneath, the jeweler included a brief summary description, presumably the sort of paragraph for use in auction or sale materials, and below that, an estimate value. "Holy bologna," he whispered. It read, "$14,000."

Thom sank into his seat, thankful for his scooter. The treasure he'd found wasn't enough to pay Elliot's creditors in full, but it may be enough to convince them to stop calling and consider the debt settled.

He scanned the jeweler's letter again and found himself wondering whether Mrs. Gregory would have been pleased with its fourteen-thousand-dollar valuation or if she would have considered that number mere peanuts. Was it small compared to other items she owned, or would she think it a gross underestimation of the piece's real worth? He didn't consider the price peanuts, of course. Frankly, he didn't understand why this wasn't one of the first items Elliot sold. Maybe Thom ought to even return to the jewelry store—it was downtown and believed to be reputable. Perhaps a piece such as this required regular appraisal; he certainly wasn't in a position to know.

He looked again for a date and spotted it, along with a line of text he hadn't bothered to read. "July 30, 2021. Property of Mr. Thomas Winslow, a gift from the estate of Martha and Elliot Gregory Sr."

"It's mine?" He ran a finger along the names of Elliot's parents. Why had they been listed as bestowing him this gift? They'd never met. They were both gone by the time Thom came into Elliot's life. Unless— Witt's voice echoed in his head, something he'd said after their chaotic meeting at the Rainbow. *Creditors can only go after Elliot's estate. Since you weren't married, anything in your name is safe.*

"You little rascal!" he squealed. "You conniving, loophole-finding stinker! How in the world did you think to do this?" He was laughing now. Fourteen thousand dollars was hardly retirement-level money, but it wasn't nothing. Even more, it meant Elliot hadn't forgotten him at all.

"Well, well, well, Mr. Gregory." He found the brooch's envelope and began to slip it back inside. "Always full of surprises, aren't you?" The pin fell to the bottom and hit with a tiny *ping!* There was something else in there. Quickly, he stood and emptied the entire contents onto the table. There was the brooch, the jeweler's notarized assessment, and a diamond ring with a circular paper key tag dangling from its band. Thom brought it close, the writing had faded, but he chuckled as he made it out. It was in Irma's handwriting and punctuated with a smiley face.

In case of emergency, break glass.

33

Irma stood at Thom's front door, calming herself before ringing the bell. She was embarrassed not to have been the one to reach out first. She should have done so as soon as she'd made her decision.

"Irma?" He opened the door before she was ready. "Is the doorbell not working? Did you knock?"

The dining room table was laid with tea, an impressive feat for a man pushing himself across the floor on a one-legged scooter. She took a seat, watching him pour.

"I appreciated your call yesterday." She figured she ought to signal her genuine intentions of peace. "In fact, I've been intending to extend the same invitation to you, and I don't have a good excuse for not having done so."

He cocked his head, genuinely surprised. "You have a bookstore to run. And a grandbaby to prepare for." Laney and Bree had stayed in touch with Thom, developed a friendship, even. They met for dinner, and cocktails (nonalcoholic for Laney), and even once, he'd stopped by the shop for coffee and a chat.

"In fact, Irma," he said, "I'm embarrassed of my own behavior. Not just recently, but going back years. I'm sure you could see that I was jealous of the attention Elliot paid to you and the Rainbow. Some of it for good reason, but I treated you poorly and that was unfair." He raised his cup. "Ms. Bedford, will you accept my sincere apology?"

Who was this man? Irma couldn't help but smile. "I will, Mr. Winslow. And may I ask, will you accept mine, as well?"

"Most certainly."

With that settled, Thom sliced the cake. Irma dived into the business of explaining herself. "As you likely know, we are moving ahead with plans to sell our building."

He mmm'd and passed her plate.

"The money from the sale is to be allocated into three buckets—one to pay off our remaining debt, one to provide a little bit of money to help Bree and Laney rejigger the business, and one bucket to help fund my retirement." She didn't know why this next part made her nervous. It wasn't as if she were asking anything of him. She took a deep breath. "I still intend to give you Elliot's share of the sale. Maybe it will help you pay off the personal debt he acquired on the store's behalf."

Thom remained quiet for a moment, running his fork along his dessert.

"Obviously, we won't get as much money as we would have liked. But if we get the price we think we can get for the real estate, it should leave you the start of a small nest egg."

She watched as he bobbled his head, considering.

"No, thank you," he said finally. "I don't see the point, frankly. If nearly all of it ends up going to pay Elliot's debts, I'd rather the money just stay with you."

"But he accrued them because of the store. It's not like he was running around indulging himself."

Thom shrugged. "We don't know that. The man loved cashmere and Italian leather. We kept individual credit cards, so I never saw what he charged, and the statements that came after he died were just documentation of its compounding interest."

"Still. I hate to think you're coming out of this with nothing."

"I appreciate that." And he did. Sincerely. "I have resentments about Elliot that I need to resolve, and I'm working on it. But, Irma, you must, too. He left you in a terrible position, at a time when you were at your most vulnerable. He made bad business decisions. Probably with the best of intentions. But bad is still bad."

He watched her take it in, trying his best to accept that it was harder for her to be critical of Elliot. They had a different relationship, one that was twice as long as Thom and Elliot's and—as much as he hated the truth of this—that was deeply, emotionally intimate.

"That money represents what you made together, the legacy you created. Don't let guilt or some irrational sense of responsibility convince you that you deserve less than you do. I didn't build the Rainbow. But you, Ms. Irma Bedford, did." He chuckled quietly, knowing this decision was much easier than if hundreds of thousands of dollars were at stake. Although, it did feel good to let himself believe he would've ultimately reached the same conclusion. Anyway, with no estate to draw on, Elliot's creditors were just going to have to swallow their losses.

"Thank you," she said quietly.

"And thank you," he answered. "Your generosity shows what a wonderful friend you were to Elliot." He sat up in his chair before his emotions got the best of him. "Now it's my turn. I can't wait to show you why you're here."

He reached into his pocket and folded the ring in his palm. "I found this in Elliot's safe-deposit box. Does it look familiar?"

She gasped when he opened his fingers. He'd taken it to the jewelers to have it cleaned before its great unveiling—it was absolutely brilliant—and the afternoon sun caught the diamond just so, flinging rainbows onto the dining room walls.

"It's our ring!"

He noted her use of the word *our*, then smiled, watching her admire it, turning her hand this way and that, the rainbows dancing about the room. "That's yours to take home. It's a pleasure to see you reunited."

"I couldn't, Thom. This was a Gregory family ring."

"That Elliot gave to you." On the subject of gift protocol, Thom was a studied expert. "It is customary for the bride to keep the ring, even if the engagement ends before marriage. Of course, in this case, you were married, making this your property."

"Formally, maybe. But what am I going to do with it now?"

He slid the key tag across the table. "You said it yourself. In case of emergency, break glass. Put the ring toward the Rainbow's future."

Irma popped from her seat and landed on him, squeezing her arms around his neck and smothering his cheek with kisses. "I don't think I was this happy when Elliot first gave it to me." She laughed. "You are a brilliant, wonderful man!"

"I know. I truly am." He chuckled at his own arrogance. "But listen—" He patted her arms, ushering her back into her chair. "There is one very important thing I'd like you do to for me."

"Anything," she gushed. "Just name it."

"Actually, it's not for me, so much as with me." Yes, that was a better way of putting it. This was something he not only wanted her to do for herself but that he felt compelled they do together. With Irma. The woman Elliot had loved so much. "I'd like you to start joining me at my weekly grief support group."

She paused, midsmile, obviously not having expected this. "Do you think I need one?"

He reached forward and took her hand. "I believe we both do. And I believe Elliot would get a kick out of seeing us walk through that door as devoted friends."

She smirked, but agreed. "I guess it's true, then. Books and rainbows are where dreams come true."

"And grief support groups," he added.

"Too morbid." She shook her head, still chuckling. "That is a terrible, terrible tagline."

The Book Haters' Book Club Newsletter

Redux
Issue #1
January 2023

The calendar isn't the only thing resetting itself…

Book Clubbers, it's been a rocky year for Over the Rainbow, and our inconsistency with this newsletter is just one sign of the trials our store and our team have endured. Thank you to everyone who showed your support while we worked to define our future—those of you who emailed and called, who shopped online and in person, who sent postcards, spoke to the media, danced in the street, and shared our story far and wide. We are grateful. We are also thrilled to tell you the Rainbow will continue to glow, bright and full of possibility, as it has since 1980.

There will be changes—in location, in the way we place the right books in customers' hands, and in the faces you'll see when you walk through our yellow door. As you may know, we were devastated to announce the death of our cofounder, Elliot Gregory, one year ago. The Rainbow will never be the same without Elliot beneath its roof, and yet neither will we allow the Technicolor magic with which he first blessed our bookshop to fade into gray.

It is with equal sadness that we announce the retirement of Over the Rainbow's intrepid and loyal cofounder, Irma Bedford (though she promises to pop in and out of the shop regularly). As she puts it, "I have one heck of a story to tell, but let's face it—my pages are worn, and my spine is creaky. It's time I give this gal some TLC."

All of which begs the question, who will take over the bookstore? And who is writing this newsletter?

Let us introduce ourselves. We are Bree Bedford and Laney Hartwell, Irma's daughters. We were raised at the shop. We grew up with books in our hands and stories in our ears. And we believe in the idea of the Rainbow. If this past year taught us anything, it's that it's true what Elliot and Irma have said all along: books and rainbows are where anything can happen.

The Over the Rainbow Bookshop is here to stay.

Of course, as your new newsletter editors, we would be remiss to not include a recommendation. This month, we are promoting only one—*The Awakened Woman* by Dr. Tererai Trent. Part memoir, part guide, it tells the story of a woman born in a small Zimbabwe village, married off as a child and mother of three by her eighteenth birthday. It was the only life she knew, and still, she found her way to the life she was meant to live instead. Her story has inspired women around the globe to stand up and reach for everything they deserve.

We are two of those women, and this book touched us deeply.

The hardship and heartbreak that 2022 brought showed us that we had surrendered our knowledge, skills, and dreams—for ourselves, for our family, for our community, and for the Rainbow. What we know, however, is that Over the Rainbow is where we want to be. You, our Book Clubbers and Haters, are who we want to serve.

Do you need guidance and inspiration, yourself? We have a copy of Dr. Trent's book for you on our shelves. Or don't wait. Order *The Awakened Woman* online and let us ship it straight into your hands.

There are many, many surprises in store for Over the Rainbow, so stay tuned. We'll make sure you're the first to see them just as soon as they're ready.

Read on, dear Haters…

—Bree Bedford and Laney Hartwell

34

1 year later...

Laney Hartwell really wanted a doughnut. She stood at the Nygaard's bakery counter salivating over a chocolate glazed.

"What do you think, Harper?" she said. "Do you want to find out what doughnut-flavored breast milk tastes like?" She leaned down and kissed the girl's downy infant hair. Harper Juliette Hartwell was three months old, and today's celebration would be her great coming-out.

"Can I help you?" the attendant behind the counter asked.

"Yes, thanks. I'm here to pick up a sheet cake. Should be under the name Bree Bedford. Or maybe Over the Rainbow?"

The attendant returned with a box as broad as their chest. It was a good thing the shop was only a few doors down, and that Harper, as magnificent as she was, hadn't yet developed the strength to kick a cake big enough to serve fifty people off the front of her stroller.

The baby wasn't the only thing kicking, either. Over the Rainbow was still alive, and people everywhere would soon discover what a wonderful thing that was. Bree had been in charge of all the changes with the physical store, but Laney had conceptualized what she had taken to calling her "second-best creation ever." Harper would always be first, obviously.

The idea began one day soon after moving home to Minneapolis when Laney finally made one too many literary references.

A customer had just said to Bree, "Isn't it wonderful? A junior college education, and still, you're able to run your own little shop." Then she'd turned on her pedicured heel and walked out.

Bree looked far more confused than insulted, so Laney explained. "You get that she was calling you stupid, right?"

She dismissed the idea.

"I'm serious. That was Southern lady code for 'I'm never coming back here because I'm a snob and you're a dum-dum.'"

"Oh, she was just—" Bree stopped. Snapped her fingers and pointed accusingly at Laney. "*Southern Lady Code*! That's a Helen Ellis book."

"I know that."

"But how do you *know that*, know that?"

"Because I read it." Laney smirked. This was just too much fun, watching Bree try to suss her out.

"Since when?"

"Since Elliot sent it to me with a note saying how much he knew I loved her first collection, *American Housewife*."

"Elliot sent you books?"

He had for years.

"And you read them?"

"He had a gift, that man."

Bree was readying a thousand more questions when Laney felt the *zap!* of inspiration flood her brain. "Holy crow. Why haven't we thought of this before? We need a real Book Haters' Book Club. We can't just wait for people to stop in to buy a recommendation here or there. I mean, we have thousands of newsletter subscribers—think of what we could do if just a portion of them started paying to have the books we recommend shipped directly to subscribers each month."

Her bookseller sister required more convincing. "There are a lot of subscription services out there already. We're late to the party."

"Not too late, though." Laney's mind and body were humming. "And it's an exact fit for our new Over the Rainbow philosophy—books as community."

Now, nearly a year later and with thanks to the seed money their mother's wedding ring brought, the Rainbow had a professionally designed and maintained online book hub. Every month, subscribers got a book of their choice in the mail. If they wanted to discuss it, they could join an online chat or live video event. Even better, real, in-person Book Haters' Book Clubs were springing up across the country. Groups had already formed in sixteen states—and they'd barely just launched.

Laney looked at her beautiful child dozing in her stroller. "You will always and forever be my favorite, but I'm telling you, this Book Haters' thing just keeps on surprising."

By the time they returned to the shop, Witt was climbing a ladder on the sidewalk, busy stringing the new banner across the front window. Grand Reopening, it read. "We may look smaller, but our books and dreams are bigger than ever."

"Thanks for the help, Witt," she called.

"You bet. Wouldn't think of letting Bree up here."

The Rainbow had moved. Not far, three blocks away from the original location, but the new shop was small by comparison. They didn't need much centralized space anymore because the reimagined Rainbow was spread out all over Lyn-Lake in the form of small, specialized pop-up shops at other neighborhood businesses.

Daisy and Lou had been the first to offer up the distillery for a trial run of the experiment. The distillery had a small selection of Lady of the Lake merchandise—T-shirts and hoodies and hats—and they allowed Laney and Bree to add an assortment of books curated especially for the distillery's clientele. There were a few bestsellers, a few books on mixology, a few DIY guides to distilling. The key to turning a profit, however, were the two iPads on which customers not only paid for their book purchases but that also directed them to the Rainbow's online catalog. It was a bookstore at their fingertips, and delivery was either free to the Rainbow, or shipped to the customer's home for a small fee.

Now, in addition to the shop at the distillery, they had pop-ups at Alstrop's Hardware, Spin Vinyl, Uptown Vintage, and the Fringe Boutique—all of the places that helped them fight the Vandaveer sale. Other stores were signing up, too.

They'd redesigned the use of space at the bookshop, as well. They still stocked the bestsellers and books backed by publisher promotions. They never wanted a customer to enter and not be able to walk out without a purchase in their hands. However, much of their shelf space they now dedicated to "show me" books—copies of the titles Bree and Laney loved to hand sell but that didn't tend to bring a customer through the door in the first place. When a customer bought a "show me" book, Rainbow staff ordered the customer's copy online and had it shipped, sometimes overnight. It was a work in progress, a business model that needed fine-tuning, but it was doing well enough that they'd been able to buy themselves about two years of runway to work out the kinks.

There were a few things they'd brought over from the original store, too, including two reading cubbies-slash-confessionals and two pews. The chandelier was too large for the space, but there were clouds on the new Rainbow's freshly painted blue ceiling. Everything they weren't able to move, they sold, repeatedly shocked at what antique dealers were willing to pay for items Laney and Bree had spent their childhood taking for granted.

Oh, and they painted the door yellow, which Laney walked through, smiling as the familiar bells tinkled overhead.

"Got the cake, Breetle-dee!" she called. Her voice was too loud in the smaller environs, and the noise of it startled Harper awake. "Oops. Sorry, Ms. Hartwell."

She placed the cake on the folding table beneath the window and pulled Harper from her stroller. She took a deep breath, taking in her daughter's sweet, baby smell. Tuck had called to video chat this morning, as he did most days, stunned that someone so tiny had captured his heart. He was going to be a long-distance father, he said so himself. California was good for him. Tires were good for him. But he was also choosing his daughter, choosing to be her father, even if miles away.

Laney had what she needed. Harper, Bree, her mother, Thom, and the Rainbow. A year ago, she thought she'd come to Minneapolis out of guilt and regret. What she'd learned was that she was finished running. She'd turned toward the people she loved, and toward the place her every instinct knew simply as "home."

Bree had just hung up with the bike shop putting the finishing touches on the two Rainbow on Bikeback mobile bookshops they'd ordered. Neither she nor Laney were in any condition to spend their days pedaling fifty pounds of literary cargo, but they'd hired two enterprising teenagers, who were ready to start as soon as next week.

She found Laney and told her the good news. "The artist doing the paint job apparently added caricatures of Mom and Elliot to the design. I can't wait to see it."

"Too bad they're not ready for the grand opening party," said Laney. "It would be fun to have them on display."

"I know, right?"

"Hey, babe?" Witt popped his head through the yellow door. "You want any balloons or anything hanging next to the banner?"

She ignored Laney, who loved to mimic Witt every time he said "Hey, babe?" Which, Bree had to admit, was a lot. "No, that's okay. The banner's going to stay up for a few weeks and balloons won't make it that long."

"Righty-o," he said, closing the door behind him.

"That man is going to enjoy fatherhood so much," Laney

said. "You may never get to hold the baby once she's out of your belly."

"You may be right." Bree looked down at her growing stomach. She was almost twenty weeks along, and she was carrying a girl. They'd gone for the ultrasound two days ago. She and Laney would be raising their daughters at the Rainbow, just as their mother had. "Mom offered to come out of retirement again, by the way. I told her she can stop by as much as she wants but to save her energy for her grandbabies."

"Yesterday she put in an order for the entire Richard Scarry collection," said Laney. "I thought she'd saved most of those from when we were growing up, but she said she wants clean copies."

"Too bad Nestor's not around anymore to build her all the new bookshelves she's going to need."

"Isn't that what Witt is for?"

"No." Bree grinned and patted her belly. "He's just for us."

Technically, the bookshop had opened at ten, but the advertisements, social media posts, and the Book Haters' Book Club site stated a 1:00 p.m. start time for the grand opening party. "No one wants to eat cake in the morning," she'd argued, to which Laney replied, "Oh yeah? What are doughnuts, then?"

Daisy and Lou came through the door with a "would you look at this place!" and set a large tray of appetizers on the front table.

"On the house," Daisy said. Lou smiled, adding, "But it's fine by us if you wanted to mention to your customers where they came from."

Of course they would. "Not sure we'd be standing here today if it weren't for you."

"Oh girls!" The yellow door tinkled again and their mother walked through, arm in arm with Thom. "How are the party preparations coming along?"

Bree accepted a peck on the cheek from Thom, while Irma went straight for Harper. "My sweet grandbaby, kiss, kiss, kiss, kiss, kiss."

"How's librarian life, Thom?" she asked. A few months ago, he'd begun volunteering at the neighborhood library, and apparently, he loved it more than he loved them. "We hardly see you anymore."

He held out his palms as if searching for words. "There's just so much to do. So much! I'm as giddy as a pig in mud."

"Your gal, Carol Ann, still there?"

"She's not my gal. She has a master's degree. And a podcast. I think she's book-world famous!"

Bree couldn't keep from smiling. Thom was like a person sent forward in time, a Victorian who woke up in a world of wonders—running water and automobiles and homes without rats. "It makes me happy to see you so fulfilled."

"Thank you," he whispered. Then, "Ah. Your mother brought something for the store." He held up a thin package wrapped in brown paper and called, "Irma? Would you like to do the honors now, or later?"

"Yes! Now, now," she chirped. "Laney and Bree, you unwrap while the rest of us watch."

Bree and her sister exchanged glances. "Together?"

Laney nodded. "Rip on the count of three. One… Two… Three."

They tore back the paper to find the backside of a frame. "Turn it over," their mother instructed. "I had it reframed, rematted, and the glass replaced."

On the other side, they found the very first newspaper article ever written about Over the Rainbow. From the *Minneapolis/ St. Paul Standard*, October 1, 1980. "Former Rivals Join Forces Over the Rainbow: New bookstore opens in Lyn-Lake." There they were, Elliot and her mom, shaking hands, smiles as wide as their faces.

Bree and Laney both told her how much they loved it.

"Elliot's mustache," said Laney.

"Mom's skirt," added Bree.

"Say what you like about our fashion," their mother said, moving in close. "But you have to admit. Those two young fools had a lot of exciting adventures ahead of them."

"Maybe you ought to write a book after all, Mom," Bree said. "Put all your stories with Elliot down on paper."

Irma winked playfully but shook her head. "No one would ever believe it."

CURTAIN CALL

Oh, my darling readers! Sadly, it seems our time together has reached the end of its final act. What a wonderful, magical, mystical time this has been with you.

I don't want it to end.

And yet it must. Because all things do. For a time, at least. Who knows what the future holds?

Judy is here. She insisted. And she wants me to remind you to—*what was it, dear?* Ah, yes. She says, "Dream on, and never quit dreaming, no matter what happens." She also wants me to highlight that she has been quoted as saying, "The greatest treasures are those invisible to the eye but found by the heart."

Isn't that so true?

My treasure lay in the people I loved, of course, and who loved me back. My wonderful Thom. My leading lady, Irma. They gave me my greatest treasure—the gift of knowing the best parts of myself.

Oh, but there was also the Over the Rainbow and all the treasure it held for our readers. That's the magic of being a bookseller: every day, you have the potential to change someone's life. It's true. It's why I spent my career trying to place brave characters into the hands of a person in need of courage; searched for stories that might bring light to those whose hearts were shaded in darkness; raised up the voices of the oddballs, the misfits, the others, and introduced them to people looking for a community to call home.

Ah, well. We seem to have really, very much come to the last page, darlings. How 'bout we don't let this end our time together. Let's keep spreading book magic to the world. Do this for me, won't you? Tell me, what librarian or bookseller changed your life by placing the right novel in your hands? Where were you? What title did they recommend? What treasures did you find within its pages?

Mercifully, I don't need social media here in angel-flyover country, but I'm told it can work wonders for those of you still breathing. Post your book treasure stories with the hashtag, #BHBCHeroes.

Judy and I can't wait to hear them.

And now, until we meet again—*Mwah! Mwah! Mwah!*

★★★★★

ONE LAST THING...

Hey there, readers. It's me, Gretchen. The one who lived with Elliot and Irma and Thom and Laney and Bree in her head, and who tried her very best to put their voices on the page for you.

If you've gotten this far, thank you—from all of us—for listening.

Now, the reason I'm popping in Elliot-style. As I drafted this story, I knew I wanted it to be full of books I loved. And it is. I could have filled three hundred pages with beloved titles alone, but if I'd done that, you would have quit reading by page two and my book team would have called a "You sure you're feeling alright, Gretchen?" meeting during which they would have taken careful note of whether my hair was brushed and then asked to see my shoes. (I have never to my knowledge left the house wearing mismatched shoes, but I did look down while standing in line at the post office to discover I was sporting slippers. And once, a woman stopped me as I was about to get on the train to ask if I knew my pants were split open down the back.)

This admission, of course, is a roundabout way of telling you that I asked real and true booksellers and librarians to step in as Elliot and recommend the titles included in his newsletters. They are the heroes of this story. Let me introduce you...

My first entry is a bit unconventional, so bear with me. *Tuck*

Everlasting by Natalie Babbitt was recommended by Carsten Anthony, who is none other than my very non-bookish middle son. He says he hates books, and yet, he took the time to make sure his book-loving mother bought and read Tuck's story. Book miracles *do* happen!

The Cape Ann by Faith Sullivan was recommended by one of my favorite Gretchens—Gretchen West of Valley Bookseller in Stillwater, Minnesota. The bookstore sits on the sparkling blue waters of the St. Croix River, and if you've never been, you don't know what you're missing. Really. Make the trip. You'll love it. ValleyBookseller.com.

Did you think I'd made up the bit about buying a set of beautifully bound classics for your favorite college grad? That, in fact, is a real and thoughtful recommendation by Paige Carda of REACH Literacy in Sioux Falls, South Dakota. Her gem of a shop is a bookstore on a mission—profits go directly into funding youth and adult literacy programs throughout the Sioux Falls area. Go find them online. They're good people. REACHLiteracy.org.

Cathy Fiebach of Main Point Books in Wayne, Pennsylvania, recommended both *The Friend* by Sigrid Nunez and *Crossing the Line* by Kareem Rosser. Cathy and I have never met in person, but I hope to change that soon. Her emails were delightful. If you get to Wayne, Pennsylvania, before me, stop in and tell them I'll be there ASAP. MainPointBooks.com.

The Garden of Small Beginnings by Abbi Waxman. What a funny, lovely writer, that Abbi. Read her books; you'll love them, love them. And when you sit down to read, be sure to send a silent thank-you to the librarian who brought her to these pages, Kelly Moore, Adult Services Librarian in Dallas/Fort Worth. Librarians are genuine superheroes. Please extend your deepest appreciation to the next one you meet.

Hollow Kingdom by Kira Jane Buxton. This award-winning slide into the absurd was brought to you by Anna Stangl of The

Bookstore at Fitgers in Duluth, Minnesota. Yes, another Minnesota bookstore overlooking the water—this time a shop on the shores of Lake Superior. Go visit Anna and her colleagues—the shop and the surrounding area are both marvelous. Fitgers-Bookstore.com.

Healing After Loss by Martha Whitmore Hickman appears thanks to Chicago-area bookselling legend Maxwell Gregory. You won't find Maxwell stocking shelves anymore, but you can see and hear and chat with her at A Mighty Blaze, the place where authors and readers meet. AMightyBlaze.com.

The Awakened Woman by Dr. Tererai Trent came with glowing reviews from all-around book champion and friend to authors everywhere, Mary O'Malley of Skylark Bookshop in Columbia, Missouri, and A Mighty Blaze. Mary conducts interviews with authors online at both SkylarkBookshop.com and AMighty-Blaze.com. Be sure to check them out.

Thanks to Mary Lee Delafield of Warwick's in La Jolla, California, and to Steven Salardino of Skylight Books in Los Angeles. Both provided wonderful recommendations that I, unfortunately, was unable to integrate into this story. Please visit them and say thanks, anyway. Independent bookstores are magical places. Warwicks.com and SkylightBooks.com.

And last but hardly least, Thom's favorite librarian. There is no single, specific entry in the newsletters from this book wonder, but nevertheless, her recommendations are sprinkled throughout these pages like confetti. Meet Carol Ann Tack of the Merrick Public Library on Long Island. Better yet, you can follow her latest book delights on Twitter @Carolanntack or listen to her heartwarming and giggle-producing podcast, *Top Shelf Live!* Don't forget your cocktail!

ACKNOWLEDGMENTS

This novel took its own, sweet time wandering the back roads of my patience, determination, and sanity as a writer, and you wouldn't be holding it if not for many wise and gracious individuals.

At the top of the list is my agent, Holly Root of Root Literary, who, sensing my desperation after a series of increasingly outlandish story pitches, pulled a single thread from my mess and gave name to it: *The Book Haters' Book Club.* My original editor at Park Row, Natalie Hallak, then recognized the potential of my fledgling idea and lifted it up, giving it breath. Without them, I may still be pitching novels in which sewer lines explode, confusion passes for plot, and all my best characters die. You both have given me so much, and this story will remain among your greatest gifts.

Standing ovation for Laura Brown, my current editor at Park Row, who took who knows how many deep breaths, then picked up the work of this manuscript and its slightly panicked author after Natalie's departure. You're a smart one, Laura B., and I sure do like working with ya a lot.

Thanks to my publicist queen, Laura Gianino. Every author should be so lucky. To copy editor, Jerry Gallagher, whose keen eye is exactly what this writer—who often gives multiple names to the same character—needed. To the Park Row and HarperCollins marketing teams, who don't shrink from promoting books in which grown women pee their pants.

Chicagoland book diva Maxwell Gregory spent the better part of an afternoon giving me color commentary on the life of a bookseller. Your insight was priceless, Maxwell. Thank you. Speaking of Midwest book champions, thank you, Pamela Klinger-Horn for sprinkling Fairy Bookmother dust on so many, many authors, including me. And heartfelt thanks to your fellow booksellers everywhere, who have not only been loyal to my work but who fight the good fight every day for all the books they love. I wasn't kidding, either, when I called librarians superheroes; they are. They may be quiet about it, but they deserve the admiration and support of every community they serve.

On that note, thanks to fellow authors Amy Meyerson and Julia Claiborne Johnson, who connected me with their favorite hometown bookshops. To Abbi Waxman, who told me to sleep more, quit thinking, and finish the story. To Josh Moehling and Laska Nygaard, my writing group partners—oh, the muck you've waded through on my pages. And to Beth and Nee, the original members of my forever book club as well as Vix, our newest coconspirator—what good is life if not filled with laughter, heartache, and memorable characters? Eventually we even get around to talking about the books!

Mom, you're my biggest cheerleader, and I'm not even embarrassed by the outfits you color coordinate with my book covers. Connor, Carsten, and J—I adore your smiles, your hugs, and the fact you do your own cooking and laundry. Chad, I just adore you. Period.

Most of all, thank you, darling readers. If it weren't for you asking, "What's next?" I wouldn't have reason to sit my butt down and write. You give purpose to the chaos, and as Laney so rightly says, "Chaos can be highly productive."

Hallelujah and pass the Jell-O salad—

Gretchen Anthony
March 2022